A GOVERNESS SHOULD NEVER... LURE A SPY

THE GOVERNESS CHRONICLES - BOOK FOUR

EMILY WINDSOR

SENARA PRESS

This is a work of fiction. All names, characters, places and incidents are products of the author's imagination. All characters are fictitious and any resemblance to real persons, living or dead, is purely coincidental.

ASIN: B0CX9BBDSZ

ISBN: 978-1-9161139-9-2

This book is written using British English spelling.

CONTENTS

NOTE TO THE PROSPECTIVE GOVERNESS…

"…to you, do I presume to offer a few scattered remarks, founded upon experience, on the particular station of life in which the Almighty has, of his divine will, been pleased to place you."

ELIZABETH APPLETON. 1815.

CHAPTER ONE

"The governess has been an instructress for some years and has deeply studied the duties of her situation."

PRIVATE EDUCATION: A PRACTICAL PLAN FOR THE STUDIES OF YOUNG LADIES.

ELIZABETH APPLETON. 1815.

No. 14 Hanover Square, Mayfair, London. May 1817.

"So tell me, Miss Jones, why should I employ you as governess?"

Curse it.

And Amelia lowered her gaze to the mahogany desk in order to portray thoughtful repose.

What a devious question.

Especially as there were countless reasons why the gentleman should, in fact, *not* employ her as governess.

She'd never educated a young lady in her entire twenty-four years of life, knew naught concerning the history of art, cared less about the proper use of semicolons, was quite hopeless at all musical endeavours and hadn't the faintest idea what… tatting was.

Yet how arduous could it be to keep a fifteen-year-old girl occupied?

Just give her a book to read, surely?

So, with a surreptitious intake of breath, Amelia clasped her hands in what she judged to be a suitably demure fashion and raised her lashes to the gentleman who prodded her so.

A Mr Hugh Cadwalader.

His lustrous blue gaze caused that intake of breath to hitch somewhat, so she pursed her lips in a prim manner and sniffed. Governesses always sniffed. But as to his question… "I am well-versed, Mr Cadwalader, in all subjects that a young lady might have need of during her Season."

Such as how to evade a marriage-obsessed mama at a ball, the varied usages for a yard length of silk sash and the extrication of oneself from the clutches of a lascivious duke with merely a dance card pencil.

"I see."

Amelia thought that reply most enigmatic. "You have my references?"

"Yes," he drawled, gathering the papers before him. "My man of affairs has attempted to verify these references, yet it seems your past employers are either not of the living or not currently residing within these isles." With agile slender fingers, he leafed through them. "Lord Fowler is pursuing parakeets in the Amazonia, Lady Bassett is sifting through sand dunes in the former Mesopotamia, Lady Clifford is combing Constantinople for the Ark and Lady Palin is combing Paris for her errant husband."

Amelia held his gaze. "How unfortunate." And tilted her head. "But if you find me acceptable on all other counts, might I suggest a period of probation until my references can be verified?"

That should give her enough time to search this townhouse, question the servants, note Mr Cadwalader's movements and read any of his pertinent correspondence, all in order to write a comprehensive report for her superior at the Foreign Office.

For Amelia's talents lay not in punctuation or musical endeavours but in subterfuge for the Crown.

She could decipher messages coded by the finest that French Intelligence had to offer, incapacitate a man with solely her reticule ribbon, and mingle unseen at society balls and gambling hells alike, just listening and observing.

"A period of probation might be a satisfactory solution," her prospective employer murmured, returning to the references with narrowed eye, his blond lashes glinting gold.

Outwardly, Amelia allowed no flicker of disquiet but within, her heart pitter-pattered and patter-pittered.

As a rule, her assignments for the Foreign Office were more…unassuming. She played the nondescript wallflower one never noticed until her seat became vacant, the disinterested barmaid who listened in as she poured, or the jaded shopgirl who asked for a signature on the bill of credit.

So to calm the pitter-patter, she turned her eye to this study.

Masculine mahogany bookcases lined one wall, crammed with gilded spines, while a few grouchy portraits fought for attention above. The leather-topped pedestal desk was a palatial affair and as she'd entered the room for the interview, she'd noted its graduated drawers with neat locks that would require no more than the most rudimental of her cracksman's tools to open.

In one corner was a luxurious chaise longue, a landscape painting of verdant hills above – was the safe hidden behind it? – while a vase of roses sat atop a Sheraton cabinet, the early blooms surely costing a pretty penny in this uncommonly chill spring weather.

Her eye drifted over a deep-green wall with white stuccoed mouldings and returned to her prospective employer.

The Foreign Office had handed her a slender file on Mr Hugh Cadwalader containing the barest details: of Welsh descent, his parents were deceased, but he'd aristocratic relatives in rural Wales as well as his own small estate where he was held to be a responsible landlord.

Within the social hubbub of London, however, he was known as the *Scandalous Hugh Cadwalader*. A patron of every gambling hell in Town, from Mayfair to Cheapside, he was also the first to arrive and the last to leave from disreputable balls and notorious soirees alike.

Deemed by the great and good of the *Ton* to be modish, debonair and an essential invitee, he was forever in demand by the gentlemen for his droll tales and by the ladies for his charm and sheer dashing looks.

Amelia had to concur with the *Ton* ladies.

For beneath tousled blond hair lay–

His eyes flicked up and caught her own lingering upon his lips.

Her breath ceased.

Not because of the lingering but…

Had he seen through her forged references?

"I must admit," he said, leaning back in his chair with leonine grace, "that I've had some difficulty filling this position."

Amelia breathed once more.

Well, yes, he would have done.

A visit to Mr Clegg and Sons' employment agency had revealed that three other governesses had applied for this job, and so Amelia had been tasked with…dissuading them.

A Miss McKenzie had simply been bribed to withdraw her

application with three guineas, a new woollen pelisse and a carpetbag from Clark & Debenham's.

A Miss Harvey had reeked of juniper and so had required no inducement to visit Mrs Gimley's gin shop in Holborn and hence forego the interview. All in all, Amelia felt she'd done Mr Cadwalader a favour with that applicant.

Then a starchy Miss Kane had been persuaded to meet in St James' Park, whereupon Amelia had bemoaned how the wicked Mr Cadwalader had ravished her up against the schoolroom's oak wainscotting and then abandoned her with child. His ninth by-blow and every single one with a governess. Miss Kane had blenched and fled.

But Amelia knew Miss Kane would find a better employer than this scandalous scapegrace.

A scapegrace with well-defined cheekbones, a straight nose, azured eyes, clefted chin and those perfectly formed lips that seemed to curve upwards with such ease.

An elegant visage, some might say, and yet the burgeoning afternoon stubble to his chin, the waning red welt to his left cheek and the dark shadows beneath his eyes all cleaved that elegant visage with a dominant masculinity.

He wore a cravat, whiter than Thassos marble and tied *L'orientale*, a silver-shot waistcoat and a dark-green tailcoat that matched the colour of the chaise silk. Before Mr Cadwalader had seated himself, she'd happened to note bias-cut pantaloons in a neutral shade that appeared like flesh.

Indeed, she'd been forced to peer thrice to make sure it hadn't been so.

She consoled herself that the fopdoodle likely padded his thighs for them to appear so muscular.

And doubtless had a corseted stomach for that trim waistline.

And cushioned his chest.

And–

That blue gaze flicked up once more.

Yet this time it held no idle humour. Just a simmering fierceness that caused an anomalous flare of flame within her.

Perhaps a warning that beneath that elegant finery and idle smile, there lay a different man.

One of dangerous nights and dangerous intent.

"My ward is..." With jaw taut, he glanced away. "I have been her guardian for less than a month, since her great-aunt became too ill to look after her, but she is...unlike other young girls."

Amelia cocked her head. She'd researched this ward already. A girl of just fifteen, her mother had succumbed to a fever two years past but her father had been lost to her only eight months ago, the circumstances of which, Amelia had not been informed of.

"How so? Is she shy?"

Those perfect lips grinned all of a sudden, eyes tempering to wicked mischievousness, and Amelia abruptly understood why a plethora of handkerchiefs were strewn in his path by the prettiest ladies of the *Ton,* and why he was pursued with invites to the most scandalous parties held by the loftiest dukes in the land.

And yet, what the handkerchief-discarding ladies failed to grasp, what the deferential dukes who chortled at his droll tales failed to realise, indeed what the entire *Ton* failed to see...

Was that the Scandalous Mr Hugh Cadwalader was also a spy for the Home Office, and the sole reason for Amelia's assignment was to assess whether he was moreover a traitor to his country.

"I'll leave that for you to decide," he said with a laugh. "But my ward did have an unusual upbringing."

"So did I," replied Amelia, her first sincere remark of the interview. Perhaps she and this ward would deal well together.

Though if the worst came to the worst and an element of governessing did happen to be required, she'd purchased a colossal tome on the subject, costing her six shillings and seven pence in expenses.

Entitled *Private Education: A Practical Plan for the Studies of Young Ladies, Edition 1815* by a Miss Elizabeth Appleton, she had read two chapters thus far and realised that the knowledge to be acquired by a future debutante would keep this young lady busier than a horse's tail in summer.

So, while this ward was occupied with finding suitable matches from Debrett's *1814 Baronetage of England,* Amelia would carry out her assignment, pen her report and depart forthwith.

Mr Cadwalader drew a hand through his dishevelled blond hair and scrutinised her with that indolent azure gaze.

Yet within those azure depths, something...dark and perilous lurked.

That flare of flame lit within her once more.

A voice whispered...

Caution, Amelia. Caution.

HUGH RUMINATED.

He ought to offer Miss Jones the position of governess without a moment's hesitation.

She held superlative if not presently verifiable references, a demure mien, intelligent amber eyes, perfect answers to his earlier questions and, to be blunt, he had more urgent demands upon his time.

Yet a certain unease had crept to his shoulders.

An innate warning that had stayed his tongue, so he glanced down to the supplementary questions that his Aunt Enid had stated were crucial in gauging the suitability of a modern educator of young ladies.

Of course, it would have been easier if Aunt Enid had conducted this interrogation herself, but the moment he'd mooted the idea, she'd dashed for the door faster than a maid on her day off.

So he frowned at Aunt's scribbles.

Gads.

"Just one or two further questions, if I may…" He cleared his throat. "Have you a broad knowledge of…tatting?"

Her amber irises widened. "But of course, Sir."

Good enough for him, and in all frankness, she could have told him it was a newly discovered moon of Saturn and he wouldn't have known better.

"What blessed fortune. And secondly, how would you address the fourth duke's third son's wife at a ball?"

Those amber irises were briefly shuttered.

A little underhand, perhaps.

Apparently, this was a test of great cunning, although Hugh had no idea of the answer. Fortunately, Aunt Enid had written it at the bottom of the page.

"May I use my notepad to chart the lineage?"

"By all means."

As she rummaged around in her carpetbag for writing accoutrements, he studied this likely candidate. Although he should amend that to sole candidate as yesternight he'd had to turn away the employment agency's Miss Harvey when she'd staggered up the steps late and reeking of gin. Then not an hour past, a promising Miss Kane had arrived, slapped his left cheek and stated she'd never work in such a filthy den of iniquity.

The injustice of it! His housekeeper kept this townhouse spick and span.

Miss Jones returned from rummaging and bit her lip. It was

an agreeable lip – sweet and pink as a rose, his favoured flower – and his eyes lingered upon her.

Dainty. Most pretty. But in a subdued manner that may cause some men to overlook her. Blond hair, lighter than his own, was sleekly knotted at her nape, and her demure eyes flickered a true amber that even from across the desk he could see harboured golden flecks. Her skin was of an English rose also, and though the gown was a voluminous rainy-day grey, he could perceive a diminutive but exceedingly well-proportioned figure.

A comely woman.

No.

A governess.

A perfect governess.

Yet...

Her countenance showed no expression. Just that perfect demureness combined with an additional stillness that surely could not be natural. He could not say for certain if she was content or melancholic, at ease or troubled.

It was...unusual, such perfect stillness, and he tapped his lip.

An enigma.

"I would need to know if he was a soldier or vicar."

"Eh?"

Her eyes shimmered like swirling whisky – smoke-infused and complex – before the shimmer vanished like a Welsh dawn mist. "This duke's third son."

Hugh peered to Aunt's scrawled question. "Er..."

"And had he a title bestowed for any other accomplishments? In natural sciences or astronomy, for instance."

"Well..."

"And was his father, this fourth duke, deceased or non-deceased? And did the son have the same mother as his siblings?"

"Might have?"

"Were the rest of the family non-deceased?"

Hugh shrugged.

Miss Jones' lips thinned. "I'm afraid I cannot possibly give an answer without full clarification of the circumstances, Mr Cadwalader. If a deadly fever had struck the fourth duke and also his two eldest sons, then the third son could now be the fifth duke for all I know, and the lady in question would therefore be addressed as Your Grace."

Which was exactly what Aunt had written at the bottom, so he should make haste and offer her the employment.

He owed his ward's deceased father so much, and Phoebe needed a governess, a feminine presence in her life now that her great-aunt had recently become too ill to provide a home for her.

But gads, why did all this have to happen now? He thrust a hand through his hair, watching Miss Jones as she sat in perfect bloody stillness. What might it hide? he wondered. For in his native land of Wales, the lakes so still on the surface could conceal a myriad beneath – dark treacherous depths or sweet restorative welcome.

Hugh shook his head.

At any other time, he would travel with Phoebe to his family in Wales, let her breathe in the pure air and allow it to heal her sadness over her father, let her regain her laugh with his kith and kin, as he could never just send her off to some soulless school. Besides which, his ducal cousin had married a governess for devil's sake, and Isabelle would, without question, offer to assist but...

The whole lot of them were in the Mediterranean and weren't due back for another month or so.

If only he could give Phoebe more, give her all his time, but he was getting closer...

Closer to the Brotherhood of Ravens and–

Accompanied by a knock, the door opened and his butler Cruikshank popped his gaunt physog around it. "Sir? A message."

With a nod to the governess, he rose and strode to the butler, read the note and pondered. Then he returned his eyes to the back of this governess' perfectly pinned blond hair, and although she must have felt the weight of his stare, she neither shifted, wriggled nor stirred.

With the corner of the re-folded note, he scratched his jaw.

Perfection did not exist; a sweet rose always hid thorns.

And that unease crept to his shoulders once more.

"Well, Miss Jones, thank you for your time. I will send word with my decision in a day or so, as it seems I have another governess to interview."

She spun in her chair and, just for a moment, he thought to see a profound golden fire burn in those eyes...before it was doused in a blink. If there had been, it blazed deep within her, and he briefly wondered if that lick of flame would scorch a man to ash.

"Of course, Sir." She rose. "Might I enquire as to her name? We governesses are most familiar with one another."

"Ah, it's a Miss Webster. Are you acquainted?"

"No." Her lips quirked, the first hint of expression he'd observed. "But I'm quite sure I'll be making her acquaintance soon."

After a shallow bow from him and a deep curtsey from her, Cruikshank held open the door and she walked from his study with measured step, before the clack of her boot heels upon the hall tiles paused, doubtless to collect her bonnet and coat from the maid.

Hugh reached for the whisky decanter, filled a glass, slugged a good measure and with it clutched in hand, meandered to stand by the window overlooking Hanover Square.

The softest of clicks sounded from behind the wall with the stuccoed mouldings and he glanced over one shoulder as the hidden door set within was pushed ajar.

Nigh-silent footsteps crept to his side.

"I suppose you were listening in, my little blackbird?"

"Of course, Uncle Hugh."

Despite the moniker of Uncle, there was no shared blood between him and Phoebe, and together they turned to watch the governess as she descended his townhouse steps, continued her measured walk across pavement and cobbled road, before pausing at a gate to the Hanover gardens in the centre of the square.

He brought the whisky glass to his lips, but then likewise paused as Miss Jones pitched her head back and scowled at the scudding clouds, the cold spring wind whipping her grey skirts, fist clenching on the handle of her carpetbag.

And that perfect demure expression fell to downright peeved as she stamped her boot.

Hugh felt his lips curve. It appeared the rose wasn't so perfect after all.

His ward merely snorted. "I don't believe she knows what tatting is, Uncle."

"To be fair, Phoebe, my love, neither do I. Some kind of feminine hairstyle perhaps?"

"That's plaiting."

"Vermin elimination?"

"That's ratting." A rare snigger emerged, a pleasure to hear, so he slung an arm around her slender shoulders, her abomination of a black dress rustling.

"Well, we have a second governess to interview tomorrow afternoon, so perhaps she'll know."

"But I don't *need* a governess for my future, Uncle. What can they teach me but endless etiquette and pointless punctuation?"

"Oh, Phoebe. You know I must, my blackbird. I agree about the punctuation but you also need feminine company and a broad education to be whoever you wish to be."

A harrumph.

Hugh pinched his nose. Perhaps it was fortuitous there was a further interviewee, as his intuition sensed too beguiling an enigma beneath the still waters of Miss Jones.

Phoebe's arm linked with his, her dark hair coming to rest upon his shoulder while his eyes shifted to the window once more.

To find that Miss Jones had simply vanished from sight.

CHAPTER TWO

"By the smallest deception, mutual confidence is destroyed."

Private Education: A Practical Plan for the Studies of Young Ladies.

Elizabeth Appleton. 1815.

"Tea for two and a plate of hot buttered crumpets, if I may."

The Hatchett's Hotel waiter turned on his heel, and Amelia removed her gloves, brought forth Miss Appleton's hefty tome from her carpetbag, placed it on the tablecloth and frowned at it.

This morning, she had attended a meeting with her superior and endeavoured to gain more insight into this governess assignment – like why the Foreign Office were involving themselves in Home Office affairs anyhow – but Lord Rainham had merely steepled his fingers and declared that she knew all she needed to know. For now.

A racket outside caught her attention and she raised her head to peer through the hotel's bow window. The ten o'clock stagecoach from the west country was disgorging its passengers like a whale spitting out bones; weary elder ladies wandered to the entrance with dusty skirts while dazed country maids gawped at Piccadilly's bustling life.

With lashes lowering once more in deference to Miss Appleton's instructional opus, Amelia opened the quarter-bound leather cover and flicked through the initial pages, past the dedication and on to the crisp leaf detailing chapter contents.

Grammar. Writing. Geography. Music. Painting. Conversation. *Morality...*

She sought page two hundred and twelve.

...for anything clandestinely begun and hastily concluded betrays a consciousness of something wrong and is the cause of many a heart-rending pang and remorse to the parties themselves.

Amelia closed the book.

Perhaps tomorrow.

During the meeting with her superior, she'd contended that she may not be the best choice for this assignment as Mr Hugh Cadwalader was too...too debonair, too sophisticated, too everything, but Lord Rainham had again steepled his fingers and replied there was no one more suitable.

No one, full stop, she'd grumbled beneath her breath.

Since the fall of Napoleon, female spies – the unsung handmaidens of the war – had become scarcer than hen's teeth. Of course, the government denied that any females had ever been involved at all, their temperaments too passionate, their passions too temperamental, their sensibilities, conversely, too delicate.

But in this world of man, what better disguise than a

woman. Hence, they had indeed worked in just such a capacity, able to enter princely palaces or society balls as humble maids, faux aristocrats or seductive courtesans.

Seduction, however, was not Amelia's forte, Lord Rainham knew that, so if she was employed as governess by Mr Cadwalader, all her abilities of observation and subterfuge would be needed.

Under normal circumstances, this assignment to search a townhouse for evidence of treason would not be too arduous but…to spy upon a spy?

"Miss Lambert, I presume?"

Amelia twisted at her true surname.

Before her stood a tall auburn-haired lady in her mid-twenties with drab-brown bonnet and even drabber-brown gown. With gloves slightly frayed at the tips and a lace collar that may once have been white, she appeared down-at-heel, but her shoulders were held straight and her green eyes were clear and astute.

"Miss Webster?" Amelia rose to her half-boots and smiled. "Delighted to meet you. Do join me."

The waiter returned and Amelia watched as Miss Webster's gaze slid over the fare with barely concealed hunger. Despite the lady residing at this hotel, perhaps she had not partaken of breakfast, so Amelia used the tongs to place a buttered crumpet onto a plate and prodded it forth.

"Oh, I couldn't," said Miss Webster, removing her gloves.

"But they are quite delicious. It would be a shame not to." Amelia smiled. "The bill is settled."

After the briefest of hesitations, the lady reached for the plate and tucked in while Amelia poured tea and contemplated Miss Webster along with what she'd learned for a guinea or two from the clerk at Mr Clegg and Sons' employment agency and a moment alone with the relevant file.

Miss Webster's former governess positions had all been in the north of England, the Westmoreland area of the Lake District, for an assortment of gentry and nobles, but now she had travelled to London seeking work.

Previously lodged at the Saracen's Head Inn where passengers on the northern stagecoach disembarked, she'd relocated here to Hatchett's on Monday, likely because they'd a special offer of five nights for the price of three. What the out-of-town Miss Webster hadn't likely heard was that Hatchett's had suffered an infestation of fleas a fortnight past, hence the special offer.

"Your message said you wished to speak with me regarding my interview with Mr Cadwalader?" Miss Webster blew on her tea whilst her shrewd eyes gazed at Amelia over the rim of her cup.

"Yes..." Amelia paused. Histrionics, she sensed, would not influence this lady, so perhaps a more direct discourse – albeit spurious – was required. "My cousin works for the employment agency and once I heard of Mr Cadwalader's search for a governess, I felt compelled to warn all applicants. He is a rake of the highest order and–"

A palm was held up. "Miss Lambert, I have dealt with libidinous dukes, groping earls and a pinching viscount who necessitated I pad my rear with a cushion. I can deal with rakes."

Amelia prodded forth another crumpet. "I have also heard rumours that the ward is–"

"Liable to tantrums? A hoyden in her prime?" With brow creased, she sighed. "I have been a governess since I was eighteen, Miss Lambert, and have seen it all." Then levelled her gaze. "So, why don't you tell me what it is you really want?"

An astute one indeed.

Amelia poured more tea. "I am asking you not to attend your interview."

The lady spluttered. "Why on earth not?"

"I cannot tell you all, but it is believed that Mr Cadwalader has been involved in…wrongdoing."

An auburn brow raised. "What sort of wrongdoing?"

"As I said, I'm not at liberty to tell you, but the…thief-taker I work fo–"

Miss Webster choked on her tea. "You work for a…"

Amelia's lips twitched, uncertain whether her superior, Lord Rainham, would chuckle or take offence at being called such, but she held the lady's incredulous stare. "Just so. And as such, I need to be employed as his governess in order to enter the household and investigate further."

"I see. Well, forgive my being taken aback, Miss Lambert, but that is not a common occupation for us unmarried ladies. If one does not wish to depend upon the largesse of relatives or has no other source of income, I thought becoming a governess or companion were our sole options."

"There are few of us, 'tis true. The work can be ceaseless and I never seem to be in one place long enough to make friends."

"Similar to a governess, so I'd best remain one," grumped Miss Webster. "But that means, Miss Lambert, I also need this job." She heaved another sigh whilst reaching for another crumpet. "I shall be frank with you. My father gambled away all the family money, including my dowry, before inconveniently dying in a tavern brawl and bequeathing a gaggle of creditors. The house I was left is falling about my ears, the roof leaks, the attics have mould, and my ducal neighbour is pressuring me to sell it to him, likely for a pittance. But I cannot and will not, for it is the only home I've ever known. It is my constant shelter and my sole hope of future security. Besides which, my uncle, who arrived on my doorstep two years ago, is slowly losing his mind, and with his meagre pension from the Royal Society has nowhere else to go. At midnight, he wanders the duke's rose garden in merely his nightshirt calling for Martha. Now tell me, Miss Lambert, who needs that job more?"

Amelia felt a sudden kinship with this lady and thrust forth her hand. "I was also left in dire circumstances at a young age with debts to settle. There must be a way we can work together – to both our advantages."

Miss Webster shook Amelia's hand. "But I do not see how. We cannot both be employed." She sipped her tea, gaze sliding to the colossal tome on the table. "Were you planning on reading that?"

With a roll of eye, Amelia chomped on a crumpet. "Indeed, but I fell asleep on chapter three last night."

"You've never been a governess before?"

"No. And I would have to retain this job for at least a fortnight in order to complete my investigation." She patted her mouth with a napkin. "There must be something we can do. You know how to be a governess but I don't, and I don't require the wage but you do."

They stared at one another for some moments before Miss Webster's lips began to curve, just as Amelia's did the same.

She hadn't the time to faff about studying this book, correcting essays or writing lists of moral instruction, which was rather hypocritical anyhow.

"I could..." Miss Webster leaned across the table. "I could write your lesson plans. Correct any of the pupil's writings and set questions."

Amelia's lips curved to a full grin. "And I would pass on the wage, assuming I get the job, of course."

"Hmm." Miss Webster played with a loose thread on her cuff, brow puckered. "Yet if you are only in the post for a fortnight, you may not receive much of a wage, if anything at all."

Amelia pondered. "If so, then my employer will stump up." *She hoped.* "And as recompense for the short-term nature of this arrangement, I could add…" Amelia mulled her assignment expenses. "One guinea a week?"

"It took me years to study Miss Appleton's book. Two guineas."

"One guinea and six shillings?"

"One guinea and a half. With ink and paper provided for the lesson plans."

Amelia pursed her lips. Paper would have to be cadged from her prospective employer as Foreign Office expenses only went so far.

"Agreed, Miss Webster."

"I'll need you to gauge the young lady's level of intelligence, of course. The lessons oft depend on the pupil, her characteristics and needs. And, please, call me Charlotte."

"I can easily send a lad with my notes on the ward when I'm there. And, please, call me Amelia."

"Perfect," they both said in unison before clinking their delicate Wedgwood cups together.

"Although…" Charlotte's nose scrunched. "What if Mr Cadwalader receives further applicants?"

Amelia winked. "I have a feeling he won't."

Her accomplice grinned while Amelia sipped her tea, most content with the morning's work, yet as she watched Charlotte snaffle another crumpet, she noticed once more the creases to her brow that refused to smooth. Amelia didn't like to pry but… Of course, she liked to pry – that was her job.

"Who is this duke pressuring you to sell your house? Perhaps I could…" *Dig up some tittle-tattle.* "…assist."

"The Duke of Shawdale."

"Not Skinflint Shawdale?"

Charlotte nodded.

"Oh dear, I've read of him in the gossip columns."

"Marcus isn't a bad sort."

Marcus? Amelia hoisted a brow.

"Well, I knew him when we were young," continued Charlotte, a blush tinging her cheeks. "We grew up together but...he changed and I do not recognise him anymore. He's become..."

"Rather a hog grubber according to the gossip rags."

Charlotte's lips trembled. "Maybe so."

Amelia would have to put her thinking cap on.

"And if I may also ask..." Charlotte winced and scratched her arm. "Could I have some monies paid upfront, do you think? I'm sure this hotel has fleas."

"I can do better than that," Amelia said, wrapping the rest of the crumpets in a serviette for Charlotte to take. "You provide the ink and you can have use of my home in Holborn rent free. No fleas."

"Done."

After a further pot of tea, Miss Webster scribbled a note to Mr Cadwalader explaining she'd been offered another position, and Amelia sat back eyeing Miss Appleton's weighty tome on the table.

What on earth was she to do with it now?

CHAPTER THREE

"Place duty first, usefulness next, ornament last."

Private Education: A Practical Plan for the Studies of Young Ladies.

Elizabeth Appleton. 1815.

A mug of tea was placed beneath Hugh's nose, its shade as murky as an old penny.

"My utmost thanks, Mrs Benson." He clasped the mug with a firm hand; there was no choice. "You certainly know how to warm a man's cockles of a morn."

The woman guffawed and winked. "Tha's what Mister Benson says too."

Hugh grinned and shifted on the incommodious bench. His superior at the Home Office had summoned him here for nine but then left him to kick his heels in the damn corridor. The bells of Whitehall Palace had just chimed ten and a restless frustration gripped him. "Do you know who's in there at the moment?"

Mrs Benson's rather broad shoulders lifted and lowered. "Big fellow with a big nose."

"Wellington returned home?"

"Has he a big nose?"

"Yes."

She sank to the bench and sidled up. "Could be but..." Beetle-brown eyes peered left. Then right. "He asked fer coffee, don't yer know." She tapped her nose. "I mean, what Englishman drinks coffee? He should have proper English tea. From England. If this country goes to the dogs, I'll blame coffee." She stood and pulled her shoulders back. "Drink up, lad."

Hugh regarded the beverage, girded his loins and took a gulp.

Gads. He could feel the tannic strength right down to the tassels on his Hessians. "As per usual, Mrs Benson, it's abundantly...strong."

"Thankin' yer. I steep it fer an hour then re-boil it. The His Nibs before, Lord rest his soul, said me brew gave a man character." She pointed at a plate of substances upon her trolley. "Biscuit? I make them meself. None of that fancy French nonsense like the new His Nibs in there orders from Mons'ur Pierre's Patipisserie."

"*Patisserie?*"

She shrugged and waggled a stubby finger at the plate.

Hugh had been in many a tight spot before – a crossbow aimed at his nether regions and a dagger held to his throat – but this called for quick wits and...sycophancy. "They appear so light and divine, Mrs Benson, as though floated down to earth from the heavens above."

"Oh, you're such a fine lad." And his shoulder was batted with fists the size of a prizefighter's.

"But as such cruel misfortune would have it, I've just this

morn been to the tooth-puller and biscuits are forbidden for...a good three weeks."

"Don't yer worry yerself. I'll keep some by till then."

Bugger.

He'd not thought that through. "Splendid."

"Well, I'd best be goin'. There's a new clerk transferred from Records who hasn't sampled me jam tarts yet." And off she lumbered.

A potted plant to one side of the bench received the remnants of the heady beverage, although with its stiff upright demeanour and hairy stems, it appeared to have already drunk its fill.

Leaning back, he stared to the monotonous white wall of the corridor, but as the creak of Mrs Benson's trolley faded, his smile did likewise.

For he used to sit here with Phoebe's father, Ross Thornton.

When first recruited to the Home Office, Hugh had been as green as the Welsh spring grass and it had been the elder Ross who'd become his mentor, taught him all – from the black arts of locks to how to wield a blade and stay alive in the rookeries of London – but Hugh had also come to know the Thornton family, watched Phoebe grow from impish toddler to mischievous child.

Over those years, he and Ross had become close friends, comrades in arms, able to know one another's thoughts and to communicate with no more than a nod. Ross had been a man of admirable strength who'd only ever seen the good in people, despite the sordid depths their missions had taken them. And furthermore, Hugh owed him his life.

Their paths had diverged over the past few years, missions taking them hither and thither, but Hugh had never forgotten the debt he owed him. Had vowed to repay him someday.

Hugh's lids closed.

But now that day would never come.

His friend and mentor had been found dead in his locked study eight months past by his butler, a glass of arsenic-laced whisky at his side along with a note – supposedly in his penmanship, though Hugh had not seen it – admitting he'd been selling Home Office secrets to the highest bidder, that he could no longer live with the guilt...

Hugh's nails bit into his palms.

Incriminating documents had also been discovered in the study, evidence overwhelming, and after mere days it had been decided by the upper echelons of the Home Office to hush up the entire affair, to shake their heads and mutter of rotten apples. But that was to ignore Ross' sixteen years of service as though it were naught, to not even consider there might be another explanation.

So along with Crown missions, Hugh had begun to look for one.

He'd pieced together Ross' last movements – where he'd been seen and what he'd been working on. According to the records, he should have been documenting the whereabouts of a vicomte in Mayfair, yet one of their shared Rookery informants told a different tale. All too often, Ross had been seen in St Giles, asking questions and supping ale with the rag, tag and bob tails who frequented those alleys.

Why?

What had he been looking for?

Another department of the Home Office had searched the Thornton household top to bottom, yet Hugh knew Ross better, so with Phoebe under the roof of her great-aunt Rebecca, he'd conducted his own search.

The study had been locked from the inside, but the Home Office search had missed minuscule but tell-tale scratch marks to the keyhole of the terrace doors. The lock had at some point been tampered with. Had someone entered and poisoned Ross? Or taken him there already lifeless?

Hugh had rifled through papers in the study, library and chambers, searched every single room in the damn house until a small portrait on the wall of Ross' wife had produced what he'd been looking for: a niche behind the wood panels, hiding a tatty notebook.

Most of it had been devoted to past missions, some they'd been on together, but then, on the last pages…

Ross had written a list of names.

At first glance, Hugh had recognised only one, that of a colleague murdered at the coast whilst pursuing wreckers, but on further investigation, he'd found that all the names had a connection with the Home Office, and all of them had come to grief in the previous year: a woman supposedly under safeguard discovered with her throat cut; an informant at the bottom of the Thames…

Ross had clearly realised this was no coincidence. That the sole explanation for the spate of murders was some traitorous lickspittle passing on reports and intelligence from within the Home Office.

Then on the next page had been a handful of further surnam–

"Number Five!"

Hugh snapped his eyes open, launched himself from the bench and dashed to the door, nigh colliding with the man departing.

Big nose but it wasn't Wellington.

His superior's office was rather ornate for Whitehall. A lavish crystal chandelier hung from a ceiling of elaborate plasterwork, and the walls were lined with gilt-framed portraits of all the previous spy masters who'd dignified these rooms.

"You wished to see me, Sir Edmund?"

"Ah, Number Five, take a seat."

Hugh did so, the leather still warm.

Papers were strewn across his superior's desk, maps of – Hugh tilted his head – Derbyshire covered the floor, and folders spilled their contents on the cabinet.

In the post for eighteen months now, Sir Edmund Twyford had white locks, stooping shoulders and perpetually bloodshot eyes. On first acquaintance, one might have thought him scatter-brained – and Hugh oft thought it on second acquaintance too – but the methods he'd brought from the admiralty yielded results and his memory for facts wa–

"Damnation!" Sir Edmund yelled. "Thomas!"

A clerk with a bilious cast about him came dashing through the door. A clerk Hugh had not seen before – the transferred chap from Records, perhaps?

"Yes, Sir Edmund."

"Get me the map of Derbyshire."

"It's on the floor," interrupted Hugh. "By the foot of your desk."

Sir Edmund peered down. "So it is. No wonder you are one of our finest intelligence officers."

"Thank you, Sir Edmund."

He commenced scribbling notes. "I'm sending you to..." A palm was thrust upwards. "Wait." More scribbling.

Hugh casually hooked his boot onto his knee but every nerve heightened as he'd not be leaving London for aught at this moment in time.

For Ross' notebook had contained a handful of further surnames scribbled beneath a title: The Brotherhood of Ravens.

Nothing further had been written about them and Hugh had wondered who the hell they were? And why had Ross been interested?

It'd taken Hugh more than a few guineas in bribery and

endless nights in various rookeries before he'd discovered they were a group of disgruntled soldiers. Feeling abandoned by the government after the war, rumours said they plotted revolution and chaos.

After learning that an Ensign named Forsyth and another man listed in Ross' notebook were regulars at an ale-house off Seven Dials, Hugh had also started frequenting the establishment in the guise of an equally disgruntled Lieutenant Davies from the Royal Welsh Fusiliers.

Only too aware of the dangers, Hugh had been patient in befriending them, always taking care to follow a torturous route home through the lanes of London to ensure he wasn't trailed.

They'd mutually complained about the corrupt government, the spendthrift Prince Regent and all those debauched coxcombs in parliament, whilst Hugh had let it be known he wanted more to be done.

Then last week, Forsyth had brought along another man.

John Roberts.

A former lieutenant in the 32nd Regiment of Foot. And moreover, leader of the Brotherhood of Ravens.

Hard-eyed and grim-lipped, he'd invited Hugh to a meeting in three days' time.

At last, he was getting somewhere.

But Ross' notebook had also contained another clue. A torn-out page, folded and stuffed in amongst the leaves, with a list of ladies' nam–

"Derbyshire!"

"Beg pardon?"

Sir Edmund glared. "I'm sending you to Derbyshire."

Not with the Ravens meeting in three days, he wasn't.

And he was also making progress on that list of ladies' names and a certain Lady Thurwood…

Justice for Ross and Phoebe came above all else and besides, if someone was still passing on information, who knew which of them could be prematurely put to bed with a mattock and tucked in with a spade.

"I am unable to–"

"It's all arranged. Lodgings and what have you. Details are sent. Number Eight is set to leave and... What are you still doing here, Thomas? Be off with you."

The clerk rolled his eyes and dashed out.

"Sir, I cannot–"

"There's talk of rebellion. Stocking frames destroyed. Riots. Stones thrown. Et cetera. So insinuate yourself with the felons. Good chap. Close the door on your way out."

Hugh remained seated. "I have a ward to consider, Sir Edmund. I cannot up sticks so quickly now."

White eyebrows shifted like frolicking lambs. "Send her off to a school, man! Three nieces of mine attended Miss Goodacre's Seminary for Elegant Young Ladies for twelve years."

Quite. Faith had recently married yet chased everything except her husband, Charity was too fond of the laudanum, and as for Hope...there was none.

"No."

Sir Edmund peered up. "No?"

"My ward needs me, and I have matters to attend to here."

Those bloodshot eyes narrowed. "Your former mentor, Thornton... He said the same when I wanted to send him to Lancashire. I hope, Number Five, you're not going to become like him."

Was that a threat? Hugh idly smiled, every knuckle wishing to punch his superior's lights out.

"There is a certain..." He leaned towards the desk. "Lady I am pursuing who is, shall we say, of a royal connection? A while ago, you wished for intelligence on the Prince Regent's private finances for parliament. I am…pushing hard to get it. But if I leave London now, she may find an alternative man to lavish her time upon."

A lie but one he could pursue should it be required.

"You old dog, why didn't you say?" His superior's eyes crinkled. "I'll give you till the end of the month. Number Eight can get started but make arrangements for your ward. Then off to Derbyshire."

With a flat-lipped smile, Hugh stood, but Sir Edmund Twyford's nose had returned to his papers. "Of course, Sir."

The monotonous Whitehall corridors blurred as Hugh strode them and descended the stairs, stepping out through a side door to the damp pavement.

A worn hackney happened to be loitering on the street, a fine drizzle repainting it in drab grey, so after shouting his address, he clambered in.

As wheel clacked over cobble, his thoughts turned to Phoebe and the shadow of sadness that hounded her. He vowed to give her back the Ross Thornton he'd known – not a scorned traitor but a brave and admirable man. A father to be proud of.

With a scowl, he shoved down the window, breathed in air redolent of damp coal and felt the light mist of drizzle upon his face.

Back in his native Wales, rain was a different commodity altogether. It could pour down as though the heavens wished to drown the populace, but the scent… Ah, the scent was of rugged moors and verdant valleys, coastal salt and fragrant heather.

As a rule, he would visit every few months to feel the sweet rain purge his jaded soul, to restore his belief in mankind, to revel in his two cousins' affection and, over the past year, to watch them each fall in love with beautiful women.

For some reason, that thought caused a pall.

Perhaps because his own life was not compatible with such romantic sentiment.

For what woman would understand the life he'd chosen? His dangerous nights and damaged body.

Hanover Square came into view and his Palladian style home, with its three floors, porticoed porch and pedimented door surround – smidgeon extravagant perhaps but expected of the Scandalous Hugh Cadwalader.

He handed thruppence to the hackney driver and loped up the steps to–

The ever-attentive Cruikshank flung open the door.

His butler had worked for all the illustrious names of the *Ton* over his career and was a bony body but corpulent mind of information. Five years ago, Hugh had snaffled him from a duke's household for fifty quid a year and a sumptuous pension, but with Hugh's employ, it had been on condition of signing a promise of confidentiality. When asked if he'd minded, Cruikshank had merely sniffed and declared it went without saying but signed nonetheless.

"Ah, Cruik, any urgent messages?"

Hugh divested himself of hat and gloves within the hall while his butler sorted through a raft of letters on a silver salver.

"I believe this is the most urgent. From a Miss Webster? Regarding your interview this afternoon, perhaps?"

Hugh narrowed his eyes, took the message and broke the seal.

I regret to inform you that...

And so on and so forth.

He tapped the paper against his lips. Which only left him with...

Miss Jones.

A vision arose of those amber eyes concealing golden flame.

An enigma.

And he found he was not quite so irritated to hear of Miss Webster's withdrawal as he should have been.

Instead, a sense of anticipation thronged his veins.

Although that could also be because Sir Edmund had solely given him till the end of the month. A short timeframe indeed.

"I'm off upstairs," he stated to Cruikshank. "Make sure I am undisturbed."

"Naturally, Sir."

Hugh ascended the staircase from the hall, shoving off his jacket.

By the first floor, his exquisitely knotted *Mathematique* cravat was undone and draped over the banister.

By the second, his waistcoat was on the rug.

He flung open double doors and lobbed his shirt over his head.

Naked from the waist up, he stretched.

Time to rid himself of some excess energy.

CHAPTER FOUR

"Poor innocent children. Look at their agitation, dread, and submission."

Private Education: A Practical Plan for the Studies of Young Ladies. Elizabeth Appleton. 1815.

Amelia muttered beneath her breath.

For No. 14 Hanover Square was so palatial that even the rainwater pipes were decorated with pugnacious dragons, the year of construction embossed in gold on the broad drain hopper: *1809*.

She'd not taken too much notice of the house for the interview, but now she admired the symmetrical façade which boasted modern sash windows, a Doric porch and a white stuccoed band above the second floor.

Charlotte had instructed that a diligent governess should arrive at the servants' entrance for her first day, so heaving her carpetbag – no mean feat with Miss Appleton's tome, clothes and other essentials packed within – she stomped past the front door and followed the elaborate iron railings to a gap giving access to basement stairs.

Yesterday, a visit to Messrs Makefare and Co., architects to the rich and famed, had resulted in plans to most of the houses in this square, and Amelia had noted that like all recent constructions, the ground floor of this house was raised up so that the basement kitchens, with their new piped water, would lead directly onto the back garden.

Even this servants' door was painted a refined dark green, as though Mr Cadwalader had personally chosen it to match his coat.

She knocked.

And waited.

Charlotte had also stated it was not uncommon for a governess to commence lessons the very same day she arrived, so Amelia had sent a message declaring she'd arrive of the eve, thereby spending as little time teaching as possi–

The door was flung open by a young maid with red cheeks, black hair and eyes the size of walnuts.

"Lor-a-mussy, the new governess! I've never met one afore. In yer come. Me name's Sally Longlane and I work in the kitchens." The effusive maid with a strong Essex accent seized hold of Amelia's arm and hauled her along an unlit corridor. "Can yer write? I suppose yer can. I can write me first name but not the other one as it's too blinkin' long." She was hustled past sitting and storerooms alike. "A word of advice. Never tell Mrs D yer've got something wrong with yer." Then a distillation room with a nauseous odour. "Ain't it a fancy gaff? It's even got an indoor boghouse fer us servants, yer realise." Before an open door led to a kitchen. "Look everyone, 'tis the new governess!" And a sturdy push on the shoulder propelled her into the room.

Amelia gulped.

Then used some choice words for Lord Rainham.

Stood there were three further maids, two thickset footmen, a plump woman who looked to be the housekeeper, the white-haired butler, whom she remembered as Cruikshank, and the cook, no skills needed to guess her job as she was dicing carrots at a stout wooden table.

She recalled Charlotte's words: *You are neither of the Servant Class nor the Upper Class. You abide between the two. Neither class are your friends, remember that. But if the servants like you, then half the battle is won.*

"Erm, good afternoon. I am so pleased to make your acquaintance."

Sally went to stand by the range cooker as the housekeeper wiped her hands on a pristine apron and hastened over. "Now then, I hope our Sally hasn't been bending your ear with all her prattle?" The housekeeper had a dulcet Welsh accent. "She's training for lower housemaid, Miss, she is." A green beady gaze perused Amelia from boots to bonnet. "And you can't be the new governess."

"W-why not?"

Her lips curved, crinkles forming by her eyes. "Too young and pretty, like."

"Oh, that's kind of you to say so."

"And aren't you short."

Amelia detested her lack of stature some days.

"Well, I'm Mrs Dawkins, the housekeeper."

"Pleased to meet you. I'm Miss Jones." She cleared her throat. "Amelia Jones."

Creases formed on Mrs Dawkins' forehead. "Have you a sore throat, lovey?"

Amelia was about to admit she did have a slight rasp but…

Sally Longlane was vehemently shaking her head behind the housekeeper's back, the footmen were wincing, the maids staring to the ceiling, and even the butler had closed his eyes in certain sufferance.

"No, no. Just thirsty, thank you. Governesses…talk so much, you know. All day. Just talking to their pupils."

"Hmm. Well, you let me know if it worsens and I'll knock up a tonic, I shall."

"That's most generous."

"Nothing like a gargle with my snail syrup for clearing hoarseness."

Amelia's lips parted. Closed. Opened. "No, I'm quite sure there isn't."

After a satisfied nod, Mrs Dawkins introduced her to the rest of the servants, and they were all so welcoming, so joyful that someone was here to look after the 'Sorrowful Miss Thornton' that Amelia had never felt such a fraud.

The butler was the sole member of the household to stare down at her as though she were a pinned butterfly. "I am to escort you to the master and his ward as soon as you arrive, Miss…Jones."

"Lawks," cried Sally, "is Mister Cadwalader back from visiting his latest bit o' fluff? That were a quicki–"

"Sally Longlane!" wailed the housekeeper. "I'll have no gossip of our esteemed master."

The rest of the crew nodded in reproach and Amelia winced – loyal servants were so much more difficult to question.

"Although," continued the housekeeper with a tut, "that *was* a smidgeon quick. Perchance he's bored and will stop gadding around soon."

As the butler led Amelia up the servants' stairs and onto the ground floor, he pointed a skeletal finger at the various rooms and Amelia feigned interest but not too much interest – though it did confirm the architect's plans.

Study to the front, drawing room in the middle and dining room to the back, before they ascended a grand mahogany staircase, the banister so polished, Amelia could see her fingernails in it.

"You will be residing upon this first floor, Miss...Jones, opposite to Miss Thornton. Another bedroom here has been converted to the schoolroom."

"That sounds perfect. And Mr Cadwalader's quart–" He halted so abruptly she ran into the back of him. "Forgive me."

The butler swivelled. "The master's quarters are the second floor."

"All of it?"

He stared down his long nose. "All of it." Raised a haughty brow. "No one, and I repeat *no one*, is allowed there without his express permission."

"Gosh," she burbled. "It's just such an impressive house. So...large."

With a roll of eye, he turned, and she followed him down the corridor, catching a glimpse of an ornate ballroom through gilded double doors. She felt rather light-headed. It had only happened once before, when an elderly peer at a gambling hell had remarked on her likeness to the famed Butterfly Courtesan of a decade past.

The butler halted.

Amelia halted.

Heart pounding.

A door was thrust open.

"Miss...Jones, Sir." And the butler withdrew.

Stepping forward into what looked to be the schoolroom, Amelia gulped as Mr Cadwalader turned, the tails of his burgundy coat swishing, fine blue eyes flashing and–

What was that?

For slouching beside the blond magnificence of Mr Cadwalader was…a crow. No, a witch. No, a…young girl? A young witch?

Black hair. Black eyes. A black crepe dress from the last century. Black jet jewellery. Black boots.

Amelia peered around for the black cat.

"Ah, Miss Jones!" enthused Mr Cadwalader. "How splendid of you to accept the position. May I introduce my vibrant ward, Miss Phoebe Thornton."

The girl scrunched her nose, lips slammed together.

"Good evening, Miss Thornton."

The girl glared.

Mr Cadwalader nudged.

"Evening," she all but mumbled.

"Well, how delightful," said Mr Cadwalader with a wide grin. "I'll let Phoebe show you to your room and allow the two of you to become better acquainted. We'll talk further on the morrow, Miss Jones, but do you have any pressing questions for me now?"

Amelia recalled the question Charlotte had considered acceptable for a first day. "Will we all be dining together, Sir, as a rule? Or do Phoebe and I dine in this schoolroom?"

The ward received an affectionate pat on the shoulder before Mr Cadwalader approached with a slight limp, breeches as fitted as bark upon a tree. "For myself, I rarely dine at home, Miss Jones, but this schoolroom is not large and Phoebe has all of fifteen years now, so I insist you both use the dining room."

"Very well, Sir."

"Uncle Hugh, you're limping." The girl frowned. "What happened this time?"

"Just an old wound, Phoebe. You don't wish to know the tale."

The girl's lip vaguely twitched. "Oh, I think I do, Uncle."

He smiled at Amelia – all white teeth and convivial eyes. "Well, truth be told, I found myself in Saint Petersburg several years ago when... I hope you are not easily put to blush, Miss Jones?"

"Governesses rarely blush, Mr Cadwalader. All the books we read."

"Good, good. Well, to cut a long story short, the then Tsar considered the fashionable new gentleman's attire of ankle-length pantaloons such a radical departure from the norm that he issued a decree forbidding them and had his troops halt carriages in order to inspect any gentlemen's leg garb."

The young girl gasped. "Were you caught, Uncle?"

"Indeed, in a pair of my finest fawn pantaloons from Ede & Ravenscroft. I was thrown to the carriage floor, would you believe, by a most bearded fellow who then cut them off at the knee with a sabre! The careless blackguard got a little carried away in his enthusiasm and the leg's never been the same in damp weather."

Phoebe Thornton sniggered, hand at mouth. "Oh, what a clanker! As if the Tsar would decree that."

Amelia turned to her employer, now stood close at her side, and narrowed her eyes. "I believe that decree was true, was it not?"

His smile lingered. "Been to Russia, have you?"

"Of course not, Sir, but as I said, governesses read so much. Books, pamphlets and...more books."

He tipped forward. "Just so, Miss Jo–" His nostrils broadened in proximity to her hair, a frown cleaving his brow. "Can I smell roses mingled with...gunpowder?"

Amelia swallowed.

That anomalous flare of flame rekindled within her.

"I wear rosewater, Sir, but as for gunpowder… I couldn't even say what it smells like."

"Wet coal and eggs."

Amelia looked him dead in the eye and fibbed for all she was worth. "Well, I partook of boiled eggs in front of the coal fire before I came. Perhaps the scents have clung to my hair?"

"Of course." He leaned back with a sudden indolent smile. "What was I thinking?" And turned. "Well, Phoebe, my blackbird, I shall leave you in the capable hands of Miss Jones. Give her a tour and so forth. I am attending the Heywood's dinner and ball tonight, so better get some togs on. It takes me an age to dress this finely."

And with a wink for his ward and a nod for Amelia, he limped from the schoolroom.

Miss Thornton turned to scowl at her while Amelia scowled at Mr Cadwalader's retreating coat-tails.

He may act the elegant dandy, may appear the epitome of a handsome gadabout with nothing more on his mind than women, *à la mode* pantaloons and select dinner invitations, but as she'd previously supposed, there was something…dangerous beneath that golden guise.

She'd *felt* it as he'd leaned near.

That elegant exterior cloaked a predatory animal. One it would be wise not to rouse.

"I'll show you to your chamber then," groused her charge.

IT WAS BLACK.

"How…restful," Amelia murmured, peering at the gothic four-poster bed with its ebony feathers, gloomy drapery and heavy oak pilasters. "I'm sure to sleep well here." If the nightmares abated for long enough.

"This isn't yours. It's mine. And it's not restful at all." Miss

Phoebe Thornton crossed her arms, bombazine material crinkling. "I ordered drapery entitled 'Deepest Night' but Uncle Hugh mixed up the lists and ordered 'Dusk Blue'."

Amelia peered again – it looked black to her – before twisting to peruse her charge.

At a mere fifteen years, Phoebe Thornton had seen much loss, been left an orphan far too young in life.

In this drab room, her young face appeared pale and wan, the old-fashioned dress drowning her in heavy lace and velvet ribbon. In general, a girl ceased wearing the deepest weeds of mourning for a parent after six months, moving to a lighter half-mourning of lavender or soft grey, so why was Phoebe still wearing a black deeper than the grave? And why was it some forty years out of fashion?

Perhaps Mr Cadwalader's luxuriant tastes had left him out of pocket where his ward was concerned?

"Well, it's a spacious room, at least." In fact, this bedchamber alone was nigh the size of her home in Holborn.

"I need the space for all the…" The girl cast a sly glance. "Tatting I do."

Amelia had been placed in charge of an imp.

An evil imp.

For although Charlotte had since told her of the lace craft, by no means could she learn it overnight. Or within a week. Or a month. She cast her own sly glance. "I'm surprised you can see to do such delicate craft in here. My bedchamber is opposite, Mr Cruikshank led me to believe?"

They both stomped across the hall to where Amelia…sighed.

"Grim, isn't it?" muttered Phoebe.

Amelia adored it.

Her mother had been so feminine and dainty, like a fluttering fay, and had wished her daughter to be the same, thus the bedroom of Amelia's childhood had been a frothy concoction of Pompadour-pink drapes, blowsy bows and winged cherubs, all festooned with yards of white lace.

At Phoebe's age, she'd suffered it, but with the passage of time, she missed the utter lightness, the soft embrace of pink.

This bedchamber reminded her of childhood, of home. One lost so long ago.

"I..." She swallowed down a clog of emotion. "I rather like it." The paperhangings were a blossom-pink while the half-tester bed was draped in deep-rose silk. A trunk was positioned at the bottom. With a useful key in its lock.

A few portraits hung on the walls while a dressing-table mirror sat upon a polished chest of drawers, and on a spacious desk was a vase of blush-pink roses.

Smiling, Amelia walked over to them, placed her carpetbag on the desk's chair and fingered the silken blooms; not a single thorn was upon their stems.

Phoebe came to stand at her side. "Uncle Hugh adores roses and as soon as they become available has them placed in every room. There are white ones in mine." She rolled her eyes. "He thinks he's funny. I'm going to paint them."

Beside the desk, a large sash window overlooked the garden with the stables at the far end, and she supposed that on the next floor up, one could view the goings-on of Oxford Street.

Amelia pressed her nose to the glass.

In the dusk light, she could make out Mr Cadwalader, dressed to the nines and following the flagstone path to the stables where doubtless a smart green carriage awaited.

So not such *an age* to dress himself then.

Black breeches clad his long legs, the artful tails of his green evening coat fluttering. His beaver hat sat at a jaunty angle and a cane tapped confidently with each stride.

What secrets did he hide? Was he a turncoat, as had been

suggested? She'd seen the most steadfast of men have their heads turned by pretty women or even prettier guineas.

"I'll be leaving you to unpack then."

Goodness, she'd all but forgotten her charge, and twisted. "Thank you, Phoebe. We will begin our lessons on the morrow."

"I don't need lessons." The girl folded her arms, lips a straight line of nothing. "Mother taught me all I needed to know. Then Father. I will have Uncle Hugh send you away as soon as I can."

The first challenge to her authority.

This was completely normal, apparently, and a professional governess ought to nip it in the bud, take a firm hand, just as Miss Appleton – well, Charlotte – advised, yet...

Amelia was no governess and she understood the pain this girl felt. A mere two years older and Amelia herself had been the one frightened of an uncertain future, the one who had wished to hide away in murky mourning clothes and never look upon the light of day.

Behind Phoebe's challenge lay grief and hurt, and Amelia vowed to treat her with all kindness.

"I agree. Nobody can teach us in the same manner as our parents do, for they know us so very well – our likes and dislikes. My own mother imparted a wealth of knowledge before I lost her when I was seventeen. But for me, there was more I wanted to learn." She cocked her head. "Is there not more you want to learn?"

"Some matters." She fiddled with the gloomy lace and then glared up. "But I wager you won't teach me them. Good night, Miss Jones. Sleep well. Although..." She paused at the doorway. "'In that sleep of death what dreams may come.'" And with a flick of shadowy skirts, she closed the door with a thud.

Amelia puffed her cheeks, opened her carpetbag and, with

reverent care, lifted out Miss Appleton's book, placing it on the desk beside the roses.

And shoved hands to hips.

Maybe she should have followed Mama in her chosen profession as assuredly one didn't have to deal with stubborn young ladies or snail syrup.

Nevertheless, she delved once more into her carpetbag and seized two squares of paper and a pencil. One was a note for Charlotte.

Miss Phoebe Thornton.
Rebellious & shrewd.
Grieving. Lost.
Appears to know Shakespeare well.
Have you any tatting samples?

And on the other...

Mr Hugh Cadwalader.
Wily & perceptive – gunpowder, indeed!
Confident. Devious.
Appears to tell embellished and droll tales to cover the truth of his activities.
Why does he need the entire second floor to himself?

She paused, lead to paper.

It would behove her to tread warily in this household, but also to make haste in completing her report as, Amelia felt, her time here would be short.

Her charge was nimble-witted.

Cadwalader did not suffer fools.

And then there was that anomalous flare of flame which his presence induced.

She must tread with care.

The scent of roses wafted from the vase beside her, spicy yet delicate, and she eyed their pink perfection before scribbling a last note.

Mr Hugh Cadwalader is dangerous.

CHAPTER FIVE

"In time, the child will feel in its little tender breast the movements of affection."

PRIVATE EDUCATION: A PRACTICAL PLAN FOR THE STUDIES OF YOUNG LADIES.

ELIZABETH APPLETON. 1815.

"I know full well how to walk," Phoebe contested.

"No, you don't," Amelia replied. "You slouch. Now place these three books on your head and pretend you are…gliding across Almack's floor into the embrace of a handsome young duke."

After all, wasn't that what every fifteen-year-old dreamed of?

Not that they existed. All the dukes Amelia knew had nose hair and liver spots.

Phoebe crossed her arms. "I'm never going to Almack's. It sounds humdrum."

Amelia brought a hand to her forehead.

As a young girl, she herself had been given all the usual

lessons by her mother's companion, a genteel lady who'd been thoroughly ruined by a rake and thoroughly enjoyed it, but those lessons had been…fun, albeit a little unusual. They'd gambled to study percentages, staggered about in mother's silliest shoes to learn the waltz and read *Tom Jones* to explore England's geography.

Charlotte had advised to begin with reading for the first day as what could go wrong? But the little imp had read Hamlet within an hour, answered every question Charlotte had prepared and then sat back with a jaded expression.

Taking a seat, Amelia contemplated her charge. Today she was wearing a black crepe dress from some three decades past that, even when fashionable, had only been worn by devoted widows after their spouses' immediate demise. It was gruesome – all black scratchy lace and black starchy collar.

"Which modiste do you visit for your gowns?"

Phoebe plucked at the skirts. "I refuse to visit a modiste. These are my great-aunt Rebecca's. She gave me her old widow's weeds."

"I was told your great-aunt Rebecca became too ill to look after you?"

"An onset of the ague, although…" The girl wrinkled her nose. "She didn't really want me there anyhow but she is my sole female relative so there was nowhere else to go. I could do as I pleased though. Wear what I wanted. No…governesses."

Which explained much.

"But Mr Cadwalader wishes you to have a governess now he is your guardian. So you may gain knowledge for the world you will soon be entering."

"Uncle just wants me distracted."

Did he? "Why is that?"

"He's other matters on his mind," she said flatly.

"And I notice you call him Uncle?"

"He was friends with my parents and so like an uncle to me," she replied yet more flatly.

"They must have been close." Amelia gave a cheery smile. "And do you have many friends?"

"No. Great-Aunt Rebecca once told me to talk with the neighbour's elder girls, said I would learn much, but they were silly as geese. Prattled of ribbons and…boys." She spat the last word as if expelling pond slime.

"Well, what would you have liked to learn about then?"

Phoebe's eyes widened as though she'd never been asked before. "Oh… I… I'd have liked to learn of… Learn about…" She wrung her hands, teeth chewing her lip, and Amelia abruptly worried she wished to discuss how babes came about.

"You can ask me anything," Amelia offered, crossing her fingers.

"I'm sure you won't know."

"But then again, I might." She crossed her toes.

"I want… I want to learn about…" Amelia closed her eyes. "I want to learn more about…mathematics."

Amelia's eyes snapped open, toes uncrossing. "Mathematics? Do you? In what manner?"

"Numerical…" Her lips joggled. "Codes and conundrums and suchlike."

"Er…"

"Great-Aunt Rebecca grumbled it was unfeminine," she blurted, "even though Mother said I had an aptitude for them."

Amelia swallowed. She herself worked with numerical cyphers all the time, so if it meant she would retain this employment for longer… "Well, I have an aptitude for numerical conundrums also. Perhaps we could work upon some?"

"You d-don't find it…unfeminine? I thought a governess would frown upon such a subject. Great-Aunt Rebecca said people would look at me strangely if I could multiply fractions. That gentlemen at balls preferred a milksop with big bosoms. Not that I care." She stared at her thin flat chest. "And I haven't any bosoms."

"It's true, Phoebe, that some men prefer milksops, but there are plenty who want more than that." She thought of Lord Rainham's mathematical genius of a wife Lily who could clear a gambling den of its profits within an hour. "And many ladies have to manage their household accounts."

"Oh, I–"

A knock interrupted and the door opened.

"Miss...Jones?"

"Yes, Mr Cruikshank?" And why did he keep hesitating before her surname? Or false surname to be truthful. She studied his elongated aspect and pale eyes; she'd never met him before, of that she was certain.

"Mr Cadwalader has requested your presence."

"Now?"

"Now."

"Very well." She twisted. "Phoebe, perhaps you could write down a mathematical conundrum that you know of and we will try to solve it together?"

Her lips formed a slight, very slight, curve. "Yes, Miss."

So, seizing Miss Appleton's book, as one should never be caught napping, Amelia followed the starched coat-tails of Cruikshank past the ballroom, down the stairs, through the hall, and into the study where she'd first been interviewed.

"Miss...Jones, Sir."

See...

And the butler closed the door.

Mr Cadwalader rose from behind his pedestal desk, all muscular male grace and confident ease.

That curious flare of flame lit once more.

Perchance she had a fever?

Gathering her composure, Amelia inhaled, only to be greeted by a spice cologne of cinnamon and leather.

From beneath demurely lowered lashes, she scoured his aspect for any signs of dissipation from his gallivanting last night as she'd not heard his return till nigh three of the morn.

Yet except for those shadows below his eyes, which quite frankly added to his dangerous aspect, he appeared in fine fettle – alert and handsome with those perfect lips perennially on the verge of a smile.

She curbed her own lips from smiling, wiped all expression from her face, curtseyed and made two wishes: that these meetings would not become a daily occurrence and that he ask naught of her plan for lessons.

HUGH SPLAYED a hand for Miss Jones to sit, shoved his own rump into the comfy leather and considered what to ask. Although his ducal cousin had married a governess, he himself had never had cause to make the acquaintance of one. What did they do all day?

"So, how do you find Phoebe? Have you a plan of lessons for her?"

The band of amber in those irises narrowed. That happened a lot, he realised.

"I am in the process of forming just such a plan, Sir, but am still evaluating Phoebe's level of knowledge. She appears keen on Shakespeare, wishes to expand on her aptitude for... mathematics and has a dislike for etiquette."

"Can't say I blame her." Hugh leaned forward. "What she needs is subjects to challenge her. Keep her...distracted."

Because Phoebe was the result of what happened when two spies got shackled and popped offspring: intelligent, ambitious and cunning. He recalled her as a tot, inspecting the four walls of her nursery as though it were a maze to find her way out of.

She had done. The window.

His governess smoothed back a lock of hair. "Distracted from what, Sir?"

"Mischief, Miss Jones."

"I shall do my utmost then." And she lowered her lashes to her snuff-hued skirts.

Hugh stared, eyes lingering on her smooth skin. Yet, like the interview, she neither wriggled, blushed nor fidgeted.

Miss Jones was inscrutable, an enigma to be unravelled, a rose of furled crimson petals.

At the Heywood's affair yesternight, Lady Thurwood had been nothing but candid, hands fluttering and words effusive. An open white flower of summer.

He'd paid her attention, dare he say flirted, as she was one of the ladies on the torn page from Ross' notebook. She had a cousin who worked in the Home Office, that young chap from Records, but he could find no connection with the Brotherhood of Ravens.

Only as a last resort did he seduce as unfulfilled promises shadowed one's heart, a short step to losing it in the darkness altogether. A touch of flattery, however, never hurt a soul. Indeed, it could bring a shy wallflower to bloom and a bluestocking to a pink flush.

He redirected his gaze to his governess who stoically studied her skirts, hair prim and hands clasped. An unrufflable closed bud.

"Are the schoolrooms agreeable? Do you require any more writing paraphernalia? Quills?"

"All is perfect, although...paper is always required, Sir."

Gads, he'd already made sure she had a drawerful. How much could two females get through?

"Very well. I shall instruct Cruikshank to procure more. And I'm afraid I shall be out again this evening – till late."

Her gaze flicked up at his words. "Thank you, Sir. That's good to know."

Hugh just hoped he would return in one piece as tonight was the meeting of the Brotherhood of Ravens and although he considered his disguise more than adequate, had told no one of his search for answers, all it would take was a slipped word from himself and he could find a dagger in his gizzards.

And from previous experience, that could hurt.

More so than his leg. Which had owed naught to sabre-wielding ruffians in Russia but blade-wielding assassins in Shoreditch.

"And," continued Miss Jones, "perhaps a visit to the modiste for Miss Thornton? She is wearing her great-aunt Rebecca's mourning attire."

Hugh shuffled his boots. "I have tried, but I… I do not wish to force her, Miss Jones. Her parents died in swift succession so if she wishes to cling to something for comfort, I will not take that away from her. I did have one small success with the 'Dusk Blue' drapery, however."

Miss Jones' lips curved to a smile.

It took his breath.

For that smile lit her face, the subdued prettiness transforming to shamelessly captivating.

Hugh cleared his throat.

Then hoped his housekeeper, Mrs Dawkins, wasn't eavesdropping in the hall or he'd find some peculiar tonic on his breakfast tray tomorrow morn. Invariably cured a fellow, mind, but best not to dwell on the ingredients.

"Well, that will be all. Perhaps just a weekly meeting will be sufficient from henceforth?"

If the previous smile had taken his breath, this one blinded him.

"Perfect, Sir," she nigh cooed, rising to her feet. "Weekly is perfect."

He stood as she curtseyed but narrowed his eyes as his governess and her well-rounded posterior positively sashayed from his study.

One could almost feel insulted.

As he'd mused, Miss Jones was an enigma but...

Too many crowded his plate as it was, so he locked the desk drawer, shoved the key to his fob pocket and left the study to ready himself for this evening.

He wouldn't be seeing Miss Jones with her captivating smile and amber gaze for another week and that was a good thing for all concerned.

HUGH SET one boot out the kitchen door and–

"Uncle Hugh, why are you wearing a tatty soldier's uniform? And why haven't you shaved? And why are your gloves holey? And why–"

"A masquerade ball, Phoebe."

She scrunched her nose as she approached him. "Are you telling me the ladies like that unwashed look?"

"Well, yes," he replied quite honestly. "And why aren't you with your governess?"

"Miss Jones is placing cutlery for me to practise with." She rolled her eyes. "I mean, there's only one way to wield a bread knife."

In fact, there were several but he digressed. "Do you like her, though?"

Her nose waggled and her arms swung as though she were about to impart a profound secret. "She's…tolerable. Although I still don't believe she knows what tatting is. Or crewel embroidery. Or tambour work. A most odd governess, if you ask me."

Hugh stifled a smile. "Well, I'm gratified she's tolerable, but you should return to her."

She stayed put and instead took up her favoured stance of folded arms. The candlelight illuminated her ashen skin and forlorn gaze. "Are… Are you going out searching for those who killed Papa?"

His eyes closed for a moment before he spread his arms wide to draw Phoebe into a fierce hug. "Ah, my precious blackbird, I can hide nothing from you, can I?"

"Of course not," she spluttered into his coat before drawing back. "That smells of mothballs. And I know… I know about Papa's death. What they said about him." Her lashes drooped. "Great-Aunt Rebecca relished telling me." Then they lifted with fierceness. "But I also know Papa would never have done anything like that."

Hugh cursed her great-aunt, knew that even if she recovered from her illness, he'd never send Phoebe back. When Ross had died, he'd not stood in the way of her great-aunt but now he wished he'd kept a closer eye.

"You are correct, Phoebe. On all counts. But this is between us alone."

She harrumphed. "Of course. Mama told me discretion is a spy's first rule."

"Please don't tell me your mother also told you of…rules."

"Well, bits and pieces. She believed some would be useful in whatever I chose to do: beware of those who seem too good to be true and always answer a question with a question."

"Gads, any more I should know?"

She pursed her lips. "Why are you asking?"

Hugh grinned and hugged her tight, despite the splutter. "I suppose next you'll be badgering me to come along on these nights."

"Lud, no. I'm only fifteen."

He heaved a sigh of relief.

"I need to learn how to handle a pistol first and Papa flatly refused to teach me." She fiddled with a button. "Would you teach me?"

Leaning back, Hugh kept a hand on each of her shoulders. "One day perhaps, but as you yourself just said, you are too young."

Black eyes dulled and she sniffed.

He recalled Phoebe before her parents' death – a bright, cheerful girl, inquisitive as hell, and how he wished to see that girl return. But he was also aware that life had, too soon, left its mark upon her; she would never be the same.

But she would be stronger for it. And with a father she could be proud of. A vanquished one. A lauded one.

He'd make sure of it.

"I have to go, Phoebe."

"I know, Uncle. Take care." A buss on the cheek and Phoebe dashed off.

Hugh pulled the kitchen door shut behind him and strode through the garden towards the stables where the oldest nag he could find would convey him to St Giles Rookery.

The night was black as chimney soot, the stars and moon concealed by a deep swathe of cloud. A prime night for footpads and–

A dim flicker of light across the lawn caught his eye and he glanced over one shoulder.

The dining room curtain dropped.

Most likely Phoebe, although...

CHAPTER SIX

"In the streets of a town, young women of all ranks must be most particular in their deportment."

Private Education: A Practical Plan for the Studies of Young Ladies.

Elizabeth Appleton. 1815.

Gamesters, thieves, jades and slip-gibbets thronged the street outside The Bowl inn of St Giles Rookery, its bow windowpanes edged with dirt, the sign swinging in a spring breeze laden with drizzle.

Dusk was drawing nigh, the daytime washerwomen, tanners and brewers scuttling home as the sins of the Rookery burst into Cimmerian life – gin shops unbolted their doors, flash houses flaunted their wares, whores scrabbled at jackets and grubby lads lifted purses.

Drawing his hat low and ragged cloak close, Hugh barged his way across the street and through the horde. Someone carped but Hugh twisted with a scowl and the lad hushed.

He knew what that lad had seen: a cut-throat with frozen

eyes and a bitter snarl. A man with a dagger in his boot and a wooden staff in his hand. One should never enter St Giles lightly as too few ever made it out – whether held by their own dark desires or because of the blade in their guts.

An odour of decay permeated, poverty ageing the inhabitants beyond their years, and yet Hugh knew many here had come to London in search of more. Irishmen driven from famine, Welshmen hounded from their land, country misses desperate to support their families.

Most ended up here selling all they had – youth, muscle, innocence...

And he sometimes wished...

But wishes were for fools, so he sidled past a blowsabella who crowded the entrance to the inn.

Hugh caught a hand at his hip and raised it. "Won't find any blunt there, you won't." His accent was strong, the sound of Wales saturating every syllable.

Rouged lips smirked. "Welshmen never 'ave any coin. Only yer sweet voice." And she swivelled away for richer pickings.

Hugh made his way through the crowd to where a tapster scrubbed the counter with a grubby cloth.

"Ale," he growled with a push of penny.

It disappeared quicker than yesteryear's summer and a tankard of nut-brown liquid was shoved across.

The Bowl inn harboured a jumble of customers beneath its low-beamed ceiling: working men propped at the bar, others slouched in a jug-bitten stupor, a few sharpers played cards at a table, and one bench held a chuckling *Ton* buck with a wench in his arms. Hugh gave him less than an hour before he found himself in the gutter – *buck* naked, out of pocket and quite possibly *sans* his auburn locks, which would fetch two shillings at the wig makers.

Hugh limped his way to the rear, to a table at the foot of the closed-in stairs with an unimpaired view of the inn's bustle. He sat heavily, thrusting the cloak over his shoulders to uncover his tattered uniform.

The ale was so bitter, it tore at your throat. Indeed, the whole establishment was barbed with malice – a dark shiver that inveigled the soul and loitered.

Situated beside St Giles Church, it was this place that had the more customers of the two and had once been a stop for condemned prisoners taken from Newgate Prison to the Tyburn hanging tree. They'd sup a bowl of ale to fortify themselves before continuing their doomed journey in an open cart. The crowds would have jeered and cheered and mocked, and though such processions had halted years back, it was said that on befogged nights, the jeers still echoed and the ghosts still journeyed.

Hugh had arrived early in order to observe other members of the Ravens, as although he'd be in a room with them soon enough, he wished to burn their faces into his memory, one by one.

Ross had written the name of this group in that notebook for a reason and Hugh could feel in his very bones they'd somehow been responsible for his mentor's death. The handful of members he'd befriended over the past months were hardened men, soldiers turned felons who no longer cared whom they hurt, others' lives a commodity.

Tonight he'd meet them all.

And as for their leader?

Allure and brutality were a potent mix, and in their brief meeting, Hugh had sensed John Roberts had both in plenitude.

Footsteps scuttled down the stairs and Hugh slouched under his hat as a rush of lavender scent assailed him and a cloaked woman brushed by, slender and… She twisted but the hood was pulled low and he could solely make out blue eyes fixed on the staircase behind her.

The tankard hovered at Hugh's lips as the men of the inn ignored her dash across the flagstones for the door. But her identity would have to wait as a fellow with a limp barged past her and made straight for the stairs. Not a moment later, a long-limbed lowlife in a tattered crimson jacket did the same and over the next quarter hour, he watched another eight ragged men enter and clamber the steps.

So he drained his tankard and did likewise.

Four doors led off the narrow corridor and at the third, he heard the grumbling of low voices so gave a strident three knocks with his wooden staff.

A sliver of a gap revealed a curled lip below one eye. "Wot?"

"The name's Davies." He repeated the lines given to him by their leader. "A brother of the blade who wishes to enter."

"Ain't never clapped me peeper on yer before."

"Let him in, Cleavers," came a voice. "I invited him."

The man scowled but opened the door to reveal his other eye was patched. Behind him was a grim room with ripped curtains, a hissing coal fire and a rectangular table with twelve or so men sat at it – some must have been there a while.

He nodded to Forsyth and the few others he knew from the Seven Dials ale-house before John Roberts strode forward with hand outstretched. "Davies."

Hugh accepted his hand. "Roberts." Knuckles cracked. "Good to see some are not taking our plight lying down."

"Not us. Come, sit."

Taking a chair at the far end, he inspected the Brotherhood – a seedy bunch of burly thugs cradling tankards of ale. With the introductions, three stood out – Cleavers with his patched eye, John Roberts himself, and a hard-eyed Scottish brute named Darnell who wore a Highland regimental jacket.

Their leader, black-haired and with eyes grey as a gravestone, strode to the head of the table. "We meet once more, my brothers, to demand action. Demand our dues." Roberts leaned low. "We made this land free for the fancy lords nigh two years ago, yet now they shove our faces in the bloody mud."

Raucous assent and slammed tankards followed.

"But we'll make 'em listen," he growled, voice now hushed as midnight, "with a blade to their throats, if that's what it takes."

Hugh slammed his tankard also but within he was a seething mass of contradictions. He felt boundless sympathy for the soldiers that trudged the London streets in their shabby red and blue jackets, men who had fought for the liberty of these isles, limbs and youth lost.

This year's spring was once again cold and wet, food prices soared, yet work was scarce for them, and all the while, the government slithered with corruption, parliament seats bought and sold like theatre tickets.

But murder was not the answer.

The Brotherhood of Ravens needed the new breed of aristocrats on their side – men like his cousin the Duke of Aberdare and others, who were fighting to get their petition for soldiers' pensions adopted.

"When?" he heard himself ask. "When do we make them listen?"

"It's begun." Roberts' lips parted to a crooked gash. "Revolution is here. With men of the north ready to fight. This Brotherhood are sending experienced soldiers, arms and coin." He drew a calloused finger across his throat. "And the devil take anyone who stands in our way."

Hugh's jaw stiffened but he raised his tankard and drank. "I came to the right place."

"Aye, you did at that." Roberts' gaze pierced him like a blade. "But we have a problem."

Silence shrouded the room and Hugh stilled.

The fire spat and Roberts inhaled.

"I've had word that a government man has been sent north to infiltrate." He turned away, fists clenching as the men grumbled.

Hugh nigh choked on his bitter ale. *How the hell did he know that?*

As Roberts swung back to the table, an ugly snarl twisted his mouth. "So I'm looking for two men who can follow and see he's silenced."

Bloody Hellfire. Twyford had mentioned the man was set to leave, yet how could Hugh go to his superior with all this until he knew where these damn leaks were coming from?

He'd have to get his own message to the man before he got his throat cut.

Hugh made to rise. "I'll do–"

"Oy," shouted Cleavers. "How do we know we can trust this bloody Welshman?"

"Aye to that," jeered a Scot's brogue. "Fer all we ken, this coward might've hidden behind another's cloak in the war and now he'll sing like a bluidy canar–"

Darnell's words halted.

Not a warble.

Because Hugh had him pinned to the wall with the staff across his gullet, a knife to his cheek.

"I've done things for this country," he snarled, "that will see me greeted by Satan himself. Never..." The blade tip bit. Blood seeped. "...call me a coward. You hear?"

The brute choked but Hugh's hold was merciless and only when the Scotsman's skin mottled red did he lessen his hold.

"I hear," Darnell rasped. "Just testing ye."

Hugh drew back, lowered his staff but kept his knife drawn. "Men who test me will meet their maker."

A hand on his shoulder and he spun, knife at the ready, but Roberts held his palms up, head nodding. "Aye, I knew when we met. Saw it in yer eyes."

"Knew wot?" Cleavers groused.

"We need men like Davies here. Men who'll do what it takes." He stared to Hugh. "But you'll not go north. I've other tasks for you."

Hugh swallowed heavily.

Was this group responsible for Ross' death? Roberts had boasted of coin and arms, so where the hell was it coming from? And where were they getting their information?

"Aye," he agreed. "I'll do what it takes."

CHAPTER SEVEN

"When she wishes to listen, she is quiet."

Private Education: A Practical Plan for the Studies of Young Ladies.

Elizabeth Appleton. 1815.

As the rosewood mantel clock struck the midnight hour, Amelia checked for the knife in its sheath and then, for one last time, shifted the curtain aside to peer from her bedchamber window.

All was still. No shadows in the garden. No movement in the stables.

No sign of Mr Cadwalader's return.

As he'd ridden out onto Oxford Street, she'd slipped the sash window up and closed her eyes to listen. Heard the single clip-clop of hooves, noticed an uneven gait and deduced the horse he rode was no thoroughbred.

Now she turned, reached for her special lantern and then crossed to open her bedchamber door, the hinges of which she'd newly oiled this eve.

Cruikshank, she had observed last night, would occupy himself on the ground floor until his master returned home, no matter the hour, so she'd decided to carry out a first reconnoitre of Mr Cadwalader's personal quarters on the floor above. His valet, Mr Towlson, would be taking a brandy with Cook, Sally Longlane being a font of gossip on the servants' daily routines.

The rug-covered floorboards neither creaked nor groaned as Amelia tiptoed down the corridor, past the ballroom with its grand double doors and to the main staircase. There, she paused to rotate a small metal dial on her lantern that brought shutters across its light on three sides and then listened once more – for distant hooves or the opening of a far door.

Silence.

A few sconces were lit for Mr Cadwalader to find his way to bed and so she crept up the stairs to the landing of the master's floor.

As per her architect's plan, one room to the front overlooked Hanover Square but a door lay straight ahead, so she commenced there, gently rotating the handle and…

Proffering her lantern high, she could make out a bathing chamber.

But what a sight.

A smart wash cabinet sat upon thick rugs, and atop a marble plinth was a colossal permanent bath with scrolled feet. How many pails of water must it take to fill?

She withdrew and peeped into the next room – a plethora of shirts, cravats, coats and other manly paraphernalia met her shaft of lantern light, but not having the time on this occasion to poke around his unmentionables, she turned on her heel and continued towards the back of the house.

At double doors above the similar ones on her floor below, she halted. Surely not another ballroom?

She reached for the handle.

In the dead of night, the door groaned like a stricken soul, so she paused, shrouding the lantern's glow against her chest.

Listened.

Not a sound.

So she pushed the door further, pivoted her lantern to the room and held it aloft.

Then stifled a shriek as dozens of Amelias within meek globes of light stared back at her.

It took a deep breath and some rapid blinking to realise that much of the room was mirrored.

Gracious.

Whatever did the Scandalous Mr Hugh Cadwalader get up to in here?

She twisted the dial to unshutter two further panes on her lantern, its own mirrors projecting light that still failed to reach the edges of the vast room.

A few cupboards could be discerned but that was all. No paintings, chairs or sofas.

Amelia turned to leave, when a lone marble statue caught her eye – Greek by the looks of him and he'd lost the lower portion of an arm, but he was the epitome of muscled male magnificence, larger than life. She lowered her eyes and lantern from his curled hair to corded neck, to his chest, to his waist, to...

She blinked.

Heraclitus was incorrect: nature was *not* wont to hide itself.

Amelia closed the door on the unusual room and hastened on down the corridor.

At the final door, she rotated the dainty knob and–

Locked.

Deciding discretion would be the better part of valour this night, she retraced her footsteps to the landing and then the room at the front of the house.

This porcelain knob acceded to her turn and Amelia poked her head in.

Then allowed the rest of her body to follow as this was…

Mr Cadwalader's bedchamber.

Breath left her lungs in a gush.

For truth be told, she'd expected crimson drapery and silken sheets, paintings of nubile ladies and a spread of velvet pillows.

What she found in the low light of lit wall sconces was an elegant bedchamber, cream damask drapes guarding a four-poster bed with a chaise longue at its end. Above the mantelpiece was a frieze of Achilles being dipped into the River Styx for invincibility – except for that cursed heel.

Skirting a fine desk, she approached the window, its shutters open, and peered out onto the square.

Lanterns flamed upon the exteriors of the surrounding houses, their glow combining to form a ribbon of citrine as a lone carriage trundled and a few gentlemen staggered.

She turned back to the room.

On the far wall hung a muted tapestry and on another a portrait: of a woman in the pendulous hat and tight bodice of a century earlier while at her side was a cherished pug dog. She had the look of a Cadwalader – the lady, not the dog – all blue eyes and curled blond hair.

Amelia crossed the chamber to a gilt-framed landscape, tilting her head at the fine rendering of a ruined gothic tower looming over a stormy coast. Raising her lantern, she read the name *Llanedwyn* carved into the nameplate and let her fingers feather over the jagged oil seas.

An ornate gilded mirror, nigh the height of herself, hung over a dressing table laden not with male accoutrements but books.

The literature of Homer, novels of Walpole and poetry of the famed Byrne.

A frown pulled at her brow. She'd imagined Mr Cadwalader to be a gentleman who required constant chatter and social entertainment, not the type to sit quietly in his chamber and read.

In fact, the entire chamber was exquisite, comfortable and...unexpected.

Amelia returned to the desk and sifted the stacked papers.

A few bills for boots and cravats and...

How much for his cravats?

Swallowing, she deftly pulled on a drawer handle with a decorative keyhole above. Locked. Not too onerous to pick, but this was just a first reconnoitre, so she merely noted which of her cracksman's implements to bring next time.

She skirted the bed but then eyed the sumptuous pillows nestled against the headboard.

Hmm.

Rooting around between headboard and mattress, she found naught concealed but breathed in a heady waft of cinnamon and spice, of leather and man.

Mr Hugh Cadwalader must recline here of an eve, shirt open at the neck. Did his eyes gleam with the idleness of the innocent? Or did they glitter with that dangerous menace which caused such a curious flare of flame in–

Amelia straightened, smoothed the sumptuous pillows, and after a last look at the genteel chamber, she headed for the door.

Listened.

All was hush. No footsteps. No voices. So she slipped out and softly drew it closed behind her.

Shuttering her lantern on three sides once more, she soundlessly made her way back down the stairs to her own bedchamber, relief rushing her as she closed the door and leaned back against it.

. . .

Shrouded in darkness, Hugh turned within the narrow gap between internal walls, pulled on a chord and pushed open the hidden door onto his bedchamber. With a wink to Great-Grandmother Agatha's portrait, he pressed it closed once more, the decorative architrave covering any evidence of the concealed nook.

Well, well, well, his alluring minx of a governess was a curious woman, indeed.

But was she simply prying or...up to something more nefarious?

The hundred guinea question.

At the conclusion of their meeting, the Brotherhood of Ravens had dispersed well before midnight and Hugh had at first thought to follow Darnell or Cleavers, but...

He'd mounted his nag and headed home.

Why?

Because someone had watched from that window as he'd departed? Or because of the fragrance of gunpowder in his governess' hair?

He knew not, just that he'd felt...ill at ease.

No point in announcing one's return under such circumstances, however, so he'd stowed his nag at the ale-house stables on Shepherd Street and walked the rest of the way, letting himself in via the basement.

Encountering Cruik in the kitchens, he'd dismissed him for the night and then quietly made for his bedchamber, leaving the sconces lit as though he was still to return.

He'd then penned a coded message for the officer headed to Derbyshire. Cruik would ensure it was on the dawn mail coach north to await the man's arrival at his lodgings, and as he'd pressed his gold seal into the melted wax, he'd shrugged off his ill-ease as concern over the Ravens.

When soft footfall had stalked his corridor, he'd thought it

Phoebe seeking a shoulder after a nightmare, but as each door had been opened and closed, he'd realised his error. After all, Phoebe knew the clothes chamber held nothing but, well, clothes.

So he'd removed himself to his bedchamber nook and watched through the pug's eyes as his governess, in naught but white night-rail and pale-pink robe, had glided in, her plentiful curves swaying, blond hair reaching her waist in shallow waves.

Such an invasion of his privacy ought to have felt like a heinous crime but…he'd heard a soft gasp as she'd entered, watched her nimble fingers as she'd smoothed his pillows, her eyes captivated by the skilful landscape of his Welsh family home, and for some reason, he'd not minded in the least.

Of course, he should boot her from his house as soon as dawn streaked the sky.

Yet Phoebe found her tolerable, which was praise indeed, and he'd forever believed in the old adage of keeping your friends close and your enemies even closer.

In fact, he'd keep her so close, she'd be breathing in his cologne, feeling the warmth of his skin.

If she was working for someone, it would benefit him to find out who. The Brotherhood of Ravens seemed improbable as she was too refined in manner. And surely he would have been gutted like a haddock if they'd known who he was.

Could it be someone who did not want him investigating Ross' death? But he'd told not a soul.

Miss Jones would get nowhere questioning his servants as he purposely kept a bare minimum of trustworthy staff at a maximum wage. He'd never informed them of his profession but there were only so many times one could stagger through the door with a bullet wound.

Could a duplicitous governess be a threat to Phoebe?

He'd more worry for the governess as though Phoebe might

be young and grieving, she was also no fool. But in addition, he'd brief Cruikshank to keep a vigilant eye.

Shrugging off his ragged waistcoat, the mirror reflected a ripple of lip – a ripple that few would recognise from him. For it was not the grin of a scandalous scoundrel or even the remorseless one of a spy. It was one he'd not seen for some while.

A carnal one.

He would discover every last secret his alluring governess kept hidden beneath that grey gown. He would rumple that inscrutable exterior and stir those still waters, as anyone who invaded his private quarters became fair game.

And games such as these were his favourite pastime.

CHAPTER EIGHT

"Let us look at vice naked, stripped of every trapping of birth and fashion, and we shall only feel horror at the sight."

PRIVATE EDUCATION: A PRACTICAL PLAN FOR THE STUDIES OF YOUNG LADIES.

ELIZABETH APPLETON. 1815.

"Taste this, will you?"

Amelia peered hesitantly at the cup of chocolate before her on the kitchen table. It looked normal. She sniffed it. Smelled normal too. "Why?"

The Welsh housekeeper, Mrs Dawkins, pursed her lips and returned to stirring a vast pot of the stuff on the stove while various servants milled about preparing for the day. "I just wish to know if it's over-sweetened, I do."

Fair enough, so Amelia swiped it up, took a gulp and...

Glutinous sludge coated her tongue, thick and potent as though horse glue was an ingredient. Maybe it was and she forced it down with a tremor.

"Is... Is that for Phoebe's breakfast?"

Sally sniggered as she sliced bread while peals of laughter rang from Mrs Dawkins. "Course not! Cook will see to that. It's my remedy for piles."

Amelia choked. "I haven't got piles."

"Not now you won't, Miss."

Gripping a hand to her throat, Amelia hoped she'd not just been poisoned by a French spy posing as a Welsh housekeeper.

Earlier, Amelia had poked her head into Mrs Dawkins' distillation room – noxious fumes had permeated, strange seed heads hanging from the ceiling, while jars of suspect items lined the wall and an array of tonics gleamed green from odd-shaped bottles.

"Have you always made herbal remedies, Mrs Dawkins?"

Amelia had descended to the kitchens this morning with the motive of ordering crumpets for Phoebe's breakfast but with the ulterior motive of questioning the servants.

"Indeed I have, Miss. Learned on my Welsh grandmother's knee in Llandudno." She sighed. "We got in a bit of trouble when Mr Llewellyn's sheep went mad but it's so difficult to try out these recipes." She paused in stirring and pointed the spoon in Amelia's direction, chocolate clinging like grass to a cliff edge. "Mr Cadwalader would be feeding the worms if it weren't for me and my remedies, he would. Forever coming home with some scrape."

"More than a scrape most times, Mrs Dawkins," prattled Sally. "Bruises, cuts, that odd gash from wot he said was a pikestaff some fella left lying around on Piccadilly."

"Well, yes." The housekeeper's gaze shifted back to her cauldron. "He is rather accident-prone, Sally, but that's gentry for you."

Amelia pressed her lips together and thought perchance the housekeeper was fully aware of *why* he was so accident-prone. "You all seem...most attached to the master."

"Of course," said Mrs Dawkins with eyes wide. "He gave me this job when no one else would. We'd all give our right arm for him. Wouldn't we?"

The broad-shouldered footman nodded.

The upstairs maid nodded.

The cook nodded.

Sally scrunched her nose.

"Wouldn't we, Sally?" nudged the housekeeper.

"Well..." She scratched under her mobcap. "I'd hope not to. I mean, I'd give a finger up, gladly. Maybe two. Especially the itty ones as they ain't much use."

Mrs Dawkins tutted. "There's gratitude for you. And after our esteemed master saved you from such wickedness."

"Did he?" asked Amelia, intrigued. "What happened?"

"Well..." Sally plonked herself into a chair and the others gathered around. "I'm from Essex, Miss, and I came ter London ter find fame and fortune on the stage."

"And did you?"

"No. I found meself in Mrs Figmore's dockside brothel with a grinagog sailor and a jug-bitten soldier who intended ter take advantage of me person fer two shillings and thruppence."

"And did they?"

"No. 'Cos I screamed. I got quite a gob on me, yer know, as I used to call fer the cows each sunset. Anyways, a golden angel, but with a whoppin' blade instead of wings, came bursting through the door to save me."

"Mr Cadwalader?"

Sally sighed. "My hero. He paid off Mrs Figmore and brought me here. I'd still like ter be an actress, though."

Amelia did have to wonder what their esteemed master was doing in a brothel in the first place.

"And he saved Lucy Tibbs here," said the housekeeper, pointing to a thin maid with blushing cheeks.

"How so?"

"I..." The blush spread down to her collar. "I were lured, Miss, and fell in ter a pit of debauchery."

The housekeeper snorted. "Fell with your legs spread for the first handsome buck, you mean."

The girl rolled her eyes. "Me fellow deserted me, Miss, fer a bleached mort with teeth like a horse. I was crying on the street with nowhere to go, destined for a life of lewdness, when Mister Cadwalader handed me a handkerchief. With his initial on and everything. I still keep it beneath me pillow. My hero."

"So he took you in too?"

"No, I followed him home as I thought he might make me his fancy piece." Her grin dropped somewhat. "But once here, Mrs Dawkins took me on instead."

And so it went on, the servants all regaling her with tales of Mr Cadwalader's saintliness.

It made one quite ill.

And more difficult to question them. "But...he is a scandalous rascal, is he not?"

"Ain't they all?" said Sally. "Cruikshank has three lady friends on his poker."

"Sally!"

"Well, he has."

Amelia blinked. Surely not.

"One day, he'll find the right one," said the housekeeper sagely. "He's a family man at heart."

"The butler?"

"No. Mr Cadwalader."

Amelia placed hand to forehead. Following a certain Monsieur Du Burgh's long-legged strides through Covent Garden on a Saturday night had been easier than this.

As though summoned, the butler himself appeared at the

kitchen door, shooed the footman for lolling and skewered Amelia with a glance.

"Mr Cadwalader desires tea."

"I'll take it," chirped up Lucy, springing to her feet as though she'd hot coals in her shoes.

"Mr Cadwalader requests Miss...Jones convey the tea."

Amelia's eyes widened. "Me?"

"You."

"Probably just wants to discuss Miss Thornton as he works, lovey," said the housekeeper. "No need to fret. Mr C's like a kitten in the mornings."

Having reared a kitten, this greatly worried Amelia as she recalled swiping claws and sharp teeth if not promptly fed.

"The master," Cruikshank continued with wintry eyes, "is located on his private floor. The room with double doors. Do not dally."

Hmm. The room with all the mirrors and Amelia innocently nodded. A chance to discover what he got up to in there.

Once Mrs Dawkins had gathered the tea paraphernalia together, Amelia seized the tray and embarked up the stairs – all three flights.

Huffing at the top, she turned and traipsed the corridor. Perhaps he inspected his attire from all sides each morn or–

The nearer she got, the more she heard...odd noises.

The slam of feet.

An exhalation.

She paused outside the door.

A growl?

Any diligent governess would knock.

But she wasn't a governess so should endeavour to find out what was happening.

Balancing the tray on one hand, she twisted the handle and slowly pushed the door ajar.

Heavens.

Mr Hugh Cadwalader was enacting some form of athletic lunge, arms stretched as though he held an invisible longbow, and faintly, she concluded that no cushioned embellishment of any sort whatsoever was used for his chest.

For it was bare.

A little moist and...rippling.

She blinked.

At all ten of them.

As although he had his back to her, his chest was reflected in all those mirrors.

Bare.

As she'd aforementioned.

She ought to remove herself post-haste, without ado, as surely he'd not meant her to enter whilst he was exercising in solely black breeches. That would be no manner in which to treat a naïve governess.

Yet...

She was not a governess.

As she'd aforementioned.

And...

Slender muscle flowed, his motion effortless, and whatever the man was accused of, she could do naught but admire such masculine splendour.

Even though that masculine splendour was rather...marred.

To his lower back was a long ridge of scar tissue; just above his hip lay a ragged circular wound; his left shoulder was flawed by the mess of a more recent injury; to the centre of his chest was another circular scab; below his ribs there looked to be a knife slash.

And Amelia realised that Mr Hugh Cadwalader's elegance and convivial eyes hid a seriousness and vigour. This practice of strength and agility was not some affectation of a *Ton* gentleman but a dedication to his profession.

He was skilled and resolute. And that body was not marred but magnificent, used for a purpose.

And by the looks of it, he'd fought for that purpose many times.

And won.

That damn flare of flame lit within her as he twisted in balletic stance, arm slicing through the air, and never had she seen anything so formidable and yet so graceful, bare feet dancing a path, his thighs beneath those black breeches taut yet supple.

He was that statue in the corner made real.

Would such a dedicated man really turn traitor?

Amelia could not reconcile that his loyalty to the Crown would be swayed by some seductress, as he had ladies aplenty on his coat-tails, but perhaps...perhaps his extravagant lifestyle had left him with pockets to let?

Pivoting, he kicked out a heel at an invisible foe, the manoeuvre uncommon and somewhat barbaric – naught gentlemanly about it – and yet he made it beautiful.

He was beautiful.

Curse it.

Perhaps as a consequence of her profession, Amelia had never felt desire for a male of the species, viewed them as a distraction, but on occasion, late at night, when the wind blew cold and sleep failed to claim her, her wayward mind would wonder what kind of man would stir her? Would understand her?

Not insubstantial ones, like the men she'd known in her childhood and grown up around, or inured ones like many male colleagues became. But capable. Strong. Devoted.

Which existed not as–

"Do enter, Miss Jones." Mr Cadwalader paused in his stance. Their eyes met in the mirror – direct and afire. "Or are you just going to stand there and watch?"

A gust of breath left her, and with it all her foolish musings.

"I have your tea," Amelia muttered.

He grabbed a towel and dabbed at his face.

Amelia covertly eyed him from beneath her lashes as he then seized a shirt from a hook on the wall and brought it over his head, shrouding those muscled arms and toned stomach behind white linen.

She glared at the teapot.

It was most improper and shameless of him to be so lacking in attire before a governess – genuine or otherwise – and she wondered if the redoubtable Miss Appleton would have anything to say about the unseemliness of employers.

"I apologise for my state of undress. I would have donned a shirt before but…" He strode towards her and tilted his head. "I failed to hear your knock."

"No matter," she stated. "We governesses are a dauntless lot. All the…anatomy books we read."

"Is that so?" He crooked a brow. "Well, I have a few more scars than you would see in an anatomy book as…" He leaned so near she could smell cinnamon cologne mingled with sultry male. The skin at his throat gleamed with exertion. "I have an unfortunate knack, Miss Jones, of impeding a jealous husband's bullet or a lamenting widow's letter knife."

A convenient falsehood. The scars came from his profession, and she glanced up to meet blue eyes…not full of teasing merriment, as she'd expected, but cold ice, watchful, and with something else she understood not but it burned to her core.

"I…" She licked dry lips. "If you have no further need of me, Sir, I must plan the day's lessons."

He took the tray from her hands and placed it on the low

cupboard. "But of course I need you, Miss Jones. I sent for you as I have a few questions."

Amelia was aware her breathing had hastened. That her palms were moist, every sense heightened.

Yet she was also aware that fear was not the cause.

This was exhilaration.

To pit her wits against the Scandalous Hugh Cadwalader.

The thrill.

The danger.

"By all means, Sir." She demurely lowered her gaze. "I am at your complete service."

A SMILE CURVED Hugh's lips at her provocation.

Of course, he'd noticed the door edge open at once, had felt her eyes upon him, yet he'd not ceased his practice, nor had any intention of donning a shirt. He'd hoped to shock her, ripple that demure still-lake surface, and indeed, any good governess would've turned and fled, not stood for such barbarism.

But this minx had stayed and...watched.

He'd felt his muscles tense.

Amber eyes now fluttered at the teapot and he took up the challenge to see if he could make them flame.

"Do you enjoy your work as governess?"

"Assuredly, Sir."

"And how many years have you worked as one?" He dragged the sleeves of his shirt up his forearms, watched her eyes follow.

"Too many to remember, Sir." She lowered her lashes. "But six, give or take."

"With four employers thus far, wasn't it?"

"Five, Sir."

"Were you dismissed from any?"

Her head snapped up, eyes dancing with gold. "I take offence at such an insinuation, Sir."

But she'd not answered his question and Hugh's lips quirked as he circled to her back. Miss Jones did not follow his movement, which was odd in itself. Most women would turn to keep an eye on him but she stayed as still as a hare caught in the open.

He bent so close that his breath ruffled the fine blond tendrils at her nape and he closely observed her profile.

"What a perfect governess," he drawled. "Have you no faults?"

Her throat moved as she swallowed. Her tongue swiped her lower lip.

A sudden urge to place a palm to her cheek gripped him. To turn her, lean in and…

Taste her.

Kiss the truth from her as to why she'd wandered his quarters yesternight.

But would those lips whisper lies?

Then she turned her head of her own accord, their mouths so close he could scent chocolate on her breath.

"I'm sure that I do, Sir. It is said 'best men are moulded out of faults, And, for the most, become much more the better. For being a little bad.'" And like that hare caught in the open, she took her chance to spring from their closeness before spinning to face him. "And you, Sir? Have you no faults of your own?"

Oh, she was a clever one, quoting Shakespeare like some innocent…governess.

"I have many, Miss Jones. In fact… I can be very bad."

He placed hands to hips, saw her eyes wander over his bared throat.

Of course, if she was simply a prying governess, then he was acting in a despicably scandalous manner.

And about to be more so.

"Do you study Greek sculpture, Miss Jones? You've just watched me practising Pankration, an ancient sport of wrestling, and this chap here was supposedly a winner of three Panhellenic Games." He strolled to the statue and heard her footsteps follow. "What is your opinion?"

The marble statue was as naked as a shorn sheep, not even a fig leaf adorning his nether regions, and any genteel-raised governess would shriek and run for the door.

Miss Jones' eyes travelled from the statue's hair, down his torso, over his thighs and landed at his feet.

Then she twisted and did the same to him.

Gads.

He felt her perusal to his every extremity and it required all his strength to quash the arousal beneath it. The need to take her hand and let her feel...

A scandalous thought indeed.

"My opinion, Sir?" She blinked and clasped fingers demurely in her skirts. "I fear that like most males, he is rather over-exaggerated." Eyes widened in innocence. "Doubtless embellished and hence an unrealistic aspiration." She bobbed a curtsey. "If you will give me leave, I must begin lessons."

Hugh nodded. Doubted he could talk.

Miss Jones sauntered from the room, head held high, and as her footsteps faded, Hugh allowed his laughter to burst forth.

"Well, well," he said to the statue. "What do you think, my fellow combatant? Just a prying governess or a liar to her toes?"

The Greek made no reply, obviously, and so Hugh spun and re-took a stance of battle.

Miss Jones was even more of an enigma than he'd first supposed, and it appeared he'd not caused the slightest disturbance to those still waters.

She was akin to a marble statue, yet of Aphrodite – desirable and coy, composed and incombustible.

But not for long because he would discover exactly what had sculpted her.

Bring her to burn with the right words and touch.

He kicked out a foot.

And his lip rippled.

CHAPTER NINE

"A gentleman must be pleased to find in the woman he designs to marry, qualities which will be likely to render her a charming and engaging companion."

PRIVATE EDUCATION: A PRACTICAL PLAN FOR THE STUDIES OF YOUNG LADIES.

ELIZABETH APPLETON. 1815.

"When are you marrying?"

From the relative refuge of the fireplace, Hugh peered over the bone china teacup held at his lips. "As yet, I've not met anyone I wish to marry, Aunt Enid."

"Well, what do you expect," she declared with a huff, "squiring sorts like Lady Tottywood around London's ballrooms."

"Thurwood."

"Precisely." She pursed her lips and raised a quizzing glass from where she sat ramrod straight upon the silk-covered sofa.

Hugh endeavoured not to squirm but Aunt Enid's beady eye

was akin to an implement of torture, prodding you with shame. And it would only get worse.

Where the hell was Phoebe to rescue him? He'd sent a message up to the schoolroom as soon as Cruikshank had deposited his aunt in the drawing room, yet no saviour in black had yet descended.

And although he adored his aunt, today he was due to visit the Military Records Office and see what he could find on members of the Brotherhood of Ravens. Read each man's file and–

Aunt Enid tutted as her quizzing glass dipped below his jacket.

Hugh's lips curved.

This lady had cared for him when his mother had died so long ago, fussed over his wounds through the years and more recently deplored his modern pantaloons.

She knew of his employment, of course, although they never talked of it as he'd vowed long ago never to involve her, never to share a whisper. It was all too easy for an innocent to let a secret slip unawares and danger then followed like a flea to a dog.

With fifty years – or thereabouts – her hair was still a ginger-red which she swore came from her maternal side but which more likely came from Mr Blenkinsop's Henna Hair Regenerator. One shilling a bottle.

Slender and tall and smothered in amethysts, Aunt often wore an odd purple turban on her head.

Dropping the quizzing glass, she harrumphed. "I have invited Miss Abigail Farquhar-Fisherwick to take tea at my abode. I expect you to be there."

Hugh rifled through the filing cabinet of his brain and found the girl under D.

Diamond of the first water. Pretty. Likely to succumb to the vapours after one look at his scarred chest.

Unlike his governess this morning. Who'd stared. Quite a lot.

"Aunt, she's scarcely eighteen and quivers at a lobster tail *hors d'oeuvre.*"

"That's as maybe but it's high time you found…anyone, as time is not on your side. I accepted my dear Bertram's suit despite him being merely a viscount." She tutted again. "Oh Hugh, what am I to do with you? I want babies."

"I hate to break it to you, Aunt Enid, but you might be too old."

"Not mine, you beggarly rascal." She brought a hand to her brow. "Odds boddikins, I feel a bout of the megrims coming on."

As did Hugh.

He wasn't against settling down one day, but he was assuredly not going to marry some meek debutante who'd faint at his grisly wounds or coarse language or rough desperate kisses after a failed mission or–

"Hugh, are you listening? Perchance I could bring along Lady Millicent Struthers and–"

The door opened, praise be, and Phoebe dashed in with her governess in tow.

After pausing to perform a dainty curtsey to them all, Phoebe ran to his aunt for a kiss.

"Good day, Phoebe, my gal. What a delight to see you. Still in that black, I see. Well, it never did nuns any harm. And what are you doing today?"

"I'm solving Polybius' mathematical conundrum, Lady Kemble."

"How unconventional." Her quizzing glass was raised once more. "And who have we here?"

Hugh splayed an arm. "This is Miss Jones, our new governess. And, Miss Jones, may I introduce a lady whom the blessed angels envy, a lady whom the saints admire, and whom I would be lost without. The estimable Lady Kemble."

Aunt rolled her eyes. "Don't cozen me, you rascal."

His governess executed a low curtsey before returning to that perfect stillness, even beneath the weight of his aunt's perusal.

Miss Jones wore a frock as grey as a badger that buttoned up to the chin and covered her toes. But, to his discerning eye, it could not hide her fine figure.

"Come closer, gal. Who was your mother?"

"Alice Jones, my lady."

"Hmm. And your father?"

"David Jones."

"How unfortunate. And what did he do?"

Miss Jones blinked. "Not a lot."

"Similar to most men, then."

"Just so, my lady."

Hugh cleared his throat.

Aunt cocked her head. "The colour of your eyes, Miss Jones, they remind me of… Hmm, I'm not sure… Which of your parents did you inherit those from?"

"M-my father."

"And what was his father's name?"

"David Jones also."

"How doubly unfortunate. And I suppose he did not do a lot either."

"No, my lady."

Even if his governess was an out-and-out purveyor of fibs, she should not be subjected to such an interrogation, so Hugh crossed to ring the bell beside the drawing room door. "I'll send for more tea, shall I?"

Aunt, distracted by the thought of Twining's Lapsang Souchong blend, nodded, then scowled. "Why are you limping, Hugh? What have you not told me?"

"Ah, well, I'm glad you asked, Aunt..." He rocked on his heels. Truth was his ankle pained from the occasion he'd liberated a ransomed member of parliament from a dockside brothel but obviously that had all been kept rather hush-hush before said parliamentarian had then relinquished his seat under the pretext of wishing to spend more time with his family. But how to explain... He cleared his throat. "A fortnight ago, I had the misfortune to be caught in a somewhat compromising position with a Swedish diplomat's wife when her stockings malfunctioned during a banquet at Mansion House."

Aunt hoisted one brow into a perfect arc.

Phoebe snorted.

His governess frowned at the Wilton carpet.

Hugh continued regardless. "Totally misconstruing the innocence of the scene they'd happened upon, the diplomat and his minions chased me down Queen Street and onto Southwark Bridge, where my sole options were either to be shot by said diplomat or jump into the Thames."

"Zooks, you did not jump, did you, Hugh?" Aunt looked aghast. "Rats frequent those waters."

His ward's lips twitched. "And if you did, I hope the tide was in."

"I did and it was." He heaved a dramatic sigh. "Colder than a frog's nose, that river, but as I dived forth, the diplomat's bullet nicked my thigh. A mere..." He flapped his hand. "Flesh wound as fortune would have it."

"But, Sir," began a demure Miss Jones, "I thought your limp due to a bearded ruffian in Russia?"

Hugh narrowed his regard on her prim expression. "That was the *other* leg, Miss Jones, but I'd not expect a reputable and vestal governess such as yourself to pay close heed to such matters. A gentleman's lower regions and so forth."

Amber eyes smouldered. "How can one not, Sir? When they are so blatantly thrust into one's gaze."

Aunt nodded and *hmm*ed in that way of hers. "I warned you about those pantaloons, Hugh. Beyond the pale." She rose, smoothed her skirts and walked to Miss Jones. "I like you, gal. Phoebe needs a governess with some verve. But I expect you to impart ladylike virtues in addition."

"Indeed, my lady."

"And tatting? How is your tatting?"

Hugh watched a shudder ripple through his governess. "Adequate."

"I sincerely hope you are not fudging me." Aunt sniffed. "I shall return to this house soon and you can show me your handiwork. Now, I will forgo more tea as I am due at the *Ladies of Mayfair Matchmaker Society*, so, Phoebe, another kiss, if you will, and I'll await you tomorrow at precisely eleven for your dance lesson. Hugh, escort me to the door and we will discuss at what hour you could meet your prospective brides. I shall also invite Miss Ponsonby-Piddlehinton. Dim as a snuffed candle but broad hips."

A shudder caught him also. "I shall look forward to making her acquaintance, Aunt."

AMELIA SCOWLED as she loitered at the schoolroom window watching Mr Cadwalader swagger down the garden path to the stables.

According to Sally, who'd *overheard* his orders for a carriage, he was to attend Lady Thurwood's literary salon tonight.

Amelia ought to search his quarters once more but...

Something had too much altered in his attitude towards her.

His questions were baited, his requests drawled and a dangerous glint lurked in his gaze whenever it rested upon her.

During their conversation in the mirrored chamber, she'd almost convinced herself that he knew she was no governess and that his scandalous conduct was to rattle her pretence...

Yet surely he would have shown her the door at once?

Or had he been toying with his governess?

Truly, she must not let herself be provoked.

She recalled his breath on her neck, his glistening chest and cool eyes. The thrill of battling wits. He was smart and wily and a man not to be underestimated.

A tut and mumble caused Amelia to turn from the window.

With a stray black curl dangling upon her cheek, Phoebe was rotating a hairpin within the lock of her rosewood jewellery box.

For the afternoon, they'd begun on Mary Wollstonecraft's treatise from which Amelia was due an essay within the week, but she was aware that the lesson plans from Charlotte were becoming rather desperate. At least Phoebe was to visit Lady Kemble tomorrow for her weekly dance lesson and so Amelia had sent a message via the kitchen lad suggesting she and Charlotte meet.

"What are you doing, Phoebe?"

"I wanted to wear Mama's cameo brooch tomorrow but I've lost my jewellery box key." Phoebe twisted the pin this way and that. "I thought hairpins opened anything."

Keeping her lips buttoned, Amelia commenced shuffling papers, for she really should not assist Phoebe in such endeavours.

But the girl huffed, and Amelia's eyes drifted back to her as she held the box to the candlelight and stabbed in the pin as though skewering a hog.

Amelia winced and cleared her throat. "Perhaps...two

hairpins might be more effective."

Black eyes slid askance. "How do you know that?"

"I might have…read something." Amelia shrugged. "Somewhere."

Another black curl fell as a second pin was drawn from Phoebe's hair. "Then what?"

"Well, if I remember rightly… You insert one and hold it against the top of the lock whilst…wiggling the other. Something like that."

"Hmm." More huffing ensued but Amelia kept hush, until with a click, Phoebe whooped. "That was fun." Another askance look. "You're a very bad governess, aren't you?"

Yes.

"A governess must have a broad knowledge, Phoebe. I can also render pupils immobile with no more than a red ribbon and a left-handed glove."

Phoebe giggled with a young girl's vigour, a hand upon her mouth, and it was such…a pleasure to hear.

"What would you like to do for the last hour then?" Amelia had earlier sifted through one of the ominous tomes on the bookshelf – *A Guide to Genteel Pastimes*. "We could embroider slippers as a gift for your guardian?"

Nose scrunched.

"Construct a paper-mâché likeness of a cat?"

Roll of eye.

"List twenty ways to amuse a gentleman with anecdotes on the weather?"

A lip curled.

"Wax flower models?"

A snort.

"Well, what then? You decide." A touch rash but if her charge was content, Amelia may last longer in this household.

"Hmm…" Phoebe tapped a lip.

Amelia fretted...

Half an hour later, Miss Phoebe Thornton proudly grinned as she locked and unlocked her jewellery box for the twelfth time with her hairpins.

Amelia placated herself that if ever the girl found herself locked out of the house, at least she might get back in.

"Now, Mama's cameo," murmured Phoebe, and she drew out a delicate brooch with the finely carved profile of a lady against a black background.

"It's exquisite," said Amelia.

Inside the jewellery box also lay ten gold bangles in an array of sizes, each with a precious gemstone. They were most charming, and Amelia sighed, remembering the baubles she'd had as a young girl – all sold now.

"Were the bangles your mother's also?"

"Oh no, Uncle Hugh gifted one to me for each birthday from when I turned five years."

"That must have been costly for him," she muttered without forethought.

Phoebe made a noise like a choking dog. "Uncle Hugh has more money than Midas. Diamond mines in Brazil, shops on Bond Street and he owns half of Mayfair's townhouses. All the swells lease from him."

Amelia frowned at this casually slung information.

For if neither money nor some seductress were a motive for Mr Cadwalader to turn traitor, what else could it be and why did the Foreign Office consider it a possibility?

What had she not been told?

She returned her gaze to the window but the roses that Mr Cadwalader had chosen for the schoolroom desk caught her eye.

Today they were an opulent yellow.

Sharp thorns on every stem.

CHAPTER TEN

"Breakfast and recreation should be one hour."

PRIVATE EDUCATION: A PRACTICAL PLAN FOR THE STUDIES OF YOUNG LADIES.

ELIZABETH APPLETON. 1815.

Hugh squinted at the cup of… "Is this my breakfast tea, Cruikshank? It's…yellow."

"Mrs Dawkins heard that your head was paining you, Sir."

Hell.

"Any idea what's in it, then?"

"Feverfew, ginger, lavender, peppermint…" Could be worse and Hugh raised it to his lips. "Valerian and millipedes."

"Millipedes?" He leaned back in the chair. "The many-toed variety?"

"Indeed, Sir."

"A miraculous concoction, I have to say, as my devil of a head pain has lifted without imbibing a drop. However, my guts are crying cupboard, so I require…toast, sausages, bacon, eggs and a pot of…" He stared at the yellow concoction. "Coffee?"

"Very well, Sir."

"And where the deuce is everybody? The house is silent as a catacomb."

For himself, he'd not arrived home till three of the morn. Thurwood's literary salon had rambled on for hours, but her recitation of *Queen Mab* had given him time to search her house. She was cousin to that clerk Thomas within the Home Office, which gave cause for concern, but he'd found nothing untoward so would commence with the next lady on Ross' list.

A Lady Tremlach...

"The hour is past eleven, Sir. Miss Thornton has left for her dance lesson at Lady Kemble's."

"Of course. And Miss Jones?"

The butler's nostrils quivered. "Miss...Jones has exited the house."

"Exited?" Hugh's noggin whirred. "Exited to where?"

"She alluded to certain...paper purchases."

Paper?

Ludicrous. He'd asked Cruik to order more only yestermorn. What was she up to?

"And when did she leave? Where was she headed?"

"Not a moment before you descended, Sir. And I happened to notice her on foot to the south-west corner of the square."

"On second thoughts, no breakfast, Cruik. I shall also exit the house."

The butler's eyes gleamed before he nodded. "Of course, Sir. Might I recommend the grey greatcoat? Less...conspicuous."

Hugh waggled his brows and stirred his rump. "You're a marvel, Cruik."

"Naturally, Sir."

Not a moment later and with greatcoat capes fluttering, Hugh dashed out the door and down the steps, boots eating up the pavement towards the south-west corner, eyes darting hither and thither.

Little Brook Street led off and he commenced down it with some speed because once she hit the juncture of Bond Street, he might lose…

Ah ha!

Snuff-coloured skirts and a carpetbag marched ahead.

To Piccadilly, perhaps?

For what? Perchance to meet with a Raven? Or someone connected with Ross' death?

He skulked twenty or so yards behind her, keeping close to the buildings and–

"Newspaper, Sir?" A grubby urchin flapped *The Times* at him.

"I have it delivered," Hugh bit out, endeavouring to keep an eye on those snuff skirts as they paused at the juncture, evaded a carriage and then…continued on.

Not Piccadilly then, and he watched as she turned right up South Molton Street.

Hugh reclaimed his stride.

For a lady of diminutive height, she walked with rapid step, compact and fluid, rarely halting, but he supposed a governess, without lady's maid or chaperone, was compelled to hasten and make herself invisible on the streets of London where all sorts of lecherous buck roamed.

South Molton was uncrowded at this time of day, so he was obliged to lag a little further behind until she reached the never-ending bustle of Oxford Street.

But why had she exited the Square from the furthest corner from their current location?

As she peered into a shop window, he dallied outside Laurie & Marner carriage makers, was offered a discount on a smart green curricle by Mr Laurie and then handed a pamphlet on the miracles of foot massage.

But his minx of a governess was now weaving through the crowds with head down and elbows out – like a bloody bull in a field of cows.

She passed the Stratford Hotel, but as he did likewise, his nostrils caught the whiff of delectable beef broth, mouth-watering chicken pie and–

With an abrupt twist of heel, she scurried into Tupps Bun Shop and he wondered if he had a moment to nip into the hotel for a pint and pie as his lack of breakfast had begun to make itself known.

No. Because she dashed out again, stuffing a box of doubtless appetising buns into that capacious carpetbag of hers.

Now she hurtled on past the plethora of stores on Oxford Street – a mingle-mangle of jewellers, tobacconists, hosiers, and tallow chandlers, the thoroughfare chock-full of hawkers, song-sheet sellers, and diminutive but odorous piles of manure. His governess seemed able to sidestep the lot of them, whereas he was halted at every moment by bawling pasty sellers, spitting shoe shiners and plucking flower girls – a lodestone for every Tom, Dick and Harriet seeking to part him from his coin.

His prey paused at the junction of New Bond Street...not for the first time. Then commenced down it.

This refined street was even more congested, for the fashionable set strutted, window shopping, prattling and getting in his damn way.

Miss Jones bustled on and he continued his pursuit.

Blenheim Coffee House tempted with its luscious scent of roasted beans.

The Green Man public house lured with its whiff of ale, liver and onions.

Even Owen and Bentley's ices appeared appetising, despite the frigid spring day.

Gads, this was torment: he was starving and–

All of a sudden, they were at Little Brook Street again.

Indeed, they'd walked a complete polygon, and he speculated if they were now heading home to Hanover Square? An utter waste of time for all concerned, although at least breakfast would be…

No such luck as she crossed Little Brook, skirted a few gentlemen on horseback and continued down Bond Street before pausing outside Barker's Repository of Sweets, where a further gaggle of females cooed over sugar-coated pink bon bons.

Behind him, a carriage horse reared and whinnied and Miss Jones' bonneted head whirled in his direction.

Hugh whirled into a doorway; a trout stared him in the eye.

"Looking tidy today, Mr Cadwalader," called the fishmonger inside Messrs Henster and Co. "Sally took a nice fillet of turbot for yer supper tonight."

With a tip of hat to Mr Henster, Hugh swivelled and popped his head from the doorway.

Had he lost her…

No, there she was, that carpetbag poking out from behind a broad lady's skirts.

With not a moment to lose, he hurried on, circumventing dogs, mincing dandies and debutantes promenading on the arms of their mothers.

So to prevent recognition and a quarter-hour prattle, he nudged his hat brim south and his coat collar north.

Along Bond Street she continued, and he was sure they were now headed for Piccadilly, until she halted at a stationer's window. *Ah ha*, was she to buy her pape–

"Coo-ee, Mr Ca–"

Hugh swung and shoved a hand over the squealing lady's lips, another to her waist, twisted and dragged her around the corner of the alley leading to Bruton Place.

The pretty blue eyes of Lady Thurwood widened over his palm. She was rigged out in the most ridiculous hat he'd ever seen, with three peacock feathers wafting about.

Although why could Miss Jones not be wearing that? She'd be visible from Cheapside.

"Forgive me, my lady," he murmured, removing his hand. "Er... Creditors hounding me, you kno–"

"Oh, Mr Cadwalader," she gushed, "how I've longed for you to do that."

"Beg pardon?"

"So dominant and manly and... Oh, do that agai–"

"Hush, my lady."

She quivered, clutched his gloved hand and rammed it over her lips, body plastered to his as though she were a paperhanging and he were a wall.

With a frown, Hugh leaned aside her to peer around the corner of the alley and observe Miss Jones re-cross the road.

Now he just had to resist the lure...

The tantalising draw...

The tormenting temptation...

The enticing invitation...

Of the Guinea Tavern behind them with its waft of grilled lamb, mint sauce and roasted potatoes.

But work first, so he deposited a bewildered Lady Thurwood back on the street and hot-footed in pursuit.

No time to dally as his quarry crossed the junction with Conduit Street and...

She stepped into Madame Devy's Modiste, which formed the corner with Grafton.

Hmm.

He loitered with intent three doors up.

How could a governess afford a modiste such as Devy's, which was exclusive and expensive?

Spending her ill-gotten gains, perhaps?

Not a moment later, she stepped out and…turned right onto Grafton.

What the devil?

Nevertheless, he tore into Devy's to encounter four shrieking ladies in petticoats and Madame Devy herself, who merely raised a brow in that distinctly Gallic manner.

"'Ow can I 'elp you, Monsieur Cadwalader?" she purred.

"Woman. Snuff-brown skirts. What did she want?"

The Frenchwoman shrugged. "To see if I 'ave any old *La Belle Assemble* for a pupil she has. With prints of modern black dresses. And I 'ave one – with a supplement for widows: *Guide to Best Blacks for Forlorn and Glum*."

Bugger.

He loathed it when his suppositions were wrong.

"And can I 'elp you in any other way, Monsieur?" she murmured, slinking a hand down her hip. "It 'as been some while since you sent a lady my way?"

"Er… Apologies for that," he called over his shoulder and lunged for the door.

Once, he might have been scandalous and flirted with the petticoats but Miss Jones was getting away.

Snuff skirts and carpetbag strode down Albemarle Street, past the Royal Institution and Kings Head ale-house. His mouth watered, stomach grumbled, yet he paced on. Was she leading him on a gastronomic tour of bloody London?

No, she was persecuting him by leading him past Grillon's Hotel, the patrons embarking upon early lunch.

Then Piccadilly.

Surely, she would rest here? Maybe pop to Hatchett's Hotel for tea as that was a respectable haven for a governess – capital dinners too, although after his last visit, he'd itched for a sennight.

No such luck as she galloped past Fortnum & Mason with all the stamina of a winner at Ascot Races.

Surely his governess would indulge in a purchase soon, or perhaps in Hatchards next door? Didn't every lady want to go there?

Yet she merely glanced in at their wares.

He pursued, past the bookseller's black-framed windows and–

"Hey, Cadwalader," called a pale-faced but pretty chap from the door, volume in hand. "Join me for a rum fuddle? I'm only here for the day to see my publishers."

"No time, Shelley, my good poet. A woman to pursue." And he winked over one shoulder.

"Still from hope to hope the bliss pursuing!" called Shelley, his laughter dogging Hugh's footsteps as his elfin minx of a governess turned into...St James' Church?

Ah ha. Was she to confess her sins?

Swinging her carpetbag, she perambulated the churchyard, inspecting headstones and admiring the flowers before ambling on down the side of the church.

He yanked off his hat and thrust a hand through his hair. "Oh, for bloody hell's sake..." Swivelled at footfall. "Sorry, Vicar."

Skulking on, Hugh followed her from the churchyard but she halted on the pavement.

As did he.

Kneeling to her carpetbag on the ground, she removed a paper bag and bit into a bun with an expression of pure hedonism.

Ye gads, the minx was slaying him.

After a pat of lip, she stood and twisted her bonneted head, and he was once again compelled to fling himself into the nearest shop doorway.

"Good day, Mr Cadwalader. Another bottle of your signature scent?"

Lud.

Whoever said one could lose oneself in London?

He hounded Miss Jones onto Duke Street and thus back to Piccadilly. A complete bloody square.

Was she addled?

And then, as though she had meant to all along, she glided into Fortnum & Mason's.

A starving man's torture chamber.

Prawns and lobster preserved in aspic jelly, scotch eggs and champagne.

He'd better wait outside.

So did just that.

And waited.

Still waited.

With a quarter hour passed, he girded his guts and entered the establishment, past the tea counter and the post shop. Past the array of champagne and wines. Through the rooms with crystallised fruit and seed cake. Past the French venison pâté and Scottish smoked salmon. Past the potted Stilton and marmalade.

She wasn't there.

Not a trace of her.

With ire rising, he approached the doorman. "I say, have you seen a woman with snuff brown skirts, carpetbag and blond hair? Pretty with–"

"You must be that fellow the little lady warned us about. I've a daughter, so I have," he growled, plunging his face near, "and you lecherous bucks pestering women are the scourge of our streets!"

And without so much as a 'by your leave', not one but two burly ruffians descended upon him.

"Have some tea, Amelia."

Charlotte prodded forth a cup, steam curling from it like a will-o'-the-wisp.

"Thank you, and I do apologise for my lateness." She stripped off her gloves, rolled her shoulders and sipped the brew.

Nigh an hour late for this meeting in Hatchett's Hotel and all due to one particular pestilence.

Mr Cadwalader.

Who'd pursued her around half of London.

He must suspect her of something. How had she given herself away?

Her lack of indignation at his bared chest, perhaps? How would a proper governess such as Charlotte have acted?

Amelia eyed the lady as she tucked into a slice of fruit cake.

Likely, Charlotte would have raised a contemptuous brow, sniffed, and stalked from the room, not engaged in a battle of wits.

"I thought to see you walk past the window earlier," Charlotte said, dabbing her mouth with a napkin.

"Hmm, it's so hard as a governess to find time for one's day-to-day errands, isn't it?" Amelia cut a thin slice of cake for herself and pushed the rest to Charlotte – her wrists were too slender. "The work is endless."

"Most people do not realise you are at the beck and call of the parents and pupil whatever the hour." Charlotte reached into a battered satchel at her side. "And then there are the lesson plans, of which I have two weeks' worth for you, along with the marked essays you sent me." And a substantial bundle of neatly tied papers was placed on the table.

"I don't know what I would have done without you, Charlotte," she said in all honesty.

"I have a hunch you would have thought of something, Amelia. I will not ask about your investigation but how is your employer? Hopefully you have not seen much of him?"

Overmuch of him, truth be told.

Amelia cleared her throat. "We've had a few meetings and he appears..." She thought of his many scars and tall tales. "Insightful, urbane and generous to his ward, but also rather scandalous."

"Quite a combination," mused the lady, and Amelia could only agree.

Whilst Charlotte finished the fruit cake, Amelia paid the bill and bundled the papers into her carpetbag. "I must dash, I'm afraid, as Phoebe will soon return from her dance lesson."

"But of course." Charlotte patted Amelia's hand and not for the first time, she wondered what it would be like to have a true friend like Charlotte. Someone to meet for agreeable conversation and mutual grumbles.

They both made for the door and stepped onto busy Piccadilly where Charlotte donned her gloves. "Good luck then, Amelia. And send word if you need more lesson plans."

"Thank you. And..." She smiled. "Perhaps when this employment is at an end, we could–"

"Ah, Miss Jones! What a coincidence."

Amelia froze. Then slowly turned.

Mr Cadwalader was leaning with nonchalance against Hatchett's bow window, a picture of elegance in claret waistcoat and grey greatcoat while fawn breeches were tucked into dusty top boots. Only his rapid breathing and dishevelled hair beneath a crooked beaver hat attested to his jaunt around London.

"M-Mr Cadwalader. How...delightful." She swivelled, aware

she was about to be frightfully rude and not introduce her companion. "Goodbye, Charlotte. So nice to have bumped into you."

Charlotte's lips pressed as though endeavouring not to laugh. "Until next time, Amelia."

And after a bob of a curtsey for the gentleman, Charlotte turn–

"Oh, but wait..." Mr Cadwalader bent to the pavement and when he rose, a white piece of lace and cotton was in his gloved palm. "Is this not your handkerchief? An item of such beauty for a beautiful lady, if I may say so."

Charlotte blushed; Amelia rolled her eyes.

"It is not mine, Sir."

"Ah, but I'm not wrong concerning your beauty, Miss...?"

"Oh... Webster."

Amelia now closed her eyes. This was why one should never involve civilians.

"Webster," the pestilence murmured. "Are you, by chance, also a governess like Miss Jones here? Indeed, were you not scheduled for an interview with me?"

Amelia opened one eye. The cat was out the bag and strolling about with a purr. Would Charlotte give her away? React to the use of Amelia's false surname?

The lady cast a beatific smile. "Yes, Sir. But I'd accepted another offer, I'm afraid. To which I must return. Good day, Sir." And with a nod, she strolled off.

Class, thought Amelia. The lady had such class.

"Well then, Miss Jones, are you for Hanover Square?" He proffered an arm as though at Almack's. "I could escort you back?"

She brought a hand to her mouth in mock incredulity. "But surely you do not wish to be seen in your governess' company, Sir?"

"I do as I please," he assured, capturing her hand and placing it upon his arm. She could feel shifting sinew.

"Men frequently do," she murmured low.

"Can you believe, Miss Jones, I ventured into Fortnum and Mason not so long ago and ended up in a light altercation."

Amelia blinked up at him, mirth and panic warring within. "How awful. What is London coming to?" She tutted for good measure. "Women aren't safe to walk the streets and gentlemen aren't safe to purchase their smoked salmon."

"Caerphilly cheese."

"Pardon?"

"I purchase my Caerphilly cheese there."

"I see."

"And may I carry your carpetbag? It appears most...burdensome."

"Books," she declared. "And I'm quite used to it, thank you. I never leave home without Miss Appleton's tome. Just in case."

They promenaded Bond Street in silence and Amelia was sure that neither of them were breathing.

A tension seemed to arc between them, a frisson far too rousing for a governess. Or a spy.

She'd best proceed apace with her repor–

Was that a rumble of thunder?

Amelia glanced to the sky.

Overcast but with no sign of a storm.

"Apologies," her employer mumbled. "No breakfast."

CHAPTER ELEVEN

"I have a word or two respecting manners in the study."

PRIVATE EDUCATION: A PRACTICAL PLAN FOR THE STUDIES OF YOUNG LADIES.

ELIZABETH APPLETON. 1815.

Amelia peered into the candle's quivering flame, its deep saffron fringe melding into gold, then white.

And listened.

As ever, when one deeply listened, the silence was not silent at all; it seemed to thrum, a pulse of something vast and immutable beneath the everyday blare of life.

She closed her eyes. Still saw the flame.

But not a murmur came from within the Cadwalader house.

Not a rustle or sigh or footstep.

The master was ensconced in his quarters on the floor above. The servants abed. Phoebe sound asleep.

Not too long past, the mantel clock had chimed one of the morn.

So Amelia opened her eyes, slipped her discreet knife into its sheath, lit her special lantern from the candle and drew open her bedchamber door.

No sconces glowed so she half-shuttered her lantern and crept down the pitch-black corridor.

Despite the elegance of this modern house, it still felt eerie to be wandering so. A moonless night, the dark was like a theatre curtain, drawing closed on the misdemeanours of Amelia.

She needed to write her report for her superior and prepare to leave. Mr Cadwalader was suspicious and although Amelia felt as though she was coming to know the household, had gleaned many a fact about the master, she'd no written document that could confirm or refute if he was a traitor.

The staircase neither creaked nor groaned as she descended to the hall and crossed to the study where she'd first been interviewed.

With care, she tried the handle.

Locked.

So, she reached for the pendant nestling in the hollow of her bosom. A butterfly in gold and blue enamel, it glittered in the faint light of her lantern, but Amelia did not pause to admire. Instead, she slid a small button on the abdomen and a hollow cracksman's key glided out.

She kneeled before the lock and inserted it, lightly twisting and turning.

"Open for me..." she whispered. A click.

The pendant fell to her décolletage and she stood, was about to push open the door when she paused.

Mr Cadwalader was no fool but a proficient spy for the Crown.

So she opened it a smidgeon and felt along the inside edge of the door frame.

Naught to the side but she stretched on tiptoes...

At the top was a cord.

Pulled taut.

Doubtless some form of pulley system that rang down to the footmen if the door was opened. She felt further along and...on the frame of the door was a hook – the daytime resting place for the cord.

She pressed herself to the door, scraping her arm in the narrow gap as she delicately unhitched the cord from the door, and as her stretched toes quivered, she looped it to its daytime hook.

Breathing once more, she stepped through, closing the door softly behind her.

But for the half-halo from her lantern, the study was ebony blackness, shutters bolted fast.

With no time to dawdle, she turned the dial on her lantern to fully unveil its light and headed for the desk. On its leather inlay was an Ormolu candelabra, unused paper and an ink pot, so placing her lantern aside, Amelia bent to the fine graduated drawers.

She must be quick.

The first opened. Naught but the interview notes of a week ago.

The second also slid open but purely held bills and...

How much for his boots?

Shaking her head, she placed a hand to the third.

Locked.

Pursing her lips, she reached up to pull two pins from her hair, one bent into waves whilst the other hooked at the tip. She pushed the latter into the keyhole and then manoeuvred the wavy pin below it, shifting and...

A click.

She drew open the drawer and sifted through the papers within.

Most were documents pertaining to the Royal Welsh Fusiliers, their postings during the war categorised by date, with a list of the men within the regiment. The name *Lieutenant Davies* was handwritten in capitals upon another sheet, together with notes on appearance and mannerisms, as if for a character in a play. She memorised the information and then returned the papers to their same positions.

With a gentle hand, she closed the drawer and once more inserted her pins in the keyhole, guiding them to and fro until she heard the deadlock slide back into its home.

She turned to the right-hand set of drawers.

The first was a little warped but opened with a soft groan. Business papers relating to his houses and mines, but Phoebe was correct... Mr Cadwalader was worth a pretty penny indeed.

The second was locked so she once again reached for her hairpins.

A folded handwritten list of names was the sole contents of this drawer and she perused them with a frown.

Most were crossed through.

Lady Tadcaster
Lady Tenby
Lady Thurwood
Lady Tremlach

Amelia was unsure if this penmanship was Mr Cadwalader's as she recalled his being more elaborate, but Thurwood was the name of the lady he was squiring about Town according to Sally and whose literary salon he'd attended, so who were the other women?

Was he seducing his way through the alphabet?

Scowling, she remembered in the nick of time not to slam the drawer shut and then commenced upon the third.

This held ledgers but also an appointment book so she skimmed through to...

On the last written page of use was a gruesome sketch of a colossal bird with rapacious eyes, blood dripping from its wings. It pecked at a sprawled dead man's chest while the name of Phoebe's father, Ross Thornton, had been written so fiercely underneath that the nib had torn the page.

Aside were the words:

If you poison us, do we not die?
And if you wrong us, shall we not revenge?

Amelia frowned. Lines from *The Merchant of Venice.*

How Phoebe's father had died, she knew not, but perhaps the circumstances had been suspicious. Was the bird a metaphor for someone? Did Mr Cadwalader suspect Ross Thornton had been murdered? Was he the one seeking revenge?

She closed the drawer, re-locked it and stabbed the pins into her cascading hair.

But naught traitorous.

So, with the lantern lending its illumination from the desk, she turned her eye to the rest of the study.

Unfastening a bureau, she lowered the front to settle on its stays, but solely paper, wax and quills were stored within.

This study also seemed to serve as the sole library of the house and she perused the eclectic selection of books – from dour philosophy to scandalous novels.

Lying atop one row was a slender volume – more verses by the poet Byrne – and she swiftly flicked the pages, for many a covert scrap of document could be found within the thumbed leaves of a book.

Yet naught.

Just poems of other people's love and passion.

And that was it, nothing else.

All his official mission documents must be behind that locked end door on the second floor, so Amelia dashed back to the desk to retrieve her lanter–

Shadow engulfed her.

Flattened her to the desk, breasts crushed to the leather, paper fluttering to the floor.

She scrabbled to lift but a relentless pressure held her; she kicked back but met thin air.

Her wrists were wrenched behind her and shackled with something silken.

She flailed, knew better than to scream until her assailant revealed himself, but she was hauled to standing, a forearm beneath her breasts imprisoning her, and…

Cinnamon cologne.

A fire pressed to her back, tied hands and derriere, her thighs rammed to the desk edge.

Amelia turned her head.

To meet the eyes of Mr Cadwalader.

That blueness which held the warmth and solace of spring when he spoke with his aunt or shone with merriment when he told a tale to his ward were…

As ice.

Impenetrable. Cold.

This dangerous warrior wore no shirt, scars ripping across him, arms bare, trapping her.

She ought to be afraid.

She ought to be frozen with terror.

Yet…

That cursed flare of flame lit within as his muscled hold tightened, keeping her crushed against his hard body. Her breath had surely ceased, yet her breasts rose and fell in rapidity above his implacable forearm.

Lips whispered over her cheek from behind her. "Well, well, my governess. What might you be doing in my study?"

HUGH SUPPRESSED A TREMOR.

With his arm tight beneath her breasts, his torso pressed to her back and tied arms, and his nether regions snug within the curve of her derriere, he could feel each swell and dip.

She was slight within his arms but she fitted, moulding to his form.

Needless to say, he'd known at once that someone had entered his study as when the bell cord system for the servants had been installed, he'd had two further cords routed for his study – one to the door and the other to the pull-down leaf of the bureau, in the event that some miscreant found another means of entry.

Hugh set the bureau each night, Cruikshank locked and set the door, and should anyone intrude, one of the cords would pull and through a rather intricate set of pulleys, tug a bell in his bedchamber.

Hauled from a nightmare about Ross, he'd grabbed his knife and breeches before dashing downstairs to the adjoining room and, in utter silence, he'd pushed open the door masked by the stuccoed mouldings.

In time to watch his governess inspect the bookshelves and then head to his desk.

So he'd discarded his knife and lunged, felt her lushness as he'd pressed her to the leather surface, felt other more primitive urges that were best consigned to the darkness until he had answers.

There had been no real need to bind her wrists with the tie from the curtains – except for his own gratification – but he'd told himself he needed to intimidate the truth from her, to have her scared and shocked and cowed and–

"Release me this instant, you clay-brained cur!"

Hugh tightened his grip.

From over her shoulder, he noted her breasts rise and fall with her swift breaths, the lantern glowing on the silken skin exposed above the scoop of her night-rail.

"How did you get in here?" he growled. "This study is locked."

"It was open, I tell you. Now release me, you buckfitch!"

"Sweet liar," he murmured, lips now feathering her cheek. "Cruikshank locks it each night." *And sets the door pull cord. How had she got past that?*

"He's indisposed, Mrs Dawkins told me." She wriggled and the pleasure nigh gutted him. "So perhaps he forgot. Now release me! This is barbaric!"

Hugh stilled. "Indisposed?"

"Just so. His stomach pained him because Mrs Dawkins added a herb to his after-dinner toddy. For his gout."

"Cruik hasn't got gout."

"He won't now."

Hugh stifled a laugh. "So, your reason for being here, Miss Jones? Let me guess… Sleep, for some reason, eluded you and hence you thought to descend to my study in the dead of night in search of a book to read?"

"Precisely." She sniffed. "That and some paper. There being no library in this house." Her hands wriggled. "And I do not expect to be so accosted for no more than a bout of insomnia and a thirst for knowledge. Now untie my hands."

"No." For he believed not a word. His lips drifted over her skin – soft and fragrant of roses. "Which book?"

He watched her throat swallow.

"A Byrne."

Hugh smiled against her… "'*Within the endless squall of eve, I wait. A writhing, nigh threshing unrest. 'Till footfall, a caress, breath of my fate. And peace, she draws me to her breast.*' I happen to know the poet Byrne dedicated that to his wife. Do you like it?"

"It's most…" Her teeth nibbled that sweet lip. "Passionate."

"The Welsh *are* passionate, my governess. About many things."

"So it appears."

Hugh shifted. "And did you take anything from my study?"

"No," she stated somewhat breathlessly. "For the last time, I demand you release me." She arched her head, their cheeks brushing, and so slowly, reluctantly, he backed from her one hair's breadth and spun her to face him.

With the lantern behind her, she was a gold-framed silhouette in the dark, and whilst some of her hair was pinned, the rest fell loose about her shoulders, breasts thrust to the fore.

"You respire most rapidly, Miss Jones," he drawled. "Through…guilt? Should I perhaps discover if your night-rail conceals any of my possessions."

Hugh was aware he was about to act the shameful blackguard but this governess was not who she seemed – he'd wager his favoured Hessian boots on it.

"How dare you! I'm no thief and anyone would breathe with rapidity if they found themselves so mistreated." She waggled her bound wrists and pulled her shoulders back with all the indignation of Joan of Arc. "I'm… I am just a simple governess."

And he was a virgin. "That I doubt."

She scowled. "I've nothing to hide."

Also doubtful. So perhaps a thorough search of her would not be inappropriate.

He reached past her shoulder and brought the lantern aside her, a curious one with mirrored plates within it. The light now glittered across her skin, highlighting a gold necklace and darting butterflies in her hair.

With leisure, he roved a finger along her smooth décolletage.

All eyes followed.

"An unusual bauble," he murmured, drawing a butterfly pendant from its luscious cocoon.

Lashes swept up and pierced him. "A gift from Lord Fowler for educating his daughter."

"Ah, yes, the earl pursuing parakeets in the Amazonia. How convenient."

He allowed it to drop.

And slid his hands to her shoulders, daring her to scold him.

"You should be ashamed of yourself, Mr Cadwalader. This is no way to treat a governess."

"No, indeed," he whispered. "But at this moment, at this hour..." Hands slid down her arms, finding naught but pliable cotton. "Are you a governess?"

Her breath caught.

As did his.

Words abandoned them both, but eyes trailed and spoke a thousand.

Fingers skimmed to her waist and unto her hips.

He could feel the warmth of her skin beneath the cotton night-rail, could imagine pressing her back to the desk, covering her petite frame with his, nipping the pendant aside, kissing the swell of those luscious breasts.

Parting her legs...

Would she whisper his name?

Would her hands explore also?

But her hands were tied so his own continued.

A breath left her but she said not a word, which told him much.

A governess would shriek or faint but she...watched.

In fact, Miss Jones had nerves of iron as his palms smoothed down her thighs.

"What have we here?"

"Er…"

He fingered the contours. A sheath of some form at her garter in the shape of…a blade?

"Have you a weapon upon your person, Miss Jones?"

"A governess can never be too careful," she retorted huskily. "Licentious employers, you understand."

Hugh suppressed his quirk of lip. He should throw her out with a flea in her ear this very moment. But he still needed to discover who Miss Jones really was, wait until she gave herself away, and in all fairness, he'd not caught her in any demonstrable act of theft.

So, he'd let her believe he still thought her a simple governess, but from this moment onwards, Miss Jones would not be able to breathe without him knowing it, feeling it.

Breathing with her.

He untied her wrists.

"Albeit that I've found naught stolen on your person, I do feel a punishment for such an intrusion should be administered."

"And I feel, Sir," she spluttered with such innocence, pressing her freed wrists and scowling, "that a punishment for such mistreatment of a governess should be administered."

His lips twitched.

Faultless debutantes wearied him, willing widows jaded him, and although Miss Jones may be a thief, a liar, a villain, or all three, there was something about her that…fascinated him.

So he brought a hand to her silken cheek.

She stilled but…turned not.

He cupped both her cheeks, mouth lowering to hers.

To punish.

Yet he did not force.

No, he tantalised. Lips brushing back and forth, his touch tender.

If she'd demurred or flinched, he would have halted.

But instead he breathed in her gasp, desire drowning him, wishing to kiss her until her lips parted in welcome.

But that did not happen.

Because all of a sudden, she took of her own accord. And it became torrid and ferocious and divine.

Her hands gripped his bare arms – skin to skin, nails clawing.

Caught up in the same dark sensual web as he.

Alone in this study.

Within the globe of lantern light.

No spies or governesses. Just them in the silence of the night, possession and need.

He threaded a hand through her lustrous hair, no control of his desire where this mendacious governess was concerned.

So he dragged her yet closer, groaning as her hips lifted and brushed against his aching hard loins, and as his hands slid to her rump, he could categorically say she'd not stolen so much as a scrap of blotting paper from his study.

He pushed her hard against the desk edge, grinding his body, heard her moan, so caging her, he slammed his hands to the leather baize either side of her to–

A crash and his eyes flicked up, too late to save the toppled candelabra from thudding to the rug. He resume–

But his governess thrust hands to his chest and shoved him away.

"Curse it," she muttered betwixt gasps.

Curse it, indeed.

And then she promptly slapped him across the cheek, all prim indignation and governess starch.

"How dare you take such a liberty!"

Which was rich.

But it was too late, he mused, realigning his jaw, for he'd tasted the real Miss Jones. Whoever she was.

So, with breath still untamed, he leaned past for her lantern, mouth brushing her earlobe before drawing back and placing it within her hands.

Lips glistened, hair tousled, cheeks flushed, and her eyes... They were molten.

If she was genuine, she'd be gone by morn and he would never see her again.

That thought...pained somewhat.

"Good night, Miss Jones," he rasped, "and no more prowling my townhouse in the dead of night." He dared lift a finger to those lips. "Because as I told you once before..." Brushed it over. "I can be very bad indeed."

CHAPTER TWELVE

"Neatness is indispensable."

PRIVATE EDUCATION: A PRACTICAL PLAN FOR THE STUDIES OF YOUNG LADIES.

ELIZABETH APPLETON. 1815.

B*leurgh.*

Amelia grimaced as she sipped black tea, heavy lashes dragging upwards as Mr Cadwalader stalked into the breakfast room and cheerily hailed his ward.

The dressing-table mirror this morn had reflected a woman in disarray – hair akin to a bramble bush, skin pale as a mountain hare in winter, night-rail creased and sallow, and some evil sprite had daubed black paint beneath her eyes.

Whereas Mr Damnable Cadwalader projected pristine splendour – an indigo-blue jacket that complemented his merry gaze, tight beige buckskins and a dun waistcoat with brass buttons. Hair smooth, chin clean shaven and cravat a perfect *Cascade*.

She yearned to apply her reticule ribbon to his throat –

although with her diminutive stature, he would have to be so amenable as to kneel.

"Ah, Miss Jones," he drawled, flipping his coat-tails and seating himself. "What an...unexpected delight to see you here this morning."

"Where else would I be, Sir?" She had no choice until this damn report was done. Then she'd leave. Without ado. In all haste. Not look back.

Mr Cadwalader reached for the buttered toast with those elegant fingers. Fingers which had caressed her hips a mere six sleepless hours previous.

"Well, who knows? I come across people in the most unexpected places."

Amelia impaled her sausage.

"And my dear blackbird," continued Mr Damnable Cadwalader, twisting to his ward, "what have you and your governess got planned for today?"

Phoebe was only too content to share, so Amelia merely glowered whilst holding a hand to her aching head.

Oh, why had she responded to that kiss?

Why had she allowed those hands to wander upon her person?

Of course, she could argue that Lord Rainham's orders had been followed, that she had done whatever was necessary to maintain her presence in this household but...the one thing Amelia never did was lie to herself.

She'd wanted his kiss.

Wanted his hands to be upon her. And not just the Mr Cadwalader of witty quips and tall tales but the midnight one – of danger and risk, with bared chest and warrior mien. Stony eyes and ruffled hair.

No other man had ever incited such need. Had aroused her

with not solely his handsome aspect but with his proficiency and droll humour.

In the dark, trapped in his lure of menace, she'd been unable to deny that need and her own hands had stalked his bare skin, feeling the muscles ripple and tense. Inhibitions had abandoned her, her lips wanton, passion erupting with such force that she'd not wished to cease, and if that candelabra had not fallen and she'd come to her senses, then she might have let…

She moved both palms to her cheeks which were heating somewhat rapidly.

"Are you well, Miss Jones, you appear…flushed?"

Utilising all her years of experience, Amelia sought calm, breathed slow and raised her lashes. "The mustard is rather piquant for my liking. I don't believe I shall ever indulge in it again."

"Oh! Such a shame." The devil hoisted a brow. "You should always try things twice, Miss Jones. As some improve upon repetition."

"And some make you ill."

Phoebe watched them with a twinkle in her eye.

"Of course," continued Mr Damnable Cadwalader, "For myself, I prefer the oyster ketchup. Vinegary on the tongue and with a hint of spice." He gave a sly glance. "My absolute favourite."

Amelia narrowed her eyes. Surely any governess should not be expected to put up with such…*irritation.*

She sniffed, ignored him and twisted to her charge. "I believe you are to visit your great-aunt Rebecca this afternoon? Has she recovered from the ague?"

A nose was scrunched. "Yes, almost."

"If your great-aunt can wait till tomorrow, my blackbird," said Mr Cadwalader with a frown, "I will accompany you. I don't like you going so far on your own."

Phoebe rolled her eyes. "I'm fifteen, Uncle, and it's only a mile. I'd rather go today. And my maid is to come with me. And a footman. And a coachman."

The frown remained but he nodded.

Massaging her forehead, Amelia speculated whether she could meet with Charlotte in order to hand over some essays for correction. "I wondered, Sir," she simpered, "since Phoebe is occupied this afternoon, if I may have an hour to myself in order to purchase some paper?"

Mr Cadwalader's lips twisted to a Cheshire cat grin. "Did I fail to mention? You have a class this afternoon, Miss Jones."

"A c-class?"

"Hmm. Mrs Dawkins wishes to learn tatting."

Amelia blinked. "She does?"

"Indeed." Mr Cadwalader dabbed his sinful lips with a napkin and rose to his polished Hessians. "I hope to see your finished works in a few days."

You can see my departing backside in a few days.

"Of course, Sir."

With a salute to them both, he strode out and Amelia brought one hand back to her throbbing head.

Her end in this house was nigh.

And for some reason, that thought made her headache worse.

THE ROSES in Amelia's bedchamber this afternoon were a deep blood red, the buds yet to open, and vicious thorns peeked from amongst the foliage.

Curious how the roses kept changing colour.

She returned her attention to the notes she'd amassed thus

far on Mr Cadwalader because a coded message had arrived this morning from her superior, Lord Rainham.

Send all you have by tomorrow eve.
R

So here she was, embarking upon her report: the documents found in the master's desk drawers, how the staff viewed him, his relationship with his ward.

And her own personal assessment.

Lord Rainham encouraged his officers to express their instincts. He trusted them.

So leaving aside other emotions, she nibbled the end of her quill, deliberated, put nib to paper and–

Placed the quill down, gathered up all the papers and popped them in a wooden box, twisted the key in her unpickable lock and popped it in the trunk.

And locked that as well.

She would do the report tomorrow.

Closing her eyes, she rubbed her still aching forehead. Surely Mrs Dawkins would have some simple willow bark for a headache?

So she trudged from her chamber, plodded along the corridor and traipsed down the flights of stairs.

Loitering in the ground-floor hall was Sally, her head flung back as she glugged wine from a crystal-cut glass, the master's half-empty lunch tray balanced in her other hand.

"Miss Longlane!"

Sally wiped her mouth and smirked. "Shame ter waste it, Miss."

Amelia grinned. "Claret, is it?"

"Hmm." She sniffed the glass. "From further north than that, I reckon."

What a refined palate. "And its taste?"

"Expensive." And with a wink, she polished it off. "Are yer off ter the kitchens? How were the tatting?"

"Mrs Dawkins had no wish to learn tatting." Amelia thinned her lips as they strolled to the basement together. "Apparently Mr Cruikshank said the master wished it and Mrs Dawkins didn't like to say no."

So instead the two of them had ventured to the distillation room where Mrs Dawkins had shown her the various jars of marinated toads, soused lizards and some grisly pickled item called an aubergine. "It has the same flower as deadly nightshade," the housekeeper had grumped, "so I'll not be using it. 'Tis the devil's handiwork."

Sally chomped on an abandoned rind of cheese from the plate. "D'yer know, I tried me hand at sewing a bodice once but halfway down Oxford Street, me bubbies fell out, so I thought it weren't for me."

Laughing, they made it to the basement and as Mrs Dawkins was now sorting sheets in the linen closet, Sally was able to procure a draught of willow bark from a jar in the distillation room.

Amelia sat at the kitchen table and drank the foul-tasting concoction as Sally nibbled at half a cracker and chatted companionably about her morning at the market. Too soon, however, voices echoed from the ground floor above them followed by a dash of feet and a distant slam of door.

Phoebe was home so Amelia stood. "I'd best go."

Sally stared to the plate. The empty plate. "I'd best wash up then."

Amelia trudged back upstairs, waiting for the draught to work its magic, but as Phoebe's door was shut, Amelia thought to leave her be and swivelled to her own cham–

A sob caught her ear.

Then another.

She turned and crossed to listen at Phoebe's door.

Crying?

Long gut-wrenching sobs…then choked guttural moans as though her charge was endeavouring to smother any noise with a pillow.

Amelia bit her lip and dithered.

On such a mission, one should never become involved in the personal trials and tribulations of the household but…

Amelia could not bear to hear Phoebe in such distress.

So she knocked.

"G-go away," a voice cried.

So she opened the door.

At the pillow end of the gloomy bed, a black huddle of cloth was scrunched over, fist in mouth and head bowed, shaking and sobbing.

Shuffling her feet, Amelia realised she had absolutely no idea what to do, had never dealt with a young girl's misery before.

What would Miss Appleton advise?

Although…

That would be what a governess would do.

And Amelia was no governess.

So, she thought back to her own younger years.

Of course.

Amelia crossed to the bed, sat and heaved Phoebe into her arms.

"Get off," cried her charge, hands flailing. "What are you doing? I don't need–"

"Cry all your tears into me," Amelia said softly. "I'm strong enough."

For a moment, she thought Phoebe might jerk away but then she felt the girl shudder and grip her arm, her head coming to rest upon Amelia's shoulder, tears falling without shame.

She just held Phoebe for a while, as Amelia's own mother had done to her.

Sometimes words were not required. Just sympathy and silent strength.

Little by little, the tears abated, hiccups abounded and Amelia produced a handkerchief.

"What happened at your great-aunt Rebecca's?"

"It doesn't matter."

"Anything that makes you cry matters. Tell me."

"She…" A tear seeped down the young girl's cheek, her nose red and lips atremble. "She said awful lies about my parents. Called my mother vulgar and my father a…a…perfidious serpent. Said I was their unnatural spawn."

Amelia closed her eyes and thought some very uncouth words. How could the woman say such things to a grief-stricken girl? She wished to meet this great-aunt – who didn't seem *great* in the slightest – equipped with a leather muzzle.

"Has she said words like this to you before?"

Phoebe sniffed. "S-she's hinted but never anything so…" She swiped at her eyes and choked.

"Your aunt is not a pleasant woman at all."

"Father once said Great-Aunt Rebecca admired the man her sister married, that she was jealous. I do not know if it is so."

"It seems to me it's your great-aunt's bitterness, her own anger, that spews forth such vileness."

A faint shrug of black shoulders.

"I…" Amelia breathed deep. She never discussed her own past and although Phoebe could use this against her, it surely mattered not. Her time here was coming to an end. "When I was growing up, many people were…unkind to me."

Her chin raised, brow knotted. "Why?"

"Well, you see…my parents did not…live together, were not exactly…married."

Black eyes widened. "Ooooh."

"Precisely. Many did not call me i-illegitimate to my face but…" She grimaced. "They made sure I heard them in corridors. At the dressmaker's or in shops. Even new maids or supposed friends. I believe it made them feel better about themselves, to demean or belittle someone else."

"How awful! It wasn't your fault." Phoebe dabbed at her eyes. "People can be so horrible. I hope you ignored them all. And it wasn't just Great-Aunt's words about me. It was m-my father too… She said my father's now in hell, being burned by the devil… That he was a Judas." Phoebe gazed up. "Because t-they say, they say…my father k-killed himself."

"Oh, Phoebe," Amelia whispered, clutching her close. "I'm so sor–"

"But it isn't true. I know it isn't. He would never have done…" The tears massed again, and Amelia held her tight.

No wonder Phoebe was so hurt by life.

And she recalled the appointment book in Mr Cadwalader's desk drawer last night – the rapacious-eyed bird ripping at Ross Thornton, the words of Shakespeare, *If you poison us... Shall we not revenge...*

But Phoebe needed her.

She drew back a touch. "You must forget your great-aunt's cruel words. Close your eyes and remember your father as *you* knew him…" She brought the girl's hand to her black-clad chest. "In here."

Phoebe did indeed close her eyes. "H-he always had time for me, despite his work. He cared deeply and hated wrongdoing. He was daring and funny. And he taught me how to write things. Mama used to call me Papa's girl as I would sit quietly in his library while he studied papers."

"The best of fathers then." Amelia frowned. Not one who would have left his daughter alone in the world had he a choice.

A nod. "And yours?"

"I... I never saw him much. As I said, he did not live with us and was a busy man. He died soon after my mother."

"Did...did they love one another? My parents did, ever so much."

Amelia closed her eyes. "Once, yes." She recalled her father visiting, Mama dashing around in silks, plumping cushions and straightening the bed. She opened her eyes. "But it didn't last and he...he let her go."

Phoebe reached up and brushed away a stray tear that had trundled down Amelia's own cheek.

Silly to be so affected after all this time and she cast her charge a thankful smile. "It was a lifetime ago."

"And do you..." Phoebe chewed her lip. "Do you think you will marry one day?"

"Me? Oh..." Amelia swallowed.

Leaving aside her illicit birth, she had always thought marriage not compatible with her life, for trust and love could not be so easily found or held onto. A spy's path was a lonely one, but sometimes she wished...she wished someone might walk at her side, to share her life and accept her just as she was and for all that she was.

"I am content, Phoebe, with my employment." Amelia wiped her charge's cheeks with her thumbs. "And as far as your great-aunt goes, in a few years' time, you will look back to now and feel sorry for the old bat... I mean Great-Aunt."

Phoebe gave a watery giggle and they just sat quiet for a while until her charge clambered from the bed, scampered to the drawer and drew out something white.

"Here, Miss Jones, this is for you. It's my best tatting work. Tell Uncle and Lady Kemble it's yours as I know you don't know how to do it."

"Oh, Phoebe." Tears smarted as she took the exquisite...

Well, it was akin to lacemaking or crochet, delicate intricate strands woven and knotted together to create a...a butterfly.

Such a piece reminded her of Mama, and she raised her gaze to Phoebe, this sullen girl in crepe black who could create such delicate beauty. She felt guilt weigh so heavily upon her shoulders like the world must have felt to Atlas, and yet all she could reveal to Phoebe of her true self was her shortcomings.

"I pretend to be a good governess, Phoebe, but I fear I am a terrible one."

"I know." Phoebe tutted and folded her arms. "Not once have you made me write letters or learn verbs." Amelia grimaced. "But we can't be good at everything and you are a kind person. Now I can solve mathematical conundrums, open locks with my hairpins and you let me read your copy of Mary Wollstonecraft." She glanced up sheepishly. "Although I've yet to write the essay."

Amelia smoothed the beautiful tatting. "Then...then, thank you."

"And everyone pretends to be something to an extent," grumped Phoebe, sitting on the bed with a bounce. "I think most people pretend in order to get through life's challenges, but... I don't believe someone can pretend kindness if it is foreign to their nature." She chewed her thumb. "Mrs Dawkins, who was driven out of Wales for being a witch, you know, says kindness is not something that can be easily feigned. I think people see through it too easily." She twisted. "Don't you agree?"

Amelia pondered. She had met many people pretending at traits foreign to them. But could one pretend kindness?

Perhaps not. Perhaps callous eyes would forever give them away.

A blue gaze floated to the fore – deadly or droll – but never unkind.

"Uncle is the same," continued Phoebe. "He may gad around,

as Mrs Dawkins says, but ultimately, he is kind and generous and honourable."

Honourable.

Amelia thought of her report. She ought not be influenced by a fifteen-year-old girl but...

Out of the mouths of babes came truths that adults oft failed to see – blinded by cynicism and suspicion.

And she knew what her report would say.

CHAPTER THIRTEEN

"Stand acquitted or condemned by your own hearts."

PRIVATE EDUCATION: A PRACTICAL PLAN FOR THE STUDIES OF YOUNG LADIES.

ELIZABETH APPLETON. 1815.

"Another decanter, if you will, Cruik."

The butler raised a brow.

Hugh raised one in return.

"Of course, Sir." And the study door closed, leaving Hugh in the muted glow of the fireplace and the lit Ormolu candelabra on the desk.

Stretching upon the dark-green chaise, he shut his eyes. He'd drunk too deeply of the whisky but frustration nipped at him. Progress on justice for Ross and Phoebe was too damn slow and he felt no closer to discovering anything significant on the Brotherhood of Ravens.

This hunt was not official business so he'd forgone the endless form-filling at the army headquarters and instead used a cod of blunt to get what he wanted: all the service records of the Ravens' members and any military offences.

Most had kept their noses clean during their service, although Cleavers had been reprimanded for fighting – within ranks rather than with the enemy.

The sole two oddities were the leader Roberts and the hard-eyed Darnell.

Darnell's file had been there but devoid of documentation while that of Roberts had not been found at all. Could their charismatic leader have not even fought in the war, fabricated his rank and record? Could he merely be a subversive who used lieutenant as a cloak to delude the other Ravens?

Hugh considered a while but came to the conclusion that Roberts' demeanour, knowledge and command made that unlikely.

With luck, their next meeting would bring something, anything, to light, as he needed to find the source of these bloody leaks from the Home Office before someone else got killed.

Scowling, Hugh got to his bare feet, stretched his arms aloft and then ambled to his study desk.

As a rule, he did both his work and drinking upstairs but tonight the chaise had appeared inviting and the desk...

A small smile quirked.

'Twas two nights ago now, and yet he could still see her there. Could still feel her against him, and if he closed his eyes, he could still taste her.

He opened the top drawer and drew out the silk curtain tie which had bound her wrists. Smiling, he brought it to his nose and swore he could smell a hint of rose.

Cruikshank had endeavoured to keep an eye on the minx but she'd done nothing suspicious yesterday, naught to cause alarm today either. Indeed, Cruik had remarked how content Miss Thornton had appeared.

A knock on the door and he bid Cruik enter, slinging the curtain tie to the chair Miss Jones had sat in for her interview.

Gads, the butler was worth every penny of his fifty quid a year, as not only had he fetched a full decanter but also a plate of cold meats, cheese and chutney.

"Will that be all, Sir?"

"Yes, Cruik. My thanks. I'll lock up and set the cord as I may be here some while."

A nod and the trusty butler turned on his heel.

Hugh poured another whisky, ambled back to the chaise and reclined, hand behind his head.

Earlier this evening, he'd pursued his other line of enquiry: the list of ladies in Ross' notebook.

Lady Tremlach, the last on the list, had been hosting an art soiree, so he'd requested an invite, done the pretty with a few guests and then turned attentions to his quarry. They'd discussed Gainsborough versus Reynolds, Turner versus Constable, and she'd appeared most amenable, inviting him to view her private collection.

At which point, he'd made his excuses and returned home.

Why?

The recollection of those molten amber eyes? The beguiling scent of rose and gunpowder?

In days gone by, the Scandalous Hugh Cadwalader might have followed such an invitation to its conclusion, but–

Footfall, light and rapid, sounded in the hall, then halted outside his door.

Was his governess to enter unbidden, searching for a book to read?

He smiled.

A knock.

Not unbidden then.

"Come."

Amelia patted her skirts, took a deep breath and...decided not to bother with the demureness of a governess.

After all, when your employer had bared his chest, shackled your wrists with a curtain tie and kissed you till your wits scattered, it seemed rather pointless.

The lad had come and gone with her report for Lord Rainham, which meant her time here was nigh at an end.

She would be departing soon, another assignment pending, and she would leave Phoebe, Mrs Dawkins, Sally and...

They had all been so kind to her, when all the while, Amelia had led a lie. But the very least she could do was assist in some small way by speaking with the master of the house.

Amelia plucked at her ugly skirts. And pushed open the door.

Oh.

For the man who lounged on the chaise in mere breeches and shirt was not the droll Mr Cadwalader but the one of darkness and danger – she could tell from his stony eyes.

And this one tempted her so.

"Miss Jones," he drawled. "I would rise to my feet but they are bare, I am drunk and 'tis best I keep my distance."

She wondered why.

"I apologise for disturbing you, Sir."

He snorted.

How boorish.

"I wished to talk about Phoebe."

He tipped his whisky glass in the direction of the chair in front of the desk. "Have a seat. Don't hesitate to move the curtain tie."

Obnoxious man.

She turned the chair to face him and sat, placing the tie within her lap. "I have been unable to arrange a meeting with you today."

"I thought our meetings were weekly?"

Amelia fiddled with the silk tie and considered throttling him with it. "It's concerning Phoebe's great-aunt Rebecca. I do not believe she should visit in the future without being escorted by yourself."

Within a blink, he was sitting upright, bare feet to the rug.

"What did the witch do?"

Amelia bit her lip. "Her great-aunt Rebecca was most vile about her parents. She returned home in tears."

He closed his eyes, throat bobbing, bare skin visible through the V of the unlaced shirt. And then he swiftly stood, turned his back, strode to the fireplace and hurled his glass into the glowing fire.

Blue flame danced; the fire spat and fumed.

"I wish... No." And he shoved fists to the mantelpiece. "Wishes are for fools, Miss Jones. I...I've not looked after Phoebe well at all since her father died. I think to do my best but..." He shook his head. "She needs me here more and I cannot do that. Not yet."

Amelia had no further need to pry into his affairs, the die was cast, yet... "Phoebe adores you and bears no resentment towards you."

He twisted. "I'm all she's got, Miss Jones."

"It's not just that. You make her laugh, are a source of comfort and a connection to her father."

A hesitant nod. "When I first came to London as a youth, her father, Ross, was a good friend to me, always there, always laughing. An admirable man." He exhaled heavily. "Not many people know the true me...but Ross did," he mumbled, before striding to the cabinet to procure another glass and replenish it. "Want one?"

Amelia shook her head. "You have many friends within the *Ton*, do you not?"

"Acquaintances, Miss Jones." He took a gulp. "They don't truly know me."

No, she thought. They solely knew the half – the debonair Scandalous Mr Cadwalader, a fabulist with tall tales and droll quips.

But she supposed that her own acquaintances in the Foreign Office solely knew the half of Amelia Lambert too – the one of deception.

They didn't know the one who'd grown up surrounded by silks and satins and rose-pink damask. The frivolous, impassioned Amelia, who'd worn pretty gowns and learned French from her mother's latest emigree lover.

"Ross Thornton knew me," he continued, "yet he's dead and I can't even look after his daughter properly. Too occupied with..." He trailed off.

"Have... Have you family?"

"The finest one could ask for. But they are all on the Continent at present, otherwise..." He glanced to her, placing his whisky on the cabinet. "Have you ever visited Wales?"

She shook her head.

"I adore London," he continued, "with its hustle and life but a part of me, a part of my soul, is forever in Wales – on the wild coast with its sweet rain and dark nights. Riding the desolate mountains with my cousins or swimming in turbulent seas." His lips quirked. "I expect you don't believe me? That the scandalous and dapper Mr Cadwalader would enjoy such pursuits?"

Amelia smiled. "Not the scandalous and dapper Mr Cadwalader, no, but the one I see sometimes, the one who's mastered ancient combat arts and has scars upon his torso, the one who drinks alone and who cares so deeply for his ward. That Mr Cadwalader, I believe, would enjoy such pursuits."

He strode over to her – all masculine elegance and raw vigour – and placed both his hands to the chair arms, caging her.

But she wasn't afraid.

"Then, Miss Jones," he whispered, "you see me more than most."

Their eyes held.

Neither breathed.

His lips parted.

Hers did likewise.

His chest heaved...

"Which," he said, letting his breath flow and drawing back, "is why you must leave. Good night, Miss Jones. Thank you for informing me of Phoebe's great-aunt Rebecca. I shall accompany her from henceforth. I should have done on this occasion."

Amelia rose, aware she'd been dismissed. And not just for tonight. "Good night, Sir."

Mr Cadwalader nodded, fetched his glass and then stood before the hearth to stare into the undiminished hiss of flames.

Gently, she closed the door behind her and stared to her hands – to the curtain tie still held within them for no reason she could discern.

A spy's emotions, she knew full well, should never become involved in the affairs of a household, and for so long she'd succeeded, yet this one had disturbed her measured existence with its camaraderie and loyalty.

And then there was the master at its core.

She sighed. Not that it mattered.

For soon, she would move on once more.

CHAPTER FOURTEEN

"We are all imperfect creatures."

Private Education: A Practical Plan for the Studies of Young Ladies.

Elizabeth Appleton. 1815.

Pall Mall at nigh ten in the morn was one place Hugh would rather forgo but his superior, Sir Edmund Twyford, had requested a meeting at Whitehall, so with little choice, he dodged and weaved through the hectic street. The spring day, for once, was clear and although a vague warmth voyaged from the sun, it still demanded a greatcoat.

At this hour, scores of clamouring merchants were abroad – knife sharpeners trundling their carts with grinders and whetting stones, baskets of hot loaves jostled beneath one's nose and Moroccan slippers brandished aloft for a shilling and sixpence a pair.

In fact, that was quite reasonable, but no time as he had to attend this meeting and then dash home in order to summon Miss Jones.

Last night, as he'd caged her in that chair, he'd desired and burned and…

To be blunt, he'd wished to rip that damn-awful gown from her and have her naked and gasping beneath him. Wished to burn away his frustration deep within her delectable body. Wished to be scorched by those gold-flecked eyes and slaked till he was smouldering ash.

But as he'd before asserted, wishes were for fools.

Therefore… He would dismiss Miss Jones.

He'd procrastinated for too long, found too much pleasure in sparring words, playing the scoundrel and…watching her.

But no more.

Hugh cursed low as Charing Cross ahead looked to be a heaving mass of tangled carriages and an overturned turnip wagon, so he nipped through Spring Gardens, a smart street with houses owned by bankers and civil servants. Then he twisted left down the narrow Buckingham Passage and back to–

Darkness. An arm locked to his neck.

He heaved scant breath, clawed at the material covering his head.

A man growled in his ear.

Hugh jabbed back an elbow.

A grunt and he was released.

He swung low, sightless, seized the knife from his boot.

Swiped.

A clout to his jaw.

Heard a snarl.

A slam to his nape.

Crumpled to his knees.

Fought to stand…

Slumped.

Wheels. A horse's snort.

Blackness...

DRIP. Drip. Drip.

The annoyance pounded into Hugh's skull like an English battering ram at a Welsh castle's gates but unable to lift his sluggish lids, he moved an arm to...

Ah.

He was tied up.

Doubting this was some widow's idea of foreplay, he warily opened one eye.

Hell.

Or to be more accurate, a windowless warehouse. Timber stacked either side. Smelled of the Thames. Sawdust on the flagstone floor. A single lantern swung from a beam. Likely to be his last resting place if he didn't stir his stumps.

His wrists were bound at the back of a chair with coarse rope, and pain arced through his nape as he wriggled his arms, fingers shifting to ascertain the type of knot.

One he could not easily release himself from.

He peered down – his boots were gone, ankles tied to the chair legs.

Bugger.

Had the Ravens identified him and brought him to this Thames-side warehouse to be disposed of? Somewhere his screams would not be heard.

He debated shuffling to a wall as best as he could to smash the chair against brick when footsteps behind him declared an arrival. Hugh turned his neck but not enough to view the incomer.

Shadows shifted on the stacked wood and a rat scuttled.

"Cadwalader," stated a cultured voice. "What am I to do with you?"

Was this the man responsible for the Home Office leaks?

"You could untie these ropes and hand me a sword."

A chuckle.

Measured footsteps resumed and the man entered into the reach of the lantern light.

Ah.

On second thoughts, maybe not a sword.

Because the chap stood before him was known to be an unsurpassable swordsman and only those not averse to a dose of humiliation chose to duel with him at Angelo's Fencing Academy.

Viscount Asher Rainham.

Bestowed with the title for outstanding services to the Crown.

Within the *Foreign* Office.

Standing with arms crossed, he had piercing hazel eyes, dark-brown hair peppered with grey and a wry smile upon his thinned lips. Whispers told that he'd once been the best tracker the Foreign Office had. Now he worked higher up but Hugh was unsure in what capacity.

"You nigh took one of my men's eyes out, Cadwalader, so I think you shall stay tied. For the time being."

"Why the hell am I–"

"Forgive the dramatic abduction but there was a sixty per cent chance you were being followed and this meeting is all highly irregular." He unfolded his arms. "We needed to talk far from any pricked-up ears or prying eyes as I am unofficially probing into Home Office affairs. In fact, I am not here at all. You have not seen me. Is that clear?"

Hugh stared at him. "How–"

"This year has been rather eventful, despite there being no

current war with France, yet eight per cent of my time is being allotted to you and the Home Office. I wish to lower that figure."

"What–"

"Revolutionists of these Isles are not within my remit, you understand, but when the Brotherhood of Ravens work with foreign spies to aid their subversive inclinations, it becomes my business also." He sighed. "I've my own man within the Ravens, you realise, and what does he report back to me? That a certain London scoundrel was regularly meeting some of them at an ale-house off Seven Dials."

"But–"

"So of course, I assume the Home Office were investigating them also, but when I ask the Home Secretary to confirm, I receive a negative. So what am I to think, Cadwalader?"

"Well–"

"Then, to make matters worse, my man informs me that the Brotherhood of Ravens were also in possession of confidential Home Office documents, and suddenly everyone, however high on the Whitehall ladder, is under suspicion of treason."

"That–"

"Quite frankly, it did not look good for you, and since it seemed...unwise to raise the matter with your Home Office superior at this stage, it left me no choice but to become further involved." He flexed his hands. "I was forced to open an investigation into you, Cadwalader, calculate the odds of whether you'd turned traitor, as I was informed another in your department had, not so long ago."

"If–"

"Well, what do you have to say?"

"I'm not your bloody traitor," Hugh growled, straining forward. "And I say the man you speak of was no traitor either, that Ross Thornton did not take his own life. I say the

Brotherhood killed him. That he grew too close to finding out who their source was. I say your man is not working fast enough and I say another of us will end up dead sooner rather than later." Hugh sank back in the chair, the rope chafing.

Opinionated spies who disobeyed orders and went off on their own were not tolerated, he knew that.

He would be given the heave-ho from the Home Office. Quite possibly locked up.

Bloody hell.

Lord Rainham heaved a deep breath. "How did you find out about the Brotherhood of Ravens?"

Hugh weighed his options. But there was no reason he could think of not to trust the man. Rainham had shared much and, quite frankly, Hugh needed the help of someone with more resources. So he cast his lot with the man before him and told him of Ross' notebook, of the list of names, all murdered, the suspicion a traitor was at large, the clue of the Ravens, and how Ross, it seemed, had begun his own investigation.

"He must have got close then," murmured Lord Rainham. "And was killed for it. I'm sorry."

Hugh hung his head. "I believe so. And I still have no idea of the source of these leaks, so...so had no choice but to keep it from..."

"Your superior, Sir Edmund Twyford." Lord Rainham pinched his brow. "You have another Brotherhood of Ravens meeting tonight, correct?"

"Yes."

"Well, it seems I either reveal your insubordination to the Home Secretary and have him deal with you or...allow you to continue."

Lips pressed, Hugh eyed him.

"On the basis of a report I have received, I shall allow you to continue your investigation. But under *my* direction. You answer to me. Is that understood?"

He nodded as Lord Rainham paced.

"Indeed, it would appear more suspicious to the Ravens should you now disappear all of a sudden and you can divert attention from my man."

"And he is?"

"Never you mind. Anything else I should know? I do not wish for further rude surprises."

Hugh stretched his toes as best he could. "Ross also had a list of four *Ton* ladies, all with surnames beginning with the letter T. The sole connection I could find was that they all knew or were related to someone who worked for the Home Office. It appeared Ross had investigated two and found nothing and neither have I. I've investigated a third and naught. There is only one left."

"Why was the letter T significant to Thornton?"

"I can solely assume he overheard something."

"Who are these ladies?"

"Lady Tadcaster, sister to an under-secretary. Lady Tenby, wife to the private secretary. Lady Thurwood, cousin to a clerk. Lady Tremlach, niece to an Office of Law bookkeeper."

"Lady Twyford?"

Hugh frowned. "My superior's wife?"

Lord Rainham cast the deftest of nods.

"I... I would assume Ross did not include the lady as she is never in Town, but moreover why–"

"An error. She comes to Town on occasion but never goes out in society. I suggest you add her to your list."

Hugh looked to the flagstones, the consequences of that suggestion not lost on him. Or the trust Lord Rainham was placing in him.

It appeared everyone was under suspicion.

"And keep this to yourself, Cadwalader, understood?"

"Yes."

"And I want a report every two days."

Two days?

"Anything else?"

"No."

"Good. And your code name?"

"Er..."

"You do have one?"

"Sir Edmund calls me Number Five."

Lord Rainham gazed into the shadows of the timber-beamed roof and heaved a breath. "And they say I lack imagination." Then lowered his head to Hugh, hazel eyes piercing. "Stoat."

Stoat?

What the hell sort of code name was that?

Hugh felt more than a little insulted, which must have been evident as Lord Rainham sighed in sufferance.

"Stoat. Fast. Furious. A deadly predator, even with larger prey than itself, pursues to the last. Courageous, with a keen intellect and sharp senses."

Better but...

"Now, I must depart," continued Rainham. "More important matters to attend to than sort out the Home Office." And he turned on his heel.

"Er, don't suppose you could untie me? In fact..." Hugh frowned. "Why am I still tied up?"

Lord Rainham paused and peered over one shoulder. "You will have one of my officers working with you from henceforth – no arguments. And as it was she who tied you, I'll leave it to her discretion."

Her?

Shoulders sagging, Hugh rammed his eyes shut to the approaching clack of boot heels.

Shook his head.

Bloody, bloody hell.

The clack halted behind him.

How could he have been so–

Something...silken slid against his cheek.

He dared to lift one eyelid.

A curtain tie. The curtain tie from his study, if he wasn't much mistaken.

"Miss...Jones, I assume?"

Bloody, bloody, bloody hell.

CHAPTER FIFTEEN

"A truly modest woman has an air of ease in all her movement; she feels her heart sound, her mind calm, her senses under the control of reason."

Private Education: A Practical Plan for the Studies of Young Ladies. Elizabeth Appleton. 1815.

"In truth," Amelia murmured to the back of her captive's tousled blond hair, "it's Miss Lambert, but for the sake of your household, and as your governess still, we will continue with Miss Jones."

The scoundrel grunted. "I knew you were up to something."

"How?" She placed her carpet bag down and swung to stand before him.

A red blotch marred his cheek, *Gastronome*-knotted cravat skew-whiff and coat undone. With his hands tied behind the chair, his broad chest was thrust to the fore.

It would be rather unprofessional to run a hand over that chest.

Although…

Lord Rainham had left him to her.

And surely he deserved a modicum of teasing after binding her wrists in his study.

So Amelia stepped near.

His shoulders tensed.

With a light touch, she trailed the curtain tie beneath his chin, over his askew cravat, along his shoulder and down his chest. It was a heady pleasure to have mastery over such a dangerous creature – even if one had to tie it up first.

Mr Cadwalader cleared his throat. "I saw you in my bedchamber." His mouth curved upwards at her widened eyes. "You smoothed my pillows."

Amelia stooped and placed lips to his ear. "I was searching for incriminating documents."

Her lips brushed his cheek as his head turned. "If you say so."

With a sniff, she drew back. "Lord Rainham has informed me fully of Phoebe's father and wishes us to work together."

His teeth gritted; a frown knotted.

"Do you not think women capable?"

"What? Lud, yes. Or no, I failed to grasp the negative in that question." He raised a wry brow. "The female can be far more deadly than the male. And do you trust me?"

She stooped once more, caged him in the chair as he had done to her only yesterday.

It affected her in the same way – a yearning that refused to be quelled.

"Not in all matters, no," she whispered. "Now, I wish to read the information you have compiled on the Brotherhood of Ravens. Where is this meeting taking place tonight?"

"If they see a gently bred female like you in the ale-house, they'll know something is amiss."

"I realise that, you lackwit." Amelia tutted. "But if you don't return, I'll need to know where to send undertakers to collect the body."

"Very well. It's the Prospect of Whitby."

"By Execution Dock?" She grimaced. "And I know about the list of ladies' names."

"I suppose you found it in my desk drawer?"

"I thought you to be seducing your way through the alphabet."

"Gads, what do you take me for?"

"A scoundrel who ties up his governess."

Mr Cadwalader's lip quirked. "Lady Tremlach is…malleable. Sir Edmund Twyford's wife will be more difficult."

Amelia smothered her scowl. He was an experienced intelligence officer and used whatever means he must, but the thought of him tangling with Tremlach caused a certain queasiness. "I'm surprised you haven't seduced Tremlach already. You attended her soiree."

"Prying governess. But I don't use seduction as a matter of course."

Amelia raised a disbelieving brow.

He gave a languid shrug. "And anyhow, my tastes at the moment seem to veer towards…"

Not sure she wished to know, Amelia drew ba–

The curtain tie looped around her nape and a somehow freed hand dragged her until she fell body-long into Mr Cadwalader's lap.

A growl in her ear. "…roses and gunpowder."

And with that, lips descended on hers – to ravish, to possess.

If there'd been some warning, Amelia might have resisted, but there was no resisting such passion, such abrupt ardour. He was all fervent male and there was nothing to be done but shove hands to his hair and…

Possess in equal measure.

His palms roamed down her back, to her rump, wrenched her yet closer.

Lips moved to her ear, urgent and–

"If you untie my feet..." he growled.

Amelia jerked back. "You did that just so I'd untie your feet?"

"What? No! I did that because I wanted to."

Breathing deep, Amelia clambered from his lap and smoothed her skirts. "There will be no further improprieties."

"Why not?"

"It distracts from work."

"So, you find me distracting?" A cocksure grin was accompanied by freed arms being folded.

Amelia glared: madder than a hornet that he'd unfastened the cunning knot of complexity she'd formed around his wrists, vexed he'd nattered on to keep her from realising what he'd been doing and mighty peeved – in her view still – that he'd kissed her purely to have his ankles untied.

So with a swish of skirts, she gathered up her carpetbag.

"Where are you going?"

Amelia marched across the shadowed warehouse and opened the door.

"Miss Jones! Come ba–"

And slammed it shut, the weak sunlight causing her to squint.

She pulled her shoulders back and set forth, then noticed her carpetbag was unfastened and so lowered it to the ground. But the deuced thing would not close.

Not with both Miss Appleton's tome and Mr Cadwalader's boots held within.

But with a smile, she clasped the handles as best she could, thought perhaps to call in at Madame Devy's for Phoebe on the way home, and strode off.

"Are you quite well, Number Five?"

"Yes, Sir Edmund." Hugh attempted to flex his toes. "Boots chafing."

White eyebrows huddled close, resembling a bank of snow. "Intelligence officers can't have chafing boots, you know. Bad form. As is arriving late for our meeting. Two hours late."

"Unforeseen circumstances, Sir Edmund."

"Hmm."

Hugh tapped his foot in order to ascertain if his toes were still attached. After untying his ankles and discovering the little minx had stolen his boots, he'd staggered to the door to find himself not in some east end warehouse but the Whitehall Timber Yard, which was located between the Thames and the governmental offices.

Not five hundred bloody yards from where he'd been snatched or where he'd been headed.

Ladies promenaded, the horse guards pranced and the aristocrats prattled.

Forced to purchase the too-small boots from a foreman at the yard, he'd hobbled down Whitehall to his superior's office, vowing all sorts of pleasurable revenge against the resourceful, deceitful Miss Jones...Lambert.

Lud, he'd known something was amiss but could hardly have expected the Foreign Office to have sent a governess to spy on him.

With the hobble down Whitehall to muse on it, however, Hugh had become more bothered by the fact that whilst he'd been burning for the minx, she'd merely been casting her practised wiles, luring him in with her demureness and drab dresses.

Had it all been a pretence?

"Number Five!"

"Yes, Sir? You were saying?"

"How is your investigation into the royal coffers proceeding? Has the lady you spoke of before given you all she has?" And he leaned forward to raise one bushy eyebrow and wink.

Eh?

Hugh gathered his thoughts. *Oh, yes...* "The Regent spent three hundred guineas on saddles last year." Information not from the fictitious lady but from the Prince Regent himself at a Carlton House affair last month. He'd been rather proud of the fact.

"What! Keep at it then. But I want you in Derbyshire as..." Sir Edmund glanced up. "Thomas!" he bellowed.

The door was flung open and that cousin of Lady Thurwood's transferred from Records, dashed in. He appeared thinner than last time with dishevelled cravat and sallow skin. "Yes, Sir Edmund?"

"Where are the documents on the situation in Derbyshire?"

"By your left hand, Sir Edmund."

"Good work. Now, Number Five, I want you in a village named Pentrich before the end of the month. Number Eight is already there, but the dissent is mounting, and this kind of talk will only grow if we don't see to it. Starts with ten disgruntled stocking workers, then fifty, and before you know it, a thousand rabble-rousers are hurtling over Westminster Bridge."

Hugh rubbed his nape, thankful he'd received a message back from the officer in Pentrich who was going to change lodgings and keep his head down. "Not possible, Sir Edmund."

"I beg your pardon?"

"I cannot leave until my ward is settled. If that means... taking leave, then I will."

Sir Edmund shoved papers aside, those bloodshot eyes narrowing. "My men do not take leave unless I say so. We have an uprising and... What are you still doing here, Thomas? Begone with you."

As Thomas scuttled for the door, Hugh breathed deep. Knew what he had to say. For he would not leave while Ross' murderer had not been brought to justice, while Phoebe needed him or while even his superior had not been absolved of involvement.

"I will take permanent leave if you force me, Sir Edmund."

"I dislike being threatened."

"So do I. Sir."

Rapping his knuckles against the desk, Sir Edmund grunted. "Come to White's tonight and we'll discuss it."

"I...have business matters to attend to tonight." Hugh swallowed. *The Brotherhood of Ravens, in fact.* "But perhaps you could come to dinner at my house this week? And with your wife, Lady Twyford?"

His superior glowered. "My wife does not attend functions, Number Five. Ever."

"Ah. I see. Perhaps next week at your club, then?"

"It will have to do. Off you go. And have your boots cleaned."

"Sir."

Hugh hobbled to the door and saw himself out before pausing to waggle his toes.

"Cramp? A cuppa'll cure that." And a chipped mug was thrust before him.

Just what he needed for once. A mug of the strongest brew in all England, and he shoved a hand around it to...

The mug was stone cold.

"Mrs Benson..."

"You've always enjoyed me brew. Always." Black stubby lashes fluttered and she gripped fists to her trolley. "I tell them all, I do. If a fellow like you says it's a brew to make the angels weep, then it must be good. A gentleman of such taste."

He *had* said that.

But not meant it in quite the way Mrs Benson had taken it.

That's where spurious flattery got you.

So he raised it to his lips.

England expects...

And downed it in one.

Swallowed.

"I'd been about to say, Mrs Benson, that I couldn't recall an occasion when I needed it more."

In actual fact, his innards were now colder than a gravestone facing north on a frosty night.

Mrs Benson dabbed at her moist eyes. "You're such a good lad. Despite what His Nibs in there says."

With a pressed-lip smile, Hugh hobbled off, down the stairs and out into the fairly fresh air of Whitehall.

Today was turning into a bloody nightmare. What else could go wr–

He narrowed his eyes, as across the road that Thomas chap was chatting to his cousin Lady Thurwood.

So he struggled over.

"My lady? What a surprise to see you in Whitehall."

Limpid blue eyes widened and a gloved hand rested upon her décolletage. Had he eliminated her from his list too soon?

"Mr Cadwalader, what a pleasure. I was just bringing my poor cousin Thomas his lunch. He never gets a moment, you know. I'd like to give his superior a good talking to."

Poor cousin Thomas shuffled his feet, a flush rising above his cravat. "I'd best return." And he rushed off as though the quill-pushers from hell were on his tail.

Hugh twisted and gave his most disarming smile. "May I escort you to your carriage?"

"Of course, and..." Her arm snaked through his, the scent of lavender drifting, lips pursing. "Perhaps home? I have the afternoon free and we could re-enact your manful ensnarement of me on Oxford Street."

"No time, my lady." He patted her hand. "I have a boot malfunction to attend to."

CHAPTER SIXTEEN

"Vice is always attended with misery."

PRIVATE EDUCATION: A PRACTICAL PLAN FOR THE STUDIES OF YOUNG LADIES.

ELIZABETH APPLETON. 1815.

A churning fog rose from the dark cobbles as though it were a phantom from the grave set with mischief. The day had been milder than most but with the onset of dusk, a profound cold had descended to settle in one's bones.

Hugh shivered as he walked down a dockside street known as Wapping Wall, and not just because his ragged once-red army jacket failed to keep out the cold.

A decade ago, with the enlargement of the London Docks, this side of town had been transformed into a modern centre of commerce – wine, brandy, spices and rice stored in endless warehouses while the new wharfs, connected to the Thames, could hold nigh four hundred ships. Foul alleys and crumbling houses had been cleared, oil streetlamps stood upon corners, smuggling...kept an eye on, and yet by night...

A malevolence lingered.

Ghosts of yore whispered.

For Execution Dock lay not a stone's throw from here.

Piracy was a dying trade, in more ways than one, but it was there that criminals of the sea were still hanged as the admiralty's jurisdiction only began where the tidal waters of the Thames splashed the banks. Thus far this year, four men had seen their grisly end, the tradition still maintained of leaving them in place until three tides had washed over their corpses.

A huddle of sailors lurched past him, their faces abruptly lit in the cloying glow of a corner streetlamp, before they were consumed by the night once more.

Pausing beside a lightless passage that led to wooden-staired access to the Thames, Hugh listened.

Though muffled by fog, water slapped and men called from their boats, for many a waterman used this passage, plying the river for trade. The Pelican Stairs – so named for the bird whom legend told fed her young on her own blood – held a strange allure that beguiled one to step into their shadows, to discover the murk high waters of Father Thames or, at low tide, the swallowing mud.

Hugh glanced up at the tavern that formed one side of the passage.

Yellow bricked and with three storeys, The Prospect of Whitby appeared from the outside to be a benign establishment, yet years ago, before a fire had burned its depravities to the ground, it'd been known as the Devil's Tavern, frequented by smugglers, pirates, thieves and cutthroats.

Many a man had never returned from an ale taken here – a knife to the guts or a sack over the head from the roaming press-gangs, and that was if the stench of the river failed to overwhelm.

The rebuilt Prospect of Whitby was now more winsomely named after a collier boat moored here, but Hugh wasn't fooled...

Your prospects were low if you frequented this place too often.

Threat still held sway over these streets, just in another guise – thieves awaited the night to plunder warehouses, doxies swung skirts on lamplit corners to lure the sailors, and footpads lingered in alleys to rob the next drunken cull.

But for tonight, these were Hugh's streets, his lone path to follow till Ross Thornton had been vindicated and Phoebe had a father to be proud of.

As a rule, he was stoic on a mission such as this, as to whether he'd survive to watch dawn rise in her blush finery, yet of late it felt more imperative: a need to return home to Miss Amelia Lambert's amber eyes and Phoebe's warm hugs.

This afternoon, Amelia had shut herself in his downstairs study to read the reports on the Brotherhood of Ravens, and he hoped those keen eyes would see something he had not.

Hugh paced to the tavern door, a rush of smoke assailing him as he swaggered in and surveyed the interior.

Aside the rear windows that overlooked the Thames, a few sailors slouched, clay pipes clamped to mouths; a table held a couple of gossiping crones; a long bench by the stairs was occupied by watermen; and at the bar, a short grubby lad in sailor's slops and with cap pulled low perched on a stool, aimlessly swinging his leg.

Quiet.

But it was still early.

The upper floor had rooms for bare-knuckle boxing and cock fighting, and one of these was to be used for the Ravens' meeting.

After sliding over a penny for an ale that tasted thrice baptised in the Thames, he settled himself on a vacant bench.

The door opened and Hugh's gaze lifted but 'twas merely another bent crone who, after flapping a hand at the other two, shuffled to the bar. The short grubby lad flinched and rose from his stool as the crone garbled for gin, skirts dusting the floor.

Hugh returned to his ale and speculated if there was a further waterman's door at the back with access to the Thames while–

The scent of damp wool, strong gin and boiled mutton drifted as the crone decided to perch on the same bench as him.

With a grimace, he glanced aside.

Brown skirts, a hood, grey hanks of hair dangling from a woollen hat, fingerless gloves that left trails of coal dust, an old soldier's greatcoat. The crone scratched her arm and Hugh made to rise.

"Got tuppence for a swig o' Strip-Me-Naked, lovey?"

Gin had many monikers so couldn't she have chosen another? The images were most disturbing.

"No," he grunted.

"The name's Mollie." And she cackled, sidling up to shove an elbow in his side, the reek of gin watering his eyes. "I bet yer'd go fer anyfink in a corset, eh?"

Odd thing to say and he shifted.

She peered at him from beneath her hood.

A scarf covered her mouth; coal dust smudged her cheeks; amber eyes blinked up.

Hugh's world tipped on its axis, a low heat swathing him, and to prevent himself yelling, grabbing or heaving, he clutched his ale and drank it down in one.

"Oh-ee," his minx blabbered. "I likes a cove who can hold his bub."

"Get away, crone," he bawled in his thick Welsh accent. "I

need a piss, I do." And he rose, barging past her towards the door.

The cold air cleared his head and he stomped past the window to the far side of the tavern, far from the Pelican Stairs passage and its malevolent ears. As he'd expected, the door opened not too long after, the crone ambling to his side.

"Need 'elp with yer breeches, do yer?" She swung her skirts like a shilling-harlot.

"What the hell are you doing, crone?" he bellowed, pretending to fiddle with his falls.

"Helpin' yer!" And she guffawed. "Me cock-bawd Rainy says to always 'elp a man with 'is breeches."

So this was Rainham's order to assist him, and he scowled. "A crone like you could get hurt on these streets."

A few burly boatmen trundled the cobbles towards them and Hugh faced the wall.

"Ooh, ain't yer got a big 'un." She chuckled. As did the boatmen. "And I'm used to these streets, lovey." The *crone* shoved a hand into her ragged army greatcoat and laid a most curious dulled metal object against her skirts. He'd only seen such a weapon once. A Duck Gun named for its cluster of four barrels, splayed like a duck's foot.

Effective if not exactly accurate.

"No aim," he said softly.

"Sorry to hear that, dearie." She cackled once more. "But it'll do fer me."

"Only if you're aiming for a flock of ducks on the Serpentine."

"And everythin' in between, lovey." She tucked the gun back into her coat, adjusted her hood and winked. "'Ave a pleasant eve." And with a swish of coal dust, she shuffled off into the fog.

Hugh gnashed his teeth.

Then let out a long breath.

She knew what she was doing. Rainham wouldn't have sent her otherwise.

And who would accost a crone with no coin?

So with a shake of head, he compelled his boots back to the tavern, ordered another ale and sat.

Not feeling quite so alone.

But odd emotions roiled.

Anger that she'd not told him.

Dread that she may be hurt.

Mortification that he'd not realised it was her until those amber eyes.

Pride for the same reason.

An anomalous lust.

The door opened once more, but this time Roberts strode in, gaze gleaming and chin determined.

He caught Hugh's eye, nodded, and as he made his way up the stairs, Hugh followed suit.

Time for work.

As THE LEADER of the Ravens rose to his feet, grumbles amongst the men waned, tankards of ale were lowered, and all eyes shifted to the head of the table.

Hugh hunched in his chair and watched as Roberts contemplated each member of the Brotherhood of Ravens, one by one, as though assessing their mettle. Meeting the wintry stare with one of his own, Hugh presumed he'd passed muster for it continued on.

Except for two older men, the faces were the same. He'd nodded at Forsyth upon entering and debated if he was Rainham's infiltrator? Or was it one of the youths with grim gaze or even Darnell with his laconic ways? Perhaps Hugh shouldn't have held that knife to his cheek…

This establishment was a better meeting place than the last as jugs of ale sat on the table while a laden fire dissipated the damp from the river. A connecting door led to another room, and a three-sectioned bay window overlooked the Thames night, a few lanterns bobbing on moored boats.

Roberts shifted. The fire sparked.

"Our two brothers sent to Derbyshire," he began with voice stern, "will soon silence the government infiltrator who seeks to betray the good men there. I say they'll have him before this sennight is out."

No, they wouldn't. The man had changed names and moved on.

Roberts nodded slow to the fists thumping the table. "Aye, they trained us as soldiers and soldiers we shall be."

"Here's to Roberts!" shouted Cleavers above the clamour, a finger scratching behind his eyepatch.

"Not me, my brothers." Their leader raised his tankard also, lids hooded. "We drink to our Lady T!"

Pewter clanked against pewter as Hugh's mind spun in turmoil – Ross' list of ladies' surnames. All beginning with T. Who the hell was she?

"The time has come," Roberts said softly, spreading his arms, neck corded. "Men of the north are rising up and we will be part of that revolution, will greet them as they sweep down the country. Nottingham Barracks will be taken, then Newark from the river and the arms depot there." With nostrils flared, he smiled. "I'm told we've a hundred thousand men to our cause – to see this land a republic."

Raucous cheers and slaps of congratulation abounded.

Roberts twisted to pace the floor. "I want two of you in Newark. To train them on use of the arms they seize." He paused, gaze shifting to Hugh. "Davies?" And he raised a brow, grey eyes glittering like a wolf's – starved and savage.

Hugh gritted his teeth. "Aye, I'll go."

"Darnell, you'll go with him. I'll send detail–"

A knock interrupted and the grubby lad in sailor's slops poked his head around the door. "Message fer Roberts?"

Their leader strode over, snatched it and read it, marched to the fire and consigned it to the flames.

Hugh clenched his fists beneath the table. What he would have given to see that message...

The half hour that followed consisted of aimless rants about the government and a few hints at riots, but naught was definite and so when a fourth jug of ale had been emptied, the meeting concluded.

Hugh rose and Roberts clapped him on the back. "Be good to see what you're made of, Davies. Our Darnell will send word."

"Glad to be of service at last." Hugh shook his hand, fingers cracking, before he filed out after Forsyth.

Some of the men piled to the bar for more ale but Hugh made his way to the street where the brume was so thick it felt like a tangible entity. He barged through it, mind in tumult from what he'd learned.

Revolution and chaos. Death and betrayal.

Rainham's infiltrator would likely inform him of the Ravens' plans to aid revolution but Hugh should also send a message post-haste.

And who the hell was this Lady T?

He should re-check the two ladies Ross had crossed off. Or it could be Tremlach, the last lady on the list? Or...was Sir Edmund's wife, Lady Twyford, slipping secrets with or without her husband's knowledge?

Hell and damnation. More questions than answers as per usual.

His lone frustrated footsteps echoed off the brick walls of the warehouses and he glanced over one shoulder as shadows shifted in the frigid fog, the glow of the streetlamp colouring it in a noxious pallor.

It was said the ghost of Captain Kidd haunted this street as nigh a century past, the pirate had met his end at Execution Dock – hanged, tarred and displayed in a cage for three years – but Hugh was more concerned with corporeal villains this night.

The type who–

"Hey, Davies!"

Hugh turned beneath a corner streetlamp to see a broad-shouldered man bearing down upon him through the fog. The figure came closer, became enveloped in the hazy globe of light and...

"Darnell?"

"Aye." A hand clamped to Hugh's shoulder. "Thought we should have a wee talk."

"About?"

A flash of silver in the sickly light and a knife tip wedged itself against Hugh's gizzards.

"About how ye ain't Lieutenant Davies, are ye?"

Hugh's breath misted. "Are you testing me again, Darnell?"

"Och no." A grim smile curved his lips. "Roberts knows who ye are. And soon enough, yer'll be feeding the worms."

Hugh returned his own grim smile. "The message he received."

Darnell shrugged. "I thought to give ye a fighting chance though, so I've only brought two of the brothers with me."

Hugh peered past the Scotsman's shoulder.

The one-eyed Cleavers and another thickset cove appeared from the fog.

Hugh nodded slowly as though ceding to his fate, then...

Flung an arm under Darnell's, twisted hard, sent the blade

skywards. With the other hand, he grabbed at the brute's windpipe with thumb and fingers.

Squeezed.

A choked howl but Darnell broke the hold, bent double, clutched his throat as the thickset cove charged, a club raised. Hugh twisted side on into a Pankration stance and before the club could swing, kicked out with his heel, slamming it to the cove's guts.

Hands to stomach, the wretch dropped to his knees, but Cleavers had sneaked from behind and a broad arm choked Hugh's neck, dragged him back, a growl at his ear.

"Turn and hit me hard as."

Eh?

Cleavers then winked with his one eye, so Hugh followed through to smash a fist to his jaw.

He toppled to the cobbles, lay motionless.

Hugh twis–

A forearm clamped his throat and a knife waved before him, nicked his ear. "Yer dirty bloody cur," spat the thickset cove. "Yer kick like a donkey."

Hugh grappled the arm, to heave him aside, to the gutter, to scrabble for his own knife, but Darnell charged, thudded into Hugh's gut and they all crashed into the brick wall and tumbled to the pavement.

Fists piled to his stomach, blade scoring skin.

He pummelled back with all he had, endeavouring to smash at eyes or throat, to reach his own knife, but then his arms were pinned. Darnell rose and crashed a fist down; blood cloaked Hugh's gaze, couldn't see for crimson…

Couldn't rise…

Another fist to his jaw.

He kicked out in vain.

Blackness swam.

His hand clawed at his boot, his knife...couldn't reach...

AMELIA SWALLOWED, braced in her stance and steadied her arm at the roiling pitch of bodies.

Then raised her aim a fraction.

And pulled the trigger on her Duck Gun.

The cacophony and recoil juddered her backwards, eyes blinded by the flash, the blast deafening, as lead shot sliced through the air in all directions, brick shrapnel from the wall showering the street in front. Her boots stumbled but she kept to her feet.

What it lacked in accuracy, it certainly made up for in spectacle as with its four barrels, it sounded like Wellington and his battalion had arrived.

She plunged the smoking gun to her crone's greatcoat and looked up as one of the men dragged himself to his feet, turned tail and fled into the night, but the other lifted his head, swivelled, locked eyes on hers and roared as he charged.

Rough hands grabbed the collar of her coat, shaking her like a rat. "Ye little bitch!"

She dangled from his grip, the coat strangling her, scrabbled at her buttons, blood from his fist smearing her jaw.

Knife, she had to reach her garter knife, fumbled, but her boots met the cobbles as one of his hands left her, the other grabbed her throat and that fist pulled back...

Amelia slammed her eyes shut, knew this was going to hurt.

A rush of air.

The fist never came.

She opened one eye to find the man being dragged backwards, an arm locked around his neck, before a formidable blond warrior spun his foe, pinned him to the wall, roared and smashed a first fist to his gut.

The man stood not a chance against such fervent anger, blows cascading without mercy, their bodies obscured and lit in strange contortions by the streetlamp.

Her warrior then planted such a punch that his foe was hurled to the side, slumping down the wall and crumpling into a mound.

No sooner had she taken breath when another broad figure lifted from the dark cobbles and Amelia bent low, felt for her garter knife and thrust it forth.

The cloying yellow of the streetlamp silhouetted a man.

A man with an eyepatch.

One who…winked at her with his other eye.

And she lowered her knife. "I could have shot you!"

"Not with that Duck thing, you couldn't."

Well, really.

"Make yerself scarce, Hare. I've got this." And he whirled, stomping off into the fog.

Which left…

"Mr…Mr Cadwalader?" He was stooped to one side, hands to knees, clothing ripped, breath panting, and Amelia dashed to him. "Are you…"

His head twisted. Still stooped.

A flint-eyed warrior stared. There was a cut to his neck and forehead, another to his ear, and blood smeared his skin.

No one would recognise this man, she realised. No one but her.

Those flint eyes sharpened. "You're hurt," he growled.

"I…" She felt her jaw. Her fingers came away sticky. "No. The blood's not mine."

His shoulders sagged and he shifted a palm to his stomach, brow crunched in pain, breath sawing back and forth in misted bursts.

With a groan from the depths, he straightened. His fingers

flexed, neck inching from side to side. An inhale grated in his chest and he faced her, expression fearsome and wild and sinister.

Until a smile split his battered physog.

"Do you not think, *Amelia,*" he drawled low, gingerly proffering an arm, "that it's time to call me Hugh?"

CHAPTER SEVENTEEN

"If she deserves your confidence, prove it to her."

Private Education: A Practical Plan for the Studies of Young Ladies.

Elizabeth Appleton. 1815.

A true governess would have demurely declined the proposal of a hot bath and rebuffed the offer of warm towels and a full-bodied wine. But Amelia was no governess and so had gratefully accepted all.

Her return with the master of the house – in her crone garments and with hair reeking of gunpowder – had not been questioned aloud as such by the servants but brows had met mobcaps and eyes had narrowed in supposition. Sally had winked.

The household now believed Amelia to be tucked up in bed, when in fact, at the behest of the master, she sat awaiting him on a silk sofa in that locked end room of the second floor, which had proved to be…

She turned her head this way and that.

A library.

But not just any library.

Restful leaf-green paperhangings peeked from behind mahogany bookcases, the ceiling edged with white and gold architrave. A magnificent desk with a vase of pink roses faced the window, currently veiled by deep-burgundy curtains, and a low fire kept the spring chill at bay.

Needless to say, there'd never been any question earlier as to whether she would shadow Hu...

Amelia frowned. She couldn't call him Hugh. It was too...familiar.

Lord Rainham had not given a direct order but he allowed his officers to make their own decisions and was not one to castigate if they put themselves in danger to aid another. Rumours were that he himself had set off on a fool's errand in French territory to liberate one of his own men from a prison set afire.

She returned her eyes to the small volume she'd removed from one of the bookcases: *Myth and Legend of Wales*.

The frontispiece had caught her eye with its fine drawing of dragons spitting fire, sweeping over jagged mountains and deep forests, fierce guardians of their treasure. And whilst she would not wish to question the decisions of her superior, she mused that Dragon might have been a more apt code name for Mr Cadwalader as he was just such a man – fierce and protective.

Yet she must beware.

For he was also a scandalous gentleman of *Ton* society, used to flirtation meaning little and kisses even less. Such kisses that spun her senses.

And although he vexed her at times, it would be all too easy for deep emotions to arise for such a man, emotions that no spy should feel, for they hindered sight and muddled clarity.

Would he kiss her again?

It should not matter.

For what was a kiss?

Just a meeting of lips? A physical act that held no lasting promise or potential for hurt.

Or did it?

Most in her profession took pleasure where they could, knew that life was fleet, but Amelia had never been able to act in such a manner, had witnessed in her childhood that hurt could too easily follow.

She slammed the book shut and stared to the mantel clock. Nigh midnight.

Mr Cadwalader had passed a fair while in his bathing chamber and she wondered if his wounds pained him? She'd not thought them too severe as he'd been at his most talkative in the hackney carriage back to Hanover.

Perhaps he was merely enjoying the lap of water against his bared skin. The cleansing soap as it glided over...

Amelia breathed deep and reopened her book.

HUGH'S GIZZARDS felt as though they'd been removed with burning tongs, spun on a cart's wheel and then shoved back in with a toasting fork.

The shallow cuts were just irritating as they stung like hell and had only ceased bleeding due to some cabbage-green sludge from Mrs Dawkins. The condition of his cheekbones was unknown as they'd numbed but his faithful housekeeper had thought nothing broken.

In fact, Hugh was uncertain how he'd made it back, just known he'd been compelled to prattle on in order to stay conscious as the hackney driver had chosen to search out and surmount every raised cobblestone in London.

He limped from his bedchamber in breeches and shirt but was halted by a lurking Cruikshank.

"I believe, Sir, that Miss...Jones is awaiting you in your library."

"Yes, thank you, Cruik. And, er... There's no need to keep a close eye on her anymore as she's...as she is..." He scrunched his nose. *How to explain?*

"One of ours, Sir?"

"Indeed."

"One did wonder." The butler clasped hands behind his back. "Henceforth, Miss Jones will be accorded all freedoms." Cruikshank cleared his throat. "Not that she wasn't, of course. Do you require tea, Sir?"

"No, no. Give my thanks to everyone and send them to bed."

Hugh made his way down the corridor but paused before the library, breathed deep...*ouch*, pulled back his shoulders...*uff*, ran a hand through his hair, stripping the remaining skin from his knuckles, and then opened the door.

What a wondrous sight for his sore eyes.

With cheeks scrubbed clean of coal dust and rosy from the fire, Amelia wore a cream robe that covered her from neck to ankle but her flaxen hair was loose and it flowed over her shoulders like the sinuous River Dwyryd in Wales.

Manfully, he strode into the room. "You look rested and unharmed, Amelia."

Her eyes began at his bruised physog, lowered to his shoulders and then to his stomach as though she could see through his shirt and to the gruesome state of his innards.

"I am. But are you yourself unharmed?"

Hugh was about to say he felt fit as a fiddle, that the occasion a crazed horse had kicked him in Hyde Park had been worse.

But there was no reason for falsehoods.

No reason to concoct a tale for distraction.

She'd been there with him. Had likely saved his life and only deserved the truth.

"I feel," he said, sinking into the sofa next to her, "horrendous. My guts throb. My cheekbones are numb. I can't move my shoulders."

A cleft of concern appeared between her brows. "You seemed in fine fettle in the hackney home."

"I was prattling. I only prattle when in pain."

"Oh. In that case, turn to one side."

He frowned but did as requested and…groaned as nimble fingers kneaded his shoulders.

Such bliss and his head sagged.

"I'm not hurting you?"

He mumbled something but she continued, so it must have been vaguely coherent.

Gads, never before had he returned from a mission to care such as this.

Fingers pressed and circled, unravelling each taut muscle and strained tendon, and an agreeable lassitude besieged him.

Except as the hands wandered down his spine, another sensation entirely made itself known.

Desire.

Rampant after the fight.

Distraction was indeed now required.

"Where did you learn this?"

"My mother. She used to suffer from megrims and this helped her. Turn towards the desk a little, Mr Cadwalader."

"I told you to call me Hugh," he groused.

But a murmur was the lone response he received.

The fire crackled and he became aware that her hands were slowing, the kneading softer, though the fire within himself raged unabated. Amelia fascinated him and he wanted to know all of her – what had formed her, how she'd come to work for the Foreign Office, what her favoured food was and which side of the bed she liked.

"Is your mother still alive?"

"No."

"Siblings?"

"No."

"Was your mother involved in our line of work?"

"No."

Gads. This was like pulling teeth with sugar tongs. "Tell me of your father?"

"He..." Her hesitation spun into a lengthy pause, then...

Silence.

And Hugh realised that whoever her parents were, she was reticent to speak of them.

"I hope you know you can tell me anything, Amelia. Or nothing, if you so wish." He twisted on the sofa and she was so near, he could smell her rosewater and the faintest hint of gunpowder still in her hair. "But anything you share with me would never pass these four walls, or indeed my lips, without your permission. I just... I just want to know all of you, 'tis all."

She plucked at her robe and chewed at a lip.

"My...my father was the late fourth Duke of Swanford," she blurted.

That did take the wind from his sails. High-born indeed. "But why are you–"

"My mother... My mother was known amongst the *Ton* as..." She paused as though seeking courage. "The... The Butterfly Courtesan."

Ah.

That would explain her reticence.

Hugh vaguely remembered the Butterfly Courtesan from many, many years ago at some demi-rep affair. An absolute beauty with dark-blond hair and jade eyes, blood-red lips and a short, curvaceous stature.

Of course, he'd been a mere cub and she'd have been in her thirties by then, but her raw sensuality had lit a room.

And Amelia...was her daughter.

He could see the likeness now. Though her amber eyes must have come from her father.

She swivelled from him, muttering.

"Amelia?"

"People always go quiet," she griped. "Whether through pity, amusement or disgust."

Hugh wished to punch someone – preferably all those *people*, but...

"You mistake my hesitation, Amelia, because your parentage prompts nothing of the sort within me. I was just taken aback, that's all." He looked to his bruised knuckles. "Let me tell you of my own mother and father. Their marriage was arranged by their parents for money and prestige, their wedding attended by the upper echelons of society. But they loathed one another. Father was a gambling wretch, Mother a cold diamond, and sometimes I am amazed they even managed one night in a bed together to beget me. They were filled with hatred for one another, bemoaned their lot for their entire lives and died miserably."

Her lips pursed to a silent *Oh*.

"I say this not to gain sympathy but so you realise that I care not a brass button for society's judgement as to what merits acceptability or happiness." He rubbed a hand over his stubbled cheek. "I presume you remained with your mother then, as..."

"As you never knew the Duke of Swanford even had a daughter? No. No one did." She turned back but her lashes swept downwards. "So you are correct, I was raised by my mother as a gentlewoman but in a somewhat...tumultuous household."

"And your father?"

Those lashes closed. "I recall little of him, did not see him much, but when I think back, I feel...sadness."

For once, Hugh stayed quiet, sensed there was so much more.

Her eyes opened to stare at him for a moment. "I suppose you will plague me until you know all."

No, Hugh would not, for he could see it caused her pain.

So willing to wait until Amelia trusted him and wanted to tell him, he merely seized her hand – small and soft betwixt his bruised and calloused mitts.

But she sighed. "My mother was an army officer's daughter, you see, left orphaned, and so she came to London for work, as a companion or some such." A grim smile. "She was seventeen, pretty and innocent, and I'm sure you've heard this timeworn tale many a time. The young duke met her in Vauxhall Gardens and became her first protector. I was born a year later. I remember him as kind but rather...soft. I remember Mama rushing around, impatient and joyful when he was to visit. I... She loved him, you see. After all, they were together for eight years, and I believe it was reciprocated, but..." She swallowed and her face became suffused with hurt.

Hugh yearned to banish it but knew not how.

She lifted her beautiful amber eyes. "A duke has to marry, does he not? One of his own class. And the duke, for all his faults, believed in faithfulness to his duchess, so he... After all that time, he just let go of my mother. Let her go and married a debutante with her faultless lineage." Her lips trembled. "I remember tears and cries; I remember being moved to a smaller house of his and Mama buying me a kitten. I…I never saw him again."

Hugh wished to tear the chicken-hearted coxcomb's head off – even though he was dead. Instead, he gripped her hand more firmly. "But your father made sure you were cared for and…"

"Money was sent for my upkeep but not enough for Mama also and we had to pay a rent. I heard his new duchess was quite…commanding. Kept a close eye on the purse strings."

Hugh now wished to punch the coxcomb fourth Duke of Swanford's decapitated head – even though he'd be twice dead – and although such contracts with courtesans were played out each year in London, her father should have had the ballocks to ensure that his past mistress, an innocent at that, need never have worked again. He should have been a presence in his daughter's life, not let her go also. It was not unheard of for a nobleman to bestow a dowry upon a merry-begotten child, acknowledging them within his world.

Amelia straightened her shoulders. "So, Mama rose from the ashes of her lost love and became the Butterfly Courtesan. Never staying with one lover for long, always playing a part: the patient confidante, the sensual paramour. But she never allowed herself to love again."

"It sounds to me," he said softly, "as though your mother was a woman of strength and courage."

Amelia smiled. "She was and although many have tried to shame me for my lack of legitimacy and my mother's occupation, I feel naught but gladness when I think upon my childhood. Unconventional, to be sure, but joyful."

He brought her hand to his lips and kissed the back. "Any shame belongs to those like my parents who spread naught but sorrow. As for your own parentage…" He smiled. "Have you heard of FitzRoy, the fourth Duke of Grafton?"

"A Whig member of parliament until he became duke, yes?"

His clever Amelia.

"Certainly, but the Grafton dukedom was only created by Charles II for the benefit of his illegitimate son. Same goes for the Duke of Saint Albans whose ancestral mother was the actress Nell Gwyn. Do they feel shame for their illegitimate ancestry? No."

Her lips quirked. "Money and title help people forget."

"Of course, but what I am trying to say is that it's damn Janus-faced of the *Ton* to disdain a child for illegitimacy when some of the most illustrious titles are due to exactly that."

Amelia smiled. "Only you could see it in such a way."

He could not help but lean forward, place a hand to her cheek.

"All I see," he murmured, "is you."

Amber eyes flitted to his – courageous and caring, and all he'd thought his chosen life would never allow him.

His head lowered without thought, lips so near, breaths mingling.

Amelia's lashes fluttered shut and it was she who closed the gap.

Brushing at first. No rush.

All was leisure and aching adoration.

As one, they drew closer.

Her robe was thin as paper, his shirt a flimsy piece of naught and he could feel her breasts, her very heartbeat, lips warm and lush, her scent of roses and gunpowder addling his wits – that blend of beauty and danger.

Unbidden, his palm slid down her throat, down her décolletage, and cupped her breast, thumb skimming the tip.

A low moan escaped her – impassioned and wanting – and Hugh wished to lay her upon this sofa, peel the robe from her skin, kiss every fingerbreadth exposed and then do it all again. He wished to watch as she cried her pleasure; he wished to sink deep. He wished to lose himself in astute beautiful Amelia until they were overwhelmed, joined, groaning and mindless.

Yet…

Those damnable wishes…

For it felt wrong.

Hearing her tale, she deserved so much more.

In the aftermath of the fight, emotions were heightened, desire tending to rush, and yet…even as he told himself all this, he was aware that something was different.

When a past mission had not gone well, he'd return home dejected at man's depravity or jaded at betrayal, but Amelia brought truth and pleasure and grace and belief.

Feelings surged and his noggin attempted to make sense of them – not just desire but protectiveness, longing, respect, need.

And he would not ruin it for a quick tup.

So, he softened his caress, drew away and kissed her cheek. "Amelia, I could kiss you all night but…"

"You're bleeding again," she said huskily.

He hadn't even noticed. "Yes. And besides, we need our rest for tomorrow."

"Tomorrow?"

"I would say for Aunt Enid who is due at the hour of eleven but also…" He stretched. "Now the Ravens know my identity, although heaven knows how as I told no one at all I was going to the meeting, we are solely reliant on Rainham's man for information from them." He raked a hand through his hair. "But what the Ravens did do tonight was raise their tankards to a Lady T."

Amelia rubbed her arms. "So Phoebe's father was right. That list of ladies' names."

"Precisely. So we must turn to discovering who she is. I must have missed something amongst those names, or there is another lady we have yet to find. And then of course, there is

Lady Twyford." He grimaced. "And unfortunately, there is only one person I can think of who'd have the nefarious means to acquire this essential underhand information on all these upper-class ladies of the *Ton*."

"Oh, no." Amelia's eyes widened. "Not…"

A grim nod. "The Prince."

CHAPTER EIGHTEEN

"The opportunities for instruction in a walk are not to be enumerated."

Private Education: A Practical Plan for the Studies of Young Ladies.

Elizabeth Appleton. 1815.

"When are you marrying?"

Du sublime au ridicule. "Did we not have this conversation last week, Aunt Enid?"

"No harm in repeating oneself," she replied with a sniff, "especially when you are seen at the art soiree of nitterwits like Lady Tremblelip."

"Tremlach."

"Just so." She raised her amethyst-encrusted quizzing glass from where she sat ramrod straight upon the breakfast room Chippendale chair.

Hugh fidgeted beneath the intense stare and briefly wondered if he could distract her by asking for any hearsay on Lady Twyford as the two were of a similar age. Yet he'd vowed long ago never to involve Aunt in his work. She was damn astute and would likely probe him further, which, considering the dangers, was unwise and–

"Oh, Hugh, you've bruises and cuts upon your person. Again."

"Ruffians in Hanover Square, Aunt."

She peered from their first-floor window to a benevolent square of tranquillity – children played hoop, ladies promenaded the central garden and a flower girl peddled daisies.

Hugh cleared his throat. "It was somewhat late."

"Pshaw! That is where gallivanting gets you, my boy. Marriage and babes. That would settle you."

Amber eyes flitted for a moment but before he could cogitate what that meant, the door opened to display Phoebe wearing her habitual black.

Although...

His gaze widened as her frock did appear to be of this era, if not this season, with a high waist and fitted sleeves. In a deep, rich velvet, it sported a modish square neck but with an ebony lace fichu. It was sombre but elegant, and suited Phoebe perfectly.

"Well, what a fine young lady," Aunt lauded while accepting a kiss to the cheek. "Been to the modiste's, have we?"

"Not quite, my lady, although if I'd known they had such a splendid selection of blacks, I might have done so. No, my governess brought this in and, well, I thought I'd try it on."

Hugh limped forward to give his ward a fierce hug. "You look beautiful. I shall have to rename you my bird of paradise."

"They're not black," she said with a giggle.

Hugh gazed over Phoebe's shoulder to Amelia with her familiar carpetbag in hand.

"I will ensure you are reimbursed, Miss Jones. My utmost thanks."

"No need," she demurred. "I first asked Madame Devy if she had any returns that Phoebe could try on, but she told me you kept an account there to charge purchases to. So, I did." Her lashes flicked up. And batted. "For other ladies, perhaps?"

Hugh grinned. "For Phoebe in the years to come, needless to say."

Wide-eyed innocence met his gaze, which he now knew to be an utter sham. "But of course, Mr Cadwalader."

Aunt's sharp eyes – with or without the quizzing glass narrowed – so Hugh sought a seat at the table as Cruikshank trundled in with the tea trolley.

"Hugh! Why is this the Wedgwood Imari? I dislike all the brash angles. The Spode Porcelain Peacock pattern is more fetching. Do you not agree, Miss Jones?"

"Er…" His minx of a governess bit her lip as she and Phoebe took a seat on the chaise. "Well–"

"Aunt, as long as they hold tea, I, for one, can't say it matters."

"Twaddle! A teacup represents your home and station in life. Men! I called upon that Lady Tremblelip's once and she gave me a chipped Coalport. I ask you! And why are you limping still? Not another pistol mishap?"

"Ah, well, I'm glad you've asked, Aunt, because therein lies a tale…" He waggled his eyebrows. "Can you believe that some wicked jade near Pall Mall appropriated my custom-made Hoby boots? I managed to purchase a pair from a lumberman but they chafed like knives, so I was forced to walk in stockinged feet all the way home. Not a carriage would halt for me." He shook his head. "Other than Lord Linton who stopped to ask if it was a new fashion."

"Bared feet? Fashion?" Lady Kemble tutted. "Whatever next? No cravat? The sky will fall."

"Oh, Uncle, what a bag of moonshine that tale is!" Phoebe sniggered. "Why would anyone want your boots?"

"Why indeed, my bird of paradise, but so it was." And he cast his elfin malapert of a governess a narrow-eyed glance. "But I cannot speak for the wicked jade herself."

Amelia cleared her throat. "Perhaps, Sir, this wicked jade felt she had just cause? Perhaps her need was greater than your own."

Aunt nodded sagely.

Phoebe snorted.

Oh, how he was going to silence that nimble tongue of Amelia's one day and images of her naked and at his mercy amidst green silk sheets beset him... He shook his head and shifted his chair further beneath the table.

"I sincerely hope," muttered Aunt, "you will desist from joggling about like that when we take tea with Miss Berrycloth-Birdwhistle next week. It's as though you have ants in your unmentionables. Though I fail to see where ants could find the room in there."

"Do you search out debutantes with the most ridiculous names on purpose?"

A small smile quirked Aunt's lips. "Be thankful I declined to invite Miss Ponsonby-Piddlehinton from Dorset. She has a sister who birthed twins."

He riffled the Debrett's bureau of his brain. "She's little more than seventeen, if I recall, Aunt. That's only two years older than Phoebe."

"Eugh!" cried Phoebe.

"Shame to quibble over years as her tatting is exemplary. Oh, Hugh, why must you be so abstruse! How about Miss Damson-Dankworth then?"

Were his saucebox of a governess' lips trembling in suppressed mirth?

Hugh could not resist. After all, it wasn't the taking part that mattered, but the winning.

"Miss Ponsonby-Piddlehinton excels at tatting, you say? Why did you not tell of this earlier, Aunt? For possession of such a miraculous skill assuredly elevates any young lady to the realms of the divine..." He placed a hand to his chin in faux thoughtfulness. "I wonder, Miss Jones, do you have your tatting work to show Lady Kemble?" And he raised his brows nigh to the ceiling.

How underhand.

And an image formed of *Hugh* Cadwalader ensnared within a six-foot roll of tatting, rather like a fly flailing within a spider's web. But with tranquil expression, Amelia reached into the carpetbag at her side, moved Miss Appleton's tome, and brought forth a folded linen cloth.

A glance passed between herself and dearest Phoebe before she rose from the chaise and crossed the breakfast room to stand before Lady Kemble. "I happen to have this on me. Just a small sample as there's not much time for leisure at the moment. All the...knowledge to be imparted and so on."

And Amelia folded back the linen to reveal Phoebe's beautiful butterfly.

"Oh, I say!" gasped Lady Kemble, raising her quizzing glass. "How superb."

Amelia felt rather than saw Mr Cadwalader arrive at her back, his nearness affecting her so.

"Exquisite," he murmured, and she twisted her head to find him not staring at the tatting sample at all but at her.

Amelia's inhalation caught; his eyes flickered.

They were so blue today. From this distance, she could see the ring of pure indigo that encircled the pupil, the hue only enhanced by the purple bruising to his cheek and the vibrant crimson gash to his forehead.

Not that she'd advocate being punched in the face to gain such vividness of colour but...

Those Cadwalader eyes managed to convey such varied emotions – teasing then serious, amiable then dangerous, and such feelings of...

Curse it.

Feelings were not what she should have for Mr Hugh Cadwalader.

"Ahem! Miss Jones!"

She snapped her gaze from him. "Apologies, my lady. Wool-gathering."

"Quite." That quizzing glass lifted in a purple-gloved hand. "It's come back to me! The colour of your eyes reminds me of the Swanford brood of dukes. Any relation?"

Cold dread drenched Amelia. "T-that family are not personally known to me, my lady."

"No loss. I was a debutante with the late fourth duke's sister."

Amelia swallowed the knot in her throat. "Oh, that's..."

"By chance, Aunt," interrupted Hugh at her side, "do you yourself have any tatting with you?"

"What? Well, of course."

"May I see it?"

"You've never asked before?"

"But now that I know of its splendiferous splendour, I'll not achieve one wink of peaceful sleep until my eyes have been graced by more. And with those delicate hands, dearest Aunt, yours must surely cause the angels to cry in envy and the cherubs to cavort in wonderment."

"Pish! You beggarly rascal." But Lady Kemble beamed and rooted in her bag.

Amelia mouthed her gratitude and he winked at her as Phoebe joined them to view the contents of Lady Kemble's tatting bag. Amelia folded the linen cloth back over Phoebe's butterfly and returned to the chaise.

The past should not affect her so, but the recollections of her father and mother last night had brought it fresh to her thoughts, and how Amelia wished she'd appreciated Mama more in her childhood and not grumped about pink and lace.

But wishes were for fools as Hugh would say, so instead she recalled the fun days of absurd hats with cloud-high feathers, music and laughter. She recalled the gentler times, chatting softly whilst soothing her mother's megrims.

A skill which had proved useful last night.

Although setting her hands upon Hugh Cadwalader's bath-dampened skin had provoked an altogether distinct sensation.

One which had demanded she return his kiss – sensuous, divine, necessary.

Within that intimacy of candlelight, Amelia had been unable to deny Hugh Cadwalader and his seductive kiss.

Yet he'd brought it to an end anyhow.

Perhaps it was for the best.

"Miss Jones!"

Amelia blinked up at Lady Kemble, who now stood over her.

"Apologies, my lady." And she rose to her feet. "I was..."

Lady Kemble pursed her lips. "Come! I require you to walk the room with me for I am old and weak."

"A pleasure, my lady." Amelia gave her best demure smile and received the lady's purple-clad arm – it was strong as a young goat's and required not one whit of support.

They stepped forth in a clockwise direction, past the windows overlooking the square.

"That tatting was exquisite, Miss Jones." Pausing in her stride, Lady Kemble turned, blue eyes shrewd. "And I would recognise it as Phoebe's work from across Hyde Park."

Amelia swallowed, abruptly tired of all the lies and subterfuge. "My lady, I..."

A pat on the arm. "If Phoebe trusts you, Miss Jones, then I do also as she is most perceptive." She peered back at the young girl who was fussing over her guardian's bruised cheek. "Phoebe is also happier than I have seen her in some while and I believe that is due to you."

"Oh, I have done little," she said honestly.

"You listen to her," the lady retorted. "Listen to her needs and that is what she requires. Phoebe will not be your conventional debutante, I think, so will need many skills to be who she wishes." She sighed. "And besides, she may be the nearest to a niece I'll have if Hugh is not amenable to any of my prospective brides." With a tut, she twisted away quite ably. "Hugh! I am for home. Where I shall also request Miss Pussett-Puddifer to attend tea next week. She is nigh a spinster at twenty-four years and dotes on a bothersome spaniel named Peril, so you might like her."

CHAPTER NINETEEN

"What is lightning? What is thunder?"

Private Education: A Practical Plan for the Studies of Young Ladies.

Elizabeth Appleton. 1815.

"Now, listen to me," stated Hugh as the hackney carriage trundled along Pall Mall. "I'll deal with this, Amelia. The fellow can be a little...irritable." He tapped his lip with the brass top of his cane. "In truth, it would be best if you stayed in the carriage."

In *actual* truth, Hugh didn't wish Amelia anywhere near this gambling hell owner known as the Prince, for despite his curt manner, scarred cheek and caliginous demeanour, women in his presence seemed to swoon to earth like geese at nightfall.

Not that the Prince seemed to notice.

And not that Hugh would be jealous.

But Amelia nodded so all was fine.

That drab snuff-coloured rag of a frock clothed her and he

imagined her in green silk, roses in her hair and emeralds encircling her neck.

"How well do you know him?" she enquired, staring out the window as dusk fell, a dank drizzle misting the windows.

Hugh would have preferred to meet within daylight hours and had sent a note to the Prince suggesting just that. The reply had been somewhat curt – a slashed cross with the hour of seven scrawled over it – and if he'd not been mistaken, the seal had been daubed with blood.

Rather theatrical.

"We've had a few dealings. Alas, I already owe him a favour."

Her head curved to him and in the dim light, he could see her lips thin. "I've heard you should never be in debt to the Prince. It's rumoured his heart is blacker than Satan's boots. That he rules half of London Town and knows all the *Ton*'s darkest secrets. That even Beelzebub himself fears him when midnight looms and–"

"Yes, yes, I'm well aware of all that. But it was for my ducal cousin in Wales. I asked the Prince if he could call in a debt to which he was...amenable."

"In return for a future favour from you?"

"Yes."

He thought to see a fleet smile cross her lips.

Shuffling in his new boots, Hugh folded his arms, his emotions and desires for Miss Amelia Lambert rather disconcerting. He yearned for her in ways he'd never felt before yet...he was utterly unsure of her feelings towards him.

Oh, she'd allowed his kiss but Amelia was adept at hiding her true feelings, her true self, and although he was fairly certain she enjoyed their banter, had gawked at his nude chest, the question remained – and this was rather galling for the Scandalous Hugh Cadwalader to have to ask but – did she like him?

"How on earth," she began, "do you think the Brotherhood of Ravens discovered you were an infiltrator?"

He shook his head. No time for moonstruck musings. "I'd say it was that note Roberts received. But who was it from? I'd told no one at the Home Office I was going." Rubbed his chin. "Perhaps they investigated the Lieutenant Davies I was pretending to be and found him to be false."

"It's odd. It feels as though someone has eyes everywhere."

"I agree." Her complexion glowed in the hackney carriage's single lantern. "Your crone garb was…inspired."

"I've used it several times but the aroma can linger."

Hugh decided to live up to his scandalous moniker and vault from his seat, swivel in mid-air, land on the cushion beside her and bring his nose to her neck. "No fragrance of vermin. Just rose, and the merest hint of gunpowder."

She cleared her throat. Surely a sign of flusterment in his presence. Good.

"Drat," she murmured, "I'll have to wash my hair again."

"Not on my account," he murmured back. "I adore the combined deadly bouquet."

Amelia looked at him oddly.

But her lips were parted so Hugh neared.

She did not withdraw, so since he was being scandalous, he placed a hand to her silken chin, then leaned in to–

"'Ere we are. The Prince's!" came a yowl from the hackney coachman, slamming what sounded like a sledgehammer upon the roof and halting so abruptly they were nigh upended to the floor.

Bloody damnation! Could a man not woo in peace.

"You'd best go." Amelia's lips quirked. "The gaming hell will only get busier after seven."

Hugh nodded, tendered her a tip of hat brim and shoved his way out.

Naturally, he was a member of this hell, but he spent little time gambling as when one's life was the wager most nights, money became rather tame.

He gave his name to the broad-shouldered henchman at the crimson door and within a trice was ushered forth.

Without pausing, he strode through the grand vestibule, on past the waiters with their silver trays of champagne, the air redolent with tuberose and leather.

Later, the air would no doubt also reek of desperation and loss but at this hour, the handful of gentlemen had elevated hopes of winning a fortune with a throw of dice rather than with labour or ledgers.

A decadent haven had been deftly created, one which beguiled, softened defences and encouraged deep play.

Swinging his cane, Hugh weaved betwixt the tables.

The Prince kept this club exclusive and expensive, the waiting list for membership as long as the Welsh winter. No house-employed doxies would saunter these rooms either, but high-class courtesans and vibrant widows were oft invited – ladies who cared not for the *Ton*'s endorsement or had enough blunt to weather the gossip.

A lanky melancholic fellow loitered by a sculpture of Orpheus, watching over the hell with vigilant eye, and one could almost be fooled into thinking he was one of the clientele, so elegantly was he attired in deepest black.

Except he wore an equally black feather in his lapel – an emblem of allegiance to the Prince.

Some, it was rumoured, had the feather inked to their skin while others were given these emblems, but such was the Prince's reputation that not even the most hardened villain dared to replicate them.

"Kian Finlay." For Hugh knew this melancholic fellow was a right-hand man of the owner.

Sombre blue eyes flicked to him. "Cadwalader. Follow me." And without another word, he spun to stalk down a corridor, past various sculptures – Cerberus the dog and Charon the ferryman of Hades – until they arrived at a grand staircase.

"You know the way."

A man of few words so Hugh merely nodded and embarked up the marble steps.

On the first floor, a scarlet door presented itself and he knocked with the brass top of his cane.

"Enter."

Hugh did as bid and closed the door.

He'd had cause to visit the Prince on a few occasions and though the gaming rooms could be termed a little ostentatious, not so was this study.

It resembled a gentleman's refuge with an immense walnut desk, decanters, bookcases, a globe, and even a pedigree bloodhound lounging by the fire.

"Wait," a voice said from behind the desk.

Hugh peered to the dog.

The dog peered back and returned to dozing, so presuming the request was aimed at himself, Hugh stayed where he was and swivelled his eyes to a painting on the wood-panelled wall.

In deepest sleep, within a field of wind-tossed wheat, lay a blond woman, her hands limp, hair spread, and it was so exquisite, so finely rendered, that with just a whisper, one could imagine her eyes dreamily opening.

"I like this," he murmured, gazing over to the Prince. "How much?"

Hugh was ignored for some while until the reprobate slotted quill in holder and then unfurled from his seat behind the desk with a certain savage grace.

"Not for sale," was the curt rebuff.

Damn it, but the sinister fellow had a glower as black as

desolation, a habitual scarlet coat cloaking his broad frame and he wore no cravat.

Some said the slicing scar upon his cheek came from the devil himself – a mark of ownership.

Hugh considered that tale for the ladies' benefit.

Though he could appreciate how that wound must have hurt when first inflicted, for Hugh had similar upon his chest – deep and torn.

Yet it wasn't the devil who made such marks but man.

"I need some information."

With long-legged stride and a swordstick jutting from his coat, the Prince made his way to the decanters, and poured two brandies.

One was handed over and they tipped their glasses at one another.

"You already owe me."

"I could pay. Or I could provide you with information in return."

The Prince merely stared with that shadowed gaze. "I've enough blunt," he grunted at last before slugging his liquor in a single gulp, peculiar scars criss-crossing his knuckles. "And there's no information I don't have."

Hugh didn't doubt it.

"There's nothing I can offer you then?"

The devil just shrugged.

Hugh clenched his fists. "This is not for some trivial game – blackmail over an earl's sins or a duchess' debt. A good man was murdered, leaving his daughter alone in this world. I want justice for them both and you might have what I need. This is about betrayal and death."

"'Death smiles at us all,'" the Prince murmured, "'all a man can do is smile back.'"

"I've not come to trade quotes," growled Hugh. "What do you

want from me?"

The Prince flicked his scarlet coat-tails to settle upon the corner of his desk and a grim smile notched his lips, pulling at the facial scar. "Why don't you…send your little drab in the hackney outside to ask me instead?"

Not on Hugh's life. "No deal."

The Prince stared with stony eye.

Hugh returned his own flint gaze.

The fire spat and the hound stirred.

Until the brigand just shrugged once more. "Good night, Cadwalader." And he prowled to the window, swordstick slapping his thigh, before staring out into the nocturnal nothingness.

"One day, Prince," Hugh said through gritted teeth, "you will need others. You will call and no one will answer. You will beg and no one will listen." He strode to the door and fisted the handle. "So let us hope for your sake that when that day comes, I show you mercy." And he stalked out, leaving it wide.

Information on these ladies would have to be gathered the hard way – through gossip at society salons and tattle at balls.

The waiters and scant gentlemen of the hell parted like the sea before Moses, as likely his expression resembled a storm, and he swept on through the vestibule, out the crimson door held wide, across the pavement and threw open the hackney door, shoving himself into the seat.

IN HER MOST LADYLIKE MANNER, Amelia cleared her throat. "Did it not go well?"

"Home, Coachman!" Hugh bit out, batting on the hell cart's roof with his brass-topped cane.

She grabbed the cane from him and batted again. "No! Wait, Coachman!"

Hugh thinned his lips. "I'm not dealing with such a terse monosyllabic blackguard." He grabbed back his cane. "Home!" And batted once more.

"No! Wait!" Amelia yelled. "What did he say?"

"Say? He's less chatty than a deceased pallbearer and if he thinks you're going up there alone, he's very much mistaken."

Amelia blinked. "He wants...me?"

"Yes. No. Home!"

"No! Wait! I'll go."

"You bloody won't." His eyes narrowed, pierced her. "He's a damnable Prince of Darkness."

"Oh, Hugh, he's just a man."

Amelia removed her bonnet and smoothed her chignon. Unfastened the top two buttons at her collar and–

"What the hell are you doing?"

"I can't go like this. I look like a governess."

"Good," he groused. "Home!"

"Wait! And–"

The wrinkled physog of the coachman appeared at the window. "I'm goin' fer a pie. Yer let me know when yer both know, eh?"

"Well, that settles it." And Amelia pinched her cheeks to blush.

"Stop doing that."

Hugh closed his eyes, nostrils flaring, and a sliver of curiosity crept through Amelia's veins. Was he merely concerned for her welfare or...jealous?

Surely not.

But just in case, she nibbled her lips to red and consulted her timepiece. "If I've not returned by the hour, come get me."

His nostrils flared once more, jaw taut as a fiddle string. "Have you the Duck Gun?"

"No. But I have Miss Appleton's tome." She suppressed a smile. "I could hit him with it."

And before he could retort, she dashed from the hackney, carpetbag in hand.

At her approach to the crimson portal, the doorman ushered her through with a flourish of hand and doff of hat.

The scent of decadence assailed her, but Amelia did not pause in the vestibule and no one halted her.

She marched on, kept close to the wall.

No one turned. No one raised their eyes.

Passing the roulette table, said to have been...procured from the *Palais Royal* in Paris, the croupier glanced up.

Uttered not a word.

She ascended the marble staircase and as the door appeared to be open, Amelia continued in.

Then hesitated.

A scarred man, stern and tenebrous, twisted from the window.

Obsidian eyes bored into her, shadow without light.

Then he stalked towards her, a hunter to a hare, and her skin prickled as though thunder approached.

Amelia stilled as he leaned close, a breath of fine brandy shivering her spine.

"So..." His voice scoured like gravel beneath a booted heel. "You work with Cadwalader now, Amelia."

"It's good to see you too, Prince. Got a brandy for me?"

His smile was imperceptible to those who knew him not, but it was there, and as he paced to the decanters, she permitted one of her own.

When she'd first met this man, she'd been terrified of his reputation and demeanour, but as time had passed, a recognition had formed, a friendship of sorts that never went beyond its bounds.

She'd heard him speak like an aristocratic lord of Mayfair and an arch rogue of the Rookery, witnessed him use his hands like a prizefighter yet wield an artist's brush with such finesse. Some whispered he was the by-blow of the devil and an angel, but who was he really?

Amelia did not know.

But if Hugh's gaze was akin to a strike of lightning, this man's was the thunder.

A brandy was proffered, her favoured, and she lowered herself to the chaise which had been reupholstered since she'd left this place four years past. Alfred the bloodhound padded over to sniff her hand and she patted his wrinkly head.

"How are you keeping, Prince?"

A shrug. Even more terse than usual, and she watched as he filled his own glass, movements precise. He appeared more… detached than before, a jaded loneliness encasing him that could never be pierced, a turbulent storm concealed by impenetrable cloud.

In years past, a compulsion had consumed him, a need for secrets and money. Now he had it all and the storm was subdued.

For the time being.

"What is it you need to know?"

"No talk of days gone by?"

"You're not here for that."

She grimaced for it was true.

"You want to know who murdered the young girl's father?"

"Do you know?"

A shake of head. "But I'll answer your questions, if I can."

"We have a list of names. All ladies of the *Ton*." And she handed over a fold of paper. "Any information on them?"

"Cadwalader has squired two around Town."

Amelia glugged her brandy. "Anything else?"

"Tremlach is having an affair with her sister's husband. Thurwood gambles too deep for her widow's stipend, so where does her blunt come from?"

Frowning, she tapped her foot and placed her brandy aside. "And the last? Lady Twyford?"

His black brow raised. "The wife of Cadwalader's superior?"

She nodded.

"Perhaps..." A scarred knuckle rasped against his stubbled cheek as he placed down his glass, skulked to the vast walnut cabinet and unhooked a chain from around his neck. Two dangling keys were inserted into its sturdy locks and turned simultaneously.

Solely once had she seen into this cabinet. The contents were ordered, methodical, and held all the secrets of the *Ton*. Rumour told he'd eyes and ears on every street – lads and servants, coachmen and courtesans.

A small card was withdrawn and handed to her.

The script was neat. Refined.

Lady Twyford.
Seen in St Giles. Meets with a man named Roberts.
Upstairs room in Bowl Tavern.
Lovers?

Amelia swallowed, stood and paced. That was it then. Lady Twyford was their traitor. But was her husband, Sir Edmund, a part of it? And if not, how did she obtain the Home Office documents?

"But how can we get past Sir Edmund to confront her?" she muttered almost to herself. "The lady never leaves the house."

"Not entirely true." The Prince perched on his desk, "When in Town, she attends the theatre. Drury Lane. Her husband rents a box Wednesday eves."

That was tomorrow.

And how did he know all this?

"Anything on Sir Edmund?"

"I leave the Home Office laggards well alone and they do the same with me."

Of course.

"And just one more..."

His glare was black as a crow's wing.

"Anything on the Brotherhood of Ravens?"

"You know I only deal in the *Ton*'s secrets."

Doubting that very much, she nevertheless nodded. "Well, that's all, Prince. I owe yo–"

"No." He stood, lifted her carpetbag and closed her hand around the handle. "You will never owe me, Amelia."

"I'm grateful then." She smiled. "But even so, if you ever need anything of me, send word."

Within the glint of candlelight, she discerned a small hitch of lip. "Cadwalader didn't want you up here with me. Why would that be?"

She produced a nonchalant shrug. "We are just working together."

"He has a danger to him under all that prinking clobber. A warrior. A good man. But beware, Amelia... He wants you."

An odd feverishness overcame her cheeks. "I'm quite sure you are wrong." It was true Hugh had kissed her once or... thrice, but surely it had meant less than naught to him. "He's used to prettier, more worldly and aristocratic ladies than I."

"You don't know your own worth, Amelia. All of us here missed you when you left."

Alfred the bloodhound snuffled as though to agree.

"You showed me the door, if I remember rightly."

His lashes flickered. "Most who come here never leave this place, hiding as they are. Some from cruelty like Hannah, or unbearable grief like Kian. But you, you were young and had your whole life in front of you. For you, Amelia, it was time to cease hiding."

She sought his pitch-black eyes. "And for yourself, Prince? When will you cease hiding?"

Amelia was more than aware he would not answer so raised up on tiptoes to smooth the black feather at his lapel.

The Prince caught her wrist. "I do not hide." His eyes held hers, unfathomable, until abruptly he released her and swivelled to stare into the night.

But after some moments, he glanced over one shoulder, that scarred cheek glistening in the candlelight. "Because no one can hide from themselves. You know that." Breath left him. "Farewell, Amelia. Take care of yourself."

"And you, Prince," she murmured. "Farewell."

CHAPTER TWENTY

"Even in her own carriage, a young lady should be reserved, her attitude always modest, easy and unaffected."

Private Education: A Practical Plan for the Studies of Young Ladies.

Elizabeth Appleton. 1815.

"Hanover," Hugh snapped to the coachman. "And make it brisk."

The hackney lurched into motion while he seethed.

Not a moment ago, Amelia had sauntered from the Prince's gambling hell with dishevelled chignon and buttons unfastened at her throat. *Three* buttons.

"Well?" he all but snarled.

Amelia settled into the opposite squabs. Night had now fallen and the dim lantern flickered with the movement of the carriage. "Your mood seems rather...agitated."

He was not agitated. He was roiling like a molten pit of Hades.

"I cannot believe," he growled, "that you…you…cavorted with that terse, surly, sly-booted, crabby, numb-skulled…"

"Oh, come now, Hugh." She tutted. "I'll give you the rest but not numb-skulled. He's most intelligent."

"Seedy, squalid, hell-bound, rum-faced…"

"And quite handsome if you look beyond the pitiless eyes."

"Perverse, raddled, immoral, mutton mongering…"

"And Prince has never been a mutton monger. He didn't so much as lay a finger on me."

"Unscrupulous, hugger-mugger…" Hugh paused as her last words penetrated his ire. "What?"

"He didn't touch me. I ruffled my hair and undid another button purely to see your reaction."

Hugh inhaled so deeply he swore he could smell the sea. "You malapert of a minx. I should take you over my knee." That threat did him no good whatsoever and Hugh folded his arms. The thought of the Prince laying a finger on Amelia had induced a green rage of possessiveness that he never knew lay within him. "Did you get the information, then?"

"Hmm," she murmured. "No debts or bargains or deals. I count myself as a friend to him, although I'm not sure it's reciprocated."

"Why the hell didn't you tell me?"

"Would you have listened?" Her lashes lowered. "So keen were you to protect me."

With a grunt, Hugh unfolded his arms. "Would you be so good as to share the information he gave you?"

Amelia did so, which led Hugh to recall the lavender-scented cloaked lady in The Bowl so long ago. Had that been Lady Twyford? She *must* be their Lady T. But was Sir Edmund complicit in all this?

At last, they were getting somewhere, and he tapped his

boot, impatient to continue but also burning with the need to ask…

"So tell me how it is, for Lucifer's sake, that you count the Prince as a…*friend*?"

"How long have we till Hanover?"

He peered out the window. The streetlamps had been lit, casting the pavement to blots of yellow, but he could discern the carriage was halfway down Regent Street, a mile or so from the Square, but this was London so there was bound to be unfinished cobbleworks…

"A fair while."

"In that case…" She clasped her hands. "When I was seventeen, a mere two years older than Phoebe, my mama came home one night from the theatre, full of joy but with a headache. The next day, it had worsened. The doctor came and bled her. She became feverish. He bled her again. And then…" Amelia swallowed. "She just…died. No warning. No time to prepare. The doctor thought it some form of brain fever."

Hugh lifted from the seat, stooped and was aside her in a moment. "Hell, I'm so sorry, Amelia."

But her eyes were bleak, lost in the memories. "A day later, I received a demand for increased rent that I had no money to pay. The monthly stipend ceased. Within a week, I received an eviction notice… I remember the terror of feeling so alone, grieving for my mother, the few servants deserting me, for they could see the way of things." She turned her head to the darkness of the window. "I called at my father's townhouse, to find out what was happening, but his son would not allow me to see him or even pass him a note. The son called me a whore's bastard and slammed the door in my face." She closed her eyes. "I discovered the duke had in fact been bedridden with the lung disease for quite some while and he died not long after. I don't think he even knew of my mother's death. So, the son became the fifth duke. And...and then he sent the bailiffs."

"That's not right," Hugh growled. "Your father must have provided for you, his daughter, in the will? Was there no solicitor?"

She shrugged and turned to him. "If there was, he was employed by the new duke so unlikely to tell me anything, and I could discover naught for myself being a lone by-blow. For all I know, my father bequeathed me nothing or the will was changed. Mama had left no money as she was not one for saving and I could not afford a solicitor of my own to investigate." Her brow puckered. "The bailiffs were banging on the door, waving documents and saying I had no right to be there, to anything. All at the behest of a man whom I shared a father with."

"I know of Swanford." Hugh clenched his fists, knuckles white. "So what did you do?"

"I thought of Mother, how she used to glance into the mirror before leaving the house and... You could see her donning the persona of the Butterfly Courtesan, playing her part to the world. So, I did the same, except I played my own part. I opened the door to the bailiffs with a courtesan's smile on my face. I told them I was to follow in my mother's profession, that a rich new protector was collecting me on the morrow. That I just needed the night to pack my clothes. That my protector would settle the debts." Her shoulders straightened. "They believed me, but as soon as they'd left, I cleared the house – I gathered jewellery, took paintings from their frames and rolled them, anything I could carry or fit in one portmanteau, all the trinkets Mother had been given by her protectors, and I left my home that very night."

Hugh placed a hand to her cheek. "No one bests, Amelia Lambert," he whispered. And then, because he had no more words for her ingenuity and strength, he kissed her.

Soft and chaste, but when their lips parted, she shook her head, eyes moist. "It wasn't like that," she whispered back. "Because I was a foolish young girl. I was not worldly wise and was swindled out of money at every turn, told certain jewels were paste, paintings fake, given pennies for them. The money dwindled on lodgings and food. I went to some of Mother's friends but they turned me away. I applied for work as a companion but was laughed at for being a trollop's daughter. I tried for scullery maid or dressmaker but was sneered at for my smooth hands."

Hugh ground his teeth. "Amelia, you were so young..."

"Eventually, I was thrown out of my final lodgings with not thruppence upon me. And...and so I went to sell all I had left..."

Anger curled Hugh's toes and fists. "Your virtue?"

She laughed. But without mirth. "Oh, no, that had no value. No, I went to the Prince with information. I knew of him as my mother used to attend his hell in her later years. So I told him of the swells who had gossiped freely at my mother's weekly salons. All the unfaithful husbands and gambling wives. I also informed him that whilst I'd been waiting, I'd noticed, a croupier was false shuffling in order to deal an accomplice a favourable hand."

"I say again, no one bests Amelia Lambert."

"Well, I'd learned the ways of the world by then and was no longer quite such a foolish young girl. I'd had to. So the Prince employed me to mingle the floor each night. Sometimes as a monied widow, others a silent waitress. Listening. Watching. I worked and had lodgings there for three years until one day, a gentleman handed me a card. The only gentleman to have ever noticed me. As *me*."

"Asher Rainham, perchance?"

"Maybe he saw my aptitude for observing the clientele. Or the Prince told him, I know not." She shook her head. "But I...I did not wish to leave. I had a…family of sorts there. Kian Finlay and Hannah the coat girl." She stared to the window. "But the Prince dismissed me, said I should go to Sir Asher, as he was then, and I was left with no choice."

"Did…did you…" Hugh loathed to ask this, but… "Did you ever have…feelings for the Prince?"

COULD anyone truly have those sorts of feelings for the Prince?

He was too detached from life. Too lost in whatever shadowed him.

"No, not at all. But I was grateful to him. I was fond of him. He took me in when no one else would."

Breath gusted from Hugh. "Then for that, I am doubly in his debt."

Amelia smiled. "Not a good position to be in, but…I thought a man such as yourself would not pay much heed to…feelings."

"A man such as I?"

"The Scandalous Hugh Cadwalader. A gentleman of the *Ton* world." She nibbled a lip. "Indeed, it's a universally acknowledged fact that scandalous scoundrels do not believe such feelings exist at all." Amelia nodded, quite getting into her stride. "That it's merely an illusory concept or a product of a female's fancies. That we mistake it for basic desire."

"I…" A gasp as Hugh clutched his chest. Wheezed.

"Hugh? What is it?"

"I can't…"

She lurched forward as he heaved in a desperate breath. "What can I do?"

"Enough," he cried, "enough of your cruel words! I can bear no more! My poetic soul is rent asunder and shrivelling to naught at your foul notions of my species." He straightened his cravat and grinned.

Amelia scowled. "You cad."

"In all truth, I suppose I might have considered more tender feelings an illusory concept if not for my Welsh family. My parents disburdened themselves of me there each summer and, Lud, never had I encountered such misty-eyed couples. The late Earl of Llanedwyn and his wife made Romeo and Juliet appear platonic friends, and their sons have both found their hearts' desires. When I start to feel…pessimistic, I always return there, for when in Wales, no one could deny the power or reality of… feelings. And it does make one rather envious."

Amelia stared at him and blinked.

He just continued grinning, all white teeth and sinful lips.

"So…" Amelia cleared her throat. "Have you…ever had tender feelings for anyone? There are more than a few tales of you and various ladies."

He fidgeted with his cane. "I'll not deny the occasional liaison over the years, that being the Scandalous Cadwalader was most diverting when young and also useful in my work as it brought me entry to exclusive *Ton* circles. But I do not play with fragile hearts. So as for those tales…" He gave a waggish grin. "The majority are utter flummery. I tell them either to cover my missions or to distract from my wounds."

She shook her head. "I did wonder."

"Well, if you'd been shot in the shoulder at St Thomas Burial ground, what would you say to friends and kin when returning to Wales injured? They started to disbelieve the highwayman yarn."

"It must be difficult…to have a family and not be able to tell them all."

His smile dropped. "Forgive me, Amelia… I am grateful to have a family, of course, but sometimes, yes. For then no one can come to know all that I am." His gaze flicked up. "Except for you, Amelia." He caressed her cheek with a single calloused finger. "And what type of man would catch your eye?" He cocked his head, blue eyes intense. "A stern blackguard like the Prince? A practical and calm man like Rainham? Or..." His eyebrows performed their habitual waggle. "A scandalous cad?"

It was a teasing question but one that had, on occasion, drifted through her mind, in that time before sleep when thoughts wandered at will. When she was alone and lonely.

"I... I'm not sure if I care whether he is stern or calm or scandalous but I..." She gazed to her lap. "I would wish that he accepts me for who I am – my birth, my past and my present." She peered up at his solemn, handsome face. "I wish for someone who would make me feel wanted and loved. I would wish that he keep hold of my hand when times became hard. If I am angry or sad. Someone who would never let me go. Never let go of my hand whatever we faced and whatever the company we found ourselves in."

Amelia closed her eyes. There was something about Hugh Cadwalader which made one blurt intimate hopes hidden deep within. Was that why he was such a revered intelligence officer? The ability to lower a person's defences with his multifaceted nature.

She'd never believed such a paragon of a man as she'd described would exist for herself, as who would want a spy for a wife? Besides which, she had no dowry, little money saved, her parentage was ignoble and her skills were not of the domestic sort. And she'd not the beauty or sensualness of her mother.

Fingers lifted her chin. "Any man," he whispered huskily, "would be a fool to let you go."

Amelia endeavoured to recall reasons for not kissing Hugh Cadwalader but they faded as though written with disappearing ink, letters jumbling into an undecipherable code, and instead she met his lips.

A sympathy kiss, she told herself. After her tale, the scoundrel was trying to make her feel better...

And it was working.

His lips were soft as snow, breaths mingling.

Yet like falling snow it built, layer upon layer, deeper and deeper, until raw ardour churned in her throat, eyes and heart, desire seeping into her very being.

Then a turbulent hunger as his broad hands swept their way to her nape, inducing a shiver, and she was pinned to the squabs by his chest.

He kissed not like the droll Hugh of scandalous tales but her warrior Hugh of darkness and sin.

"Hell, Amelia..." And the kisses dragged down her neck, drugging her senses with mint and cinnamon, his scruff of stubble abrading her skin.

She knew where this was leading...

His mouth lingered in the hollow of her throat, one hand brushing her breast, the other at her hip, tugging her closer. She could feel his want, his need. And she wanted also.

So when he unfastened her fourth button, she merely breathed her acquiescence.

A kiss loitered on the skin exposed, a brush of tongue.

As the fifth button loosened, the ribbons of her stays were bared – a dusky rose pink – and he groaned, deep and low and dangerous.

So she shoved hands to his hair, urged him on as lips skimmed the swell of her breasts, his other hand yanking at her drab skirts.

Fingers stroked their way above her stocking.

Mouth tugging at her stay ribbons, hips pushing and–

"Oy!" A hammering brought her spinning back to the hackney carriage – and not for the first time – a gruff voice burbling from above. "First you wanna come here, then yer don't. Then yer do. Then yer don't. Now we're here and yer ain't getting out. Swells," he grumbled. "Mazed as brushes."

Hugh's chin lifted, his cheeks a scarlet hue, eyes glazed as though drunk, hands atremble. "Amelia?"

She gulped, reality raising its nasty little head. "We...we are home and h-have work to do. We need to prepare for the theatre tomorrow night. Confront Lady Twyford."

For a moment, she thought he might disagree or kiss her again or sweep her into his arms and dash with her to his chamber.

Instead, with a grunt, he shoved back to the opposite seat.

"I...I've no option but to let you go."

CHAPTER TWENTY-ONE

"The young girls are growing into women; they must depend upon themselves for subsistence."

PRIVATE EDUCATION: A PRACTICAL PLAN FOR THE STUDIES OF YOUNG LADIES. ELIZABETH APPLETON. 1815.

"I don't suppose you've seen any lemons lying around, Miss Jones?"

Amelia peered up from marking a mathematics test while her charge was at the modiste. She was endeavouring to complete all her governess duties by noon as tonight, she and Hugh would attempt to confront Lady Twyford at the theatre.

"Lemons, Mrs Dawkins?"

"Aye, lemons." And the housekeeper placed a mid-morning tray laden with tea, crumpets and scones upon the schoolroom desk. "There's no lemon for your tea as they've all disappeared."

"Disappeared?"

"Aye, like the maid Lucy's virtue. There one moment, gone the next."

Amelia's lips twitched. "Well, I am quite content without, Mrs Dawkins, but do you think them stolen?"

The housekeeper pursed her lips. "I trust all my girls, I do, and Cruikshank runs a tight ship with the lads." She tapped her foot. "Do you reckon I should ask Mr Cadwalader? Perhaps he's lightening his hair with the juice."

Amelia's lips more than twitched. "Worth a try."

With an assured nod, Mrs Dawkins departed, and so sipping her lemon-less tea, Amelia finished marking Phoebe's test. All correct, and she stared to the timepiece held on a chain at her waist. Phoebe was due back from Madame Devy's at any moment but there might be time to assess her essay on Mary Wollstonecraft's treatise.

She seized the paper and–

It was blank.

She turned the paper over. Still blank.

Frowning, she sifted through the other sheets; no essay anywhere so–

"Oh, Miss Jones!" And Phoebe rushed in, eyes bright and cheeks pink. "Never have I seen so many glorious shades of black – charcoal and ebony and raven. Sable, ink and dusk, although I'd call that one dark grey." Then she clasped hands to her head. "Madame Devy tried to dress me in *white*! Can you believe it? But Lady Kemble agreed that I can wear what colour I like until my Season. And I have no intention of having a Season."

Amelia blinked. "I'm glad you had a pleasant time."

"Yes, indeed." And she plopped down on the chaise. "And it's all thanks to you."

"Oh, Phoebe, I merely showed you some pictures of different styles."

The young girl leaned forward. "But you did it in a way that didn't seek to change...*me.* For black is a part of me now. And it seems so many people have to change their true aspect for others: whether it be a debutante suffering white for Almack's or a modiste pretending to be French for the *Ton*, as I'm sure Madame Devy is from Essex. But you don't mind me how I am."

Amelia smiled. "Then thank you and I am glad you are content." And she hoped that Miss Phoebe Thornton would always stay true to herself – unlike so many people who felt obliged to suppress or hide their true selves in order to please or conform, herself included. "Although..." She waved the blank paper but kept her lips curved. "It seems someone has not been writing their essays."

Phoebe's eyes glinted, her expression as sly as that of a fox loitering aside a henhouse. "But I did, Miss Jones. I wrote two whole pages."

"If that is so, then..."

Amelia paused.

Disappearing lemons? The little rascal!

So, with a narrowed eye at her charge, Amelia stood and marched to her carpetbag, rummaged around and... Ah ha, her tinderbox.

On occasion, this procedure could cause a dash of smoke, so she opened the window to allow a cool spring breeze into the schoolroom.

Then with quick fingers, she struck flint and steel against the cotton inside and as it caught, Phoebe waggled a splint within the flame, such animation to her pale features.

Two candles were then lit side by side and Phoebe clasped her hands in excitement as Amelia passed the blank sheet of paper back and forth over the flames.

Quick enough not to burn but slow enough to warm the paper.

A waft of smoke did indeed curl but as though by magic, brown lettering appeared. The penmanship was a little scratchy and hard to read, but it was not easy to write with transparent lemon juice or maintain it on a quill nib, so an excellent first attempt.

As a governess, Amelia was unsure whether to approve or not, but as an intelligence officer…

"Very clever, Phoebe."

"I've been reading *Magia Naturalis* on secret writing and invisible inks." She scrunched her nose. "But…how did you know that heat would reveal it? And…you must also have known it was written in lemon juice? Have you been reading that book also?"

Amelia cleared her throat. "A governess reads many a book, Phoebe. Besides, Mrs Dawkins is lamenting her missing lemons. You need to speak to her before she accuses Mr Cadwalader of pilfering them."

"Oh. I'd best go now, if I may." She grinned at the charred paper. "I've written the essay in normal ink as well, so might I keep this? My first attempt."

"Of course. But correcting the essay will have to wait until the morrow now as I shall not be here this afternoon or evening. You are to depart for Lady Kemble's at dusk, yes? I believe she has a certain Monsieur DePont arriving with a desk telescope in order to familiarise you with the night sky?"

Phoebe swished her skirts. "Hmm. But where are you going?"

Amelia garnered a deep breath, so disliked lying to Phoebe now. "Well… I have a…"

A small hand enclosed her own. A hushed whisper. "Is it… Is it to do with my father?"

Amelia's gaze flicked up. "Phoebe…"

"Uncle Hugh told me he was searching," she gushed quietly, "and…and I know you came home with him the other night with blood on your cheek, Sally said so and…and you know so much about invisible inks and locks, and…and Uncle Hugh allows you to use his study, so you must be helping him."

Amelia sighed and rubbed the chill hand betwixt her own. "All I can do is nod." She nodded. "And no more."

"I understand. But there's no…no risk for you tonight, is there?"

"No, I do not believe so. We are purely looking for someone at the Theatre Royal."

Phoebe's hand pressed. "I wish I was old enough to help. To do…*something*."

"You help by being here for your uncle – safe and content."

"I am content, so much more than before, but there must be… Oh!" And she abruptly fled from the schoolroom.

Bemused, Amelia followed the flapping black skirts as Phoebe dashed to her bedchamber, flung open the door, kneeled and rummaged under her bed. A battered valise was dragged forth and she commenced hurling papers about.

"What are you doing?"

"The Theatre Royal on Drury Lane or Covent Garden?"

"Drury Lane."

"Well, I started collecting useful bits and pieces a while back. Cuttings and… Ah ha! Here it is! A plan of Drury Lane Theatre that was published in *The Times* when it reopened last year."

Amelia grinned. "Perfect, Phoebe. Thank you. We are alike as I keep a book with pasted newspaper cuttings too, but I do not have this theatre. Well done."

Phoebe grinned back. "Is there anything else? I would lend you a dress, but all I have is black. Have you something suitable?"

"I have dresses at my lodgings, which is where I am going this afternoon. And…perhaps you should call me Amelia."

"Such a pretty name. I will, thank you. And… Hmm." An assessing eye was cast from Amelia's head to her toes. "Green would suit you. Dark green." She batted her lashes. "And Uncle Hugh likes green."

Rascal indeed. "We are merely working together, Phoebe."

"Oh. I thought… Well… It seemed to me…" And she lapsed into silence.

Amelia would not ask.

She would not.

Definitely would not.

"Yes?" she asked.

"Weeelll…" Phoebe hemmed and hawed. "Well… It's just… You do look at each other a lot. Then try and hide it. And you tease each other a lot. Then try and hide that too."

Amelia cleared her throat again. "It's merely the repartee of work colleagues."

"If you say so, Miss." Phoebe waggled her pursed lips in the exact same way her guardian waggled his eyebrows. "But like writing with lemon juice, nothing stays hidden forever."

CLAD IN SHIRT AND PANTALOONS, Hugh scowled at the array of waistcoats upon the bed – claret, saffron, canary, Pomona, azure and violet – yet none quite suited.

This afternoon, before heading off to her lodgings, Amelia had met with Rainham to discuss their findings while Hugh had invited himself to a meeting of *The Berkeley Square Ladies' Benevolent Fund for Orphans, Wounded Soldiers and other Poor Persons*.

Promising a substantial donation to a new hospital for soldiers and a new Dalton tea set for the ladies, he'd endeavoured to dredge up any gossip concerning Lady Twyford, but most had not seen her for years whilst others were rather tight-lipped.

All were agreed, however, that she almost never ventured from the house and never accepted visitors. *Most odd.*

Something to do with her clandestine activities, perhaps?

After all this time, could he be near to an answer?

No more deaths.

Would Ross' honour be restored?

Would Phoebe have a father to be proud of?

He strode to the dressing table, flipped a box lid and took out the cufflinks which lay within – the gold was tarnished and one of the minuscule emeralds that formed a clover leaf had been lost. But they'd been Ross' and he fastened them to his shirt cuffs.

It felt as if he'd been blundering in the dark for an age but perhaps tonight, the light was a short step away. With Amelia at his side.

"Ahem, the *Maratte*, Sir?"

"Eh?" And Hugh twisted to find his valet standing with yards of cloth over his arm.

"Your cravat knot, Sir? The *Maratte*?"

"No, the *Trone d'Amour*, if you will, Towlson."

His valet heaved a sigh. "I shall return henceforth with different cloth then, Sir, as a more liberal dose of starch is required for such perfection. If you will excuse me?"

Nodding, Hugh returned to the waistcoats and reached out for the saffro–

The door opened behind him and nigh-silent footsteps came to a halt at his side.

"None of those, Uncle."

"Phoebe, my blackbird of paradise, what would you suggest then?"

She was draped in a black cloak, presumably awaiting Lady Kemble's carriage, but there was a pinkness to her cheeks that cheered him and her eyes were buoyant.

"A dark green?"

"Why?"

Innocent lashes batted. "It suits you."

Hugh cast a sideways glance. "And…"

"And you'll match Amelia's dress."

He grinned. "You call her Amelia now?"

"She asked that I call her that as her name's not really Miss Jones."

"Ah. She told you or…you guessed?"

"Both. But I believe she will wear green tonight. Stay here and I'll go fetch yours."

Hugh absently nodded as an image of Amelia, not in drab governess grey but in green silk came to the fore, her skin radiant, blond curls falling upon her décolletage.

Damn it, but Amelia Lambert had tumbled into his life from nowhere and he had no idea what to do about it. Never considered that such strong feelings could besiege him.

What was he to–

"Uncle?" A green waistcoat was thrust in front of him. "My coach has arrived."

"Ah. Perfect. Thank you. And be good for Lady Kemble."

"I'm always good." Phoebe's lips curved. "And you be careful tonight, Uncle."

"I'm always careful."

A snort. "And remember to compliment Amelia's dress."

"I'm famed for lavishing the ladies with flattery."

A small hand laid on his chest. "No, Uncle. No flim-flam flattery. Just truth." And she was gone in a swish of black.

"THE BLUE?"

Amelia peered at the silk dress Charlotte brandished.

"Too demure for tonight."

Charlotte sighed and rummaged for another while Amelia eyed her rather diminutive, terraced home. After the elegance of Hanover Square, it felt a little shabby but at least it was all Amelia's – the deeds in her own name, paid for with her own earnings – and no one could take it from her. Unless, of course, she chose to marry.

For propriety's sake, she'd hired a maid when she'd moved in and informed the neighbours that she'd a brother in India who actually owned the property. That had been enough to ensure she met the standards of respectability for the area – which weren't all that lofty, this being Holborn, not aristocratic Mayfair.

"This one?"

Amelia turned to a poppy-red gown. "Too bold for tonight."

With a grump, Charlotte folded her arms. "I wish you'd tell me why you are attending the theatre with Mr Cadwalader. Are you to be his...his ladybird?"

"No! Not at all." Though 'twas true, Amelia would indeed be viewed as a ladybird tonight, attending the theatre unchaperoned and unknown. She rose to clasp Charlotte's hand, for how she so wanted to tell Charlotte all, how she longed to have friends to just talk with, but... "I wish... I wish I could tell you more... I wish it were different."

"Tell me one thing then. You're not in any danger from Mr Cadwalader, are you?"

In some ways, yes, but...

"No," she replied, clasping the lady's hand tighter in gratitude for her concern. "For my investigation has taken a different turn."

Charlotte looked deep into her eyes and nodded. "The dark green then. It suits you."

"That's what Phoebe said."

"Well then."

Amelia's nose twitched. "But she also said Mr Cadwalader likes green and I wouldn't want him to think..."

Charlotte released her hand and hastened to the wardrobe. "Your charge is just being mischievous and doubtless told him you like green, so I wouldn't worry." And a dress the colour of ivy and pure white swished into view.

Amelia tilted her head. "I've never worn that one."

"Was there a reason?"

"No. It's perfect."

With much laughter, they endeavoured to slip the gown on without creasing the luxurious satin, although the full sleeves slid awry and the fluted lace snagged on her stays, but at last, Charlotte was busy with the laces at the back, teeth nibbling lip in concentration.

Amelia studied herself in the long mirror opposite. "I read that your Duke of Shawdale is in Town."

An unladylike curse came from behind. "He's not *mine*."

"The lady doth protest." And Amelia raised a brow to the reflection. "You had feelings for him though?"

Charlotte scowled over Amelia's shoulder. "Have you ever had a man gaze at you and felt such an unspoken accord? Have you felt his hand on your waist and experienced such a passionate frisson?"

With a sigh, Amelia nodded.

"I felt all that for Marcus after we danced just thrice at the Ambleside Christmas Ball. I was young, 'tis true, a mere seventeen, but that night..." She gently pulled a lace through its eyelet. "He was so intense, devoted, and I thought his eyes had declared such emotion." Her forehead creased. "He went to London soon after, for some Town polish, and how keenly I awaited his homecoming, how I thought we'd..." She shook her head. "Yet it must have all been a fanciful notion of my own making, for a stern and aloof nobleman returned. A duke who did not even glance my way. A duke who cared for naught but coin and land. And had become a..." Amelia winced as Charlotte pulled hard on the gown laces. "Crabby hog-grubbing nipcheese!"

"I'm sorry."

Charlotte led her to the dressing table chair. "Pah! I see him now and then when I am in the Lake District and even his hazel eyes have changed. They used to smoulder green but now they just glint with avarice gold."

They stayed silent for a while, Charlotte curling Amelia's hair with hot tongs from the fire, both lost in their own thoughts.

"There we are. All done."

At that moment came a rattle on the front door, likely the coachman, so while Charlotte descended the stairs to answer it, Amelia took her chance to grab the key hidden inside the handle of a hairbrush and open the bottom dressing table drawer.

An array of elegant hairpins, rings and necklaces nestled in velvet compartments, so after choosing three butterfly pins, she carefully placed them in her coiffure. A faux diamond ring topped with a sizeable faux sapphire was next, and...just in case, the long necklace.

She straightened to assess her aspect in the mirror and tucked the pendant of the necklace into her cleavage.

"Amelia, were you expecting flowers?"

"No." The most exquisite pink rosebuds were clasped within Charlotte's hands. "Who are they from?"

A foolish question for she could guess.

A card was handed over.

A rose by any other name would smell as sweet.

To place in your hair.
H.

Oh. "Erm, well…"

Charlotte chortled. "I wish I'd gone for that interview if the governess perquisites included roses and theatre trips. Shall I place them in your hair?"

"I'd better do it myself," she murmured as she twisted. "These hairpins can be quite lethal."

They fastened the last bud to her bodice and then primped and groomed until no more could be done and the trot of horses' hooves could be heard coming to a halt on the cobbles outside.

"Prince Charming is here," said Charlotte, misting the small window with her breath. "In a green town coach pulled by four handsome bays. Have a grand time."

"Thank you, Charlotte. For everything." Amelia smiled and crossed to the hook on the wall for her velvet cloak, her habitual composure a little…flustered.

But this was work. Nothing more.

CHAPTER TWENTY-TWO

"Loud talking, laughing, gazing after people; all these are improper."

Private Education: A Practical Plan for the Studies of Young Ladies. Elizabeth Appleton. 1815.

The golden glister of a theatre could hide a thousand misdeeds: a gilded private box shrouding whispers of treachery or a satin-gloved hand shielding a blade.

With hands clasped, Hugh rubbed a thumb over Ross' cufflink and watched – the debutantes in fine silks who sighed over the handsome actors, the gentlemen in pristine cravats who chuckled at the ribald jokes, the courtesans who flicked their lace fans and the Corinthians who lounged in practised ennui.

Three tiers of boxes encircled the stage of the Theatre Royal, cradling the haughty elite of London, their attention focused upon the ongoing play while Hugh focused on them.

And he could not help but wonder what lay beneath all the splendour and society sparkle.

The theatre seemed to breathe and murmur, mirroring the emotions enacted upon the stage – desire, deception, melancholy, disguise – all scented with perfume, smoke and beeswax.

A rustle of skirts and his gaze was drawn.

Trimmed with lace, a bottle-green bodice clung to Amelia's curvaceous form, a lengthy gold necklace forming a beguiling pointer into her fine cleavage. White satin underskirts were covered with a diaphanous silk which shifted and slid above clocked silk stockings, while slippers with silver rosettes shod her modest feet.

Hugh had sensed a certain shyness when she'd first removed her cloak in the lobby yet had no idea why as she was stunning. So much so that words had fled his tongue and he'd wittered some nonsense about her looking *nice*.

Dunderhead.

Applause rippled through the audience and Amelia glanced to him.

And he was undone.

Amber eyes sparkled with gold flecks, cheeks gently glowed, and lips were tinted a soft pink. One of the rosebuds he'd sent was fastened to her bodice while the rest nestled in her hair with green ribbons and slender pins tipped with butterflies. In the low light of the box sconces, the ringlets framing her face were lit to gilded threads and how he longed to unravel them.

A hundred cliched expressions of flattery were on his tongue but...he recalled Phoebe's advice.

"Amelia," he whispered. "I could not say earlier for I'd not the words but... You are perfection."

Her lips curved yet she shook her head. "It's the dress," she whispered back.

"No. It's not the dress." He grasped her white-satin-gloved hand and brushed his lips over the back. "'Tis you. And I'm pleased the rosebuds were delivered in time, for they look..." He reached up a finger to touch.

"I wouldn't," she said softly, staying his wrist. "Those hairpins are tipped with a surprise. Not fatal and they are capped, but you would be insensate for several hours."

How he loved having her by his side. No longer alone.

"Any further hazards I should know of?" *Other than to his heart.*

She brought forth her gloved left hand. On the middle finger was a gold ring with what looked to be an oval-cut sapphire atop, surrounded by diamonds.

"Pretty. But I'm guessing..."

"The faux sapphire hides a compartment. One push of a certain diamond would deposit opium powder into a glass."

Hugh shifted in his chair.

"And then," she continued low, "you already know about the knife in my garter."

All he could do was return a repressed smile, having wondered on more than one occasion about the contents of her garter.

AMELIA FLICKED her eyes to the occupants of the box two to their left – Lady Twyford and her husband. At least, she presumed it was Lady Twyford as the couple had arrived later than themselves and she wore some type of veil, their wall sconce snuffed.

Hugh's own private box was apparently further towards the stage but he'd managed to swap with an acquaintance for this perfectly placed position.

It allowed a view of the entire theatre, and one became

almost overwhelmed with the richness on show. Each time Amelia blinked, another facet caught her eye – the magnificent chandelier, the golden décor, the crimson relief on the theatre boxes.

To watch a play was not the sole attraction for the sophisticated aristocrats in the private boxes or for the swaggering bucks with their chattering ladybirds in the pit. It was also for the vibrancy and sheer occasion.

All seemed possible while watching the thespians enact scenes of unfeasible bravery or deepest emotion, and the audience was filled with aspiration.

Well, most were… Corinthians larked about, quaffing furtive nips of liquor and inspecting the debutantes with far-reaching opera glasses while those same debutantes hid behind fans, eyes flitting like dragonfly wings. But even their stern chaperones leaned upon the velvet balcony cushions, beholding the play with dreams of what might be…

Smiling, Amelia turned her attention to the stage. The opening scene of Shakespeare's *Twelfth Night* had been a marvel, a mechanically shifting painted coast of Illyria spitting out the shipwrecked Viola who'd disguised herself as a boy.

Amelia had pursed her lips. A very feminine-looking boy with hairless chin and wide hips who wouldn't have fooled the eyes of a potato but the audience had cheered and the men had whistled.

For much of the play, Amelia had felt Hugh's gaze linger upon herself like a concealed caress, kindling that flare of flame within, but she supposed he was playing his part, a gentleman enamoured with his Cyprian companion.

His hair gleamed like guineas in the chandelier light, blue eyes more sensual than blithe and with a hooded slant. Clean shaven, his cuts and bruises were still evident but they lent his refined visage a potent air.

A complex *trone d'amour* cravat festooned his throat and a notion drifted that if a woman did happen to be in a hurry to extract him from it, a knife would be quicker than unravelling that knot. His jacket was coal black but the green of his waistcoat matched her dress and it was threaded with ebony silk, while his fawn pantaloons were so tight it was a wonder he could sit. A knife might be required for them also...

She swallowed.

On the stage, Duke Orsino had now been thoroughly hoodwinked by Viola, the boy who was a girl, even complimenting him on his smooth and rubious lips.

But that was dukes for you.

From the corner of her eye, Amelia caught Sir Edmund Twyford lifting a hand to adjust his wife's veil. Why did she wear it?

Amelia slanted towards Hugh. "How long will the interval be?"

No answer and she turned her head to find him now intently staring through a brown-leather spyglass at – Amelia reached for her own theatre glasses – a box on the far side which contained a sylph beauty with hair akin to deepest night and skin like marble. Wearing crimson, she appeared like a Venus descended from Mount Olympus.

"Who is she?" whispered Amelia in her most professional tone.

"Who is who?" He still stared.

Applause rippled the theatre. "The woman in crimson?"

Hugh twisted to her, a frown creasing his brow. "What woman in crimson?"

"Over there."

He peered over the top of his spyglass. "That's Lady Tremlach. Niece to a bookkeeper at the Home Office. The last woman on Ross' list."

Oh.

"I see. That is fortuitous. I suppose you could..." Amelia smoothed her skirts, the green silk feeling rather restrained compared to crimson. "We could kill two birds with one stone tonight then."

"What are you talking about, Amelia?" He still held a frown until... "Ah." Hugh shuffled his chair till it clattered against her own. "Take my spyglass," he whispered as the last scene before the interval commenced, "and close your viewing eye."

She complied and Hugh placed a hand around her shoulder, his breath disturbing the tendrils of her hair and likewise her peace of mind.

He adjusted the direction of the spyglass so it was aimed at Lady Tremlach.

"Now close your other eye. And look only through the eyepiece."

Amelia frowned as the circular image was not of Tremlach at all.

But of the Twyfords' box.

"How..." She drew back to check the spyglass pointed at Tremlach and then stared through it again. Yet the magnified image was of the Twyfords who were absorbed by the play. "How does this work?" she whispered, twisting the spyglass this way and that.

His lips were nigh at her earlobe. "There's a lens with an oblique mirror inside and a side aperture so you can stealthily watch to your left or right. It's called a polemoscope. Some chap called Hevelius came up with it."

"A wonder," she murmured. "And with it... I can see Lady Twyford leaving their box. Sir Edmund is not following her."

Hugh's warm breath left her. "Time for Act Two then, Amelia. Good luck."

CHAPTER TWENTY-THREE

"The mind has no confidence in itself, and at the same time it is not aware of its own debility."

PRIVATE EDUCATION: A PRACTICAL PLAN FOR THE STUDIES OF YOUNG LADIES.

ELIZABETH APPLETON. 1815.

The actor's voices fell to muted as Amelia crept down the theatre hallway in pursuit, statues of Shakespeare's characters watching her furtive movement with marble eye.

From Phoebe's plan, Amelia knew Lady Twyford was headed for the ladies' retiring room and as the interval had not yet begun, solely a few maids scurried about with trays.

Perfect.

It had been agreed that if the lady did not leave her seat until the interval, then Hugh would keep Sir Edmund occupied while Amelia would lure his wife away, but such a ruse might have been rife with difficulty.

This way, the lady would be alone.

The retiring room door was closed when Amelia reached it so she softly twisted the handle to peer inside.

A lone maid dried chamber pots while Lady Twyford was seated on a chaise, veiled hat cast aside, skirts hitched to her knees and a shoe flung to the floor. A groan emerged as she massaged her stockinged foot.

Entering the room, Amelia could not help but grin. "New shoes?"

The lady startled and glanced up, but then smiled in such a winsome manner that Amelia blinked. Twice.

Their suspect was not at all what Amelia had expected. In her early fifties or thereabouts, she had gentle blue eyes, but with more than a few lines about them attesting to some hardship, and she'd such a…fragility that Amelia could not imagine the hard-edged Roberts as her lover.

"All I did was walk from the carriage," the lady said in a hushed voice whilst removing her other shoe, "and it felt as though the back of my heel was being rubbed by a hedgehog."

With a laugh, Amelia sat herself on the chaise also. "I know the feeling." She waggled her feet. "These are new and feel as though they've shrunk from when I tried them on at the cobblers."

Lady Twyford returned a low chuckle. "Are you the lady I saw with Mr Cadwalader?" She chewed her lip. "I suppose you are his… Well…" A blush tinged her cheeks. "Friend."

Amelia smiled but her mind was whirling as this woman seemed so sheltered and fledgling in speech. "I am indeed with Mr Cadwalader, but…" Amelia tapped her lip, knew she must hurry before the interval was upon them. "I'm sure I recognise you from somewhere."

Creases appeared upon the lady's brow. "I doubt it. I reside in the country and do not go out much, but I-I do so miss the theatre."

"Ah," Amelia nodded. "But I'm sure I've seen you before." She cocked her head. "The Bowl Tavern, perhaps?"

The shoe clattered to the floor. "T-the Bowl?"

"Why, yes. That was it. And your lavender fragrance is the same also."

Those blue eyes swung swifter than a weathercock in a storm, from ease to...fear. "W-who are you?" And she backed away along the chaise.

"I mean you no harm, my lady. I–"

"Go away," she whispered. "Please, go away. Am I not punished enough in life?"

"My lady? I..." Amelia frowned. "Roberts is a dangerous man and–"

"I know that!" she shrieked, causing the maid to peer over. Lady Twyford shoved a hand to her mouth. "He...he's a cruel monster but..."

Amelia bit her lip. The Prince had assumed wrong. They were no lovers.

So she rose to her feet, opened her reticule, approached the maid and placed a cache of coins into her palm.

The maid nodded and left them.

Amelia turned the key in the lock and spun on her heel.

"What are y-you doing?" Lady Twyford rubbed her arms as though a frozen north wind had gusted.

"Roberts, my lady, why do you go to him?"

Her head wrenched up – blue eyes bleak. "Why should I tell you?" Her lids fell, a tear trailing, and a look of such misery lined her face.

Amelia rushed to kneel by her. "Because I can help you."

"No, you can't. No one can. I...I have been so careful. How did you..." She wiped a trembling hand over her eyes. "Oh, what does it matter if you know this much already. He is...b-blackmailing me. Knows things about me that..."

"And you give…what in return? Information?"

"What? No!" The woman shook her head, opening her eyes to display pure confusion. "What information would I have?"

"I know of your husband's–"

"Of course not! He tells me nothing, if that is what you mean." She pressed her face into her palms. "Money," she sobbed. "I give Roberts my pin money, but it's not enough. He's demanding more and I have to… I will have to sell my precious family rings."

Lady Twyford wept into her hands and Amelia perused her.

Could it be an act?

But her fingers trembled, lashes flapping like the wings of a captured moth and her quivering voice held truth.

So Amelia reached out a hand to her shoulder. "What is he blackmailing you over? If you tell me, I can help you."

"How can you help me? I do not even know who you are."

"But I know people. People with influence."

"I… I cannot." She stuffed a fist into her mouth, her breathing ragged. "I-I do not feel well. I must go home. I have to–"

"Leticia?" The door handle rattled. "Are you in there? You've been some while."

"My husband!" Lady Twyford jumped to her feet, wiping her eyes and shuddering. "He mustn't know… I… Edmund is…" She grabbed hold of Amelia's arm. "If you mean me no harm, as you say, prove it. Help me with my hat. My shoes."

Amelia nodded and the lady breathed deep. "I'm here, Edmund. Just one moment."

Together they replaced her shoes, wiped her eyes, positioned the hat atop her curls and straightened her dress.

"My lady," Amelia whispered, "Roberts will be brought to justice and this wretchedness will soon be over."

A hand touched Amelia's cheek. "Sweet girl," she said softly. "But my wretchedness will never be over."

The lady brought the veil down over her eyes and trudged to the door while Amelia hid herself behind a screen.

She heard the key turn and the door open.

"Leticia?"

"I f-feel unwell, Edmund. Can we go home?"

Amelia strained to hear the response but the door clicked shut behind them, and so she returned to the chaise to straighten her clocked stockings and muse.

This investigation was like a Rookery labyrinth, twisting and dead ending, secrets unveiled and new ones to uncover.

Yet one thing Amelia felt sure of was that Lady Twyford was not who they were searching for, so with a sigh, she meandered to the mirror, pinched her cheeks and made for the door.

She poked her head out.

Curse it.

A herd of vibrant colour was bearing down the hallway like silked jockeys at Ascot: the interval must have commenced. Amelia gulped, darted out into the hall, and then veered for shelter behind a statue of King Hamlet's ghost before the ladies entered *en masse* into the retiring paddock. Even then, there formed a queue outside the door.

"Did you notice," a lady in jonquil yellow began, "the... woman with Mr Cadwalader?" She sniffed. "He's not attended the theatre in an age and now he turns up with some fresh ladybird. Pretty enough but not up to his usual standards by any stretch of the imagination."

Amelia frowned.

"Oh, you know how Hugh is," said her companion. "Takes pity on wallflowers so is likely just doing her a favour. Maybe he hopes one of his friends will take her off his hands."

They both chortled, and although Amelia knew envy when she heard it, the words still stung.

She refused to cower behind statues, however, so she stepped from behind, head held high, and walked with measured step, past the queue, until the line of ladies ended, and–

"Hey, my lovely," slurred some buck, grabbing her waist. "Are you the interval entertainment?"

Not appreciating the mauling in the least, Amelia growled and swung her standard-issue Foreign Office reticule – with its five-pound weight sewn into the base – up into his ballocks.

As his eyes bulged, breath gone, she fled from his grasp and dashed on down the hall.

Upon reaching the safety of their box, she was about to swish back the curtain when…voices murmured – a rumble and a purr.

"Oh, those bruises, Hugh," a woman lamented in a Scottish lilt. "Do you have more beneath that waistcoat? If you would allow me, I could attend to them most diligently."

Lady Tremlach, by the sounds of it, and Amelia bit her lip, hard, could not catch Hugh's response, but the lady's laughter tinkled like shards of glass.

Glass that pierced Amelia, jagged and deep. For that is what her jealousy felt like. A physical pain. An ache of longing and impossible envy.

This was why spies should never become involved, why the heart should remain in a locked box. For they had their parts to play and Hugh must discover if Tremlach was their traitor by whatever means necessary. Do what he must.

So she swiped at her eyes and straightened her shoulders, knew she must play her own part.

Amelia swished the curtain aside and dramatically halted, fist to beating heart, face awash with hurt.

It required no act.

Hugh was standing in profile as the lady in crimson, Lady Tremlach, caressed his lapel with a black-gloved hand, her bosom nigh brushing his chest, sultry lips pursed.

To see him thus lacerated Amelia, but…

"Hugh?" she gasped as he twisted. "Who is this lady?" She placed hands to hips. "I'm gone for but a moment and am usurped. How could you!"

His blue eyes were wide. "Amel–"

"It appears there is naught to keep me here." And she gathered her shawl from the chair.

He reached for her arm but she snatched it away.

"Amelia, I–"

"Our mutual friend went home, Mr Cadwalader, nothing to report, so I should leave you to it." She stared brightly at them both. "You should stay and d-do what you must."

And with that, she strode from the box, heard her name called once more but refused to turn.

The hallways and stairs were heaving with ladies, gentlemen and waiters, champagne spilling and laughter too loud. Amelia dodged them all, kept close to the walls, until she reached the lobby where chortling Corinthians were abandoning the theatre for more salacious entertainment.

Not bothering to collect her cloak, Amelia fled. A doorman doffed his hat and cold air smote her skin.

The pavement was likewise heaving, doxies readying themselves for departing bucks, hawkers selling ribbons and song-sheets, but Amelia swung around the corner and into Russell Street, where a line of hackney carriages awaited trade.

Ignoring the first sly-looking three, she found a fellow dozing upon his carriage step, a dog on his lap.

She kicked his booted foot. "Hanover Square."

"Eh?" One eye opened to drift over her curls, down her dress and land on her silk slippers. "Yer ain't running aways, are yer? I don't want Bow Street on me tail. Show me yer coin."

Amelia muttered beneath her breath as she'd given all her coin to the maid. "The butler at Hanover can pay you."

"And me brains are in me ballocks. Night." And he closed his eyes.

With a scowl, she began to draw the long necklace from her cleavage. As a rule, she would not resort to this but when needs must. "I do have this, however."

"I don't care if yer've got–" His eyes widened at the single black feather dangling from her necklace. Then he scrambled to his feet, the dog letting out a yowl. "Bloody hell, the Prince... Yes, me lady...er... Princess. I mean..."

"I'll pay when we reach Hanover."

"No need." And he opened the door with a swish, nose at knees. "Always a pleasure to do service fer His Highness."

Amelia clambered inside. It smelled of wet dog but not much caring, she sat back against the squab.

It had been a useful evening, she told herself, albeit with more questions than answers. Lady Twyford's confession had been unexpected and now Hugh would focus on Lady Tremlach.

This was their work. She knew that.

Her hand quivered upon the reticule ribbons as she fumbled for a handkerchief.

This was what they had to do.

A senseless, foolish tear seeped and she palmed it away.

Do what they must.

Another followed. Then another.

Amelia let them flow.

Her one chance as Cinderella in silks had come to an end.

And just like that night in the fairy tale...

She was alone.

CHAPTER TWENTY-FOUR

"The lovely evenings of summer are the best calculated for the unfolding of beautiful truths."

PRIVATE EDUCATION: A PRACTICAL PLAN FOR THE STUDIES OF YOUNG LADIES.

ELIZABETH APPLETON. 1815.

Hugh flung himself from the carriage, thundered up the steps to his townhouse and flew through the abruptly opened door. He'd given the household the night off but his faithful Cruikshank still held fast to his station.

"Where is she?" he growled, straightening his crooked cravat and tugging his tousled hair flat.

The butler cocked a brow at his master's lack of hat. "Miss Jones was to retire, Sir, but recalled some documents she wished to peruse in your library. I believe she is still–"

Hugh tore up the two flights of stairs, stalked down the corridor, threw open the library door and slammed it behind him.

Standing aside his desk, an array of documents spread, Amelia clutched a folder in one hand, hair loose and with all the pink roses gone apart from the one still pinned to her green satin bodice. She gazed up. Her throat bobbed. "That was quick."

A swell of such anger and hurt surged through him. That she could be so damn calm, so bloody unaffected, so hellishly impassive, while he...

He frowned.

Amelia's eyes were red-rimmed.

The folder trembled in her hand.

Her skin ashen pale.

Breath light and hitching.

And his anger abated.

"What was quick?"

"L-Lady Tremlach. I hope you understood me. Lady Twyford is not who is providing the Brotherhood of Ravens with information so you n-needed...needed to..."

He prowled towards her, snatched the folder from her fingers and threw it to the desk.

Enough was enough.

"Amelia, listen to me. I was in fact attempting to disentangle myself from Lady Tremlach when you walked in and granted me carte blanche to seduce her or, to be more accurate, gave *her* carte blanche to seduce me. I declined the lady's invitation and dashed off in search of you but was delayed by–"

"Hugh." She placed a hand to his chest, lashes lowered. "There is no need for a tale. Not with me. Your *trone d'amour* cravat is askew and half your waistcoat buttons...gone." She swallowed. "I unders–"

He placed his palm to her lips. "No. You do not understand. I am dishevelled because as I was dashing down the stairs after you, I happened upon the fifth Duke of Swanford ascending. Your half-brother. Expecting me to move aside for him to pass, I was overcome by such rage and a most curious compulsion to land a fist upon the blaggard's jaw. As misfortune would have it, he had two cohorts with him and so there ensued a bit of a… skirmish on the landing." Now was not the time to detail the broken window, the ruin of his hat or the loss of Macbeth's head.

Eyes widened above his palm. "Youwallopedtheduke! Atthetheatre!"

He smiled. "Damn it, Amelia, do you not know how much I want you?"

And he realised she did not. As a matter of fact, he realised that for all Amelia's confidence, for all her ingenuity, she had no idea at all of how much he desired her. Perhaps growing up, she'd unknowingly felt eclipsed by the brilliance of the Butterfly Courtesan, denting self-belief in her own beauty and allure.

Was that why she'd not followed her mother into the profession? Little did Amelia know that if she chose, she could have the whole world at her slippers.

"I desire no one but you, Amelia Lambert. I want your beguiling lips upon mine and your lethal hands all over me." His own shifted to cup her cheeks. "What do you say to that?"

"Oh."

Good enough for him. "And for yourself, Amelia? Are you truly so…" He whispered lips over hers. "Unaffected by me? Do you not…shiver when we touch?"

Her eyes met his. Clear. Honest. "No, Hugh. I do not shiver."

"Oh."

His hands dropp–

"I burn," she said softly. "Like Hellenic fire. Uncontrollable and unceasing, and however much I endeavour to quench it, the flame returns at your touch. It feels…that if I allow it freedom, it may burn me whole."

Hugh growled low. "Then, Amelia Lambert, let us scorch our bodies with the flame that sears between us. Set the Thames ablaze and reduce this whole damn world to ash."

So to light the touchpaper, he kissed her. Not tenderly, or softly, or hesitantly but with all the pent-up passion that seethed within, that had gathered and raged since Amelia had sat so demurely in his study, a rose-scented enigma with amber eyes, a blade at her thigh and pins of poison in her hair.

And at last, he knew by her avid kiss and exploring hands that he wasn't alone on this path of desire, that there was no need for pretence or tales or lies.

He walked her backwards, a base need to feel her crushed against him as his lips slid down her throat, the fragrance of her skin igniting his every sense. A gasp as her back met the wall, tugging fingers within his hair, the tussle of hips, her satin bodice hindering his need for her naked skin.

Lips met again, tongues clashing and hands clasping. His mouth hunted, soft skin and the swell of her luscious breasts. He dipped to them, teeth grazing over lace then satin and the firm crest beneath.

She cried out his name.

And he could wait no more.

Knew it had to be now.

He shoved a knee between her legs so she rode his thigh, kissed her rosy lips and commenced yanking at satin and petticoats, skin afire and loins hard as the devil's nagnails.

"Hugh…"

"Forgive me, Amelia," he snarled. "I have to… Hell, I need you. Now. Here."

His hand skimmed her thigh, higher, found such welcoming heat and he ground his palm against her.

She bucked and cried out, so ready for him; his hand rushed to his falls and–

"H-here?" came a faint gasp.

He wrenched his head up.

Amelia's eyes were glazed but with a smidge of...concern?

"Talk to me," he rumbled. "Or by hell or high water, I will be inside you within a moment."

She gulped as he lifted her by the rump, nudged his hips against her so she'd know he spoke the truth.

No answer so he commenced on the buttons of his falls once mo–

"I... I'm not exactly experienced," she blurted.

Hugh paused at the third button. "How not experienced?"

"N-not at all."

A long, slow breath and he removed his hand to place it at her chin, searching her eyes. "Never tell me you are an innocent?"

"Is t-that rhetorical?"

Beef-witted, clod-skulled, thoughtless addlepate.

How could he have not even considered that?

"I thought all Foreign Office spies were versed in..."

"Well, some are." Her gold-tipped lashes lowered. "But it wasn't my forte. I was better at being the shopgirl you never noticed, or the wallflower."

"You underestimate your charms, Amelia, as you'd have me babbling like a brook."

She bit her lip. "But also... I-I could not run the risk of being with child. Not just because of my employment but...but because..."

Beef-witted, clod-skulled, thoughtless addlepate.

And dolt.

Because of her upbringing. Because she would never want a child to feel as disparaged as she herself had felt.

"Amelia…" And he stroked a curl from her forehead. "Do you trust me?"

"Of course." Her lashes flitted up. "Completely."

"Then trust me this night through." And he swept her into his arms, ignored her squawk, stalked to the door, fumbled for the handle, strode down the corridor, kicked open his bedchamber door, and then, only then, did he allow her body to slide down his with maddening slowness.

He grabbed her hand. "Forgive such audacity but…" And slid it over his aching manhood. To show her his need. "I want you, Amelia. You are the woman who makes my skin shiver and heart thud. The woman I have no intention of letting go until dawn searches us out. Until you are thoroughly ruined. Until we are breathless and sated. Until you beg me for rest."

"And if I don't," she whispered with a shy twist to her mouth.

A groan escaped him as her hand flexed. "Let us see, shall we?"

AMELIA NIGH WHIMPERED as Hugh kissed his way down her throat, murmuring how exquisite she was, how silken soft, and she would defy any woman not to believe his words.

This man made her feel beautiful and desired as his hands skimmed her hips and drew her so close, she could feel every taut sinew.

His hands were tugging at her laces, lips insistent, words compelling and…and he'd walloped the Duke of Swanford for her.

No one had ever sought to avenge her, to protect her.

And she wanted him so, this fierce defender and droll scoundrel. This warrior of the night and gentleman of the day.

But was it really that simple?

She lifted her hand, cupped his clean-shaven cheek and brought his eyes to hers. "Hugh…" Yet she had no words.

His features were bathed in golden light from two lit candles while a low fire glowed in the grate.

"Amelia…" His blue eyes burned.

And she realised it *was* that simple.

"Show me," she whispered.

His lips curved, almost feral, and she trailed her hands down his chest, pushed off his jacket and unfastened the remaining buttons of his waistcoat. He stood motionless as she yanked at the cravat which, having been afore dishevelled, unknotted quicker than she'd feared, let it drop to the floor and then pulled the shirt from his pantaloons.

"For a woman who claims to have no experience," he said huskily, "you are doing most admirably." He leaned near. "You nigh unman me, Amelia."

Nigh? She'd see about that and so smoothed hands over his rippling stomach, began shoving his shirt aloft. "I'm a quick learner," she said breathlessly. "Although it was easier when you were tied up."

A deep chuckle singed her ear. "Any time you wish."

And words were lost as he wrenched the shirt over his head to expose his magnificent chest in the candlelight – marred, to be sure, but with wiry muscle and a dusting of golden hair.

She kissed his scarred shoulder; he shuddered.

She reached for his fall buttons; his hand forestalled her.

"Oh, no, Amelia. Now… Now we slow."

With an agile turn, he was behind her, loosening laces until her dress sagged and fell to the floor in a slew of white satin and green silk. Then her stays and petticoats were discarded until she stood in simply her chemise and stockings.

Scandalous.

A kiss at her nape and she sighed, his arms entwining her

waist and drawing her back against such heat, his manhood nudging her buttocks in impatience.

She twisted in his embrace, impatient also, and kisses shifted from slow to swift, soft to searing.

"I adore your hair." He groaned, fingers threading through her loose locks before they moved to tug at the sleeves of her chemise and it fell, caught on her hips, exposing her breasts to his intense gaze.

A crawl of nerves impinged but then Hugh's lips were at her collarbone, nibbling and flooding her with pleasure before roaming lower, brushing her breasts, finding the crests and laving till the world burned bright white behind her eyelids.

"Please..." she gasped.

Her plea was granted as she was urged rearwards to that fine bed, her chemise pushed to the floor, Amelia's derriere meeting the cotton sheets and–

A muttered curse as Hugh turned from her to yank at boots and tug at pantaloons.

Sat in solely her stockings, Amelia trailed a single finger along his spine, watched his shoulder blades flex as though wings were attached.

With a tortured moan, he bent to his bedside cabinet and she smiled because despite his fierce ardour, Hugh had kept his word and would not betray her trust.

Then he swivelled and before she could gasp, she found herself flat on her back, covered by muscle and heat and a torrid arousal that should alarm her but instead caused such aching need. A warrior whose broad hand skimmed over her breasts, causing her spine to arch, her eyes to close, before smoothing down her stomach and lower.

To tease and torment.

Palm grinding, fingers demanding. Every nerve heightened as she chased the pleasure. Her eyes opened, met his, the blueness lost to shadow but with such intense possession, it stole her remaining breath.

"My Amelia," he growled. "My Amelia of roses and gunpowder, solace and fire." His lips descended to her breast. "Blaze for me."

Her spine bowed as ecstasy gushed, crying out, his lips and hand unceasing and binding her with words and touch and torment.

She sank into the crisp sheets, malleable as wax.

Then his ardent body covered her, nude and lithe.

He nudged her stockinged legs wide, his expression wicked and fierce, and she welcomed him, fingers kneading firm upon his shoulders, chest, stomach and–

"No," he snarled, catching her, to slide his palm over hers and draw their hands to the sheets at her shoulder. "Don't let go."

She did not.

She did not let go when hard hips settled upon her, when she felt him nudging, retreating, persistent. She did not let go when a gasp of pain departed her lips or when he kissed it away.

She did not let go when he forged forward, gentle at first, then stronger, deeper, more. Till she was filled by him, moaning and twisting her legs about his hips.

A brutal grunt left him before he began to thrust.

And then...

Then she did let go, wrenching her hand free to dig her nails into his taut arms, to watch his vehement eyes and pounding hips.

Such pleasure, rough and incendiary, seized her, and she drew her nails down his back, to his flexing buttocks, scratched her wild ecstasy into him.

He'd warned they'd set the Thames ablaze, reduce the world to ash, and she felt it, the roiling all-consuming burn as he thrust again and again, deep and turbulent, all vestiges of the gentleman stripped away to reveal her fierce Welsh warrior of sin and danger.

Her leg was wrenched higher, sensation soared, and she was lost...

Scorched as rapture ripped through her, nothing left untouched, and she cried out, eyes slamming shut, flame over water as the whole damn world blazed.

At her gasped name, she dragged open her lids, to watch Hugh as his chest rippled, every muscle taut as his hips thrust with savage possession, his head rearing, a shudder, eyes closed as he roared his own pleasure to the inferno they'd lit.

Ragged breaths meshed. Time slowed. Hands clasped, and although Hugh's shoulders slumped, his hips still ground in leisure.

Then his lips searched for hers – tender and soft as ash.

He shifted to nuzzle her neck, her skin now sensitive as petals, and she quivered, felt his lips curve, but before she could take another breath, his hands gripped her waist and that muscled body rolled so she was draped atop him like a concubine to some decadent king.

Although Amelia was the one to feel decadent, lying upon this elegant bed with Hugh, the scent of roses and cinnamon mingling. She swept a hand over his chest and down his arms, a low rumble – like that of a lion at midday rest – emanating from him.

Never had she felt so...replete, and her hand continued to wander the ridges and flaws, the brawn and scars, the chronicle of this man's life.

But she was not alone. For Hugh's broad palms also wandered her back and then derrière, rough fingers circling upon her skin, and she realised the fire within had not been wholly doused.

With every caress, it caught and sparked.
She lifted to her elbows and gazed down.
His hair was tousled, skin glistening.
Their gazes met. Intimate. As one.
And he growled low words.
"Our fire still rages, Amelia. The night is young..."

CHAPTER TWENTY-FIVE

"Never, my child, be concerned in torturing your fellow creatures."

Private Education: A Practical Plan for the Studies of Young Ladies. Elizabeth Appleton. 1815.

A fist met gut and Hugh fell to his knees.

Then onto his back.

He stared at the ceiling. It had been newly painted.

"Cadwalader!" a voice boomed. "Where the hell is your concentration this morning?"

Absorbed by rose-blush skin and flaxen hair, nimble fingers, stockinged legs and a soft gasp in his ear as he–

Ice-cold water sluiced his skin and he sat bolt upright, shaking his head like a dog with ear mites. "Damn it! What was that for?"

Seth Hawkins, the owner of this fine boxing establishment on the edge of Piccadilly and with whom he practised every Thursday morn, stretched out a broad hand. "To clear your head. Your footwork is sloppy, your fists are slapdash and your concentration is adrift."

With any other man, Hugh might have disputed such outright fibs, but Seth had once been a champion prizefighter so grudgingly, Hugh grabbed the hand that hauled him to his feet. "I'll concentrate."

"No, we'll stop there," said Seth. "Your face and guts don't look as though they'd take another bashing and besides, my next client is here. I'd wager, however..." He lifted the simple hemp rope which surrounded the boxing ring so Hugh could step beneath. "It's a woman on your mind. Always the same. I'm thinking of changing the name of this place to *Hawkins' Advice for Bachelors*. Five guineas per enquiry."

Hugh merely grunted and began unfastening the scant strips of cloth from his knuckles. Seth was one of the few who allowed him to fight more or less bare-fisted because, believe it or not, most criminal lowlifes refused to wait for him to don boxing gloves. He and the retired prizefighter had also discovered they'd become vaguely related when Seth had married a certain Miss Matilda Griffin last year, a distant relation of his own Welsh cousin, but he wasn't sure that gave Seth cause to bestow unwarranted advice.

Besides, he knew his own mind.

He'd fallen head over heels for Miss Amelia Lambert.

Last night had been...everything. Fervid and intense. Then achingly slow and tender. A shuddering possession that would never lose its allure and–

"I do hope," an aristocratic voice rumbled, "that your gruesome face was previously marred and not the result of your bout with Hawkins?"

Hugh glanced up to the Duke of Shawdale.

The lofty gent merely wore shirt and breeches yet exuded aristocratic power. His ducal seat lay in the Lake District but his reputation in London was of a man ruthless in business deals, a miserly shagbag to the last ha'penny and not one to suffer fools gladly.

"Shawdale." Hugh shook his hand. "Have no fear, Hawkins took pity on me because of my erstwhile bruises, so he'll pull no punches with you."

One ducal eyebrow raised. "I would expect nothing less for the coin I pay."

Hugh rolled his eyes and trailed Seth to a wooden tub of water to slosh his arms and chest. "Seth, for your five guineas an enquiry, tell me what you would gift a lady you hoped to woo?"

The former prizefighter scratched his chin. "I gifted my Matilda tender poetry."

With dark hair, firm jaw, muscles the size of Hercules and olive-hued skin, it likely wasn't the only thing he'd gifted Matilda, but Hugh grimaced. He wasn't so proficient at poetry himself.

"If she requires costly poets and their scribble," the duke drawled from behind them, "you'll be beggared soon enough."

Hugh twisted. "Never gifted a woman anything, Shawdale?"

"Nev–" The duke's hazel eyes swirled green for an instant before settling to golden brown. "Long ago, perhaps. Before I learned better."

"Well, any other ideas? Tender poetry's not my forte."

Seth slapped him on the back; Hugh nigh drowned in the tub.

"'Is love a tender thing? It is too rough, too rude, too boisterous, and it pricks like thorn.'"

Damnation, and Hugh realised Seth – or Shakespeare – was correct. Amelia would likely prefer lethal hairpins to a *tender* gift.

"Seth, you should charge ten guineas."

Shawdale winced but the prizefighter gazed around his

sumptuous room with its brown velvet curtains, pristine racks for dumbbells and the latest weighing machine. "Could do with some extra coin. The sash windows need painting, my daughter needs another set of gowns and..." A smile split his features. "Matilda is with child."

"What!" Hugh slapped him on the back; Seth barely flinched. "Congratulations. Is she well?"

"Eating for five."

"That'll cost," grumped the duke.

Hugh ignored him. One day, a woman would bring that pinchpenny duke to his knees and Hugh for one would pay a damn fortune to see it.

After further manly slaps on the back, Seth and his client departed for the ring while Hugh made his way to the basement changing rooms, thoughts restless as he exchanged his loose boxing breeches for daytime wear.

When he'd awoken this morning, Amelia had afore departed his bedchamber, leaving rose-scented sheets. He couldn't blame her for making herself scarce before dawn as maids made their rounds at first light, but he wished he could have awoken to her amber eyes and silken kiss.

And furthermore, they needed to talk of what she'd learned from Lady Twyford at the theatre and how to proceed with Lady Tremlach.

He tied a rough cravat for once, shrugged on his jacket and made for the door.

Their hunt continued.

A GIMLET EYE PERUSED AMELIA. "Where is my nephew, Miss...Jones?"

"Mr Cruikshank informed me that the master has left for his regular early appointment at his Boxing Club, my lady."

Amelia herself had crept from his bedchamber when she'd heard the household stirring at five of the morn but then had fallen asleep in her own bed until Sally had brought tea at eight.

Hugh had departed the house at a half after seven.

"Harrumph."

Amelia could only concur. "I believe, my lady, the master thought you were not returning Phoebe to us until the hour of twelve."

The hall's longcase clock broke the quietude of the drawing room as it struck a quarter before eleven.

"One arrived early," Lady Kemble stated, sitting bolt upright in the Chippendale chair, "as one has...questions."

Lady Kemble's attitude towards her appeared to have changed somewhat, and Amelia sensed not for the good. She made to rise. "Perhaps I should attend to Phoebe and–"

"Sit."

Amelia sat.

Clasped her hands and sought the demure governess.

Though after last night, she wasn't sure that *demure* could ever be included within her repertoire again. She shuffled and–

"Cease fidgeting. You are as bad as Hugh. Has this abode fleas?"

"I don't believe so, my lady. Perhaps the chair cushions are lumpish and need re-upholstering."

The lady's brows elevated to her henna hairline before she retrieved her quizzing glass and scrutinised Amelia from her booted toes to her simple chignon.

"Hugh attended the theatre last night, I hear. Do you know which play he saw?"

Amelia recognised an interrogation when she heard one.

"Also," Lady Kemble continued, "there were reports of an unseemly rumpus–"

The front door closed, a deep voice rumbled and Amelia launched to her feet. She'd been trained to withstand questioning under duress, but Lady Kemble and her quizzing glass were a test of any spy's button-lipped resolve.

"Mr Cadwalader's home," she said brightly. "I should go and...educate my charge. With a book and–"

"Sit."

Amelia sat.

Silence stretched, like that before a summer storm, until the drawing room door swung open and Hugh strode in, handsome in a blue jacket and cream buckskins.

Scowling at her ugly grey governess skirts, Amelia rose and bobbed a curtsey.

Their eyes met and his lids hooded, lips twisting to downright sensual. Amelia's breath caught before she cleared her throat and nudged her gaze towards his aunt on the far chair.

His head swerved as though struck by a fist, "Ah, my favourite aunt!"

Lady Kemble tutted. "Your *only* aunt."

"What brings you here so early this fine morn?" He hastened over to buss her cheek. "And dressed in the splendour of an aubergine from paradise."

"Pshaw! You devilish scoundrel." She patted her purple skirts as he turned back. "I want words with you."

Amelia rose. "I should..."

"Sit!"

Amelia sat.

"Concerning?" And flipping his coat-tails, Hugh seated himself beside her on the sofa.

Lady Kemble narrowed her eyes. "Letty Harcourt."

"Do I know her?"

"Lady Twyford to you, young man. I wish to know why you have been inquiring about her at *The Berkeley Square Ladies' Benevolent Fund* tea and crumpet meeting? And why I found her in tears when I went to call this morn while Phoebe was at breakfast?"

Amelia gulped but Hugh merely leaned back into the sofa and laid his arm behind her, fingers brushing beneath her shoulder.

"How do you know Lady Twyford, Aunt?"

She pursed her lips. "We had our first Season together and along with some others were... Well, you would not imagine it now, but..." Her lashes fluttered. "We were known as the Dashing Debutantes."

"I certainly could imagine it, my dear Aunt, but I don't recall you ever mentioning her?"

"No. I do not speak of Letty, for a reason. And in any case, she mostly keeps to the countryside so I hardly ever see her. However, when she is in London, we meet for breakfast once in a while. And this morn, she tells me that *you*..." A purple-gloved finger was thrust at Hugh. "Have been asking questions about her. And furthermore, that she was accosted last night at the theatre by a woman that you had escorted there." The finger stabbed to Amelia. "A blond woman with amber eyes."

Hugh sat forward, hands clasped, hesitated... "Lady Twyford was suspected of deeds that have caused great harm to others, Aunt."

"Breadcrumbs and fishhooks, what twaddle! *She* is the one being harmed."

A furrow rutted Hugh's brow.

"Blackmail," Amelia murmured. "The lady is being blackmailed for money."

"Precisely! Honestly, do keep up, Hugh." Lady Kemble folded

her arms, purple fingers tapping. "And I presume you, young lady, are no governess at all, but some...colleague of Hugh's?" That haughty eyebrow rose once more.

Amelia would not crumble.

Hugh closed his eyes. "You're correct, Aunt. This is Amelia Lambert. We are working together. But I tell you this only because I know I can trust you with our lives."

"Of course!" Lady Kemble leaned back in the chair. "And poor Letty? What is all this about? She does not need the two of you plaguing her."

"We had no choice, Aunt. This is a serious matter. But I do have connections that might be able to help Lady Twyford if I know what it is she's being blackmailed over. A secret lover or–"

"Don't be ridiculous." She unfolded her arms, the chair creaking as she sighed. "I myself was sworn to abject secrecy over this, yet I can see it is important..." A sniff and that finger was speared out once more. "But I want your solemn promise this goes no further. Both of you."

They both nodded.

Lady Kemble garnered a long breath and gazed to the window. "Dearest Letty, you should know, was the diamond amongst us Dashing Debutantes. The diamond of the Season. Not just a beauty but kind and gentle too. Her parents had a marquess lined up for her. Then, on the third day of September, she departed with a maid to Lock & Co. for a new hat." The lady's eyes closed. "The story was that a dog ran into the road, two carriage horses were startled and charged onto the pavement. Letty was knocked down and her maid, Sarah... Sarah was killed outright."

Amelia brought curled fingers to her lips. "How awful," she whispered.

"That poor maid," murmured Hugh.

"Yes. Sarah had but sixteen years to her name." Lady Kemble fumbled for a handkerchief within her sleeve. "Then as for Letty herself, she was gravely hurt and rendered insensate as her head had struck the kerb, causing a deep gash. We all feared..." She dabbed an eye. "But then, thank the heavens, on the third day she awoke. All seemed well. She recovered and appeared right as an adamant, but then..." A hand lifted to her brow. "There was a dinner to celebrate Letty's return to society. The marquess, myself, her parents and a few others attended. She was quietly listening to the conversation, when... I do not know how it started but all of a sudden, her chair crashed and Letty was...upon the floor, her body shaking, limbs contorting, spine arching like some wild creature. She had no control and, oh, I was so scared for her. We all were. Letty's mother slapped her and..." Lady Kemble wiped at her eyes. "We got her to a couch, held her and little by little, it lessened but..." She stared up. "In time, it became clear the accident had provoked some form of falling sickness and poor Letty, it was awful. Her life fell apart within those months that followed. She was prodded and poked by quacks, the marquess and his parents refused the marriage, citing she was mad, and her own parents... They were ready to send her to an asylum, believing Letty was now possessed by evil spirits."

Amelia put her head in her hands, felt wracked with remorse for upsetting the lady last night. She had read of such conditions, knew many were sent to an asylum as they were deemed to be a danger. "What happened, Lady Kemble?"

"Edmund happened, that's what. He'd been dotty about her from day one of the Season but was a mere fourth son of a viscount. A handsome fellow and Letty enjoyed his company but knew naught could come of it as her family would never approve of such a low match. But he... Well, he just swept in and saved the day." She leaned forward. "He came to me as her friend and said that with my compliance also, he could end any talk of the matter. I know not how he accomplished it but all the dinner guests who'd witnessed the events that night were compelled to silence, including the marquess. Her parents moved to the coast, and Edmund and Letty were married with all haste."

Hugh whistled softly beneath his breath. "I wondered why he was so guarded of her."

Lady Kemble snorted. "Edmund worships the ground she walks on. And she him. He whisked her off to the country in the hope the air would help her and to an extent, I believe it has. She prefers the peace and is less fearful of witnesses to her illness there, but she misses the theatre and her friends. Episodes of her sickness are rarer now, but she is...delicate still and easily distressed."

Amelia looked to her toes.

"Forgive us, Aunt." Hugh paused for some moments as his aunt nodded. He tapped his fingers on the sofa. "So I suppose should it become known that a high-up official in the Home Office is married to a lady many believe should be in an asylum..."

"Just so." Lady Kemble grimaced. "And that is where this heinous blackmail comes in. A year past, Letty received a note. It claimed to know of her condition and demanded she meet alone with a certain Mr Roberts. This fiend convinced her that Edmund would lose his job, that his peers would believe him mad also, for why else would he marry a woman possessed by spirits? How the reprobate found out about her condition, I do not know, but after all Edmund had done for her over the years, Letty decided to pay for this Roberts' silence. Still pays for his silence." She shook her head. "Indeed, it is one of the reasons she has come to London more often of late."

"Damn it all, the poor lady," murmured Hugh, digging hands

into his hair. "This investigation of ours just goes around in circles."

"Perhaps it would help," Lady Kemble whispered, "if you could tell me what it is you are investigating?"

With a sigh, Hugh rolled his shoulders and Amelia could see the struggle within him – to protect his aunt from the danger that any involvement in their work could cause her but also a yearning to unburden his soul and find justice for Phoebe's father.

"I believe," said Amelia, placing a gentle hand to Hugh's arm, "that Lady Kemble's knowledge of the past can only be of assistance to us."

He exhaled. And laid his hand over hers. "I told you, Aunt, that Phoebe's father had died in suspicious circumstances, which were then hushed up by the Home Office, but... Ross was murdered. I am sure of it."

Lady Kemble closed her eyes and nodded. "My poor, poor Phoebe."

"We believe this Roberts had a hand in it. He is also somehow obtaining information from the Home Office and I could not go to Sir Edmund with any of this because..."

"You suspected Letty?" Her chin dropped. "I can understand that. But I can also tell you that Edmund says not a word of his work to her. Never has done. To protect her and because of her fragility." She peeled off her purple gloves. "So who else could this Roberts be obtaining the information from?"

Silence fell, only punctured by the light step of a maid in the hallway and a dull rattle of cartwheels in the Square.

"I..." Hugh hooked a boot on knee and Amelia turned to him.

"Yes?"

"It's just..." He breathed deep. "Aunt, you say Sir Edmund

worships the ground Lady Twyford walks on, would do anything at all for her?"

"Of course. Always has."

Amelia met Hugh's eyes and understood the reason for his question.

"So what if," she murmured, "Roberts is also blackmailing Sir Edmund over his wife's sickness. Information in return for a secret kept."

Lady Kemble shook her head. "Never. He is too smart."

Hugh frowned. "I confess it still leaves a host of unanswered questions but... We must at least consider it."

She shook her head more vehemently. "I'll not believe it, Hugh."

Amelia bit her lip.

Men had betrayed their country for greed or lust, envy or wrath, all manner of the seven deadly sins, so why not love?

Her gaze roamed over Hugh, his broad shoulders and blond tousled hair, another bruise on his cheek, and the endless blue of his eyes.

What would a man, or indeed a woman, do for love?

CHAPTER TWENTY-SIX

"The power of a book is supreme."

Private Education: A Practical Plan for the Studies of Young Ladies.

Elizabeth Appleton. 1815.

Hugh tapped his Hessian booted foot, gaze darting from floor to desk to ceiling as he waited within his superior's office.

An urgent message had arrived at the house after Aunt had departed, requesting he attend Sir Edmund in Whitehall with all haste and yet here he sat alone. Solely the clerks rushed about like headless chickens.

He glared at the desk strewn with papers and maps.

At this moment, he'd like nothing more than to confront Sir Edmund, but Amelia had been adamant she should talk to Lord Rainham first. After all, they'd no proof for their suspicions.

With a deep frown, he stared to his brown as a nut beverage. Hugh didn't mean to be finicky with his tea but this morning, Cruikshank had served him a delicate Twinings special blend of

Pekoe and Bohea leaves, so Hugh stirred his stumps and sidled for the potted plant behind the door, a quintessence of health and lustre, which signified Sir Edmund never partook of Mrs Benson's brew either.

He was about to toss the contents into the soil when an approaching kerfuffle in the corridor caught his ear.

Hugh watched from where he stood as the clerk Thomas darted into the room, cheeks flush and eyes angered. Without glancing around, the fellow headed for the desk and flung papers about, stamped his foot and–

"Can I...help you?" Hugh murmured.

Thomas startled and abruptly swivelled. "No, not at all, Sir." The man gulped. "Just...maps." And he lunged for one teetering on the corner of the desk and dashed out again.

Hmm.

With the potted plant quenched, Hugh returned to the chair and drummed his fingers against his thigh, feeling all was not well for some reason. Nothing within this investigation completely made sense. Perhaps they ought to revisit the list of Ravens' members and search for any correlation once mor–

"Ah, Number Five." Sir Edmund himself stomped in, flumped to his seat and heaved a sigh.

Hugh speared him a glance and endeavoured to imagine Sir Edmund as a love-struck young man, saving his beloved from an asylum and silencing all threats.

Impossible.

"Sir Edmund." Hugh nodded.

"Derbyshire. Tomorrow. Before all hell breaks loose."

At least Hugh knew this wasn't some ploy. Insurrection was undeniably afoot but...

"No, Sir."

White eyebrows shifted like cumulus clouds. "This is no time for debate, Number Five. The Midlands are in a rebellious mood and revolutionists from London are aiding their cause."

Indeed, and Hugh wished to discover who exactly was leaking confidential information to those revolutionists. "I cannot, Sir Edmund."

"Cannot? Or will not?" His superior leaned forward, a raft of desk papers tumbling to the floor. "If you will not take this mission, then… Then you are dismissed."

Hugh let a gust of breath gently flow.

For nine years, he'd been employed within the Home Office, put his life on the line countless times.

It *was* his life.

But perhaps it no longer needed to be.

So, rising to his feet, he straightened his waistcoat and nodded.

"Then so be it, Sir Edmund. Good day."

A splutter of "Come back here" followed him down the corridor but Hugh refused to turn.

This was for the best and his boots instinctively continued.

He needed to be free to pursue his investigation, find Ross' killer.

As though in a trance, he descended the stairs, trailed a finger along the gilt-framed portrait that hung there of Sir John, the spymaster who'd recruited him, and wished him farewell.

He pushed opened a hefty door, traipsed down steps and found himself on the Whitehall Street, a chill wind buffeting his frame.

Felt…odd.

The corners of his lips wilted.

"Hugh?" a soft voice called. "Are you well?"

Those corners lifted.

"Amelia…" She wore that dire grey dress, hair neat as a ninepence, and that habitual carpetbag was clutched in her hand with all her governess paraphernalia inside. She looked beautiful. "The Home Office and I...have parted company. After all these years."

An arm laced through his, Amelia not seeming to care one whit for gossip in the middle of hectic Whitehall. Horses pranced, maids giggled with soldiers, and...was that the back of Lady Tremlach with a broad-shouldered fellow?

He couldn't be certain.

"And how...how does that feel?"

"Adrift, if I'm honest."

"Let's stroll in Saint James' Park." And he let her guide him down Parliament Street, turn onto Great George and then through Storey's Gate and into the wide avenue which bordered the royal park, plane trees and bushes prettifying the edges.

A gaggle of ladies sauntered, tucked up against the cold spring breeze in redingotes and muffs, while a boy played hoop, and the place all seemed rather affable by day. Alas, Hugh knew by night it teemed with penny doxies and footpads.

"Ross and I used to come here," he murmured. "We'd practise fencing at dawn when no one was about but the pelicans."

"Were they to judge the winner?"

He smiled, for the park had been home to those birds for some two hundred years. "Yes, usually Ross as he was excellent with a sword." He breathed deep. "Better than me."

"When did you begin working together?"

"I was recruited after Oxford. They were looking for young, non-titled men with naught to do but gad around London. I seemed to fit the bill. Ross had been with the Office for five years and he was to be my mentor. But we became firm friends and it all felt...such a lark at the beginning."

"Then the reality of what men can do to one another sets in, doesn't it? The desperation and the depths."

Hugh peered down at her. "Exactly so. I have enjoyed the

work but…" He needed this, he realised. To be able to talk with someone who understood, to know she wouldn't be repulsed by the deeds he'd done for King and Country, and he felt profoundly grateful Amelia had plunged into his life. "Lately, I've felt…jaded."

She nodded, carpetbag and skirts swirling against his boots in a sudden gust. "I was once told by a Foreign Office colleague that one should retire within fifteen years of service regardless. That it was more than enough."

"And did he?"

A smile. "Yes. Lord Kelmarsh now lives in utter rusticity with his lovely wife. He even digs up his own potatoes."

Hugh laughed. "Not sure that's for me." They weaved around a wooden hoop as it spun down the path, then dodged the lad who chased it. "So what did Rainham have to say?"

"That we must continue to gather evidence." Her nose scrunched. "And if Sir Edmund is involved in some way, it still doesn't explain why Roberts raised his tankard to a Lady T, unless he was referring to the money he receives from Lady Twyford." She paused in her stride. "Perhaps we should review the file on each of the Ravens once more. Last night, before we…" She cleared her throat; Hugh's lips twitched. "I re-read of there being no service record on Roberts?"

"I had that same thought."

"But you believe Roberts when he says he served in the army?"

"Yes. His bearing and knowledge certainly point to it. And he was no private either but someone with command. He says lieutenant and I don't believe he'd veer too far from the truth."

"Then we should search the more detailed records of the division he says he was attached to. I believe there's an office for the Thirty-Second Regiment in London."

"A fine idea but..." Hugh twisted. "Official permission is required, takes an age to obtain and...I've just resigned."

She sucked on her bottom lip and he imagined doing the same. "In that case, we will need to be more..." Innocent amber eyes blinked up. "Unofficial. After dark, perhaps?"

Hugh smiled, for she was a woman after his own wicked heart and he placed hands to her shoulders. "Amelia Lambert, I–"

Clouds parted; a glint caught the corner of his–

"Down!"

He whirled to shield Amelia, dragged her to the ground, landed on top of her as a pistol roared and his arm stung.

Ladies screamed; a child cried; all rushed for the gates. Hugh lifted, spun on his haunches.

A man in uniform and low cap stood to one side of a tree, a smoking pistol discarded to the grass.

Another cocked in his hand.

Sighted at Hugh as he crouched.

The man's lips curved.

There was no cover.

Protect Amelia.

He threw his arms wide, stared down the brute, felt something rest on his shoulder and–

A blast so loud, so blinding, tumbled him backwards and he lay for a moment, staring up at the pale-blue sky amidst the spring leaf canopy.

A breeze whispered over his skin.

Was he dead?

It felt as if he was resting upon the softest of clouds.

"Get off me, you great oaf!" yelled Amelia above the ringing in his ears. "I got him! In the leg it looks like."

Hugh sat up and–

Scraps of charred paper fluttered all around them. "What the bloody hell was that?"

"My governess tome." An elbow heaved into his ribs. "Quick, he'll get awa–" The elbow dug again. "Oh, look!"

Hugh gathered his senses and spun.

To see that Scotsman Darnell slammed up against a tree, a leather-gloved hand gripping him by the throat, a pistol pointed at his chest.

All belonging to the one-eyed Cleavers, black cloak billowing from his shoulders.

Hugh stood and stretched a hand to Amelia. On the path lay her hefty governess tome, open and missing half its leather cover but revealing that the inside had been hollowed out, a metal frame with the mechanics of a shortened flintlock pistol fixed within.

As they approached Cleavers, he could see Darnell's breeches were rent and stained with blood above the knee.

"I 'eard of their plan," bit out Cleavers, "got 'ere quick as."

Hugh clapped him on the back. "And thank hell you did." He twisted to Darnell. "Rather desperate, no? To attack in broad daylight?"

The man groaned and eyed Hugh and Cleavers with mortal distaste. "Bluidy traitors. We'll get ye all," he rasped. "And the Miss too. I'll carve ye up like–"

Leather creaked as Cleavers tightened his grip on the brute's throat, woollen jacket straining at the seams. "Nah, yer won't."

Hugh dusted down his buckskins. "Have we compromised your mission?"

"Nah." Cleavers winked. "No one knows I'm 'ere, and not a sparrow's tweet gonna be heard from where he's goin'."

Amelia reached up to his shoulder. "We owe you."

"Aye. Add it to the bill," he said with a wink, before in a swirl of black cloak, he grabbed Darnell's collar and dragged him off through the deserted park.

Spring leaves quivered in a gust; a hoop lay abandoned.

Amelia closed her eyes. "He could have...have killed you. How did you see..."

"I caught a glint of sun off the barrel but..." He cupped her cheek with one hand; her lashes raised to reveal bright amber eyes. "Where the hell did you get that book... gun...contraption?"

"I made it," she said softly. "I needed a weapon a governess could carry at all times without drawing attention. The bookmark is metal and hooks to the trigger. The spine is the sight, although I required your shoulder for steadiness. Rather a waste of a good book some might say, but I'd no othe–"

Hugh kissed her – voracious and carnal.

There in the middle of the park, pelicans squawking their return overhead.

Amelia's forehead met his, the wind still gusting the odd blackened shred of paper until with a deep exhale, she drew back and placed a trembling hand to his sleev–

"Hugh? You're bleeding!"

He nodded. "Bullet caught me. Just a scratch."

"You should have told me!" Amelia slapped his shoulder.

"Ouch."

She glared. "We need to get you to Mrs Dawkins and–"

"No, no. It's naught and she'll only fuss." He clasped her hands within his. "This is not over, Amelia. We are close to finding Ross' murderer so let's go somewhere to gather our thoughts." He drew her near, felt her body curve to his. "Some calm before the coming storm is in order. I'll clean this up there and..." His lips curved. "'Tis on the other side of London but I know the perfect place."

CHAPTER TWENTY-SEVEN

"The governess has not, you know, many enjoyments."

Private Education: A Practical Plan for the Studies of Young Ladies.

Elizabeth Appleton. 1815.

"Keep still!"

"It's a scratch."

"It's a hole." Amelia huffed. Honestly, men. Give them a dose of the sniffles and they wailed for their sick bed but get shot and they puffed out their chests and called for brandy.

She wrung the cloth out into the bowl, the water tinging an alarming crimson. In truth, the bullet *had* solely winged his upper arm, the blood ceasing when they'd bound it with Hugh's cravat in the hackney carriage. Yet the gash was lengthy and had reopened upon washing, likely needing stitches, but for now she re-bound it as tightly as she could with clean bandages.

His muslin shirt had been removed so he sat in merely his buckskins and although Amelia considered herself a capable, self-reliant woman, there was something about his abundant masculinity that made her feel she could lean upon his strength once in a while and he'd never even notice.

This *perfect place* of Hugh's happened to be on the east side of town where merchants and trade held sway. Far from the aristocratic parishes, it was obviously a place where Hugh could be anonymous.

They'd stepped from the carriage into the madness of Smithfield Market where every type of livestock could be found and it'd been hard to believe they were still within the modern metropolis of London as huge pens had contained braying cattle, bleating lambs and snorting pigs, the dome of St Paul's cathedral upon the skyline looking on in faint disgust.

Hugh had guided her to an impressive stone archway with a rather nondescript, two-storey, brick-clad building constructed above it. The cobbled path through led onto the ancient St Bartholomew's churchyard but beneath the arch they'd veered to one side, where Hugh had unlocked a door to stairs leading up into that same nondescript building.

A disguise for what had lain beneath.

She gazed around and smiled as those bricks were merely a façade, the interior displaying the structure to be pure Tudor London, one which somehow had escaped the Great Fire a century and a half ago. Black beams hung low, floorboards dark and gouged, and wattle and daub walls were dissected by curved oak timbers.

The furnishings matched the historic age, sheepskin rugs and sturdy trunks but there were also modern comforts – a coal fire, which they'd gladly lit, and a sofa with velvet upholstery.

"What is this place?"

Hugh prodded his bandage. "Well, it's said the arch below us used to form part of the southern nave of the church, but after King Henry got his way, half was knocked down and someone built this house on top instead. The timber frame exterior must have offended a previous owner so they had it clad in brick. I needed a house no one knew of as despite me having to live up to the sobriquet of the Scandalous Mr Cadwalader..." He waggled his eyebrows. "Sometimes I feel a need to...escape, to be unknown, to think, to escape the *Ton* world, and so when Wales is a mite far, I come here. I don't get the chance often, but there is something about this place which brings me peace. As it did after Ross' death."

"You miss him, don't you?" Amelia lightly brushed his arm.

"Yes." Hugh's mouth pinched. "We met less often in the last few years, which I now regret, but he taught me all. Saved my life once." His eyes strayed to an oil painting of a ship setting sail on the Thames. "Left me that in his will. His favoured painting of London." Hugh rubbed his creased forehead. "When I viewed the inside of this place, I knew it had to be mine."

"It's beautiful. I prefer these old houses with their secrets. What they've seen. What they've heard."

"Are you saying you prefer this ramshackle old place to my Messrs Makefare and Co., architect designed Hanover Square townhouse?"

A snigger escaped her. "I would never say no to piped water and windows that keep the draughts out but there is a... romance to these places."

"Amelia Lambert is a romantic?"

"Only on a new moon."

He chuckled and flexed his arm. "My man of affairs pays a neighbour here to dust, keep the cupboards stocked and–"

"Place roses in vases?" She cocked her head to the white blooms upon one of the oak trunks.

"A weakness of mine," he said huskily. "They remind me of summers in Wales. Innocence and life. Joy and beauty."

Amelia felt her lips softly curve – at a man who was a

warrior to his core and yet could still speak of the joy and beauty within life. At a man who she had nearly lost today.

As that Darnell had aimed his pistol at Hugh, her heart had ceased to beat, vision blurring and hands trembling, and she'd heard of only one emotion a woman could have that could cause such profound fear of loss for a man.

Dare she speak of it?

Yet perhaps such an emotion whilst working together was… normal? Perhaps Hugh had experienced this a hundred times with other female colleagues. Would it fade when their mission was done?

His lips were upturned as he studied her face.

With thoughts in tumult, she cleared her throat and breathed deep. "I cannot believe I failed to see Darnell by that tree. I'm normally alert to such threats but I was…distracted by our conversation."

Distracted by you.

His lips levelled, gaze darkening. "Yet if you'd not been there with your governess tome, I'd be dead, Amelia."

She shuddered and closed her eyes. "That's why I smelled of gunpowder on my first day, you realise. I'd been assembling it." She pulled back her shoulders. "The Brotherhood of Ravens must know we are close to have sent Darnell and will not give up. We could have them arrested and jailed tomorrow with the evidence we have of their sedition."

"But then we would not have the source of the leaks, and it is the Ravens who will lead us to them. If we remove the Ravens, the betrayals will not cease. Another set of willing hands will accept the information instead."

"I know. But…" She trailed a hand over the many scars upon his torso. "I don't like it when you get shot, Hugh."

A finger raised her chin and he leaned forward to gently kiss her lips. "To tell you the truth, neither do I." He winked. "And I do try to avoid it." She smiled but Hugh frowned. "I thought to see Lady Tremlach as we left Whitehall, which could be no coincidence."

Amelia scrunched her nose. "We still need to investigate her."

"Indeed, but that must wait as my stomach is emptier than the Regent's coffers. Let's see what Betty has left for us."

They searched the cupboards to find a round of hard cheese, jars of pickled quince, dried crackers and a bottle or two of wine, so they spread them upon the low table in front of the sofa.

Amelia kicked off her boots and stretched her toes, watching as Hugh – all glinting muscle and slick damp hair from his wash – placed a shovel of coal on the fire.

Then he stepped through to the next room, delved into a chest of drawers and returned, alas, with a shirt, and while he opened the wine and Amelia sliced the cheese, they chatted of Phoebe and her future, Hugh's years in the Home Office and Amelia's past missions.

It was all rather intimate and cosy.

"This is nice," she said with a yawn, stretching and allowing Hugh to fill her glass once more. "I never seem to have time to just rest."

Hugh rotated his shoulders and settled back into the comfortable old sofa. "So what does Amelia do when she has a day to herself?"

"I…" She frowned. "I practise with my cracksman's tools and read the papers."

"That's work." He cocked his head, those eyes far too penetrating. They saw her loneliness, she knew. "What would be your dream day then?"

"Oh, I don't know. Reading a novel?"

"You can do better than that," he countered. "Tell me your

most cherished dream? Even if it's one that could never be." His manner was jovial and yet his question touched deep.

"I...I haven't the faintest idea."

He leaned near; she could count the stubble hairs on his chin even in the fading light. "Yes, you do," he whispered.

"It's foolish," she whispered back. "Rather a feminine dream."

"Dreams are not foolish. They are a cornerstone for us, why we strive and fret and toil. To chase that dream and make it real."

"Well, I..." She stared into the molten red of the coals. "I dream of...attending a glamorous ball. Not for work but for the pure occasion. I spend the day bathing and washing my hair in rosewater. I dress in vibrant silks that are my own." She closed her eyes. "The atmosphere of the ball is imbued with thrill and merriment. I would dance without fear of scornful stares. I would be amongst friends, amongst laughter and commonplace chatter. I would hear no derision for my past or receive looks of disdain." She rubbed her cheeks. "Do not mistake me, I am proud of who I am and of my mother, but...I dream of it sometimes, the feeling of being..."

"Accepted." His voice was low. "For all you are."

"I told you it was foolish for society cannot be changed on Amelia Lambert's whim." She closed her eyes, wished not to speak of it anymore. "But tell me of your perfect day. A morn at Ascot Races? Then an afternoon at the club followed by an evening at some exclusive society event?"

Amelia sensed his hesitation before broad arms drew her into the muscular fold of his linen-clad chest. She did not protest. His heart thudded, strong and faithful, and all her uncertainties dissolved into him.

"My perfect day," he murmured, "would begin with a dawn gallop along the coast of my cousin's estate in Wales." His voice was a soporific rumble at her ear. "Not a summer's day but one of spring when the cliffs are carpeted in pinks and yellows, the wind whipping the timeless sea to a deep grey, the sky boundless and pale with the rising sun."

Amelia stretched in lassitude. Could see it in her mind's eye. Could see him relishing the freedom. "Sounds beautiful…"

"I'd return to the house where Mrs Pugh the housekeeper there has prepared me a breakfast of egg, bacon, toast and butter so golden you can taste the scant Welsh sunshine."

A smile curved her lips. Men and their stomachs.

HUGH CLOSED his eyes to feel the peacefulness. "I'd walk to the nearby cove with my two cousins for a swim, feel the cold saltwater invigorating me, healing me, cleansing my soul. We'd dress and perhaps play cricket on the sands, gulls circling in the soft sky. Then we'd look up to the cliffs and sight three ladies weaving their way down the stone steps cut into them. They'd be chatting with one another, skirts swirling, picnic baskets clasped in their hands. We men would all stand motionless, breath caught, possession and passion searing like dragon's fire in our veins." Hugh paused, breathed. "Two of the ladies would be the wives of my cousins, and the third… She is laughing, without fears, flaxen hair blown loose by the mischievous fingers of the Welsh wind, verdant green skirts swaying above bare feet. She looks up also. Our eyes meet and I feel such pride. Because she… She is mine."

He stilled, waited.

Waited for Amelia perhaps to ask…

The coal crackled.

Gentle breath flowed from her.

Amelia's head lolled.

Sound asleep.

With a sigh, he stared to the ancient, beamed ceiling that

must have witnessed so many lives unfold beneath it, observed struggle and valour, time a meaningless concept.

It could wait, he knew, wait until they were free from the menace, free from danger and lies.

But he vowed that one day…

One day he'd somehow make Amelia's dreams real.

A LIGHT PITTER-PATTER of rain woke Amelia to…

Darkness. Warmth. Cinnamon. And Hugh.

She blinked and wriggled, her eyes adjusting to find a chamber tinged with the crimson glow of a coal fire somewhere. Dawn seemed far off as no light seeped but she could just make out a small bedside table, a vase of roses atop, and she appeared to be lying upon the most enormous bed known to womankind.

Her eyes drifted upwards. A four-poster, its drapes and coverlets were green with paisley gold detail and the wood frame a polished oak brown. Surely the house had been built around the bed for it would never fit up a staircase.

Somewhere downstairs, a clock chimed two and with a bottomless sigh of contentment, Amelia stretched her toes and then realised she only wore a chemise. Not even her stockings had been left in place.

Never had she slept so profoundly but then never had she been in possession of a personal bed furnace.

For behind her, woven to her back, was Hugh.

She wriggled again and–

A broad hand slid over her shoulder, down her arm and to her hip, lips nibbling her earlobe, suckling on the skin and kindling that damn flame within her.

She arched as a sensual need seeped through her like the

spill of molten iron, her buttocks encountering firm loins and naked skin, and she twisted her head to kiss him, not caring about the awkward tilt of her neck or the clumsiness of her kiss.

Then all of a sudden and with a scold of himself, he was gone, and Amelia could not think of a single man so caring, who'd recalled her concerns and would allay them without fuss.

Within a moment, he'd returned, woven to her back, and if the first night had been impatient desire, this was measured seduction, intoxicating touch as his hand roved, cupped her breast over the chemise, teasing the nipple.

His mouth shifted, lips brushing her nape, and her head lolled as his teeth grazed her skin, shivers of longing besieging her. The dark lent her boldness and her own hand swept where it could – his naked waist, slender hips – as their bodies began to move as one, curving back and forth, that flame fanning.

Palms hoicked her chemise, hips grinding against her, breaths now gasping and swift.

With little preamble, her thigh was clasped and drawn back, chemise riding up further. Her ankle locked with his shin, open to his exploring palm, his jutting manhood.

This arrangement might have felt awkward yet it felt so right and she pushed back...then gasped as he slid inside her – fitted and unique.

Their moans mingled and her head slumped as he commenced a languid motion, rousing and searing, hands at her hips and breath upon her nape.

It was tight, like this, tight and exquisite, and as his hand slid the chemise aside to hold her breast, she flung her arm to his nape, the slow shallow plunder a maddening possession.

More, she wanted more, so she ground against him, felt his stubble at her shoulder, eyes devouring her arched breasts, and she felt beautiful and wanted and desired.

"Hugh..."

He lunged, hand at her waist, steadying her as he pressed deeper, his pace intensifying.

She kept hold, cried out as his hand now delved to her heat, heard a growl in her ear and wished this would never end just as much as she wished for the flames to consume her.

And they did, fire devouring, fusing her to Hugh and all that he was. She slammed her eyes shut to the exquisite bliss she never wished to be without.

Teeth grazed her shoulder, a deep thrust, a muffled grunt, and Hugh tumbled into the fire also, his broad frame shuddering over and over.

Amelia savoured it all, allowed the bliss to undulate and flow.

Little by little, the pitter-patter of rain began to resume in her ears, the fire crackled and the bedchamber settled back into shadowed focus.

Hugh still languorously thrust but his laboured breath eased and his grasp upon her slackened.

Yet she wished to hold onto this moment forever, to return to it when the future loomed unknown – Amelia Lambert had been desired and wanted for who she was and this memory would always be hers.

As she pushed at the crumpled chemise encircling her waist, a giggle emerged.

"Let's get rid of that," a gruff voice proclaimed and before she could so much as lift a buttock, it was yanked over her hips and flung none-too-tenderly across the room.

"I've only five chemises to my name," she grumbled breathlessly.

"That's five too many as far as I'm concerned." Hugh leaned over to seize something from the bedside table, and in the dimness of night, she could make out the whiteness of a rose.

He trailed it over her neck, brushed her lips with its silken petals, and in the crimson light of the fire, she could discern dark eyes caressing her face.

With breath hitching, Amelia reached up and slid her hand into his, fingers entwining, the rose crushed between their palms, its heady scent all encompassing.

“Don’t let go,” she murmured. “Don’t ever let go.”

And his mouth descended.

CHAPTER TWENTY-EIGHT

"The fingers go naturally to the right keys after a few trials."

Private Education: A Practical Plan for the Studies of Young Ladies.

Elizabeth Appleton. 1815.

The silhouette of a ragged cloaked figure crept through the darkness of the Hanover Square kitchens, their features hidden by a slouched hat.

Hugh's tread was soundless as he approached, the shadows his accomplice as he moved over the flagstones.

The ominous figure opened a drawer, black-gloved hands searching…

For what?

He thrust his lantern high.

Then muffled a snort for Amelia's cheeks were daubed with coal dust, her beautiful hair tucked tight within the confines of that horrendous hat, and she wore some peculiar black skirt with pleats.

"Hugh!" She swished her cloak over her shoulders and

shoved those black-gloved hands to her hips. "What *are* you wearing?"

With a mutter of pot and kettle, he peered down at his rather natty charcoal-black waistcoat with silver thread, ebony-black jacket and fine jet-black breeches. He'd forgone the ink-black greatcoat as the night felt warm for once. "My informal wear? And what are you searching for?"

"Tapers," she hissed. "And we are breaking into a Regiment Office, not attending Almack's."

"I realise that," he said, somewhat affronted. "I'm wearing boots and not my diamond-buckled shoes. But if I'm stopped by the watch on Piccadilly, then I'm merely a gentleman wandering at his leisure. Whereas you'd be taken to Bow Street without so much as a 'by your leave'. I've never seen anyone who more resembles a heinous footpad on the prowl."

The long black leather gloves folded across her black jacket and he couldn't help but speculate on the colour of her stockings.

"I'm a female on the streets after midnight. My choices are limited. It was either footpad, doxy or crone."

Er... "Footpad then. In fact, those leather gloves make me ra–"

"Where are you off to?"

Hugh turned to find Phoebe tapping her slipper at the kitchen doorway, arms folded and plaits jiggling.

"Why aren't you in bed, young miss? It's gone midnight."

"I heard Amelia tiptoe past my door."

"Ah." He folded his arms also. "Well, we are just off to do some…reconnoitring."

She scrunched her nose. "From what I heard, it sounded more like burglary."

"It's not burglary if it's official business." Which it wasn't as he'd resigned but that was by the by.

Phoebe narrowed her eyes. "Semantics. And shouldn't you be wearing something a little less…refined, Uncle Hugh?" She hurried to Amelia. "I do so adore that skirt. Do the pleats mean you can run in it?"

"Precisely," Amelia said, splaying the material out. "An Irish lady designs them for us. So easy and–"

"Could we perhaps debate the fashion choices of an *à la mode* footpad on the morrow?" No one had even noticed Hugh's new boots. Which he'd scuffed especially.

Phoebe nodded and shivered, pale hands rubbing her arms. "Will you be gone…all night?"

"No, just an hour or so."

"And…are you close, do you think?" Her lips pressed, black eyes shimmering. "To finding out what happened to Papa?"

Hugh strode over and wrapped her in a hug. "Yes, my blackbird," he whispered into hair that smelled of smoke and lemon juice. "I believe we are."

"Then be careful." She tightened her hold around his waist. "I couldn't bear it if anything happened to either of you."

Amelia laid a hand on Phoebe's shoulder. "Do not fear, tonight should not be too perilous for us."

"That's good." She drew back, wiped her eyes and stiffened her spine. "I need to toughen myself up if I wish to do this type of work. Like you and Papa."

"Not at all, Phoebe," Amelia said softly. "Compassion and concern for others are just as important. Those must be retained also in order to keep our humanity. To remember why we do this."

Phoebe's eyes lifted. "I understand." She nodded. "For…for my father. Then thank you. Take care and Godspeed." She bussed Hugh's cheek and gave Amelia a tight hug before departing with coal dust on her nose.

Amelia blinked. "She hugged me."

"My ward is most fond of you." Hugh bent to kiss her lightly. "As am I. Now, no more dallying. I detest being late for breaking and entering. Best done at precisely one of the morn." And he turned on his heel.

"A quarter past," murmured Amelia as she sashayed out the door behind him. "The watchman does his rounds on the hour."

THE LONDON OFFICE for the 32nd Regiment of Foot was a smart abode on Sackville Street, but within the rather malodorous back alley, Hugh gave his footpad on the prowl a foot-up over the wall, wincing as his wounded arm protested.

Amelia clambered over in those pleated skirts before a thud signalled her boots meeting earth. So, without ado, Hugh lugged over her bag, and then with his superior height, grabbed the wall top, hauled himself up and swung his legs over.

Amelia harrumphed.

The moon drifted from behind a cloud, illuminating them to any neighbours yet to seek their beds so they hurried over the grass towards the back door.

Two stout locks, one upper and one lower. With luck, no further bolts on the inside as jemmying the door with the paraphernalia in Amelia's bag of tricks would no doubt cause a commotion.

"I'll do the upper," he rumbled low. "You do the other."

A nod and she reached into her bag to reveal a small velvet pouch.

Hugh's brows raised as she unravelled it to reveal a neat row of picks, hollow keys and other cracksman accoutrements.

With a rueful smile, he shoved a hand to his inside pocket to produce a more rudimentary three pick keys on a brass ring. As a rule, one of them would fit.

Selecting his favourite, he inserted it and slowly twisted, lips parted, feeling the mechanism shudder against the key's curves. A bit more joggling and lifting and...

The lock clicked.

Hugh peered down with triumph only to find Amelia had already done hers and was tidily stowing away her items, so he withdrew his key from the lock and kissed the brass-cast of a scantily clad woman adorning its bow. "My Kate never leaves me wanting."

Amelia merely rolled her eyes while he tested the handle.

And let out a breath as it ceded to his hand, the door opening without a creak.

They stepped into a deserted kitchen and Amelia cocked her head to the far door. It was ajar so they hastened through and headed for the stairs, Amelia's black cloak swirling.

Being Regiment Offices, all was spick and span, the staircase treads oiled and door hinges greased. The 32nd, he knew, was a regiment renowned for bravery, having fought in many a battle on the Peninsula – Roliça and Vimeiro under Wellesley. They'd been struck by malaria but had still been back in Spain to help storm Salamanca and then fight for victory at Waterloo.

Hugh shook his head. If Roberts had been part of this regiment, which Hugh had no reason to doubt, he was a valiant man and yet... Violence seethed within him still, a need for destruction and death.

They emerged into a hallway as black as Phoebe's hair, but Amelia was akin to a cat, stalking for a door at the far end, leaning her ear against it and then rotating the handle.

He didn't ask how she knew which door to head for.

It opened and they stepped into the room.

Black as tar.

No moonlight entered through cracks around the shutters; all was bolted tight.

Hugh closed the door behind him and heard Amelia delving

into her bag, so he blindly felt his way forward until his thigh knocked into what was likely a desk. There he burrowed into his pocket for his tinderbox.

As a young man, he'd practised this over and over with a blindfold so he placed the box to the desk, flipped it open and took out the damper and splints, placing them to the left. He then felt for the flint and steel striker, held them close to the box with its tinder contents and struck them together.

First strike and sparks ignited the scorched linen inside and he quickly lit the splint, handing it to Amelia who'd brought that curious shuttered lantern from her bag.

He damped the flaming tinder and returned everything to the box, snapped shut the lid and slipped it to his pocket.

"Neatly done," whispered Amelia, her face lit by the lantern's glow.

A smile and he stalked to the first cabinet against the wall to open its door.

Surely no man could entirely wash themselves of their pasts.

"Let's see what we can find on Roberts."

With true military spruceness, the files were sorted by rank, which was fortunate as with some five hundred men in the regiment, it would have taken all night to sift through.

First Major, Captain and then…

"The bloody Lieutenants are missing," he growled. "It skips straight to Ensigns." Had someone removed them? Or was there some innocent bureaucratic reason for their absence?

He tried other cabinets but they contained naught but regiment deployments and dates. Hell, were they never to–

"Hugh," came a hiss, and he twisted to see Amelia running a gloved finger along a row of vast leather-bound volumes upon stout shelves. "These look to be the pay ledgers. They might have something."

Together, they tugged out one of the more recent volumes,

its spine etched with the gold numerals 1814–1816, and laid it upon the desk, placing the lantern to one side.

It was indeed a written record of payments, sorted by month and rank.

"Let's try March 1815, just before Waterloo," murmured Hugh.

First came Majors, then Captains and then...

He turned the crisp page.

Lieutenants.

Amelia lifted the lantern, held it close and tilted it for best light while he drew a finger down the list, now sorted by date of enlistment.

"James Robinson. Henry Brooks... Edward Stephens. Theobald Butler." He sighed. "Samuel Lawrence. George Barr. John..."

He frowned.

Swallowed.

Closed his eyes. Oh no...

Bloody, bloody hell.

"What is it?" Amelia's hand pulled at his sleeve, peering over the lantern.

He pointed to the page and lifted his head.

"We have him, Amelia. We damn well have him."

CHAPTER TWENTY-NINE

"No one can long sustain an assumed character."

Private Education: A Practical Plan for the Studies of Young Ladies.

Elizabeth Appleton. 1815.

Hugh took a gulp of his tannin-laden brew, grimaced, stretched his legs and…

Waited.

A warm spring day had at last prevailed and Sir Edmund's office was stifling; even the potted plant looked to be wilting. Hugh muttered to himself as he sat kicking his heels, a lack of sleep causing a vague head pain to gather.

Impatience seethed within, to confront the culprit, for it to be over, and his thoughts spun to last night, when he'd viewed that name upon the regiment ledgers.

Were they right?

Were all Ross' nights spent hunting in the Rookery, and then his own, soon to be worthwhile? Would the treachery and death soon end?

A light-headedness overcame him at what that end would signify.

The recognition Ross deserved. A father Phoebe could be proud of. And for himself, a missing sense of peace, allow the memory of Ross to rest at last.

Then, he could begin a new chapter in his life...

He'd vowed to sweep Amelia off her pretty toes and declare himself, whisk her off to Wales with its verdant cool hills and crashing cold sea.

Wiping perspiration from his forehead, he–

"Oh, pardon me."

Hugh glanced up and narrowed his eyes. "Ah, Thomas, how are you?"

The man hopped from foot to foot. "Quite well, Sir."

"Working your way through Sir Edmund's papers, I see." Indeed, one could actually view the leather baize of the desk.

"I'm endeavouring, Sir, but 'tis a monumental task."

"Hmm. And how's Lady Thurwood? I've not seen her in Town of late."

"F-fine, Sir... Our family are attending the races together next week." A ruddy flush enveloped the chap's cheeks. "Excuse me, I hear my name called." And the young man fled.

Hugh took another gulp from his mug, paused with it at his lips and–

"Such a good lad, yer are," wittered Mrs Benson from the door. "I added sugar as yer look a mite under the weather to me."

With a grin, Hugh tipped his mug to her, swigged down the remnants, leaves included, and then frowned at it. "Odd taste today, Mrs Benson."

"Must be the sugar. Smidge expensive, so don't tell His Nibs. I gave yer two spoonfuls."

"Hmm. And the arsenic?"

Her head jerked. “Eh!” Beetle-brown eyes widened as her hand clutched her chest. “Come again?”

“Arsenic, Mrs Benson. In the same manner Ross Thornton was murdered. Or was it your son…John Robert Benson who gave him the fatal dose?”

Her bosom rose and fell in agitation, fingers plucking at her apron as she lurched forward, shutting the door behind her. “What on earth yer talkin’ about?” Her voice rose, cloudy brown eyes bulging. “I adored Mister Thornton, I did.”

Hugh got to his feet and peered at the nigh-dead potted plant in the corner. “I’m sure you did…until he got too close to the truth.” He placed the mug on the desk. “For Lady T was no abbreviation but simply a play on words.” A grimace twisted his lips. “The Tea Lady.”

Mrs Benson merely flapped her hands. “Sure yer not ill, lad? Yer lookin’ a bit peaky to me.”

“Of course.” Hugh swayed. “Because you put arsenic in my tea, did you not? And now you’ll concoct some tale about my being sick. See me to a hackney? Is that what you did with Ross? Will the driver be your son? The leader of the Ravens, a Lieutenant John Robert Benson.”

Mrs Benson shrugged those broad shoulders and stared to the ceiling before heaving a sigh. “Yer always were a clever lad. Aye, John’s my boy and has called me Lady Tea since he were a cub. Thought it were funny.” Her gaze dawdled back down. “And dear Mister Thornton were a clever one too. He were close, I could feel it in m’bones, sticking his nose where it ought not to be, so I dished him my special tea after some meetin’ and off he toddled. My boy picked him off the streets puking his guts not a half hour later, told Mister Thornton he’d take him to a quack.”

Sheer fury pulsed within Hugh, nape clammy with abhorrence. That such a good man, an honourable man and father, had been slain with such cold forethought. That Ross had died alone, in pain, with Benson looking on. "But he let him die," Hugh rasped. "And then you set the scene in his study."

Mrs Benson smiled. "It were a magnificent plan."

"You stole maps, documents, read private letters. I talked with the other clerks who said Thomas has been getting increasingly frustrated as documents were going missing from this desk."

"His Nibs is a weak old codger," she muttered. "Always leaving his desk unattended and no one noticed me. But it don't matter now as you'll be meeting Mister Grim soon. I even doubled the dose. And don't think to be calling out or my boy will visit yer young ward. Thornton's little girl, ain't it?"

"You wretch–"

"Look, yer already lurching in them fine boots o' yers. So aye, I'll just say yer've got the pukes and see yer to a hackney. But it'll be John again and this time he'll just dump yer in the river. When they find yer, bloated and half nibbled by fish, no one will know what happened."

Hugh frowned and placed a steadying hand to the desk. "My one question, before I meet Mr Grim, is how your son knew I was an infiltrator?"

She laughed, a girlish incongruous shriek. "I were there, dearie. In the Whitby tavern by the river, havin' a sip o' bub in the corner the second time yer attended a Ravens' meetin'. I always inspect the new recruits and what a shock I had when yer blond mop strolled through the door in all that clobber." Her lips flattened to a slit. "Be glad to get rid of yer."

"Well, I'm loath to disappoint you, Mrs Benson, but I fed your tea to that potted plant and re-filled it from my hipflask."

She floundered, stumbled back against the wall before a scuffle and shouts carried from the corridor.

The door burst open and Lieutenant John Robert Benson,

scowling and with his hands roped, was thrust into the room by two thickset Home Office soldiers with Sir Edmund following, fists clenched and face taut.

Amelia marched in as the soldiers nodded and left, her lips curving in a triumphant grin. "We got him, Hugh. He was waiting outside in an old hackney."

"Don't say a bloody word, Ma."

"Too late," Hugh drawled, and he strode to Mrs Benson, who stood her ground, face scrunched to a sneer.

"You also tried to kill me when I was last here, did you not? Knew I'd soon discover your family connection, but I poured your tea into the plant. So your son sent Darnell to shoot me instead. You were getting desperate."

"Bloody traitor, yer deserved it," shouted Benson, bound wrists straining. "I'll slit–"

"No, you won't," boomed Sir Edmund, eyes afire and lips a twisted snarl. Hugh had never witnessed him thus, but for the first time, he could see the vehemence of that young swain who'd saved his wife from an asylum. "And as for you, Mrs Benson…"

She folded her arms and pressed her lips together.

Amelia stepped forward. "She's been selling the information to whomever she could, Sir Edmund. Riffling through documents for her son and his revolutionists. Leaking officers' names and locatio–"

A crash and Benson swivelled to charge at Amelia.

Hugh yelled, wiped sweat from his eyes as the whoreson rammed his head into her chest.

She tumbled to the floor as Benson spun for the door.

Vision red, Hugh hurtled, grabbed the whoreson's collar, swung him around.

A knee sought his groin but he punched a fist to Benson's jaw, another to his gut. With a growl, he shoved the thrashing man against the wall and pulled back another fist.

To finish it.

For Ross.

For Phoeb–

"No!" shouted Sir Edmund at his shoulder. "I'll take care of this." He grabbed Benson's neckcloth. Drew back his broad knuckles clenched to white... "This is for blackmailing my Letty." And crunched them into Benson's face with such force that the murderer's head left a dent in the plasterwork as he sagged to the floor.

Sir Edmund stood back, neatened his jacket, realigned his waistcoat and set his cravat to rights. "Well, that was quite a morning. Good work, Number Five, and I'd say you're due an apology..."

But Hugh was gazing to Amelia who'd risen and was tying the wrists of a ranting Mrs Benson to a chair with aplomb.

Hugh needed to hold her. See if she was hurt. Kiss her.

He frowned and stared down as his boots refused to lift.

Each limb felt as though formed of sodden flour.

His arm speared with pain, rupturing as if wire tightened around it. He swallowed, throat dry, that vague ache to his head now gouging a fissure.

"Number Five?"

He turned his head but the room tipped, nausea pitched and his knees failed him, crumpling to the floor.

Then Amelia was there, amber eyes so wide but...shadowed figures surrounded her – cavorting and ghoulish.

His lips parted to tell her he was fine, he was always fine, just needed some sleep and a stiff brandy, but his tongue refused to comply. Confused and lame.

"Hugh!" He heard fright in that voice. Such a chill palm on his forehead. "You're burning up, Hugh! Why didn't you say!"

Amber eyes… With fewer flecks of gold today, just profound amber.

His head fell into softness, muffled words drifted.

Looked up to Amelia as she cradled him in her beautiful lap.

Wanted to say…

Everything.

But his lids drooped.

Her lips moved, though no words that he could hear.

She blurred, those shadows crowding her, and he clung to her eyes, desperate to focus.

Those amber eyes.

How he loved her amber eyes…

How he loved Amelia.

His own drifted shut.

Yet still that amber. Vibrant and aflame.

And then…

Then…

Those shadows snuffed them also…

CHAPTER THIRTY

"Look not sad. Why should you fear?"

Private Education: A Practical Plan for the Studies of Young Ladies.

Elizabeth Appleton. 1815.

"When d-do you believe he'll wake from this delirium, Amelia? It has been two days now."

Biting her lip to stop a tremble, Amelia patted Lady Kemble's arm, the candlelight casting her movement in shadow upon the wall. "I'm sure it will be soon, my lady. Sleep is best, and the doctor has tended the wound most judiciously." Yet she twisted in her chair so that Lady Kemble would not witness the terror that surely haunted her eyes.

A candle gutted and smoke curled in the sombreness of dusk, Amelia returning her gaze to Hugh as he lay supine upon his elegant bed, cheeks so flushed, hair dark with sweat and yet conversely shivers wracking his body.

When first brought home, the household had all remained buoyant. After all, this was the Scandalous Mr Hugh

Cadwalader who'd survived knife slashes, pike wounds and apparently a crossbow bolt to his nether regions, yet… Amelia had discerned the fraught creases to Mrs Dawkins' brow as she'd undone the upper arm bandages and seen the state of the inflamed wound, she'd heard the hitch of breath from Sally as cold cloths upon his forehead had heated within a moment, and she'd despaired when Cruikshank's long face had leached to grey as the doctor had departed, mumbling to him and shaking his head.

"H-he is all I have," Lady Kemble whispered, her fingers quivering as she reached out to hold Hugh's limp hand. "His parents were too busy squabbling to care for him so he always found his way to my home. He was so mischievous and yet…so deuced charming, even as a boy, that you forgave him for playing cricket in the long gallery or drawing on your Caravaggio."

A soft splutter left Amelia. "I can imagine that all too well, my lady. But he will get better." She swallowed and breathed deep. "He has the best care there is, what with the doctor, Mrs Dawkins and all of us."

"Between you and me, Amelia, I have never entirely trusted those…tinctures of the housekeeper."

"But Hugh does, and if Mrs Dawkins had looked after the wound to start with, he may not be… I wish…" Amelia blinked away moisture. Wishes were for fools, as Hugh always said. "I should have informed her. Sent him to her straight away."

A return pat on her arm. "Hugh's nature has always been carefree, my dear. He considered it naught and so it was naught."

"But any wound should be seen to, for the bullet may have left shreds of cloth or… I washed it as best I could and…"

"Do nor fret, Amelia. We all know you did." Her eyes roamed

Hugh's pale face. "My nephew has never been the best of patients and would have insisted it a scratch."

Amelia smiled softly. "Yes, my lady. He did." Yet how she'd castigated herself: she should have ignored Hugh's protests, demanded Mrs Dawkins attend to it. For that so-called scratch had festered beneath the binding till it'd become swollen and raw, noxious fluid seeping.

The doctor had cut into his arm until crimson blood had run and then tied it with the same binding, which Mrs Dawkins had then untied and disposed of. She'd dabbed a green ointment upon the fresh raw cut and then wrapped it with clean boiled cloths.

For the first day and night, Amelia had refused to leave his side but Lady Kemble had ushered her to the hall for, as she'd termed it, 'a good talking to'. How an exhausted Amelia would be no use to anyone, how they could all take turns.

Now, by day, Lady Kemble, Mrs Dawkins or Phoebe sat with him while the valet and Cruikshank brought much-appreciated trays of strong tea, bowls of cool cloths and stoic encouragement. On occasion, they'd been able to get some broth down him, but his azure eyes had dulled to clouded sapphires, scarce mumbles unintelligible.

Then there were the nights when Amelia cared for him. When the fever raged and she alternated between covering him with cool sheets and piling on woollen blankets, bathing his forehead with cold well water and biting her lip till it bled to stop herself from...

She would not cry.

For Hugh was alive and he *would* recover.

A soft rumble came from the chair beside her and Amelia turned.

Lady Kemble's head had lolled to one side, turban askew and

face shadowed in the dim light. She seemed to have aged ten years in the last two days. All of them had.

Amelia patted her arm and–

"Hugh!" Her eyes flared wide, skin ashen.

"He's the same, my lady, but you should go home and rest. Or I will be forced to give you a good talking to."

The lady pressed her lips together. "You are right, Amelia, dear. Forgive me, I slept not a wink last night." She rose, her purple skirts creased from sitting all day. "I will ask Sally to bring up some fresh roses. Those have wilted in the heat of this room. You will let me know if…"

Amelia got to her feet also. "As soon as he wakes."

Lady Kemble leaned forward to embrace her and Amelia felt tears sting her eyes. "Until tomorrow."

"Of course."

Amelia did not return to her chair but perched upon the edge of the bed as Lady Kemble quietly closed the door.

Hugh was too still. So unlike his usual self, whether it be the droll eyebrow-waggling scoundrel or the dangerous flint-eyed warrior. Only the minimal rise and fall of his chest attested to life. She placed a hand to his cheek – too hot, and so grabbed a cloth, rinsing it in the bowl of cold water.

With a slow hand, she stroked it over his forehead, down his face and over his bare chest.

He murmured and she drew close.

"Hugh?"

"Am…Ame…"

But he fitfully turned, words incoherent, and the moment was gone.

As the room darkened, Amelia resumed her caress of cool water, night falling like a gossamer veil of black as she did so.

A knock on the door and she bade whomever it was to enter.

Frothy pink roses came first, followed by Sally. "Hot enough ter boil an egg in here."

"The doctor said to keep the windows closed."

"Maybe when the fog's drifting, Miss, but 'tis a clear evening and the breeze ain't from the Thames. Smells o' spring out there."

With a smile of accord, Amelia ambled to open the window. Here on the second floor, it was high enough to catch the breeze and with less of the London street odours. Amelia breathed deep.

Spring indeed.

She twisted as Sally removed the faded white roses from the vase by the bed, the buds having wilted to grey without even blooming.

"Thank you, Sally."

"Not at all, Miss. And...beggin' yer pardon, but seeing as how...close yer are to the master now, I were wonderin'... Do yer think we ought ter send a message to his folks in Wales?"

Amelia felt her cheeks blush. "A good idea but Lady Kemble said they are all on the Continent. By the time they receive it, he'll either be better or...or be better."

"Of course, Miss." And with a soft smile, she left.

Amelia returned to her chair beside the bed, breathed in the scent of the fresh roses, picked up the slim volume of his favoured poetry, turned to the bookmarked page and began to read to him...

"'If love is not to be my fate
Oh, why bestow a yearning heart?
A bleak soul wearied at the wait,
An ardent spirit cleaved apart.'"

She closed her eyes tight, blinked, willed the moisture to depart.

For tomorrow Hugh would wake, those eyebrows would waggle, blue eyes merry as he apologised for giving them all such a fright.

Tomorrow.

Surely tomorrow…

Three days later.

FEAR HAD an acrid taste and it slid down Amelia's throat in knots as she watched Hugh flail and thrash, sweat beading on his chest, arm so swollen that the merest touch pained him.

It was nigh six of the eve but today Amelia had not departed his side.

For the second day, they'd not been able to coax him into swallowing Mrs Dawkins' tincture.

Or the broth.

He was weaker.

Earlier, with Cruikshank supporting his arm, she and the housekeeper had changed the bandages but a vivid crimson now flared from the malevolent wound, encircling skin slick and pulled taut. Mrs Dawkins had muttered beneath her breath, cleaned it and applied her latest dark-brown poultice.

Hugh had shaken and mumbled incoherent words of death and blades and blood.

Amelia had sent a sobbing Phoebe away for rest, fought to keep her own tears at bay.

She had to stay strong. For Hugh.

Lightly, she lowered to the bed and stroked back his damp hair.

With a low moan, he flung himself onto his back, lids parting to reveal slashes of briny blue.

At first, such signs had brought them all joy that he was recovering, and Amelia had talked to him, told him how the roses were blooming in the garden and that Lucy the maid was being courted by the footman. How Phoebe longed to hear one of his waggish tales and...how much she herself missed him.

Occasionally his lips would move and she'd been sure he'd heard, wanted to answer, but too soon the fever would possess him and he was lost once more.

"I-I never told you my code name," she whispered as his dipping eyes appeared to seek her. "I was rather vexed with Lord Rainham...when he named you Stoat as I'm...I'm Hare, you see, and everyone knows hares are a stoat's prey." She swallowed. "But now I find it somewhat...almost as if Lord Rainham knew. They say stoats mesmerise their prey with some sort of dance..." His lids sank. "And...and you did likewise to me, Hugh." A tear trailed and she scrubbed at it. "Mesmerised me with your jollity and bravery till all of a sudden, I was yours and–"

A knock on the door and she swiped away the stupid tear, sat straight, patted her skirts.

All would be well. Hugh would be well.

"Yes?" she called rather too brightly.

Phoebe's head poked around the door. "I thought I might sit with him while you rest, Amelia."

"No, 'tis fine, I..."

But Phoebe was marching in with purpose, a book beneath her arm. "You need all your rest for the night. I fell asleep for a half-hour so am wide awake now."

Amelia gave a watery chuckle. "You are right." For a weariness seemed to have settled into her every nook, limbs heavy and mind sluggish.

"I know I am." Phoebe sat on the chair by the bed but then stood again, tutting as she removed a book from under the seat cushion. "Byrne? The poet?"

"Hugh enjoys his work, doesn't he, so..."

They were silent awhile, solely listening to his shallow breath like sandpaper on rock.

"He managed no broth today," whispered Phoebe.

"No." Amelia grasped her hand, had to stay strong. "But tomorrow is another day and then...then he will surely sup two bowlfuls."

The young girl smiled, although her lips quivered. "He has to...has to get better, Amelia. He must. Because I need to thank him. For all he has done for my father. Now I can tell the whole world that Papa did not..." She wiped at an eye. "Not do any of those things. So, Uncle Hugh has to get better, you see, to know how grateful I am to him."

"And he will," said Amelia fervently, rising from the bed to seize Phoebe in a hug. "You know Hugh, he's probably enjoying all the fuss being made over him, so..." She forced a smile as Phoebe quietly giggled. "Sally is coming up soon, so she will be with you while I rest and then... Ask Sally to come get me in an hour, yes?"

"Of course."

They embraced again and stared to Hugh for a while, their hands entwined.

"Now, Uncle Hugh," Phoebe said fiercely, "enough of this teasing us and get better. And I'm afraid you'll have none of this romantic poetry twaddle from me. We'll read *Treatise on Ciphers* by Leon Battista Alberti and enjoy it." With which, she plonked herself into the chair and turned to chapter one.

Amelia smiled, touched Hugh's hand, whispered her thanks to Phoebe and with quiet tread left the bedchamber to the soft pitch of the young girl's voice.

Once outside, she leaned back against the door and rammed her eyes shut to halt the tears, so sick to the stomach with fear.

Such a heart-wrenching fear.

That she would *not* allow.

So she blinked, straightened both her skirts and her shoulders, and hastened for the stairs.

Sally had left a cold collation in Amelia's chamber but she felt little hunger, her stomach in such tumult, so she kicked off her slippers and dragged the chair to the window. She snuffed the lit sconces to leave just one lantern and then settled into the chair with a cushion, tucking her legs beneath her.

Staring out through the glass, Amelia watched day slip into dusk, the pink blossoms of spring dulling to grey, the jasper-green leaves fading to ash.

She must sleep, she knew.

Ready to hold strong through the forthcoming night.

So she shuttered her gaze to the dwindling day and willed herself to dream of blossoming roses and unclouded azure eyes.

AMELIA WOKE WITH A START, her room dark, the hall clock chiming its quarter before nine of the eve.

Hugh.

Why had Sally not come for her?

Surely he was...

She sprang to her feet, the cushion falling.

Hugh.

Amelia scurried down the corridor, up the stairs; all was dark and quiet. Thrust open his bedchamber door.

Phoebe still sat there but tears slid down her pale cheeks, breath hitching.

"No!" Amelia cried. "He can't..."

With eyes awash, Phoebe twisted. "No, Amelia, he's

breathing but… But he is weak. I-I thought he wasn't… Sally has only just left and I couldn't see his chest lift…" Phoebe wiped her cheeks with her cuffs. "But then his hand shuddered for a moment."

Hugh was so motionless, his skin pale as a corpse except for the red flush upon his cheekbones, but his fingers again twitched in whatever thrall imprisoned him.

"He's still with us, Phoebe." She hugged the young girl's shoulders. "You did well. And he will get better. Now, it is your turn to rest."

A small nod. "Thank you, Amelia." She dried her tears, rose and clenched Hugh's hand. "Good night, Uncle. I'll s-see you in the morning." And after a tight embrace for Amelia, she left the room with dragging feet.

Taking up watch in the chair, Amelia just gazed at Hugh for a while and listened to the sounds of eve – horses neighed in the mews, a nightwatchman hollered the hour and a nightingale sang his goodnight.

Life continued around them in the Square, hours ticking relentlessly by, unaware of how time had come to a halt within this house – those hours a meaningless number, attributed solely to the light of day or the dark of night.

With a deep breath, she lifted from the chair and re-arranged the roses in the vase, straightened the bed coverlet and the spare blankets, opened the curtains to allow the moon to shine bright and plumped the cushions on the chaise.

Having read him all the Byrne poems, Amelia opened his bedside drawer to see if there were any other books that…

A dried pink rose rested within. The rose she'd worn upon her bodice to the theatre that night.

With trembling fingers, she brought forth the flower to her lips.

A tear seeped.

Another gathered.

This time, she let it fall.

And now she could not stop them.

Fear and fury raging through her.

Not Hugh. Please God. Do not take Hugh from her.

She shoved palms to her face and just wept for a while.

If Hugh… If h-he were to be taken from her, she'd move far, far from here.

A cottage in his beloved Wales where the summer sea would always remind her of his eyes and–

"Miss?"

She'd not even heard the door open and frantically scrubbed at her cheeks. "Mrs Dawkins, I was just…"

"I know, Missy, I do. Just something in your eye, eh?"

"Yes," she sobbed, placing the rose back in the drawer. "Because…because he'll be well in the morning."

"Aye, so he will." And Amelia was enclosed in an embrace such as she'd not felt since childhood – comforting and maternal. "Now then…" Mrs Dawkins placed her firm hands on Amelia's shoulders. "I've one more tincture to try, I have. So, dry your eyes as I want you to bathe his skin with it. Maybe a few drops to swallow as well, aye?"

"Will it work?"

"It's all I have left, lovey." A small brown bottle was tucked into her hands. "Took me a while to gather what I needed but 'tis the very best I know of."

Amelia uncapped it and sniffed, half expecting horse dung or wet dog. "Roses?"

"Aye 'tis in there. Now, Sally put new bedding on earlier, and more clean cloths and fresh water are on the chest, but if there's anything you need, we're all sleeping with one eye open. Although Mr Cruikshank sleeps with both open apparently."

Amelia's lips curved. "Thank you, Mrs Dawkins. For everything."

The housekeeper nodded, and after blessing the master with a Welsh prayer, she shuffled from the room.

With a long exhale, Amelia fetched a clean cloth and returned to sit on the bed. She uncapped the bottle and moistened the cloth with the tincture, the scent of roses rising like a benediction.

Gently, she laved Hugh's chest and arms, the motion calming her. His muscles were just as strapping, his chest still broad, but his face was gaunt, black smudges ringing his eyes like storm-laden clouds. She dabbed his stomach and legs and down to his hairy toes.

Then she tipped some of the tincture onto a spoon and dribbled it between his lips.

It hopelessly ran from the corners and her teeth gritted, tried once more, willing him to swallow.

"Hugh," she whispered. "*Please*, Hugh."

She clambered further onto the bed for better reach and attempted once more.

A few drops and his throat bobbed. Amelia's resolve firmed. "Just a little, Hugh, please."

Another dribble slipped into his mouth but he choked, twisting his head to her, eyelids quivering.

"Hugh," she murmured softly, seizing his hand in hers, knowing he would never hear. "Let's try some more?"

His eyelids paused aloft and his lips moved, a faint rumbling in his chest.

"Hugh?" She leaned near, put her other hand to his forehead but it was still burning like wildfire.

His lips mumbled. "I…"

"Save your strength, Hugh. Save it for the night."

But his head pitched to the side and the corner of his mouth curved. "I…never…"

"Hugh?" She lowered her ear to his mouth. Did he need something?

A whisper… "I never…I would never let you go if…" His hand imperceptibly pressed her own.

"W-what?"

"Y-your…hand. Never…let you go…"

A tear dripped onto his face, her tear, and she cupped his cheek. "Hugh? Hugh!"

But his grip loosened.

Fell limp.

"Hugh, don't you dare!" She shoved the tincture to the bedside chest, scrambled back to his side.

He was breathing, no more than scant rasps, body trembling, and she seized his hand, plastered herself against him.

"Then don't let go, Hugh," she cried. "Just don't because… because I should have told you this long ago, but… I love you. I love you so much. And I never should have waited to tell you. So don't you dare let go. Not now."

Amelia kissed his knuckles, held his shuddering body.

He might not have the strength to hold on to her hand, but she would do it for both of them.

And never let go.

She kissed his arm. Wrapped both her hands around his and closed her eyes.

"Don't let go, Hugh," she sobbed. "Please…please. *Never* let go."

CHAPTER THIRTY-ONE

"The clock gives the signal for rest."

Private Education: A Practical Plan for the Studies of Young Ladies.

Elizabeth Appleton. 1815.

Birdsong trilled.

Vague warmth stole over her skin.

The first milkmaid shouted of her wares.

Yet Amelia was so afraid to open her eyes.

Hugh was motionless.

She'd drifted in and out of a restless sleep all the darkness through and now a tepid dawn light touched her closed lids.

Amelia still held onto his hand.

Held it tight.

But it was limp and…cold.

So cold.

The fever could have left him or…

Bravery was a curious concept, for it was not just to be found in facing battle with fortitude. It was also to keep the light of hope within your heart when it seemed all hope was lost. It was to face each moment anew and carry that light of hope into the dark. Bravery was recognising one's emotions, telling someone you loved them, wherever it led, whatever the risk to one's heart.

Amelia's moment to be brave was now.

So, her lashes lifted.

Shafts of daybreak shimmered through the window and she squinted, shifted her head to...

Cerulean-blue eyes met hers from the pillow.

Watchful.

She was almost afraid to move.

"Hugh?"

His lips parted, naught emerged.

"You're thirsty, I'll–"

He shook his head, then winced. Closed his eyes.

She waited.

They reopened. "Amelia..." His voice was a whisper, lids heavy but eyes lucid. "You...you never let go... Never let go of me."

A tear seeped. "No." She shook her head, clenching his hand yet tighter. "I did not."

His lips curved. "I feel..."

"Yes?"

"Awful."

A weak laugh escaped her and she sat up to kiss his knuckles, before feeling his forehead with the back of her hand. It no longer burned. She dragged her hand lower – over his cheek and throat, to his chest – cool skin and weak but steady breath.

Her eyes briefly shuttered and gentle relief swept her. He'd made it through the night. Was coherent and... It seemed the fever had left him. "I must let everyone know you're awake.

They'll be so overjoyed." She swallowed the lump in her throat. "What would you like from me? Broth? Anything. Anything at all."

With a grimace, he lifted his wounded arm, unsteadily but enough to show that perhaps the worst was behind them.

Then he crooked his smallest finger…

"Come a little closer," he whispered.

NOT ONE MOMENT LATER, Amelia was dashing down the stairs, tears streaming and breath hitching. She flew into Phoebe's chamber but the bed was empty, so she raced along the corridor, joy nipping at her heels, ran down the next flight of stairs, past a footman in the hall, hurtled down the basement steps and into the kitchen.

The sombreness was tangible and she felt like a bird about to chirp at a funeral.

At the table, Mrs Dawkins and Phoebe pushed back their chairs and stood.

Lucy and Mr Towlson put down their mugs.

Mr Cruikshank twisted from the range, face waxen, and Sally shoved hands to her cheeks. "Yer crying, Miss…"

Amelia couldn't speak, breath panting and throat dry. "He's…"

"Nooo!" wailed Phoebe, burying her head into the housekeeper's bosom.

"No, no!" Amelia sobbed. "Awake. He's awake!"

Phoebe's head lifted, eyes wide. "You mean…"

"The fever's left him," Amelia cried. "He's talking! Or whispering, to be precis–"

Everyone jumped on her, hugs abounding as she promptly burst into another bout of tears, and even though Hugh was far from healed, it still felt like a battle had been won.

Cruikshank drew back from a fervent hug with Mrs Dawkins, gave a refined cough and strode for the open door, calling for a footman. "A message to Lady Kemble. Fast as you can. The master is without fever and coherent. Go, go. With all haste."

Amelia and Phoebe held each other so tight. "I was so scared." Phoebe's eyes were puffy, lips trembling into a smile. "Mrs Dawkins and I were just gathering the courage to come up."

Wiping her eyes, Amelia turned to the housekeeper. "But, Mrs Dawkins, other than rosewater, what else was in that tincture last night? For it surely worked."

The housekeeper blew her nose on her apron and shook her head. "Just some ginger and yarrow, Miss. Naught else as I'd tried everything I had. But all of us, we...we all added our prayers to it, our hope. And that's all the tincture was, lovey. Strength and hope."

Sally waved a hand in front of her eyes. "I'm gonna cry again."

Cruikshank passed her a handkerchief. "Did the master manage to say anything? Did he ask for anything?"

"Yes." Amelia bit her lip. "He asked for toast, bacon, sausages, a shave and...and..."

"And?"

"Well..." Amelia swallowed as Sally cocked her head, Mr Cruikshank frowned, and Phoebe hopped from foot to foot.

Mrs Dawkins patted her shoulder. "Spit it out, lovey."

"Well, he also..."

"Yes?"

"He also asked...asked if I would marry him and I said ye–"

Amelia was jumped on once more, shrieks of joy, Phoebe whooping.

"Lawks-a-mussy!" cried Sally. "I knew it. How I love a

weddin'." And she burst into tears all over again as a beaming Mr Cruikshank passed her a new handkerchief.

Mrs Dawkins sagely nodded. "I told you all, I did. Eh, Mr Cruikshank?"

Amelia swiped at her cheeks as she was fussed over. Just like the entire household, she needed to sup some breakfast, breathe in the fresh air of spring and sleep for a week.

But Hugh would still require all their care and support for some while yet. He'd need to be coddled with kindness and patience.

It would be a time of togetherness and tender healing for them all.

Eight days later.

"HUGH CADWALADER, if you do not eat that porridge, I will tie you to that bed and force it down your gullet at knifepoint."

Hugh wouldn't object to being tied up but the porridge… He peered at the unappetising bowlful before returning his eyes to his beloved, who was tapping her foot, arms folded and with a militant gaze. "It's grey," he grumbled. "Why is it grey?"

"Mrs Dawkins might have added a few drops of castor oil but–"

"Can't I have bacon?"

"Porridge first."

With a grimace, he devoured the lot in three spoonfuls.

Gads…

Castor oil wasn't the sole added ingredient, he felt sure. "Now can I have bacon?" His arm still twinged but was healing. A headache oft plagued but sleep aided. His back ached but he blamed that on lying in bed for so long. Hunger, however, seemed constant.

"You are the worst patient ever." Amelia huffed. "And don't think I haven't heard about you walking around the room and pestering Towlson for your slippers."

"You hid them."

"You..." A finger pointed like a sabre, words stabbing. "Were told to stay in bed."

He patted the coverlet. "Amelia, come sit by me."

Ignoring his pat, she perched upon the chair instead, glaring daggers at him with those beautiful amber eyes.

Not that he could blame her as Hugh knew he wasn't the best of patients. Never had been.

The days and nights he'd been lost in delirium were now bewildering recollections – of torment and bliss, burn and chill, rage and peace. Nonsensical dreams had plagued him – poetry-reciting hares lolloping around a Welsh mountain while numbers and letters had swirled in a mass of cyphers.

But he recalled Amelia on that foreboding night. When his will to see dawn had ebbed, when the fever had coiled, twisting him in its deathly embrace, whispering of release...

Yet Amelia's hand had never let go.

He owed her his life. He owed everyone in this household his life – for all their care. And although he knew he was acting the curmudgeon, he was now impatient to get on with that life.

The sole problem was convincing Amelia that he was ready to leave his sickbed.

"I feel much better. I had a bath this morning, a fresh nightshirt and–"

"Little more than a week ago you almost died."

"I heal quickly."

Her lips pursed. "Lady Kemble told me that when you broke

your leg, you walked on it too soon and put the healing back a month."

"I was twelve years old!"

She crossed her arms.

He was doomed.

Amelia was all starch and prickle, a grey-frocked nurse on a mission, and when he'd endeavoured to kiss her, she'd told him not to overexert himself.

Bugger that.

"Hellfire, my head," he whimpered, abruptly flinging himself onto his back and groaning. "I need…"

"Oh, Hugh, what?" She jumped to her feet and leaned over him, touched a hand to his cheek. "All this pettifogging between us isn't good for you. In fact–"

It ended in a shriek as with his uninjured arm around her hips, he yanked her down to the bed, executed a proficient Pankration move, twined their legs together and rolled so he was above her.

"A kiss," he growled.

And without ado, he met her protesting luscious lips with his own.

"No!"

No?

He drew back. "Why not?"

Gads, she was divine, lying there with a halo of blond hair, lips rosy, breath panting and–

"The doctor said no strenuous activity for at least a month."

A month!

"Damnable quack," he muttered, and leaned down to kiss her exquisite–

A palm slammed over his mouth.

"A month, Hugh. No strenuous activity. No absconding down the corridor – and don't think I didn't know. I'm a spy for heaven's sake – and no kisses." The palm crept to his cheek and all of a sudden, he felt an utter blaggard as her eyes shone with moisture. "We almost lost you, Hugh," she said softly. "You may be improving and that's wonderful, but it's taking all of us some time to recover too."

With a kiss on her nose, he drew back – humbled, chastened and... "Amelia Lambert, I love you."

Those amber eyes softened. Her lips curved. "And I love you, also." She brushed a hand down his still-bandaged arm. "I should have told you sooner but I... I was not...brave."

He kissed her again, a butterfly touch. "And I should never have waited to declare my love. I should have told you that night after the theatre, over and over till you proclaimed yourself tired of hearing it. And in fact, I will say it each and every day of our married life."

Her eyes caressed his face yet her smile had waned a touch. "Hugh..."

"Amelia..."

"I... I want to m-marry you, so very much, but...are you... still sure all will be well? What about your family? A duke. The truth remains, and can never be ignored, that I-I'm illegit–"

He put an end to her words with his lips, cupped her cheeks, had to make her understand.

"I love you, Amelia Lambert, for everything that you are. My family will adore you. My friends will cherish you. And to hell with anyone else." He brought his forehead to hers. "I will fight any aristocrat who dares to cut you. Any nobleman who dares to hurt you. Anyone who dares to look down on you. And not just because we stand as one and they would be daring to insult me also, but because they would be daring to insult the bravest woman I know. A woman who has served her country, her fortitude and ability beyond refute."

Hugh felt the salt of tears upon his hands but her smile had returned, so shifting back against the headboard, he brought her to his chest and settled her into his embrace.

He kissed her hair and closed his eyes.

Sir Edmund had told him his job was still there for him if he wished and also expressed his sincere remorse on behalf of Whitehall for the conclusions drawn over Ross Thornton. Changes would be made, he'd asserted with steel in his eyes, and Hugh believed him.

As to the future, Hugh had asked for some time to think on it.

With Amelia.

So yestereve, they'd discussed their hopes and found their sentiments were in accord. No more deadly missions. No more fear for one another. No more bullets. They'd done their service and new adventures beckoned.

This morning, Amelia had given Lord Rainham notice that when possible, she wished to resign her position. But her superior, seeming to have been hitherto aware of what she was to ask, had steepled his fingers and stated that though she would be missed, Amelia could relinquish her position whenever she chose.

Then he'd offered an alternative for them both to mull…

The clock chimed five and Amelia stretched. "Lady Kemble is due to arrive at a half past the hour. Do you feel well enough?" She sat up, having regained her nurse mien but it was betrayed by her curved lips.

"Aunt's company is a delight now she's not trying to marry me off to Miss Bunwell-Birdwhistle-Blacktoft."

A smirk. "I shall leave you to it then."

She twisted but Hugh caught her hand and kissed the wrist, heard her hitch of breath.

"I cannot wait, Amelia Lambert, for the night you will be my bride."

A blush and that delicious backside sashayed to the door.

HUGH THREW *THE TIMES* ASIDE, having previously read it thrice and–

Frantic footfall in the corridor and he glanced up, just as a knock rattled, the door was flung open and a black figure with pale wet cheeks dashed in, closing the door behind her.

Sobs intermingled with hitched gasps.

"Phoebe! Who's hurt you? I'll throttl–"

"No...No..." She came to a halt by the bed, waving what looked to be a letter, and although tears still gathered and tumbled, he could now discern a quivering smile to her lips.

"My blackbird?"

"I..." She swiped at her face, sniffed and bit her lip. "A letter came for me just this afternoon. From Sir Edmund."

Ah.

Hugh patted the bed aside him. "And what does he have to say?"

With a distinct snag to her breath, his ward settled herself and smoothed the letter across her knee. "He a-apologises to me on behalf of all at Whitehall." She swallowed. "That Papa was wrongly accused." Her awash black eyes gleamed. "He says that my papa was a true hero."

"And so he was, blackbird."

One tear escaped its confines. "And not only that but...h-his name will be given to a new Home Office honour of gallantry, one to be presented each year. To only the most dedicated officers, that my father will be the first recipient and...and..."

Hugh twisted, arms outstretched, and she fell into his fierce hug, tears plummeting once more.

"Ah, Phoebe. That is wonderful news. 'Tis fully deserved. He will be remembered forever. As a loyal man dedicated to justice and his country."

Her face rubbed up and down on his shoulder.

Hugh held her. "I know it won't return him to us but…"

"No, but it helps me," was the muffled answer before she drew back. "He was brave and honourable, we know that, and we don't have to hide it anymore. No one can tell lies about him. Papa was taken from me and I shall miss him every single day but those who did it were brought to justice." She frowned at his damaged arm. "And it's all thanks to you and Amelia."

He reached for her hand. "Your father saved my life, Phoebe. I owe him so much. But more than that, he was my friend and I will miss him also." He wiped her damp cheeks with his nightshirt cuff, his own emotions an odd sense of loss and triumph. Ross had indeed been vindicated but a good friend and loving father was gone. One who could never be replaced.

Phoebe rubbed at her forehead with one thumb, exactly like Ross used to, and Hugh smiled – maybe not entirely gone as this young girl was truly her father's daughter.

"He would have been proud of you, Phoebe."

"I've not done anything. I couldn't help with your investigations or–"

"You have coped with his loss with such strength. A loss that no young girl should have to face. And you never once surrendered the courage of your convictions in your father's innocence. Ross always said that to have the courage of your convictions was a cornerstone of this profession. That it was needed in order to remain committed to integrity and truth. You have your father's strength and courage in abundance."

A smile wobbled. "Thank you, Uncle Hugh."

"Now, my blackbird, hop over to the dressing table, will you, and bring me that brass inlaid box."

She did as bid before bouncing back onto the bed.

Hugh opened the lid, lifted out the clover cufflinks and then held them forth within his palm. "I think you should have these now."

"No." Phoebe shook her head. And folded her arms. "They are yours."

Hugh attempted his best overbearing stare. Rather devalued by the dowdy nightshirt. "He gifted them to me when I had a dangerous mission, said they brought luck and they did, but I feel they belong with you now."

With fingers tapping on her black velvet sleeves, Phoebe's overbearing stare was rather superior. "No."

Stalemate.

Until those black eyes narrowed. "I know…" She hummed and hawed before reaching for the cufflink with the missing emerald. "We shall each have one."

"A fine idea, my blackbird of paradise. And since I'm bound to this bed till…eternity if Amelia has her way." He dramatically sighed. "I'll ask Cruik to have two identical boxes made for them."

"Thank you, Uncle Hugh. And being bedbound is for your own good, you realise, as when you were twelve years old with a broken ank–"

"Yes, yes. I've been reminded of that many a time."

She sniggered. "I'm so happy you're to marry Amelia."

A strident knock accompanied an even more strident, "Ahem! Are you decent, Hugh?"

"Lady Kemble!" Phoebe sprang off the bed.

The handle turned and a purple bonnet popped around the door. "Ah ha! There you all are." And in a dress the colour of spring violets, she strode to his bedside.

"You look a little peaky, my gal. Have you been crying?" Aunt rested a hand to Phoebe's shoulder. "Are you well?"

"Yes, my lady." A wide smile tugged at his ward's lips. "I think

I shall be very well from now on. I had a letter from the Home Office. They will honour my father with an award and name it after him."

"What splendid news." Aunt drew her into a gentle hug. "We can all be so proud. And I'm so proud of you." She patted her shoulder. "So how is our patient today? Not very patient according to Amelia. That poor girl."

They both turned but Hugh merely eyed them, head cocked to one side, fingers tapping.

After a buss to his forehead, Aunt perched on the chair. "Odds boddikins, I recognise that look. It signifies trouble."

A giggling Phoebe sat on the end of the bed.

"I was just wondering..." Hugh waggled his eyebrows. "I need some assistance with a cunning plan of deceit, subterfuge and hoodwinking."

"Hmm," said Phoebe. "Will you let me borrow your polemoscope?"

Cunning indeed.

"Done."

Phoebe patted his foot through the bedsheet. "Then, Uncle Hugh, you've come to the right people."

CHAPTER THIRTY-TWO

"I now claim your indulgence."

Private Education: A Practical Plan for the Studies of Young Ladies.

Elizabeth Appleton. 1815.

Ten days later.

Amelia peered at herself in the gilded mirror.

Fiddled with her lace-edged sleeve.

Fidgeted with the gossamer net over her pink satin skirts.

Faffed with the ribbon beneath her carmine-hued bodice.

"This is ridiculous," she mumbled, pulling taut her gloves of white silk. "To be so anxious. It's just a ball out there."

Albeit quite a grand one.

With Hugh still recovering, an invitation had arrived from Sir Edmund for an impromptu ball to be held at his townhouse. A handwritten note to them both had been attached, explaining that no more was his wife to hide away from the social whirl, that they would pay no heed if the *Ton* gossiped about her condition or if the Home Office considered it a hindrance to his position.

And this ball would be her debut.

Hugh had groaned and clutched his arm, so Amelia had sought her quill in order to send a return message, to convey their sincere regret and wish them well but they could not attend, not with Hugh still infirm. But…

Lady Kemble had proposed that Amelia accompany her to the ball. That the two of them must attend as Letty would require their full support.

Phoebe had folded her arms and declared it a splendid idea.

Hugh had nodded and agreed it was for the best and that Sir Edmund would greatly appreciate the gesture.

So here she was alone in the retiring room, cloistered from the hubbub of the ball, smoothing the beautiful dress that Lady Kemble had provided for her and rearranging her choker with its enamelled butterfly.

The afternoon's preparations, she would have to admit, had been wondrous.

Aided by Mrs Dawkins and Sally, she'd been bathed in rosewater and then primped, powdered and perfumed till she hardly recognised herself.

Phoebe had then rouged Amelia's cheeks and lips. "I wish I could come," she'd said with a leaden sigh. "Although would I be allowed to wear black?"

"I suppose it depends on the host," Amelia had replied. "And I wish you could come too, but it won't be long now until you can attend all the balls you want during your Season."

"Bleurgh." Phoebe had wrinkled her nose. "I want to attend this ball, not others. And I'll not wear white. I'd faint. Now…" She'd tweaked a hairpin. "I'm going upstairs to sit with Uncle and read him *The History of Locks.* So have a lovely time." And with a buss, she'd left.

Whilst awaiting Lady Kemble's carriage, Amelia had gently knocked upon Hugh's bedchamber door as how she'd wished for him to see her in all her finery rather than the drab governess gowns that she'd worn each day for nursing him.

Phoebe had popped her head out. "He's asleep," she'd whispered. "Nodded off on page three so we mustn't disturb him. As you've always said, he needs his rest."

She had said that but surely...

Then the carriage had arrived in the Square to collect her while Sally had draped a cloak over her shoulders and led her downstairs. Cruikshank had held open the door and Amelia had departed for the ball with a small sigh as–

A rattle of handle and the retiring room door opened, chatter from the hall bubbling, and Amelia grabbed her shawl, should cease loitering here.

"Good evening. Miss Lambert, is it not?"

She glanced up to meet the amused blue eyes of Lady Twyford herself. She sank into a curtsey. "Oh, my lady. Please do excuse our deception."

Wafting a silk-gloved hand, she smiled and closed the door. "It was my own fault. I should have told Edmund of the blackmail but..." The lines were still about her eyes but a burden seemed to have eased from her, softening her pretty features. "I only wished to protect him, as he has always protected me. And..." A soft exhale. "I have hidden away for so long that it was second nature to continue hiding from everyone."

"But no longer?"

"No, my dear. No longer," she said huskily. "I shall always have this affliction but I shall no longer be bound by it and hide from society, for I adore company and balls and the theatre."

Amelia smiled. "I am so glad, Lady Twyford."

"And why are you yourself hiding in here?" She sat upon the sofa in the middle of the room and wiggled her feet.

"I wasn't... Well, maybe..." Amelia hesitated and crossed to sit aside her. "It's that... I have never attended a ball just as myself. I've been a wallflower and widow for the Foreign Office, you understand, but never just...Amelia Lambert." She clasped hands in her lap. "You likely do not know this, my lady, but the truth is I'm... I am the daughter of the Duke of Swanford and... the Butterfly Courtesan."

"Of course I know," the lady declared. "Edmund told me."

"Oh..." Amelia unclasped her hands. "And...that does not offend you?"

"Of course not, my dear. Malice to others offends me. But you worry what the *Ton* will say?"

Amelia nodded. "I am content with who I am, truly, yet upon introduction as Miss Lambert, will guests ask of my family? What should I say? Should I speak the truth or...fudge a bit? In the past, I have always had a false story to tell." She straightened her shoulders. "But like you, I do not want to hide anymore."

Lady Twyford patted her hand. "We have much in common, us two. We have both been made fearful of others, their judgements of us, made to feel shame for who we are." She tutted. "But I say we should fear no more." And rose to her feet. "Do not think me naïve, for I know some will seek to belittle me, perhaps even here tonight, but we will draw strength from each other and our friends and not let anyone make us feel...less. It is time we stopped feeling shame for who they perceive us to be, Amelia, and not who we are." With a smile, Lady Twyford held out her gloved hand. "Shall we?"

"Yes." Amelia returned her own wide smile and clutched the lady's hand. "Yes, we shall."

Arm in arm, they departed the retiring room to be faced

with a hall crammed with guests, every room having been opened to accommodate.

Lady Twyford hugged Amelia's arm tight. "I confess, we've more here than we anticipated and–"

"There you both are!" A purple turban joggled from side to side as Lady Kemble weaved her way towards them, a vision of plum perfection. "Letty, what a success, my dear!"

"Oh, Enid. It's just like old times."

"The Dashing Debutantes! And do you know, I..." She leaned in, a purple feather brushing Amelia's nose. "I thought to see the Duke of Wellington. So gallant and handsome, is he not? I came over most peculiar, nigh had a fit of the vapours."

"It was indeed the duke, Enid, and I'm sure he'd be delighted to meet you." Lady Twyford reached out her hand to her dear friend. "I'm so grateful to have you both here for my...debut of sorts. It's...it's like being all of seventeen again."

"Isn't it just!" Lady Kemble firmly clasped her hand. "Though back then, I could eat apple fritters without fear of dyspepsia."

Amelia hid a smile behind her hand but Lady Twyford chuckled. "I must return to Edmund or he'll worry. But I will see you both soon. And, Miss Lambert, remember what we agreed." Then with a squeeze of hands, she twisted away to be absorbed into the crowd.

"Now..." Lady Kemble smoothed a wrinkle in Amelia's glove, yanked at her bodice and straightened a tassel. "You look delightful. How are you faring, my gal?"

"All is well, Lady Kemble."

"Splendid. Now hold your chin high, your bosom out and I told you to call me Enid."

Amelia did as requested – on all counts.

Her purple feather nodded. "Let us make for the ballroom. It's as stuffed as a jar of asparagus but I thought to see Wellington stride that way. He cuts such a fine form in those shiny boots of his. Do you think he keeps them on when making… No, surely not, although it's said…"

Amelia followed the chatter and plum-purple skirts as they pressed their way towards the open doors of the ballroom. The throng was a hotchpotch of finely dressed nobles and soberly dressed parliamentary bigwigs, peacock feathers wafting in ladies' coiffures.

Sir Edmund was certainly well-connected.

The ballroom was not vast but the walls were pure white with gold-painted mouldings in elaborate swirls, vases of full-bloom roses within the plaster niches. A chandelier glittered over the dancers stood awaiting a quadrille to commence, and it all appeared like a magical dream – the gowns so vivid against the backdrop of white.

"Oh, what a superlative crush," proclaimed Enid, "And, ah!" Her fan pointed into the midst of the ballroom. "There's the champagne. Do come along."

Amelia darted after Enid who seemed to have a unique ability to part the throng with merely a perilous stare whilst at the same time nodding her regal turban at acquaintances.

With eyes darting hither and thither, Amelia glimpsed Lord Rainham and his lovely wife Lily but a wink was all she caught before the prelude to the quadrille could be heard and further guests blocked her view as they took their positions in lines.

Champagne was procured and Amelia sipp–

"If I may," a low rumble interrupted. "Would you honour me with your hand for this dance?"

Amelia spun.

Nigh dropped her glass…

Blinked.

Muscular legs clad in black.

A crimson waistcoat.

Collier de Cheval neckcloth.

Clean-shaven chin and a twitch of lip.

Two eyes.

"Cleavers," she hissed. "What are you–"

"Yes, of course she will, Lord Cleavers." Lady Kemble snatched away her champagne glass, nudged her in the ribs and bent to her ear. "Such a well-mannered young man," she whispered. "I was introduced to the viscount whilst awaiting you in the vestibule. He esteemed my purple plumage. Off you go."

Amelia barely had time to gape as *Lord* Cleavers tugged her to the dancefloor. She'd not danced in an age and nerves fluttered within. Would she recall the steps?

From all sides, Amelia felt watched as ladies assessed and gentlemen perused.

A curtsey. The dance began.

Forward. Clasp hands.

Closely circle one another.

Circle tw–

"Wot a barrelful of rum coves, eh?" growled a voice in her ear. "And mind out fer yer toes! I ain't the best at this."

Nerves lifted and she grinned. "Rum, indeed, *Lord* Cleavers. It does seem that all and sundry have an invitation to this ball."

"Wot invitation?" And with a wink, he stepped back into the line of gentlemen, his feet most lithesome for a man built like an ox.

Rolling her eyes, Amelia looped with the lady aside her and then twisted to face her partner once more.

"I say," Cleavers intoned with aristocratic tenor. "I do declare you the belle of this ball, Miss Lambert, as pink as a…as a newly boiled ham. Succulent and savoury."

"Oh, *Lord* Cleavers…" She batted her lashes. "Such fulsome flattery! But I do hope I'm not merely the latest in a line of ladies who've been brought to a swoon at such words?"

"*Moi?*" was his response before they were required to circle another once more and he bent to her ear. "Well, yer look a right spruce wench ter me and I ain't tellin' no clankers."

Amelia smiled at him just as the music's tempo lifted and all the ladies were required to swap positions, the dance bestowing a different partner.

To and fro, the steps continued in simple elegance until the gentlemen swapped places and she was once more returned to Cleavers.

They clasped hands. "Got me peepers on that cockish countess over there. D'yer reckon I should make meself a duke? All the morts swoon at them rum fribbles."

"Worth a try." And chuckling at his devilry, she twisted back to the line of ladies as the dance concluded, the last pull of violin bow fading.

Cleavers bowed with a deep flourish.

Amelia dipped into an equally low curtsey – after all, he was a duke now – and then rose to…

With his lady wife aside him, Sir Edmund was standing in their midst, his smile broad. "Forgive the interruption, my friends, but before you all depart for refreshment, I would like to say a few words…"

Dancers shuffled back just as other guests shuffled forward to stand at their shoulders, until Sir Edmund and his wife were encircled by an attentive throng, waiters weaving between with trays of champagne.

The Duke of Cleavers grabbed two glasses and crossed the circle to hand one to Amelia.

Sir Edmund cleared his throat. "Welcome all and thank you for attending at such short notice. I have the utmost pleasure in hosting this ball tonight for two special reasons." He splayed an arm. "The first is to celebrate the return of my beautiful wife to our London social whirl. Since we met so many years ago now, she has been my constancy and my strength, and to have her by my side once more tonight has made me a man both proud and humble. I ask you all to join me in a toast." He raised his glass. "To my beloved wife, Lady Twyford."

The lady blushed but smiled as glasses were raised high in her direction.

"But there is a second cause for celebration tonight." Sir Edmund's white eyebrows shuffled like swan's down. "For I also have the utmost honour in announcing the betrothal of two of the finest people I know."

Amelia frowned. Especially as Lady Kemb... Enid was winking at her from across the circle.

"So it is with great pleasure that I do hereby announce the betrothal of the honourable Mr Hugh Cadwalader of the Welsh Cadogan-Cadwaladers..."

A low murmur of anticipation swept the ballroom. Amelia's fingers numbed, Cleavers catching her champagne glass.

Her mouth dried as Sir Edmund's eyes tur–

"And the estimable Miss Amelia Lambert." His arm now swept in her direction. "Daughter of the Duke of Swanford and Alice Lambert."

Her throat seized as a hundred eyes snapped her way. A light-headedness consumed, heat enveloping, and the white room blurred to–

Fingers entwined with her own.

A firm arm to her waist.

Broad chest to her back.

She dared to turn.

Met resolute azure eyes.

"Hugh?"

"We stand as one, Amelia. For eternity."

She felt tears smart. In a simple *Cascade* cravat, an amber silk jacket with a white rosebud in the lapel and a waistcoat of cream silk, he looked in fine fettle…most fine. And undeniably not asleep in his bed.

And Amelia realised the wool had been quite thoroughly pulled over her eyes, that she'd been spun a yarn by them all – Lady Kemble, Phoebe, Mrs Dawkins, Cleavers, Sally, Cruikshank and…

Hugh's hand cupped her cheek. "I love you, Miss Lambert."

Then he kissed her. Quite rigorously.

There in the middle of the ballroom. The most *Scandalous* Hugh Cadwalader.

"A toast," Amelia vaguely heard Sir Edmund proclaim above the hubbub.

Glasses clinked but a wave of murmurs waxed and waned, a minor commotion seeming to sweep the ballroom. Whispers gusted and skirts flurried as ladies turned their backs. Was the gossip of her mother wending its way amongst the guests?

Feathers dipped from sight and gentlemen's heads lowered as though a maelstrom blew through the ballroom, knocking them like dominoes.

Amelia frowned and…and…

Oh heavens.

And she dropped into a deep curtsey.

"Your Royal Highness," she spluttered, now staring at the Prince Regent's sizeable stockinged knees. "I…"

"Up. Up." He wafted a beringed hand. "I want to see the petticoat this scandalous fellow has captured. Introduce me, Cadwalader, won't you?"

Hugh arose from his profound bow and assisted his beloved with hand outstretched.

Sir Edmund had mentioned he'd sent an invitation to the Prince Regent but Hugh really hadn't thought…

"Your Royal Highness, may I present Miss Amelia Lambert."

The Prince Regent removed his quizzing glass and inspected Hugh's betrothed from slippers to bosom – lingering there rather too long for Hugh's liking – then from bosom to butterfly hairpins.

"Well, well, what a beauty. Good effort, Cadwalader," he pronounced as though Hugh had caught her in a net.

Amelia demurely smiled.

The Prince Regent beamed. "Sir Edmund and I met in our salad days, you see, and I've been informed of your recent…fine work." He leaned low. "Well done." And a protuberant eye winked.

"Thank you, Your Royal Highness."

He nodded. "D'you know I met your mother once, Miss Lambert. A beautiful woman who took pity on a younger me when others were mocking, and I never forgot that kindness." He tapped his extensive stomach, lifted his head and surveyed the onlookers. "I will look forward," he said in a most strident manner, "to seeing you, Miss Lambert, on our London scene. Now, Twyford, fill up my glass, if you would, and then I'm afraid I must leave you all for Madame Luridesque's masquerade."

Hugh bowed once more, Amelia held a low curtsey, and with another satisfied nod, the Prince Regent lumbered off.

Whispers rose to murmurs, murmurs to babble, as debutantes gossiped behind fans and society matrons collapsed into chairs lining the wall.

"Did I dream it," whispered Amelia, "or did the Prince Regent just give me his seal of approval?"

"Not that you need it, my beautiful Amelia." Hugh seized his beloved around the waist. "For I love you just as you are. For all that you are."

"Odds boddikins!" Aunt Enid's hands were clasped to her

purple bosom, a tear rolling down her cheek. "That all worked so splendidly!"

And at her side, a blackbird of paradise hopped from foot to foot.

"Phoebe, you're here!" Amelia broke Hugh's hold to hug her hard.

"Of course! I wouldn't have missed it for all the black silk in France," she gushed, eyes a luminous obsidian. "Although I'm only allowed to stay for an hour. I shouldn't even really be here. And no dancing. Or drinking ratafia. And I have to stay beside Lady Kemble now. In fact, you haven't seen me."

"I cannot believe I didn't realise what you were all up to."

"Our hoodwinking was a success, Uncle!"

They were joined by Sir Edmund with his wife, and Lord Rainham who bussed his beloved's cheek and clapped Hugh on the back.

Amelia turned to him, amber eyes aflame, and Hugh could do naught but reach for her hand once more, his betrothed and the one woman who knew him.

All of him.

AWASH WITH JOY, Amelia felt breathless. Hugh at her side, his hand steadfast in hers.

She caught Lady Twyford's eye who winked and Amelia smiled in return. No longer would either of them allow anyone to make them feel…less.

Tonight, Amelia was no one but herself.

"Congratulations!"

Amelia turned to a stunning gown of russet. "Charlotte! How did you…"

A tip of auburn hair. "Your Mr Cadwalader here. He

deduced our little ruse and invited me and… Oh, the waltz is about to start and I have a partner. We will talk soon, yes?"

Amelia nodded and clasped her hands. "I should like that very much."

"Good. I must dash as my dance is with…" A frown appeared. "Have you heard of a Prince Cleavers of Hapsburg?"

With a bite of lip, Amelia shook her head but as Charlotte twisted away, she turned to Hugh. "Should I tell her?"

"Well, it could be true for all we know." He caressed a curl in her hair. "Anything is possible tonight, my love."

"And how will it end? This perfect night?"

Hugh drew her near. "I'd propose we go somewhere to gather our thoughts. Find some calm after the storm." He winked. "'Tis on the other side of London but I know the perfect place."

Amelia smiled and brought her palm to his chest, her warrior and her gentleman.

"But before that…" Hugh proffered an arm. "Waltz with me? Though I warn you, I shall be scandalous and hold you most close."

She laid a hand upon his sleeve of amber silk. "I'd expect nothing less of the Scandalous Hugh Cadwalader."

Lips curved to that sinful smile. "From henceforth, we shall be scandalous together, my beloved Amelia." And with that… and a waggle of eyebrow, Hugh led her to the dancefloor.

EPILOGUE

"Do you not feel amazement on contemplating the works of nature?"

Private Education: A Practical Plan for the Studies of Young Ladies.

Elizabeth Appleton. 1815.

A breeze laden with salt and autumn caressed Hugh's skin, healing him and cleansing his soul. Gulls squawked overhead, the sea rhythmically swashing the secluded cove's beach with its eddies of white while the sun bestowed a weak September warmth.

Flowers of blue sea holly, purple aster and golden samphire still stippled the Welsh cliff tops behind him, but an ancient hawthorn warned that the colder months would soon be upon them, laden as it was with ripening berries.

While he lay on the sand, Hugh's Welsh cousins – Rhys and his twin brother, Tristan, once mourned as lost to the sea but now blessedly returned to their fold – wandered the cove gathering driftwood for a fire. In his mind's eye, Hugh could still see them all as young lads, playing on this very beach, yet Tristan was a father himself and Rhys a duke of the realm.

They'd both not an hour past thrashed Hugh at cricket before the three of them had then thrown themselves into the sea, and gads, it had been cold but also invigorating and life-affirming.

With a smile curving his lips, he stared up at the sky, felt the sand moulding to his back and shoulders.

A profound peace overcame him and he closed his eyes.

In the drifting shadow behind his lids, he saw Amelia in her wedding gown of sage green and their honeymoon in the south of Wales, just them and a cottage with red roses around the door. Endless days of carefree laughter and nights of passionate love.

Opening his eyes, he watched a butterfly flit hither and thither. Soon it would disappear for the winter but while the autumn sun still shone it would live life to the fullest, feasting on nectar from the sweet sea-spurrey that still flowered amongst the cove's shingle.

"Hugh! Cease daydreaming and get this damn fire lit," shouted Rhys. "We don't have much time."

Jumping to his feet, he grabbed a tinderbox from his pocket and made his way to their pile of sticks upon the sea-smoothed pebbles at the back of the cove.

Within a trice, it was lit and the three of them sat to warm their hands, well satisfied with their manly deed of the day.

"Do you remember," began Tristan in his rasping voice, "when we sat in this very spot as boys, ten years old or so, and debated girls?"

"I deemed them unnecessary," said Rhys with a wry smile.

Tristan smirked. "I thought them incompatible with being a pirate."

"What was my opinion?" Hugh's brow creased. "Can't damn well recall."

"Well, you were younger." Rhys' lips quirked. "So you thought a girl might be useful. A damsel you could pretend to rescue from the Welsh lake monster Afanc."

"Gads, how chivalrous." He rubbed his hands and held them to the flames. "Although as it's turned out, my damsel could rescue hersel..." Hugh glanced up. Stilled.

Rhys turned his head.

Tristan's eyes pivoted, a tender smile upon his lips.

Three ladies weaved their way down the stone steps cut into the cliff, picnic baskets clasped in their hands.

Two were the beautiful wives of his cousins but the other...

Laughing with such freedom, flaxen hair blown loose by the fingers of the mischievous wind, verdant skirts swaying.

She looked up.

Their eyes met.

And she... She was his.

AMELIA FELT her husband's gaze like a fervid caress and she blushed, smiling as her new cousins-in-law nudged her with a laugh.

In fact, since the moment she'd stepped through the magnificent portal of the Llanedwyn manor house, she'd never stopped smiling.

None of Hugh's family had batted an eyelid at her parentage yet she'd still felt compelled to ask the duke tentatively one evening if her marriage into a noble family such as themselves would be an encumbrance or bring disrepute upon them.

He'd not dismissed her question as foolish but turned his black eyes thoughtful. "People will always seek to judge but it matters naught to us. You are joined with our family now, joined with the Cadwalader and Llanedwyn heritage. And *we* are honoured to have you." He'd rested a hand upon her shoulder. "*Cousin* Amelia."

And no one could argue with a duke.

His duchess, who'd insisted on being called Isabelle, had been a governess too, a true one, but to the duke's niece and possessed her own revered copy of Miss Appleton's educational tome. Amelia had been rather hesitant to explain how she'd blown hers to smithereens, but Hugh had regaled the tale with his customary flair, hoots of laughter ringing around the dinner table.

Rhys and Tristan had bussed her cheek and thanked her for saving Hugh's life, their eyes attesting to the regard and love they held for him.

And now she was included in that regard. Included in this family.

Phoebe had, of course, travelled with them to Wales, as had the entire London household, for their wedding here at the duke's estate. She still dressed in her habitual black but the vindication of her father had lightened her soul, and she and Tristan's daughter, Mari, were now thick as thieves – both dark-haired and beautiful, and bound to cause a storm of trouble for the young gentlemen of London one day.

Amelia adored them all. The thoughtful duke and welcoming Isabelle. Rough-hewn Tristan and his kindly Gwen.

And Amelia loved Wales, incandescent in the pure light. A place, she was discovering, of dragons and wildness, beauty and legends, and…

Hugh.

"Oh, look," cried Isabelle, "they've even lit a fire."

But Amelia only had eyes for her husband.

Wearing solely shirt and breeches, the breeze plastered the dampened linen against his muscled chest. His hair was wet from the sea, face no longer so pale after their honeymoon on the coast, and one would hardly recognise the debonair London gentleman. Here, he was akin to the wild land with its sweet rain and dark nights.

Her Welsh warrior.

Gwen and Isabelle left her side to greet their husbands with affection, while she and Hugh approached one another like a couple meeting for the first time, that flare of flame within her igniting as it always would.

"Walk with me, Mrs Cadwalader?"

"A pleasure, Mr Cadwalader."

She hooked an arm through his, kicking off her shoes so they could paddle their way through the shallow water, the soft waves rippling the shore on this calm autumn day as they had done, and would do, for eternity.

"You seemed deep in thought when I saw you from the clifftop, lying upon the sand. Mulling on Lord Rainham's idea, perchance?"

Her superior had suggested a year-long diplomatic post in Spain might be of interest to them. No danger involved, just utilisation of their more innocuous skills – Amelia's observation and Hugh's effortless camaraderie. With passage for three, of course.

It was a fine offer and one they would almost certainly accept.

But Hugh shook his head. "I was thinking…what if someone else had come for the governess interview that day?" He puffed a breath of horror. "Someone with truthful references and exemplary tatting."

Amelia smirked. "The odds were somewhat weighted in my favour."

With a grin, he twisted, caught her around the waist and kissed her, the salt breeze twisting her skirts around him. "And

I'm glad of that because..." He clasped her nape, fingers caressing, gaze serious. "I cannot now imagine a life without you, Amelia. I have been blessed, both with you and a new beginning, and I intend to make the most of it." And his lips descended for–

Two butterflies flitted between the diminishing gap before they surged skywards, fluttering about their heads in a mutual dance of joy and life.

Amelia and Hugh laughed, watching as the breeze gusted the ephemeral creatures onto their next adventure – the yellow gorse upon the coastal headland, new pastures, the world.

"Cousins!" came a ducal shout on the breeze. "Come on!"

Her husband held out his broad hand and those lips curved. "Shall we commence, my beloved?"

And she knew he spoke not just of the picnic but of their life together.

A new beginning. A less perilous one, to be sure, but still filled with adventure and laughter.

Passion and love.

She clasped that hand and his fingers wrapped snug to hers.

Fitted and as one.

Never. Never to let go.

The End

THANK YOU

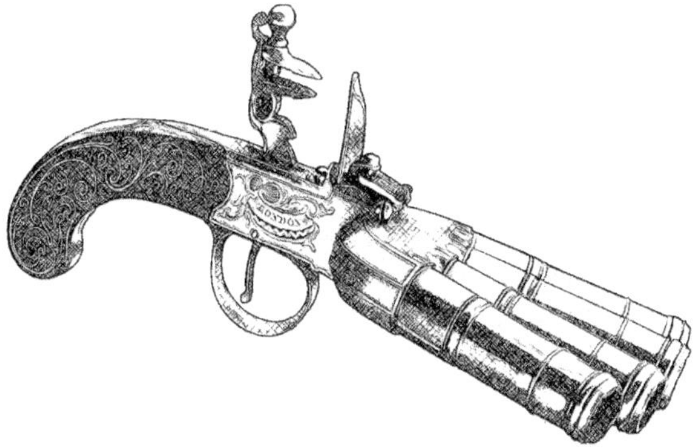

Amelia's Duck Gun. What it lacked in accuracy, it certainly made up for in spectacle...

Thank you for reading *A Governess Should Never... Lure a Spy*. I truly hope you enjoyed Amelia and Hugh's tale.

ALSO BY EMILY WINDSOR

THE GOVERNESS CHRONICLES SERIES

A Governess Should Never... Tempt A Prizefighter (Book 1)
Seth and Matilda's Tale

With scandalous kisses in midnight carriages, tavern jaunts, whifflers, nobblers and dressing as a nefarious footpad on the prowl, the vocation of governess for Miss Matilda Griffin has never been so exciting...

A Governess Should Never... Deny A Duke (Book 2)
Isabelle and Rhys' Tale

The Prudent Governess and the Passionate Duke.
One should never judge a Welsh duke by his Mean, Moody & Mysterious reputation or a governess by her tightly pinned hair, for beneath both tamed façades lay wildness and shared passions – not to be denied.

A Gentleman Will Never... Forget A Lady (Book 3 - Christmas Novella)

Get swept away to a romantic and rugged land in this joyful and heart-warming Christmas tale...

A Governess Should Never... Wager A Duke (Book 5 - Christmas Short Story)

Coming November 2024.

A LADY TO SUIT SERIES

The Duke of Diamonds (Book 1)

Casper Brook, the eighth Duke of Rothwell, has forever spurned frivolous pleasures, his restless emotions remaining buried beneath duty and command.
Yet when a titian-haired minx perches upon his ducal desk and claims to know the whereabouts of his one burning obsession, a game of wits and passion erupts...

The Rake of Hearts (Book 2)

RULES OF THE ROGUE SERIES

An Earl in Wolf's Clothing (Book 1)

From the hallowed halls of London's Almack's to the unkempt taverns of Drury Lane, from whispered words in glittering theatres to seductive encounters at Vauxhall Gardens – an earl must pursue his love.
A determined lady. An even more determined gentleman.

Let the pursuit begin…

Merry Christmas, my Viscount (Book 2)

Seduce a rogue? By Christmas Eve? What a troubling resolution for the most proper widow Mrs Lily Mereworth to be left with… How? And more importantly, who?
Ghost stories on a windy night, swordplay down the Great Portrait Gallery, a lady and a spymaster with no thought to love… Merry Christmas.

Let Sleeping Dukes Lie (Book 3)

"Strait-laced. Ruthless. Arrogant." – The Duke of Rakecombe has forever spurned love…and with good reason.
"Forthright. Impudent. Capricious saucebox." – The fiery Miss Aideen Quinlan refuses to be spurned, unable to erase the memory of the duke's vehement kiss…
An unlikely couple, an unquenchable passion.
Resistance is futile.

Marquess to a Flame (Book 4)

The Marquess of Winterbourne has long been guided by his *Rules of the Rogue*, but as spy for the Crown, his next mission will break every single one. Sent to the wilds of Cornwall to beguile secrets from a lady, the last thing this rogue expects is to unearth his own buried heart.

CAPTIVATING DEBUTANTES SERIES

Captivated by the Viscount

ALSO BY EMILY WINDSOR

My Captive Earl

Her Noble Captive

ABOUT THE AUTHOR

Emily grew up in the north of England on a diet of historical romance and strong tea.

Unfortunately, you couldn't study Regency slang, so she did the next best thing and gained a degree in Classics and History instead. This 'led' to an eight-year stint in engineering.

Having left city life, she now lives in a dilapidated farmhouse in the country where her days are spent writing, fixing the leaky roof, battling the endless vegetation and finding pictures of well-tied cravats.

Happy Reading,
Love,
Emily
x

facebook.com/AuthorEmilyWindsor
pinterest.com/EmilyWindsorBks
instagram.com/emilywindsorwritesregency
bookbub.com/authors/emily-windsor
goodreads.com/EmilyWindsor
amazon.com/author/emilywindsor

Printed in Great Britain
by Amazon

43704163R00199